A Blessing to Cherish

LAURAINE SNELLING

BETHANYHOUSE

a division of Baker Publishing Group
Minneapolis, Minnesota

© 2020 by Lauraine Snelling

Published by Bethany House Publishers
11400 Hampshire Avenue South
Bloomington, Minnesota 55438
www.bethanyhouse.com

Bethany House Publishers is a division of
Baker Publishing Group, Grand Rapids, Michigan

Printed in the United States of America

Library of Congress Control Number: 2020936848

ISBN 978-0-7642-3289-3 (trade paper)
ISBN 978-0-7642-3290-9 (cloth)
ISBN 978-0-7642-3291-6 (large print)

Scripture quotations are from the King James Version of the Bible.

This is a work of fiction. Names, characters, incidents, and dialogues are products of the author's imagination and are not to be construed as real. Any resemblance to actual events or persons, living or dead, is entirely coincidental.

Cover design by Dan Thornberg, Design Source Creative Services

Author is represented by Books & Such Literary Management.

20 21 22 23 24 25 26   7 6 5 4 3 2 1

A
Blessing
to
Cherish

Books by Lauraine Snelling

A Blessing to Cherish

UNDER NORTHERN SKIES

The Promise of Dawn
A Breath of Hope
A Season of Grace
A Song of Joy

SONG OF BLESSING

To Everything a Season
A Harvest of Hope
Streams of Mercy
From This Day Forward

An Untamed Heart

RED RIVER OF THE NORTH

An Untamed Land
A New Day Rising
A Land to Call Home
The Reapers' Song
Tender Mercies
Blessing in Disguise

RETURN TO RED RIVER

A Dream to Follow
Believing the Dream
More Than a Dream

DAUGHTERS OF BLESSING

A Promise for Ellie
Sophie's Dilemma
A Touch of Grace
Rebecca's Reward

HOME TO BLESSING

A Measure of Mercy
No Distance Too Far
A Heart for Home

WILD WEST WIND

Valley of Dreams
Whispers in the Wind
A Place to Belong

DAKOTAH TREASURES

Ruby • Pearl
Opal • Amethyst

SECRET REFUGE

Daughter of Twin Oaks
Sisters of the Confederacy
The Long Way Home
A Secret Refuge 3-in-1

I dedicate *A Blessing to Cherish*
to three women
who have held big places in my life,
both in writing and in living.

First to my mother, Thelma Moe Clauson Sommerseth, who lived the example for me of loving unconditionally. Her sister, Inga Detschman, lived her life with joy and saw the good side of life and all that is living. Ingeborg grew from these two women.

The third worked on these books with me from word one and, like the two above, has gone on to glory. Sharon Asmus, my editor at Bethany House, helped in more ways than she probably realized with ideas, story wisdom, and constant encouragement. While she kept so much information on her computer, her brain held far more. When she was no longer here, I was almost hesitant to keep going on this series without her.

God gives us people in our lives
for so many reasons and so many blessings.
I rejoice in these gifts.

Chapter 1

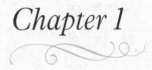

"Grandma, tell us a story."

Ingeborg Bjorklund loved that request, because she had so many to tell. "Which one would you like?"

Inga and Emmy, both in their usual position on the porch floor, grinned at each other and nodded. "The one where you met Mr. Gould." The two girls, one nearly white-blond, the other dark of hair and eyes due to her Sioux heritage, wore white aprons over their faded summer shifts, their crossed legs giving them something to prop their elbows on. The back porch, in the shade of the cottonwood tree, was their favorite summer gathering place.

"You've heard that story so many times." Sitting on the two-person porch swing, Ingeborg shook her head, her smile so full of love for these two girls that her face no doubt glowed. She wore her deep golden hair, now bearing streaks of silver, braided and wrapped around her head like a crown.

"But I haven't." Thorliff, her elder son, sat on the top step, leaning against the porch post with his arms crossed over his bent knee. He grinned at his daughter and her best friend. "Good choice." He winked at the man in question, who sat on the porch rail behind the swing. "Don't you think so, Mr. Gould?"

"Oh, I most certainly do," David Gould agreed.

Ingeborg could feel his teasing gaze on the back of her neck. Leave it to these girls. "Should I begin with 'Once upon a time'?"

"How about 'A long time ago in a city far away'?" Gould offered.

Refusing to let him fluster her, Ingeborg continued. "All right, a long time ago in a city far away, a young woman, newly immigrated from Norway, was searching the streets of New York City for the way back to the docks where her son had accidentally stolen an apple and she had promised to pay for it. She now had the penny in her reticule, but by this time she was hopelessly lost. The streets and sidewalks were covered in slush, and a cold wind sneaked through her coat, so she was cold all through. The docks were not within sight, and she had no idea how to find her way back to the boardinghouse where her family was waiting to board a train to North Dakota. She knew if she started crying, she would melt into a puddle of tears, but what could she do? She waited on a street corner, trying to decide which way to go. Since she spoke little English, she could not ask for directions or read the street signs."

"Why didn't her husband go with her?" Thorliff asked. "Or just take the penny himself?"

"She snuck out while he was gone, because he said she was foolish to want to do such a thing and she should let it go." Her voice hardened even after all these years. "She was mighty upset with him."

"But maybe he was right. After all, a penny." Thorliff, the boy who had stolen the apple, shifted his weight against the porch post.

Inga turned and shook her head at her father. "Shh, Pa, let Grandma tell her story."

He held up both hands, palms out. "Sorry. Just need to get my facts straight."

"You're not interviewing her for a story for your newspaper, you know," Inga said, her tone scolding.

"I don't know. I think I have an idea beginning to stir." He nodded slowly as he spoke.

Ingeborg stared at her son. The excitement on his face confirmed something was bubbling behind his Bjorklund-blue eyes.

"Come on, Grandma, back to your story," Emmy urged.

"Now, where was I?"

"Lost in New York City in a snowstorm," Gould answered.

"I finally decided which direction to go, but just as I stepped forward, someone bumped me, and I started falling into the street. Suddenly two strong hands grabbed my upper arms, and a man lifted me right back up on the sidewalk. Without thinking, I said, 'Takk,' and he answered, 'You are welcome' in Norwegian. I looked up into the man's face and stuttered, 'How do you know Norwegian?'"

Gould chimed in. "And he said, 'That's a long story, miss, but my nanny taught me.' I half-carried her back to the protection of the building, because every time she put her weight on her foot, she started to collapse again."

Both girls stared at him, their mouths in matching *O* formations.

"And so the charming young man hailed a cab and helped me up into the carriage. He asked where I needed to go, and I told him the docks to find the apple vendor to pay him what I owed."

10

"And did you find him?" Thorliff asked.

"We did. Mr. Gould tried to ignore my penny, but I insisted and . . ."

"And, polite young man that I was, I took her penny and paid the vendor, who sputtered and tried to refuse. But I was so disgusted that this young woman was out on the streets alone that I would have stuffed it down his gullet. I wanted to take her to the hospital to make sure her foot was not broken, but she insisted that it was just sprained and would be better in no time."

"I knew it wasn't broken, but it sure did hurt and was swelling up like a balloon. We should have gathered some of that snow and packed it around my foot."

Gould moved from the porch railing to sit next to her on the swing.

Ingeborg continued, "Instead he hired that hack to drive us around the city, and he showed me all these wonderfully huge build-ings and parks and even a college, and I was so amazed. I could have ridden around like that forever, but I gave him the address of the boardinghouse and asked him to take me there."

"I did so reluctantly. I considered taking her to my home and calling for a doctor to come look at her foot, but she was getting frantic to get back, so I did as she asked. When

11

we got to the boardinghouse, two young men came striding up the sidewalk. I helped her out of the carriage, and she introduced me to her husband and his brother. Her husband was really put out with her, hardly even civil in his thanks to me. After the introduction, she hobbled over to the entry and went inside."

"I about collapsed just inside the door, but the woman who owned the boardinghouse took pity on me and helped me up to our rooms."

"That was Grandpa Roald, right?" Inga asked.

Ingeborg nodded. "Right. He was Thorliff's father."

"You snitched an apple?" Inga stared at her pa.

Thorliff shrugged. "I would never have stolen anything, but some boys who were playing there grabbed apples off the cart and tossed one to me. I was so proud I caught it, and oh, it tasted so good. And then I looked up, and my new mother was coming after me with fury on her face. You see, she had told me to stay in one place because she had to go back for something, and I disobeyed and followed those boys, who had invited me to play."

"I thought I had lost him for good," Ingeborg said, "and I could have paddled his behind, but I was so thankful to have him back that I hugged him instead."

"But still . . ." Inga shook her head. "Pa, you sure caused a lot of trouble."

"Be that as it may, that penny gave me a chance to meet that determined young woman, and now here we all are today." Gould gave Ingeborg a smile that made her heart flutter.

Thorliff locked his hands around his bent knee. "All over an apple. Now that I think of it, isn't there another story about an apple that changed history?"

Ingeborg shook her head. "Thorliff Bjorklund, you can't mix that story with this one."

"Just a comparison, to test the Bible knowledge of our two girls." He nodded toward them.

Emmy giggled. "Adam and Eve. But that was different."

"Very good!" Ingeborg turned and smiled at the man sharing her swing. "How does a glass of lemonade sound?"

"And cookies?" Gould asked hopefully.

All three females laughed. "You knew we baked cookies this morning, Mr. Gould," Emmy said with a grin.

"I distinctly remember the fragrance of lemon." He smiled.

"We'll get them." Both girls stood straight up without a hand and pulled open the spring-held screen door.

"First summer-warm spring day. It's been chilly for April." Ingeborg pulled her shawl closer around her shoulders as a breeze tickled the growing leaves of the cottonwood trees. "To think we're sitting out here today when it froze a couple of nights ago."

Thorliff chuckled. "I think spring finally got fed up with playing tug-of-war with winter and scared it away."

"Interesting mental picture, Thorliff." David Gould draped an arm across Ingeborg's shoulders. "Good thing my chicks didn't hatch early. This is the first time I've ever watched a broody hen sit on eggs. Say, are Grace and Jonathan back yet? She's the one who teased me into keeping chickens."

"Well, after you built them such a fancy henhouse and pen . . ." Thorliff chided.

"They had to have a place to live," Gould argued.

"Right. And you needed something to build. Lars says teaching you woodworking is easy; you're an apt pupil." Thorliff took a small pad of paper and a pencil stub out of his chest pocket and wrote some notes. "So I don't forget. How long are you here?"

"I have to leave for New York the first

week of May to attend to several business matters. It will be a lengthy stay, but I put it off as long as I could. Why?"

Beside him, Ingeborg sighed. He'd tried to talk her into coming along, but she'd told him the garden wasn't all in and she had too much to do here. It was the truth, mostly.

"We need to hire another teacher for next year. Actually we need two more, but one may have to wait. I'm putting out advertisements and have gotten one reply so far. I sure wish Jonathan's cousin had stayed on. He was an excellent teacher." Thorliff nodded to his mother. "And you, Mor. I think you're one of the favorite teachers at the school."

"But I only teach one class a week."

"I know, but the students sure look forward to it. You want to teach more, we'll find a place for you." As head of the school board, Thorliff was always on the lookout for new teachers. "Hmmm, I just had an idea." He looked at Gould. "You ever thought about teaching a class on economics for, say, a semester at the high school?"

"No, can't say as that has entered my mind. An interesting thought."

Ingeborg nodded to her son. That would keep Gould in town for an entire semester. The thought made her smile.

"The first lemonade of the year," Inga

15

said as she and Emmy pushed open the screen door. "Grandma, do we have any juice in the cellar for swizzle?"

"I'm not sure. If we do have juice, that would make a fine tapioca pudding."

"I've not had tapioca pudding for years," Gould said as he took the glass of lemonade Emmy handed him. "Thank you."

"Will you be here for supper?" Ingeborg asked.

"If I'm invited."

Ingeborg grimaced. He was so polite, sometimes too much so. "Of course you're invited. You have a standing invitation."

"Could we play cards after?" Inga asked.

Ingeborg nodded. "We need to get some baking done for the dinner tomorrow, but of course."

The girls joined Thorliff on the steps to enjoy the repast. "Grandma, there are buds on the rosebushes."

"I know. I warned them it could still freeze, but they don't seem to listen."

The girls looked at each other and giggled. Thorliff bounced his eyebrows and shrugged.

Let him make fun. She knew not everyone talked to their flowers, but Ingeborg always had. That was why hers always grew so well.

"Grandma, can we start a rosebush for

my house? You know, for when I am grown up and married?" Inga asked.

"Well, of course we can, but it will be a mighty big bush by then. So don't you go getting any ideas for a long while yet."

"That's for sure!" Thorliff gave his daughter a stern-father look and nudged her with his elbow.

Inga rolled her eyes. "I'm still a child, but I'm just looking ahead. I love Grandma's rosebushes." She inhaled as if sniffing rose blossoms. "And the ones at Tante Astrid's. Of course, those really belong to Mrs. Jeffers." She tipped back her head and stared at the sky. "There are rosebushes all over Blessing from Grandma's roses and Mrs. Jeffers'. That's pretty special, isn't it?"

"It is," answered Gould. "I've heard many comments from visitors about the beautiful flowers here. They say Blessing is a very welcoming place."

"Well, if people keep wanting to move here, we're going to need more houses and more jobs." Thorliff stood and dusted off the seat of his pants. "I have a paper to put together. Takk for the visit and the refreshments." He looked down at his daughter. "Why don't you and Emmy come eat at home for a change? Your little brother needs some company."

The two girls looked at each other, then to Ingeborg, who nodded.

"You go ahead," she told the girls. "I'll see you at church in the morning."

"So, do you need some help with the paper?" Inga asked her father.

Thorliff nodded. "That wasn't my intention, but it would be appreciated. If you want a ride, I'll wait a couple of minutes."

"I'll get my dress. Last time we cleaned the newspaper office, I got ink on my apron. It never came out, so I'll get that too."

When they were all in the cart, Thorliff backed up the formerly dozing horse, which turned around to trot up the lane.

They all waved at Ingeborg and headed for town.

"And so life changes in an instant. I thought we were going to make tapioca pudding and play cards." Ingeborg reached for the tray, but Gould beat her to it.

"Is there any coffee?" he asked.

"There is always coffee. And if there isn't, we know how to make a fresh pot." She watched the cart disappear. "That child always amazes me."

"I would say she is no longer a child, and the way time flies, she will be wanting those rosebushes sooner than you think." He carried the tray inside as she held the door.

She pulled the coffeepot to the hotter part of the stove. "About time for new." She swished the pot around and poured the leftover coffee and grounds into a small bucket, which would later be dumped around one of the rosebushes. She did this even when snow covered the bushes, and as the snow melted, the roses were fed. The bedding from the barn that they banked against the house every fall also helped feed the bushes of lilac, bridal wreath, and snowball.

"We need to get some starts going to plant around your house," she commented as she prepared the fresh pot of coffee.

"You know, you could let Freda make the supper."

"I know, but she baked pies this afternoon and started the roast beef for tomorrow, so I told her to go lie down for a while. Her back is bothering her again."

He nodded. "I know. And you and the girls worked in the garden all morning and much of the afternoon."

"Planting a garden gives me such joy. Each little seed saved from last year is now starting on its new life. I put them in the ground, and God sends the rain and the sunshine. As if He's my gardening partner. Or rather I am His. I've wondered sometimes if He helped Adam and Eve in their garden. He said He met them in the garden to visit. I think of that when I see the tiny green sprouts, and then you can see the rows of lettuce and radishes. I love to see the beans with their curved stalks and the seed at the end poking out. You can almost see them straighten up and reach for the sun."

"To most people a garden is work." His head moved gently from side to side. "You make it sound like pure joy."

She turned to stare at him. "You are an amazing man." *How can I help but love you?*

Chapter 2

Rolly, Thorliff's young son, was hanging on the front gate when Thorliff arrived home. "You went to Gramma's without me."

Thorliff swung his son up in the air and around once. "I wasn't planning on staying long."

"But you did stay long."

"Next time. What is Thelma making for supper?"

"She says Esmeralda and dumplings."

20

Thorliff laughed. "Esmeralda!"

Rolly followed him up the walkway. "That cranky old hen pecked Thelma one time too many. Did Gramma send me cookies?"

"How'd you guess?"

"I can smell them and you have a package. She said she sends me cookies 'cause she loves me."

"That she does, Rolly. That she does. We'll be out at her place tomorrow for dinner and the ball game."

"Will I play too?"

"Probably not. Wait till you get a little bigger."

Rolly gave his pa a dirty look and pulled open the screen door.

"Go ask Thelma how long until supper. I think I'll go out and work for a little while."

"Oh-kay." Rolly was a genius at making one word sound like a pout.

Thorliff inhaled. Something sure smelled good. He headed toward the back steps and down them to the newspaper building.

Inga and Emmy met him at the door. "The horse is taken care of. We fed and brushed him and turned him out into the pasture. You need some help in here?" Inga asked.

"If you're suggesting the printing room needs cleaning, you are right. You could probably file type too."

Cleaning and filing type was a messy job that both girls had learned to do faster than anyone else he'd ever employed, and they worked for time on the typewriter in the newspaper office as wages. Emmy wanted to learn to type, so he had drawn out a keyboard for her to practice on. Since then he'd had the cleanest office in all the years he had produced the *Blessing Gazette*, a biweekly newspaper that had earned a goodly number of awards. But ever since Father Thomas Devlin had moved to take over a parish in Michigan, Thorliff had not had regular office help other than a couple of students from the high school class he taught.

He sat down at his desk and picked up the article he'd been working on. He had yet to develop the habit of typing rough drafts rather than hand-writing them. When his hand was moving across a sheet of paper, good thoughts flowed. When he had to peck at that typewriter, the thoughts were like a rain cloud as he struggled.

"Pa!"

The tone was exasperated. Thorliff looked up to see Rolly standing in the doorway. His frown said it all.

"Were you calling me?" Thorliff asked.

Rolly glared some more. "Thelma says come to supper. Now!"

Thorliff fought the laughter from his face and tone. Rolly took anything he was asked to do very seriously. Other than pick up his toys. "You better tell Inga and Emmy." He looked over his shoulder and watched his son march to the print room doorway.

"Come eat!"

"Now?"

He nodded. "Now."

Thorliff laid his pencil at the top of his pad of paper, since pencils had a habit of disappearing, and pushed back his wheeled chair.

"We can come out and finish after supper, can't we?" Inga asked as she and Emmy took Rolly's hands and started skipping with him between them.

"If you want." Thorliff shut the door behind him. Small critters had sought out housing in his office before. "Rolly, is Dr. Commons here yet?"

Dr. Jason Commons had come out from Chicago after he finished his schooling and set up a practice here in Blessing. He was living in Thorliff's upstairs room until he could have his house built. A second doctor in town was greatly relieving the pressure on Dr. Astrid, Thorliff's sister. Besides, Jason and Thorliff had become good friends.

Gremlin the cat met them at the top of the steps, meowing, asking to be picked up.

23

Emmy scooped up the armful of fluff, which had a purr loud enough to be heard across the street.

"Smells awful good, Thelma," Thorliff called as he stepped into the kitchen.

Thelma came from the dining room. "Wasn't sure how many there'd be for supper, so I set up in there. Dr. Commons was called in for an emergency."

"Any idea what?" Thorliff asked. He was one of the men always on call for emergencies when extra orderlies were needed.

"I think it was a baby, but not sure." She checked something in the oven before reaching for potholders. "Rolly, you and the girls go wash."

Thorliff picked up the earpiece on the wall telephone. "The hospital. Shouldn't you be home by now, Gerald?"

Their telephone operator replied, "My replacement asked if she could come in late. I'll hook you up right now. Have a good evening."

There was a click.

"Hospital." The young woman on the desk sounded rushed.

"You need any help over there?"

"I think they're all right. Baby was choking. Dr. Commons got here just in time. Baby was blue."

24

Thorliff heaved a breath of relief. He clicked the ear prong. "Gerald, could you please call Reverend Solberg and ask him to go by the hospital? There was an emergency, and I'm sure that family would appreciate his coming."

"Of course." Gerald Valders clicked off, and Thorliff hung the earpiece back on the prongs.

"All is well?" Thelma asked as she carried the pot to the dining room table.

"Ja, it is now." He sank into the chair at the head of the table. "Rolly, you want to say grace?"

Rolly rattled off the table prayer in Norwegian. Thorliff didn't catch all the words, but they all said the *amen* together.

As soon as all the plates were filled, including Thelma's, they set to eating as if they'd not been fed for days, rather than hours.

"Esmeralda is mighty good, thanks." Inga grinned at Thelma. "Served her right for being nasty."

"Inga Bjorklund, what a thing to say." Thelma stared at her, but when Thorliff snorted, she shook her head.

"But we eat all the chickens after a while. That's part of our food."

"I know but . . ." Thelma shook her head again. "It just . . ."

25

"No matter. This chicken and dumplings is better than others I've had." Thorliff poured more oil on the troubled waters. "So how far did you get on the type?" Changing the subject seemed like a good idea.

"About half. We didn't have much time out there, but we can finish it after supper," Emmy answered. "Do you have something you would like me to type?"

Thorliff looked at her. "Are you sure?"

"I'm not very fast because I strive for accuracy, but the more I type, the faster I get. Unless, of course, you would rather I cleaned."

"I will give you this article as soon as I've written it. Thank you." He studied the food on his plate. The girls were growing up so fast, especially Emmy. "So, are you really not going to your tribe this summer?"

Emmy replied, "We're planning to take a wagonload of clothes and food up there, probably in August. Grandma is hoping to talk with the older and wiser women of the tribe and share some ideas with them. We won't be gone that long."

The two girls returned to the newspaper office after supper to finish cleaning and filing the type. Thorliff completed his article and started to work on the layout. He found himself whistling as he worked on the drawing board. A light bulb with a shade hung above the table.

"I'm going to walk Emmy halfway home." The two girls stood beside his table. "We're finished here."

He looked at Emmy. "I thought you were spending the night."

"I need to help Grandma in the morning. I finished typing your article. It's on your desk."

"What time is it?"

"Almost nine." Inga grinned at her far. "Grandma says you go off into your own world when you come out here. And she's right."

"Your grandma is always right. Thank you both for cleaning. Emmy, the typewriter is yours whenever you want." He paused and studied his daughter. "Are you enjoying learning to type, Inga?"

"I am. I have the practice keyboard now. It's just like the one Mor used for the piano. She said she'd teach me to play the piano when I got older and could sit still long enough."

"I remember that. So many things we planned to do." He wagged his head. Time flew too fast.

"But at least we have you back." Inga hugged him. "I'll be home soon."

He watched the two girls leave, feeling

the tears building at the back of his eyes. He blew his nose and stuffed the handkerchief back into his pocket. *Thank you, Lord, that you brought me back from that pit I was drowning in.* When Elizabeth died, years ago, his world had turned black. Even now, the grief grabbed him at times and tried to drag him back in. He would never be able to thank his sister and mother enough for waking him up before the damage was so severe that his children were wounded beyond healing.

He shut off the light and closed the door. He'd planned to stop earlier to spend some time with Rolly, but like Inga said, he got lost in his own world. The perfume of something baking met him as he mounted the steps to the back porch.

"What smells so wonderful?" he asked from the door.

"Pa!" Rolly charged into him, his nightshirt flying behind him.

Thorliff gave him a hug. "Aren't you supposed to be in bed?"

"I was waiting for you. Thelma said you would come put me to bed. We have cookies and milk."

"I see that." Thorliff sat down at the table beside his son.

"Would you rather have coffee?" Thelma

asked as she pulled another sheet of cookies out of the oven.

"No, this is fine. You've been busy." He nodded toward the three pies cooling on the counter. "For the dinner tomorrow?"

"I said we'd bring pies, and cookies are always welcome."

Rolly took a cookie off the plate and grinned around the crumbs from his first bite. "Thelma makes good cookies."

Thorliff dunked his cookie in the glass of milk and nibbled its edges, a habit his Rolly had picked up.

Thelma asked, "Where's Inga?"

"Walking Emmy partway home."

"Dinner at Gramma's tomorrow, right?" Rolly stuffed the rest of his cookie into his mouth.

"Right."

"Please, I wanna play ball. Can I? Huh?"

Thorliff shook his head. "You never give up, do you?"

Thelma cleared her throat, clearly trying not to laugh. She slid the last sheet of cookies into the oven and wiped the moisture from her forehead. "Now I can let the stove go out. It feels almost like summer today, not just spring. Good night, Rolly."

Rolly stiffened his legs and slid off the chair. "'Night. Good cookies."

Thorliff stood with him and headed up the stairs.

Rolly snuggled down in his bed and clasped his hands on top of the covers. "Story? Please?"

"What about?"

"The goats."

"Aren't you tired of that one? All right. Once upon a time, three goats lived on a farm near the mountains of Norway. Spring melt had turned the dancing creek into a raging torrent. The goats wanted to cross the bridge to the better grass on the other side, but they knew a mean old troll lived under the bridge."

As his mouth talked, his brain circled back to a different thought. Stories. Inga and Emmy had asked for a story. From infancy, stories had informed the children's lives. Stories preserved history and memories. Stories kept people from being forgotten. Stories were so important. Crucial, even. The tiny flicker of an idea that had come to him on Mor's porch began to grow.

Rolly's eyes had drifted closed, so Thorliff paused and waited. "Sleep well, my son." He left the room. "Lord bless and keep him. I forgot to say prayers."

He fought back a yawn of his own. Why didn't he just go to bed now too? He heard

Inga laughing in the kitchen with Thelma, so she was home safe—not that there had been any doubt.

"I give up." He turned from going down the stairs and entered his bedroom across the hall from Rolly's. Why on earth was he so tired? He draped his clothes over the chair and slid between the cool sheets. The lace curtain danced at the window, inviting him to look outside, where the smiling moon hung not even halfway to midnight. Instead of rolling over and reaching for Elizabeth, which he so often did, he picked up his Bible and flipped it open at a marker ribbon. Thanks to his mor, he started with a psalm. All those years he'd not even glanced at his Bible except on Sundays. He read the psalm out loud to help keep him awake. "Praise the Lord, O my soul." Did one ever praise God enough?

"Lord, please open my eyes to see all I could praise you for. Every day is full of great and marvelous things, especially my family and my friends. Thank you, Father, for . . ."

He drifted off to sleep before he finished.

Chapter 3

"That's it!"

David Gould's eyes popped open. Of course, that was it. The missing piece in the puzzle. He glanced at the clock. Too soon to call Daniel Jeffers. And besides, this was Sunday. And this really wasn't his problem anyway, but what a perfect solution.

He grabbed his notepad off the nightstand and wrote enough to bring in the clear picture. He sat up and swung his feet over the edge of the bed. This house was far too quiet. When he got back from New York, he would find someone to be cook and housekeeper. Perhaps he should do as Inga suggested and get a cat or a dog, some other living creature. She'd said she would take care of it when he was traveling.

Which brought up another subject. Perhaps it was time to cut back on the traveling. For business, at least.

Marrying Ingeborg would solve the quiet and loneliness issues. He closed his eyes and heaved a sigh. He'd pounded the gates of heaven with entreaties. He knew she loved him, but she was content with things the way they were, and he was not. *Lord, I want her here beside me, to share the jubilation of this puzzle piece, to make this house a home, which would happen just by her being here.* He sighed. He knew God had heard his prayers, and he felt sure marriage was in His plan for both of them. "I want to take care of her the way she deserves to be cared for, not just caring for everyone else. And yes, I know she is happy where she is. She loves that farm and the children." He paused. Were Emmy and Manny, Ingeborg's other adoptee, afraid of losing their home if Ingeborg married him? Might they want to live here too? That was a new thought.

Going into the bathroom, he stropped his razor. When the blade had regained its edge, he lathered his face with the soap-filled brush and set to removing the mask that had grown overnight on his cheeks and chin. He splashed aftershave into the palm of his hand and patted it over his face. Hair combed, he returned to the bedroom and chose his shirt for the day.

In New York, his valet saw to this job. Should he bring him out from New York too? Not that he wanted to strip that house of its amenities. While he much preferred life here in Blessing to living in New York City, a valet might be pushing the customs too far.

His son Jonathan had adapted to life here as if he hadn't grown up in New York. But then, he had a wife and more than enough to do. They had nearly finished the new building for the deaf school, allowing for nearly a third more students, increasing the need for more teachers and aides. That meant more work for Jonathan. While Jonathan had planned to run their farm, where students were trained to work in spite of their handicap, he was learning that running the school along with his wife, Grace, took more and more of his time. Their latest enterprise was the bakery, which had grown enough both in quality and quantity to open a storefront on Main Street near the soda fountain. Rumor had it their bread was almost as good as Ingeborg's. Which was not surprising, since she gave them her recipes and trained the bakers.

David fought with his tie to get the knot just right and, when it was perfected, made his way downstairs to start the stove for breakfast. But halfway down, the fragrance of coffee caught his attention, and he realized someone was in his house. He followed his nose to his sunny kitchen and found Emmy sliding something into the oven.

"Well, good morning," he said. "What a nice surprise."

"Good morning. We wanted to surprise you." Emmy grinned brightly.

"You certainly did. We?" He glanced around, hoping to see Ingeborg, but Emmy was the only one present.

"Grandma and I." She poured him a cup of coffee. "The rolls are in the oven, so they'll be hot in a minute." Her dark eyes twinkled. "She said she'd see you at church."

He took the cup and saucer and leaned against the counter to hold and sip from it. "Surely she didn't get up early enough this morning to bake rolls."

"No, we made them last night and kept them in the icebox, then baked them this morning."

"Have you already had breakfast?"

"Some, but I'll have a cinnamon roll with you. I could fry you some eggs, if you'd like."

"No, thank you, this is plenty. I must have been sleeping hard, that you could start the fire without me hearing you."

"I tried to be quiet." She poured another cup of coffee and added cream. "The table is set in the dining room. We can take our coffee in there, and I'll bring the rolls."

He picked up both cups and carried them into the dining room. They could have eaten at the table in the kitchen, but he knew she was trying to do what was proper by city standards.

He sat down and glanced around this room that was used so little. He knew every piece of the walnut moldings, the flocked burgundy wallpaper with gold medallions, the crystal chandelier, because he had helped finish this room. For the first time in his life, he knew how to choose the wood, use the proper tools, and apply all the coats of finish. He had not hung the wallpaper, but he had picked it out. It wasn't surprising that this looked much like his house in New York. And yet, the distance from New York to North Dakota was im-measurable.

"May I warm up your coffee?" Emmy asked as she set the platter of rolls beside him.

He looked in his cup. Empty. And he didn't even remember drinking it. He handed it to her with a smile. "Thank you."

She brought back a full cup and set it by his plate. "Would you like cream and sugar?"

"No, thank you. I prefer it just like this." He waited until she sat down and then pushed the platter halfway between them. "Are these as good as they look?"

She smiled at him and nodded. And waited until he picked up a roll before taking one of her own.

She is so polite, he thought. *Ingeborg has trained her well. But what will happen to her after school? She's an Indian. Indians are not well received.* After his first bite, nearly smacking his lips, he sipped his coffee and smiled at her.

"Any idea what you plan to do after high school?" *Please don't say go back to the reservation.*

"I want to go to teachers' training so I can return and teach my people."

"Thorliff said you are getting good on the typewriter." He finished his roll and reached for another. There was no way he could eat only one.

"I like it."

Ideas paraded through his mind. What if he were to purchase enough typewriters for a class at the high school, say five or six or however many they would need, and find someone to teach the class? Time to talk with John Solberg again. The idea kept growing. Since the deaf students went to the public school as soon as they learned sign language, they could take the class there, but several more typewriters at the deaf school would be a good idea as well. The office staff needed to transition to modern methods and machines.

"Would you like more coffee?" Emmy asked.

"Please, one more cup." He watched her return to the kitchen. "I ordered rolls from the bakery for the dinner today. I said I would pick them up at Grace's place after church. Can you think of anything else I could bring?"

She thought and then shook her head. "Everyone is looking forward to the dinner but really the ball game."

"Lars and I will be the umpires. Him behind the plate, me on first base." Gould shook his head. "At least this way I won't be on a team." He thought back to last year. No, he did not want to be on a team again. Besides, they never had a lack of players. This was a young man's game. What he'd like best to do was sit next to Ingeborg and cheer. "Maybe I could ask John Solberg if he would like to be an umpire this year."

"He, Lars, and Haakan—Mr. Bjorklund— used to share the umpiring. I think he was happy to find someone else to do the job."

"Oh." So much for that idea. "Guess I'll just take my turn." He drained his coffee cup. "Thank you for bringing me breakfast, Emmy. You're a treasure." He pushed back his chair. "Are you going home before church?"

She shook her head. "I will clean up the kitchen before I go."

"Not that there is a big mess."

"Grandma wouldn't be happy if I didn't."

"I have a meeting with John before church, so I will see you there." He lifted his hat from the hat rack standing by the front door. "Thank you again."

"I could pick up the rolls for you after church."

"Thank you. If you want."

"Inga and I will."

He nodded and stepped out onto the front porch. Settling his hat on his head, he inhaled the fragrant air and listened to a robin singing. He would never experience such peace and beauty from his house in New York. He inhaled again. Never. Even if he couldn't convince Ingeborg to marry him and live here, the thought of moving back east was anathema to him. Even returning there on business was getting more difficult. He locked his hands behind his back and whistled his way over to the white church with a bell in the steeple. Why, he had gotten to know more people here after only a few months than he'd known in all the years he'd attended the big stone church in New York. Geraldine, his second wife, was known for her philanthropy through the church. Their children had been baptized there, but they were true Sunday-only members there because that was the proper thing to do rather than because of faith.

But here? John Solberg often gave him black-and-blue shins in his sermons, and

David had told him so. But John lived what he preached. He worked right along with the people of Blessing in whatever needed doing. All these years, he'd taught in the school in addition to his church duties. Blessing would be at a real loss if John were called elsewhere. Besides, he had become a good friend. *Perhaps I need to go walking more often if it triggers deep thoughts like these.* But when he thought about it, he had no real friends in New York City. Social and business contacts, but not true friends. What a shame.

"Do I need to be wearing shin guards?" he asked John after their greetings.

"Now, David, surely you jest."

"Should I show you the scars?" They both chuckled.

John asked, "So why are we having this conversation?"

"When I asked to meet you, I had something else in mind, but now I want to share a new idea with you. I want to buy as many typewriters as needed so the young people here can get trained to use them and qualify for jobs in other places, should they decide to move. Just looking ahead."

"Sounds good to me, but we don't have a teacher."

"I'll find one. I'm thinking especially of

the deaf students. This could open whole new vistas for them."

"Thanks to you and Thorliff, I guess we are being thrust into the new age of machines."

"Now, if only this country can keep out of the coming war so that our young people aren't destroyed."

"I keep praying that the president will have the wisdom to manage that." He pulled out his pocket watch. "I better get robed. Thank you for your time." He clapped Gould on the upper arm. "Thanks too for agreeing to umpire today. It's not a job I've liked that well. I get involved in the game and forget to pay attention."

Gould watched him go around the church to the office door.

During the service, he had a hard time keeping his mind on the sermon, more aware of the woman sitting beside him. When they sang the closing hymn while Jonathan played the organ, Gould felt pride for his son warming his heart. He knew his son had been practicing, transferring his piano techniques to the organ, but still he amazed his father with his skill.

Gould greeted the folks around them as they made their way to the front door, where Reverend Solberg made sure to welcome everyone.

"Say, Daniel, I had an idea this morning. Perhaps we can talk about it after the game."

Daniel Jeffers studied him. "You've aroused my curiosity."

"Good. You coming to the game?"

"He wouldn't dare miss it," Dr. Astrid answered with a smile at her husband. "He is captain of the red team."

Gould nodded. "Guess I forgot that. You want to umpire, and I'll captain the team?"

Daniel shook his head. "Not really. We have to beat Thorliff's blues."

"I heard the teams will keep the same players as last year. That's rather a modern idea. I was surprised."

Daniel nodded. "Me too. The next thing you know, they'll start practicing before the games begin. With the boys playing baseball at school, the competition starts early."

"Inga and Emmy insist that the girls play too." Which reminded Gould . . . "Emmy said she and Inga would pick up the buns I ordered."

"On foot? How about Astrid and I stop there with the buggy? It'd be a lot easier."

"I appreciate that. Excuse me, I'd better tell her before they take off." Gould looked around for Emmy. She and Inga were talking and laughing with a group of girls. Should he interrupt or not?

42

Ingeborg stopped at his side. "Are you ready to leave?"

"Thank you," he said in relief. "Would you please tell Inga that she and Emmy could ride with Astrid and Daniel to pick up the buns?"

"Flummoxed by a group of girls?" Ingeborg patted his arm and walked over to tell the girls, then returned. "All right?"

"Thank you. How come you always know what to do?"

"Ah, you put me in front of one of your board members, and I'd faint."

He smiled at her, slightly shaking his head. "No, you wouldn't. You'd have them eating out of your hand in no time."

"I doubt that, but it's a moot point. I'm not going to New York again. For some strange reason, I don't have good memories of that city." She paused. "Except for being saved by a young man who spoke Norwegian. Did your brothers and sister learn to speak Norwegian too?" They started walking toward the farmhouse.

He shrugged. "Some odd words and phrases, but they most likely don't remember them." *They don't have the incentive I do. Perhaps I should practice asking her to marry me in Norwegian.*

A small voice in the back of his mind taunted, *If you ever do ask her.*

Chapter 4

"**M**or, I have an idea to talk over with you." Thorliff laid down his fork, his plate empty.

Ingeborg smiled. "Another new idea? Will I like this one?"

Thorliff nodded. "I hope so, but it's going to take a lot of work."

"Grandma, when are we going to play baseball?" Carl, her eldest grandson and Andrew's eldest child, asked.

"Why are you asking me?"

Thorliff answered for her. "As soon as everyone is finished eating. You could help carry the dishes into the house. I think they have already started washing up in the kitchen." He kept from laughing at the look on his nephew's face. But Carl didn't argue; he joined Inga and Emmy and let them load him up.

Ingeborg nodded. "I heard Inga ask him to help too." She looked out at the field where some of the men were measuring off the baseball diamond. "I was hoping we would get the backstop built before the first game. But I know—spring field work always comes first."

Thorliff waved a hand. "We should build a baseball field at the school. That would make more sense." He pulled his ever-present tablet out of his shirt pocket. "Then anyone could use it. Building some bleachers for spectators would be a good idea too. Guess we better start a fund."

"Pass around the hat after the game while everyone is excited."

"Good idea." Thorliff checked his pocket watch. "We said the game would start at two, and it's getting close." He snapped the watch closed. "You coming to watch?"

"I wouldn't miss it."

As folks gathered at the ball diamond, Emmy and Inga rounded up the smaller children and took them to the barn, where Joker and the ponies waited in the corral. Manny had saddled and bridled his horse, Joker, and the girls slipped bridles on the two ponies.

Thorliff watched them. Rolly had gone with them, much to his father's relief. While they played catch with him at home and were teaching him to bat, he could get hurt when the game began. And he was endlessly insistent that he should play. Was Thorliff that persistent when he was little? Probably.

Andrew appointed Carl and a couple of the other younger boys to be ball fetchers for

45

when the pitched ball got by the catcher. That kept them happy and out of trouble.

At the playing field, the older boys joined the teams lined up from last year, Thorliff's blue team and Daniel's red.

"All right, everyone, they've asked me to bless this game, so let us pray." Reverend Solberg's voice could most likely be heard in town. As the crowd settled down, he began. "Heavenly Father, we thank you for this day and a sport that can bring us all together. We ask for your protection over all those gathered here, both the players and those cheering. Help us to remember this is just a game. O Lord, we praise your holy name. Amen." He paused for a brief moment. "Play ball!"

Everyone clapped and cheered, and both the team captains joined Gould at home plate, where he tossed a coin to see who would bat first. When he slapped it on the back of his hand and lifted his other hand, he announced, "Blues are up first!"

The red team headed for their field positions, and the blues lined up for batting. Gould umpired first base, while Lars took his place behind the batter. The pitcher threw the ball, and Lars called, "Strike one!"

By the end of the game, the players were dripping sweat, and those cheering were hoarse.

While the ice cream was set out, Reverend Solberg motioned to Manny for his whistle that sounded like a stream train. The blast got everyone's attention immediately, and he raised his voice. "To make this game easier to play and safer for everyone, it has been suggested that we build a ball field at the schoolhouse. Since there is no money budgeted for such a project, today we are passing the hat. Put in what you can, and starting tomorrow, there will be donation boxes at the newspaper office, the mercantile, and the ice cream parlor. The sooner we have the money, the sooner we will begin to build the backstop. It'd be nice if we could build some seats for the spectators too." Applause broke out. "Okay, so here it goes." He took the hat off his head and handed it to Manny. "We'll give you the honors, son."

While the folks gathered, Manny went down the line. Those who had money with them dropped some in, and others said they'd use the donation boxes.

Several of the women stepped up to dish out the ice cream donated by Rebecca from the ice cream parlor. The red team lined up first as the winners, and everyone else waited until both teams had their dishes filled.

Thorliff went down the line, congratulating his players and thanking them for a good game. "We'll do even better next time."

"Can we play again next Sunday?"

"I think so. At least, we're planning on it. As you know, it all depends on the weather."

After all the good-byes had been said, Thorliff, along with Andrew and his wife, Ellie, joined the family on the porch. "Did anyone count the money collected yet?"

Ingeborg shook her head. "John dumped it from his hat into the bowl on the table. Looks like a lot."

"Let's get it counted, and tomorrow I'll open an account at the bank for it." He paused. "I have a better idea—you kids can count it. Emmy, you want to find a tablet? Carl, you can help."

The girls eagerly set up at the kitchen table and started sorting out the change. Manny carefully counted the bills.

Thorliff leaned against the porch post and looked at his mor. "Good. This way, we can talk about my great idea."

"I wondered when I'd get to find out what it is." Ingeborg smiled at David Gould as he settled in beside her on the porch swing.

"I'm all in favor." He too was smiling.

Thorliff wondered how much of Gould's smiling was from the good camaraderie of the game today and how much was because of his mor.

How to approach this? He broke off a

48

piece of the branch he'd picked up in the yard. "You know when we were talking about your life—well, mine too—back when we first came to this land?"

Ingeborg nodded. "The grandchildren are always asking me to tell them the stories."

"We grown-ups love stories too. I would say it is stories that make the world go around." Gould mindlessly set the swing to swaying back and forth, back and forth.

"They even shape how we approach God." Ingeborg smiled. "Jesus taught in parables. Stories."

Thorliff nodded. "Even little Blessing is full of stories. Especially your story, Mor. You have had a massive presence in this town's existence. I want your story told. But not just my take on it. Everyone's. I want to write letters to the people who know you, asking them to tell their stories. People like your cousin Gunlaug in Minnesota. Andrew and Ellie, your stories too. And Mor, I want your story told by you. Then I will compile them and build a historical memoir."

"Well," she mused, "if anyone could do that, you could."

Thorliff had just given himself a massive task.

And he could hardly wait.

Two days later Thorliff was working at his desk when he got a call. "Thorliff, Fritz Stauffer just fell off the roof out on the Hanover barn." It was Toby on the phone, a friend who worked in construction.

"Have you called the hospital yet?"

"The operator did. We have him loaded in the wagon with as much padding as we could find, and they are leaving now."

"Thanks, Toby. I'll meet them at the hospital." Thorliff clicked the earpiece of his telephone. "Call Ingeborg, please." He waited until she picked up. "Mor, that construction worker Fritz Stauffer just fell off a barn. Please call John and set the prayers in motion. I'm on my way to the hospital."

"Do they have a telephone where he lives?"

"I don't believe so. I'll send someone over there."

"John and I should be there shortly."

"Thank you." Thorliff hung up and stepped into the press room, where Inga had been setting type since she got home from school and Emmy was typing a stack of letters he had given her. "One of the construction workers fell off a barn roof, so I'm heading to the hospital. The story will probably be front page. You're okay here?"

"Of course." The two girls spoke almost in unison.

"Any questions, call me there."

His mind raced faster than his feet as he strode to the hospital. How badly was Stauffer hurt? Thank God for the X-ray machine the hospital in Chicago had sent to them when it got a new one. He tried to think of Stauffer's family, or was the fellow one of the single men living in the apartments? He used to know everyone who worked for the construction crews, but not so much anymore.

Swinging open the door to the hospital, he saw Dr. Commons pushing a gurney to the emergency entrance. "Any more news?" he asked.

"No, so we're ready for anything. I'll be handling this, as I have more training on the X-ray."

"Isn't there danger in using that machine? I read somewhere . . ."

"We wear lead protection. And before you ask, I sent Astrid home earlier today. She said she doesn't feel well. Just in case it's something catching . . ." He let the sentence fall.

Thorliff nodded. "Thank you." But he was smiling inside. Dr. Commons had sent Astrid home, eh? Although he had to admit, once they knew they would have a new resident again, she had been more amenable to taking some time off.

"When will your new crew arrive?" Thorliff asked.

"Tomorrow, I think. One resident, three nurses, and some kind of new machine that records blood pressure."

"The wagon's here." Thorliff opened the double doors, ready to assist with transferring the patient from the wagon to the gurney.

Benny, who had lost his legs from the knees down when he was little, was driving the wagon.

"Hey, Benny, how did it go?" During the summer, Benny drove wagons for the construction crews. He'd started doing it when they built the Monster, as they called the three-story building at the deaf school.

"He came to about a mile out. The pain is pretty bad."

Dr. Commons climbed up in the wagon to check Stauffer's vitals. He gave the patient a shot of morphine, all the while talking in a gentle voice. "Tell Toby they did a good job here. We can lift him with the quilt."

"I will." Benny stayed on the seat, ready to signal the team forward.

"Do you know anything about him?" Thorliff asked.

Benny nodded. "He's single and lives at

the apartments. He's been here for about a year and is learning English from Mrs. Jeffers. She told me he's a good worker. He just sent back to Germany for his fiancée. She's supposed to arrive soon." He frowned. "In fact, maybe tomorrow. I think that's what he said."

By now, several other men stood around, waiting for instructions. Dr. Commons checked Stauffer's pulse again and lifted an eyelid. "Okay, four men up here, and we'll hand him off to four on the ground. We do not want to bend him or shift him in any way in case there's a spinal injury. Ready?"

He and Thorliff took the upper body, rolling the quilt to form handholds. "On three. One, two, three." They lifted as one and shuffled their burden to waiting hands. "Now, all at the same time, lower him to the gurney, and we'll strap him in." That took a minute as the doctor stuffed bedsheets under the small of Mr. Stauffer's back. "Now, Benny."

As the team pulled the wagon out of the way, they turned the gurney and wheeled it inside and down the hall to the X-ray room. Four men again lifted Stauffer from the gurney to the X-ray table. Dr. Commons donned a heavy lead apron, and he and a nurse got everything in place, then stepped out of the room. The machine whirred and clicked. He set up for another shot and repeated the process.

"Do you have any information on him?" Nurse Deborah asked the gathered men, clipboard and forms in hand.

Thorliff told her what Benny had told him, so she filled in the form. "The usual billing," he added. His policy was that anyone injured on the job did not have to worry about paying the expenses.

Ingeborg arrived.

"He's still in the X-ray room." Thorliff answered the question before it could be asked. "And Dr. Commons sent Astrid home."

"Really?" Her eyebrows tickled her hairline. "She feels that ill?"

"Apparently she didn't object. So I'd guess so." Astrid was notorious for following the old saying, *Do as I say, not as I do.*

Ingeborg gently shook her head. "Uff da."

John Solberg arrived slightly out of breath. "We'll be over at the window." He nodded toward the end of the hall, where several chairs were grouped at the wall of windows. "Send anyone down who wants to join us."

Thorliff walked with them. "His fiancée is scheduled to arrive on tomorrow's train. John, has he talked with you about a wedding?"

"Yes, he was planning to have her stay in his new house, and he would remain in the apartment until they were married."

"Is his house finished?"

"Not quite, but enough that they were going to move into it."

"She can stay with us at first," Ingeborg volunteered. "I'll meet her at the train when she arrives. Poor Mr. Stauffer. He's been working so hard to get things ready for her. I wonder what all needs to be done."

"There you go, Ingeborg." John grinned at her. "I'll ask Mary Martha to join you."

"Are you thinking what I'm thinking?"

"Most likely. Let's pray for him now."

Thorliff left them with their heads bowed and stopped at the desk to see Nurse Deborah—who was now Nurse Deborah Valders, since she and Toby had married. "Never-ending?"

"That's for sure. I'm working our new nurses into the schedule. You want me to call you as soon as we know anything?"

"Yes, please. And ask Mor if she would stop by my office on her way home. I have a feeling she has something up her sleeve."

Deborah smiled. "Are you going to interview the new resident and nurses for this next edition?"

"Just mentions in this edition. Inga is

typesetting it as we speak." He would have to redo the front page and insert an article about Fritz Stauffer, but that was why he always left it until last. "See you later," he said as he walked out the door.

He turned off Main Street and was almost to his gate when Astrid called to him from her front porch.

"Can you come over? Amelia has the pitcher ready to pour."

Instead of turning right into his gate, he turned left and crossed the street. "I see you are doing what you were told."

"Oh hush. Danny is sleeping, and we are enjoying the breeze. I'll take a nap as well in a bit, try to shake this exhaustion."

"I'm impressed you obeyed Dr. Commons and came home. Thank you. You usually don't let anyone else run the show." Thorliff climbed the steps and sank into one of the rocking chairs.

A sly smirk eased onto her face. "I haven't told Mor yet, so you should feel special that you get to hear it first. But I suspect I might be pregnant."

Thorliff felt happiness swell in his chest. "That's wonderful! I promise not to spill the beans and take away the fun of telling the rest of the family."

Astrid gave him her sternest doctor look,

then relaxed back into her chair, shaking her head. "I feel so sorry for Mr. Stauffer."

"It's such a pity."

"James hasn't read the X-rays yet?" Astrid, chief administrator of their hospital, had a lot of trouble sitting when everyone else was hustling.

"He hadn't yet when I left, but he sure set them up and took the pictures mighty quick." Thorliff shrugged. "Mor and John are praying. Deborah promised to call me with the diagnosis. I should be able to get it in this week's edition."

The screen door opened as Amelia Jeffers, Astrid's mother-in-law, backed out with a tray.

Thorliff leaped to his feet and took it from her. "Why didn't you say something?"

Amelia shrugged and thanked him. "You'd think, as close as we live, we'd see more of each other." She tucked a strand of her gray hair back into place.

"I know. Crazy, isn't it?" He held the tray so they could take their glasses and then set it on the table. He sat back down, glass in hand. A sip turned into swallows, and he sighed. "Now, that hit the spot. Thank you."

"Here, try these." Amelia held out the plate of cookies. "All right, now, what is the news?"

"New hospital staff arrives tomorrow. Mr. Stauffer's fiancée arrives sometime soon, probably tomorrow, and I'm sure Mor will enlist your help with whatever she is thinking about. She and John are at the hospital praying for him as we speak."

"Busy time." Astrid leaned against the cushions of her chair. "Oh, this feels so good. I've been nauseated all morning. Thank you, Amelia, for insisting."

Amelia took one of the cookies. "The bedrooms here are ready for our new nurses, since their rooms at the boardinghouse aren't quite finished. Sophie decided to get the rooms painted while they were vacant, and the project is taking longer than she expected."

Astrid nodded. "Projects always take longer than you expect. And we are planning on the social on Saturday to welcome them all to the community. The resident will stay with you again, right?" She looked at Thorliff.

"For as long as he can put up with Rolly. Or, if he'd rather, he can stay at the boardinghouse for the year."

Thorliff finished his glass and brushed the cookie crumbs off his shirt. "Well, I better get going. Toby will be by with daily reports pretty soon."

"How many crews is he running?"

"Three. One on that barn, one finishing

up the Webster house, and one starting another block of houses out past the church and schools. We're going to buy the one-and-a-half-floor Sears packages this time to speed things up. Digging the cellars now."

"And I suppose they're all sold?"

"I think so." He pushed himself to his feet. "Thanks again." He ambled out the walk and paused to shut the gate securely. Astrid's son, Danny, loved being outside and tended to wander off.

"Hi, Pa!"

He heard Rolly's voice before he saw him. "Hi to you too." Thorliff pushed open his gate, setting Rolly to giggling as he clung to the frame. Thorliff realized that Rolly was now big enough that he was going to pull the hinges loose one of these days. The boy needed reprimanding. But not today.

"Inga and Emmy came home from school to have dinner with me," Rolly announced.

"Good. Are they still working?"

"Uh-huh. Thelma took a pitcher of ice water out to them, and some cookies. I wanted to go, but they said they're busy. What are they doing?"

"Inga is typesetting the paper, and Emmy is typing letters for me."

"I want to go to Tante Sophie's, but nobody would go with me."

"Sorry." Thorliff tousled his son's hair. "You are growing up so fast."

"Can Hanny and Olaf come play with me?"

Thorliff headed for his office. "Let me think about it. We'll figure something out." After all, they were cousins.

This town really was growing. He could remember when there were no playmates Inga's age. Now there were half a dozen children nearby, many of them relatives.

"Your mail is on your desk," Emmy announced as Thorliff stepped into his office. She stretched her arms over her head. "All the letters are stacked there for you to sign, the copies in a separate stack. I addressed the envelopes too."

"Thank you. Are you finished?"

"One more to go."

He could hear Inga still at her task.

"She's on the last page," Emmy said.

"Well, I'll be. You two sure know how to keep working."

"How is the man who fell?" Emmy asked.

"We don't know yet." The phone rang. He waited to hear the pattern of the rings and then picked up the earpiece. "Thorliff here."

"Dr. Commons," Gerald said.

"Thanks."

"Thorliff, the X-rays show three cracked

vertebrae, but the spine is still in alignment," Dr. Commons reported.

"Thank God."

"Yes, our prayers have turned to praises. I told John and Ingeborg first, then Dr. Astrid. We will keep him here for a few days, get the swelling down. He won't be going back to work for a while. We are devising a brace like a stiff corset that he can wear, but he will have to take it easy."

"Is he conscious?"

"Yes, somewhat. The morphine is fogging him up."

"Has anyone asked him when his fiancée is coming? I heard maybe tomorrow."

"I think Ingeborg is taking care of that."

"Good. How long will he be down?"

"At least a couple weeks, maybe longer. He's young, so his bones should knit fairly fast."

"Okay, thank you." Thorliff hung up and nodded. Leave it to his mor.

The next morning, Thorliff joined Astrid, Ingeborg, Reverend Solberg, and Deborah Valders at the train station to meet the new nurses who were interning for a year, along with the resident doctor. Would Stauffer's fiancée be on the train? He didn't know.

Dr. Commons had planned to come, but one of the farmers had brought his son in for stitches in a long gash in his arm.

"How does it feel to know another doctor is taking care of the emergencies so you can do this?" Thorliff asked his sister.

"A big relief. And a new resident is another blessing. We'll have a third person to share the night shifts. We've come a long way."

"That we have." Thorliff turned to his mother. "So what are you planning for Stauffer's new house?"

"Whatever made you think that?" Mor looked downright coy.

"I know you. And John said Mary Martha was going with you."

Ingeborg half shrugged. "You want to help too?"

"Do you need some construction work done?"

"We do, actually. We need doors hung, floors painted, along with woodwork. He doesn't have much furniture yet. We need a bed, a kitchen table and chairs, and a chest of drawers would be good. The women will gather up linens and kitchenware. Curtains would be nice too, but they're not as necessary. We were planning on a kitchen shower anyway, so we will announce this in church on Sunday. Fritz says she will arrive next Monday, so that gives us some time."

"That's true. It's only Wednesday. I'll ask Toby to send over a crew tomorrow. Is the paint there?"

She shook her head. "Penny is donating paint. She called in an order yesterday, so it should be here on Friday. A bed is critical, as he will not be able to get up and down easily or sleep on the floor, as he has been doing."

"Did you ask Sophie?"

"No, but that is a good idea. Or the crew could build the frame and stretch ropes, and we'll find a mattress for it somewhere, or at least a straw pallet. But it has to be firm, Dr. Commons says."

"Have you mentioned any of this to David?"

"Not yet. I'll see him at supper tonight. I know there is a quilt in the mission barrel to send to the reservation. We can use that."

They looked up as the train whistled the long blast when the engineer put on the brakes for the approach to the station.

"Is there any way to contact the fiancée?" Thorliff asked.

"Doubtful. Oh well, we'll deal with all this the way we always do—let God provide."

"And has He ever let us down?" John asked.

They all shook their heads. "He's been right down to the wire at times, but never late," Ingeborg said.

So why is it hard to trust Him when we've seen so many prayers answered? Would he ever be able to trust like his mor?

Chapter 5

"Come home soon."

"As soon as I can." David Gould kissed Ingeborg on the cheek, wishing he had the right to kiss her lips.

"I'll miss you."

Enough to say yes when I finally get up the courage to ask you to marry me? He just felt he should mention his desired life change to his children before he really set it in motion. He'd invited them to come visit Blessing, but in spite of Jonathan's raving about life in the small town, and his as well, they firmly believed everything their mother had told them after her brief visit for Jonathan's wedding all those years ago. She'd definitely poisoned their minds.

"You need to be boarding, Mr. Gould," the conductor said softly.

"Yes, I know." He squeezed Ingeborg's hand. "I so wish you would come with me."

"Perhaps another time. You know how busy it gets here as summer sets in." She stepped back and blew him a kiss.

He climbed aboard and took a seat in his private compartment so he could wave to her out the window. He was already missing her. *Just get busy,* he ordered himself. *You have plenty to do, and at least here on the train you won't have any distractions.*

His mind immediately jumped back to Sunday night, after the game was over and all the other folks had gone home. Manny and the girls had been counting the donations for the baseball field at the school. How easy it would have been to just say he would pay for it. It wasn't like he couldn't, but he truly believed that was not the best way. The community had to know they were an important part of it happening.

That was the way Blessing had grown all through the years—hard work and people caring for each other. And look at all they had accomplished. His mind wandered around the town. The hospital. The new grain elevator, after the first one blew up and started a fire that nearly took out the town. The machine company, the school for the deaf, all the farms. He smiled. Ingeborg's cheese house. The town had a feeling all its own, what with the hotel and the train station and the other stores and businesses along Main Street.

He looked up at a tap on the door. "Yes?"

"Can I bring you anything, sir?"

Gould didn't recognize the black man wearing a waiter's uniform and a tentative smile. "Is William about?"

"No, sir. Not sure why, but he isn't working right now. My name is Carver, and I'll be your server for this trip."

"Come in, please." Gould smiled. "I think I've seen you before."

"Yes, sir, in the dining car. Would you care for coffee and one of the pastries Chef just brought out of the oven?"

Gould nodded. "Thank you for offering. I'd appreciate the coffee." He paused. "Oh, go ahead and bring a scone too. And, Carver, after that, please ask if anyone else knows what has happened with William."

"Yes, sir."

As the waiter backed out into the hall and shut the door, Gould began to think. William was a fine man who had accepted the assistance Gould had offered for the education of his children. All of them were now in college or some kind of training thanks to an education fund Gould and his wife had set up for those who couldn't otherwise afford it.

He wrote himself a note to check in to William's situation. At least he had an address for him at the house. Then he extricated a sheaf of papers from his briefcase and set to reading but was interrupted by a tap on the door.

"Come in," he said.

Carver lowered a tray to the table and set out a cup and saucer along with a small plate and napkin, then poured the coffee and placed the coffee carafe on the table with a plate of small, fragrant pastries.

"Is there anything else, sir?"

"Not for now. Thank you. I'll ring if I want something."

"Yes, sir." Carver gently clicked the door closed as he left.

Gould sipped his coffee and eyed the assortment of delicacies. If only Ingeborg were here, the time would fly by. She would be figuring out how to make the new kind of specialty and teasing him about eating more than one.

He deliberately set his cup down and picked up the papers. *Just get through this trip*, he ordered himself. Why was this trip bothering him more than the others? That question set him to contemplating, which was best done while sipping coffee and staring out the window. Fields were growing green, cattle and horses grazed, and small villages flew by.

Turning back to his work, he wrote his responses to some project questions and reached for another of the pastries. The coffee had gone cold. Without a thought, he pressed his bell to summon the server. When the coffee carafe was hot again, he leaned back, cup in hands, and let his thoughts return to Ingeborg. The desire to see her, hear her voice, ate at him like the mosquitoes of North Dakota.

Only two nights before he would be back in New York and a house he no longer called home. That brought up another thought. The house still had Geraldine's stamp all over it. He hadn't changed a thing since she died, but now was the time. Actually, it was past time.

Since Geraldine died, he was looking at many things differently. All the things he had worked so hard for. All the years he had spent building an empire. *Admit it*, he told himself, *you thrived on the challenges*. His mind flipped back through the years of travel that kept him from being home with his wife and children. And when he was home, all the hours at the office or the club, all the conquests, the dreams fulfilled, the people he had run over. His motto had been *join me or you'll regret it*. One thing he was pleased with was he had always paid his staff well; after all, that was the best way to get and keep good people who wanted to work, to build.

He watched lights from houses and towns slowly parade past his window.

But now? Now would be different. He slapped the palm of his hand down on the table. The cup rattled in the saucer. He blinked. Why were all the dishes sitting here? Shaking his head, he pushed the button to call Carver. How many hours had he been sitting here thinking?

A tap at the door.

"Come in."

In a matter of moments, Carver cleared the table and wiped off the crumbs. "Can I get you something to drink, or perhaps supper?" He handed Gould a menu.

"What time is it?"

"Going on six, sir."

"Give me half an hour, and I'll make up my mind. In the meantime, where are we?"

"Chicago in a couple of hours."

He settled back and, only barely hearing the door close, returned his other papers to his briefcase and pulled out fresh pages to write down all his thoughts and questions from these hours of contemplating. This skill had enabled him to keep track of all the various threads of his life. All his journals were lined up in the library at the New York house. While there, he would have his valet pack them all to be shipped to Blessing. Those and anything else he wanted to keep with him. He started another list. It would be a short one.

Should he bring household staff from New York to the Blessing house? That might make life there easier. But he shook his head. Easier for him, but none of them would fit in. Surely he could find someone in Blessing to tend to the cooking and cleaning.

I thought you were cutting ties with life in New York. Sometimes an inner voice had good ideas, sometimes it badgered him. He and Ingeborg had talked about those inner voices one day. She seemed to think women had them more than men. The things they discussed; never in his entire life had he given a moment's thought to what went on in a woman's mind. Had he ever cared? And yet . . .

Interesting that his inner voice had seemed absent for quite some time. Perhaps . . . He shook his head. Right now he did not need any obnoxious voices intruding. But then, when *did* one have time for such distractions?

Dusk settled as he ate the dinner he'd ordered. Carver had served him well, but . . . but he no longer wanted to eat alone. In

Blessing he had a standing invitation at Ingeborg's, and he'd joined Thorliff's family, and Andrew's too, at times. The Solbergs often invited him, and Grace and Jonathan always set a place for him. Life was so different in Blessing. There had been frequent dinner parties in New York—Geraldine saw to that. She was highly regarded as an excellent hostess. When he was home, they had dinner at seven, in the dining room, with at least four courses. And everyone dressed appropriately. That was just the way it was. As the children grew up, they joined their parents in the dining room, dressed and proper. Their nannies trained them in proper etiquette and manners.

What was going on with him? All this introspection.

The first thing he would do when he reached his office at his house was to put in a call to Ingeborg. That thought firmly in place, he nodded and pulled a copy of *Pilgrim's Progress* from his briefcase. He and Thorliff had a challenge to read this and meet with John Solberg to discuss it, and it should help pass several pleasant hours on his trip.

He tipped the cab driver generously and led the way to the front door of the gray granite house. He hadn't yet struck the knocker before the door opened.

"Welcome home, sir," his butler greeted him. "I hope you had a comfortable journey." Mason reached for Gould's valise.

"I did, as always."

"Shall I draw your bath, sir?" Walter, his valet, who stood right behind the butler, took David's hat from him and hung it on the peg.

"Not yet."

"Will you want refreshments?"

"No. I'll wait for dinner."

"Very good, sir." The gentleman disappeared upstairs with the valise.

David was accustomed to the services of a staff; he had grown up with one at his beck and call. But what did the butler do that David could not? Nothing. How much time would it have taken Gould to carry his own valise upstairs? Two minutes? His butler and valet were conveniences, not necessities. He pictured a butler in the Bjorklund home and nearly snickered aloud. Emmy, Inga, and Ingeborg would bump into the butler a few times, declare him to be in the way, and shoo him outside. They saw to David's needs and took care of him not because they were in his employ but because they loved him and enjoyed doing those things. What a difference!

Instead of going up to his rooms, Gould retreated to his office and picked up the telephone. "Ingeborg Bjorklund in Blessing, North Dakota. Yes, I'll wait."

He tapped his pencil against the blotter on his cherrywood desk, but as the wait stretched, he flipped the pencil to the sharpened end and drew concentric circles on the first paper he pulled out of the drawer. He joined the circles with curving lines. He should have told the operator to call him back. He drew stars around the circles.

A tap at the door stopped his pencil. "Yes!"

"I brought you something to drink, sir," a stuttering female voice answered.

"Good. Bring it in." He knew he was being rude, so he smiled at her when the door opened. "Thank you." He pointed to the corner of his desk.

"Your call to North Dakota is on the line," the operator said.

"I'm here." He looked at the maid. "Thank you." He'd never seen her before. What had happened to the other maid who'd been with them for years? He needed to have a talk with the housekeeper.

"Go ahead," the operator said.

He stared at the telephone as if he could see through it. "Hello, Ingeborg?"

A young voice answered. "No, this is Emmy. Grandma is out in the garden."

He rolled his eyes. Of course she was outside. It wasn't dark yet. "Don't worry, Emmy. Nothing's wrong. Please go call her."

He heard the earpiece bang against the wall, flinched, and heaved a sigh. Why did everything have to be so difficult? *I am never coming back here without her again, even if I have to hog-tie her and—*

David Jonathan Gould, for crying out loud, calm down.

His stern order made him draw another breath. *Lord, give me patience. This is not like me.* Shaking his head, he reached for the glass filled with an iced drink of some kind. Lemonade? No . . .

"Hello?"

He studied the molding above the fireplace and sucked in a deep breath.

"Hello, David. Mr. Gould?"

"Forgive me, Ingeborg. I . . . don't know what came over me."

"Are you all right?"

"I am now." He could feel the truth of it relax his shoulders and settle him deeper in his chair. "I am now."

"You concerned me there for a minute."

"Are you sitting down?"

"No, why?"

"Because we might be talking for a while, and I want you to be comfortable."

Her chuckle made him relax his head against the back of his chair. *You have no idea how much I needed to hear your voice.* That realization caught him up short. What was going on with him? All that ruminating on the train, and now . . . *Face it, Gould, this woman has you wrapped around her finger. No, her heart.*

"So what is going on there?" he asked.

"A beautiful day with just enough breeze to make the curtains dance. We were sitting out on the porch during the warmer hours, so we ate dinner out there too, and just now I was weeding the carrots. It takes finesse to weed carrots so early. I hate to lose even one, since my mouth is watering for fresh carrots. Have you ever pulled a carrot, wiped the dirt off on your clothing, and eaten it right there? That first sweet bite makes up for all the canned carrots we eat during the winter."

"No. I'm sorry to say I never have. But then, I've never weeded a garden." Why did he feel like he was missing out on something of value? What was wrong with hiring a gardener? He wondered for a moment how many gardeners and groundskeepers he was paying to keep this place looking like it did. He assumed he had put money in the account established to maintain the house and grounds. Or had he?

He jerked himself back from rapid-fire thoughts and questions to the present conversation. "Excuse me, what did you say?"

Her chuckle made him wish he were there. Not here in this study that he used to see as a needed place. Where he could close out the day and not be bothered with the goings-on around him.

"What time is it there?" Ingeborg asked.

"One hour ahead of you. Here we are on Eastern time, North Dakota is on Central."

"So what are you having for supper?"

"I have no idea. But the cook and butler fully expect me to eat in the dining room when I am home. I'm sure Cook has prepared enough for the entire staff."

"What do they do when you are not there?"

"I-I don't really know." *But*, he told himself, *I do know that some things are going to change around here, starting tomorrow.*

Chapter 6

"What's wrong, Grandma?" Emmy asked.

Ingeborg set the telephone receiver back on the prong. "Nothing is really wrong. . . ." But she shook her head. "At least I don't think there is."

"Mr. Gould got home all right?"

Ingeborg nodded. *He just doesn't sound like himself.* But it was nothing she could put her finger on. The telephone rang again. She paused to see if the ring was for them, then lifted the receiver. "Hello."

"Call from Thorliff, Ingeborg. Busy time, eh?"

She smiled at the operator's comment.

The line clicked, and Thorliff's voice filled her ear. "Mor, I have some things to discuss with you. Would now be a good time?"

"Good as any. As long as the telephone keeps ringing, I can't get back out in the garden anyway."

"I could come later, if you'd rather."

"Bring Rolly with you?" she asked.

"If you'd like."

Ingeborg nodded, then remembered he

couldn't see her. "See you soon. The girls have been baking cookies. Stay for supper? You can bring Thelma too. She needs a break."

"Guess I'll hitch up the horse, then. Can we bring anything? You know Thelma always has to bring something."

They hung up, but Ingeborg hadn't had time to walk across the kitchen before two long rings and a short called her back. "Hello?"

"Ingeborg, I have a chicken about to come out of the oven. You want I should bring that?" Thelma always sounded brisk.

"Sure. We'll have potluck."

She'd just hung up the telephone again when Manny came through the door.

"I knew it! Gingerbread cookies. I could smell them up the road." He picked up one that Emmy was just sliding off the cookie sheet. "Ow."

Emmy rolled her dancing eyes. "You should know better than that by now. Take one of the cooler ones."

Still juggling the hot cookie, he picked up another. "You want to come help milk?"

"You want supper?" Inga countered.

"Inga, you haven't milked cows for years." He chomped the head off the second gingerbread man.

"You haven't made supper for years, if ever."

"Just thought I'd ask." He snatched another cookie and headed for the barn. Freda called to him from the cheese house, so he made a detour over there. He helped with the cheese house whenever needed.

Ingeborg shook her head. Manny had come to them a broken boy, but now, even fully grown, he loved to tease the two girls, especially Emmy. Their stories also needed to go in The Book, as they had all come to call it. Perhaps that was what Thorliff wanted to talk with her about. He'd probably bring a couple of newspapers along. Today the biweekly paper was released. What could they do to celebrate?

"Emmy, Inga, you two go get ice for making ice cream. I'll mix up the other ingredients. Make sure you cover up the ice again, or Andrew will be after you."

The icehouse was a cellar dug into the ground, well insulated and with sawdust and burlap bags covering the ice that had been cut and stored during the winter. They all used the ice in their iceboxes in the kitchens. What a grand day when Haakan had insisted they buy an icebox so they could have cold things in the summer. Until then they had kept jugs of milk, cream, and buttermilk in the trough in the well house. The windmill pumped water into the rock trough, then out to the cattle tank. Eggs kept cool enough there too, as did smoked meat.

When the girls ran out the door, Ingeborg gathered the eggs, cream, sugar, and vanilla. Once those were on the counter, she set the rest of the eggs to boil. Deviled eggs were always appreciated. They would eat supper out on the porch. It was a shame David wasn't here. He loved ice cream and impromptu meals like this.

The thought made her pause. What was it about their conversation that concerned her? She cracked the eggs into the bowl and started beating them to a froth. *Lord, you know all things. Please keep David in the palm of your hand. I can watch out for him here, but only you can oversee such distances.* She smiled at the memory of his shoulder against hers, sitting in the swing on the front porch.

She added the sugar, then the cream and vanilla. It was a shame the strawberries weren't ready, but surely they still had canned ones down in the cellar. A strawberry sauce would make the treat even more special. Putting the bowl of batter in the icebox, she went down the cellar stairs for canned strawberries and found one jar of strawberry jam left too. They still had a few jars of dill pickles left, but none upstairs. Clutching the jars in her arms, she climbed the stairs more slowly than she had a few years ago. It was hard to admit she might be slowing down a bit.

"Ingeborg?"

"Coming, Freda."

"Why didn't you call me? I could have gotten that for you." Freda took the jars from Ingeborg. "Where are the girls?"

"Gone to get ice. It's beginning to look like we're having a party here tonight."

"What's the occasion?"

"Thorliff called to say he was coming out, and I said bring Rolly, and so now Thelma is coming too, and perhaps I should call Kaaren and Lars."

"He is down at the barn, milking."

Lars, Andrew, and Manny, along with two boys from the deaf school, took care of the milking these days, with each of them milking three to four cows, and Manny now in charge of the calves. Carl, Andrew's oldest son, helped him, and he and his pa took care of the pigs and sheep at their barn. Emmy and Ingeborg fed the hens and picked the eggs. Inga helped whenever she was at the farm, which was most of the summer. If she had her way, she'd be there all summer.

Since Ingeborg had bought two ponies for the grandchildren, and Manny let both Emmy and Inga ride his horse, Joker, three or even four could go riding together. They especially loved riding up and down the rivers, both the Red and the Little Salt, and packing picnic lunches for the day. Ingeborg knew where the wild strawberries grew, but they'd take a horse and cart to go there. Later in the summer, they picked and canned Juneberries, after baking pies and cakes and cobblers. Emmy had taught them how to dry the berries and mix them with dried meat and tallow to make pemmican.

Ingeborg watched as the girls trundled a block of ice back in the wheelbarrow. They fetched the axe and whacked off a couple of large pieces to put in a burlap bag. Using the flat of the axe blade, they smashed the ice in the bag into small enough pieces to fill in around the metal ice cream maker. Ingeborg brought out the canister filled with the cream and egg mixture to set in the middle, and they packed the ice in around it. They sprinkled rock salt on the ice and started turning the crank to turn the canister.

As soon as Manny washed up, he took turns cranking too. "Isn't this supposed to be the men's job?" he asked.

"If we waited for you to get here, we'd be having ice cream for breakfast." Emmy took her turn again.

"We need more ice," Inga said. Both girls looked at Manny, then at the burlap-shrouded ice block with the axe beside it.

"All right. You think we'll use all of this?"
He whacked off a chunk.

"I hope not. Then we'll have some for the
icebox."

They heard Thorliff's cart arrive, Rolly
shrieking, "Gramma, we're here!"

"So what are we celebrating this time?"
Thorliff asked when he joined them on the
back porch.

"Here, Pa, your turn." Inga grinned at her
father. "I think we can say we're celebrating
spring. Or perhaps it's because you came for
supper, and then the group grew. Onkel Lars
and Tante Kaaren are coming too."

Thorliff winked. "As if Grandma really
needs an excuse to celebrate. The next one
will be strawberry season, and we'll all have
strawberry shortcake."

Rolly pushed open the screen door and
stood on the top step. "Ice cream!"

"Right you are. Here. You crank awhile."
Thorliff moved aside for his son.

Rolly cranked for a minute, two at most,
then stepped back. He looked at Emmy.
"Your turn."

Ingeborg watched from the screen door
and joined the others in chuckling. She
opened the door and sat down on the upper
step with Thorliff.

"Isn't it beautiful out here?" She watched

the barn swallows dipping up mud from beside the cattle's water tank to build their nests under the eaves of the barn. Birds sang in the cottonwood tree at the corner of the porch. Its branches arched up and over to shade the house from the coming summer's heat. Just what she had dreamed when she planted it.

Thorliff watched as Rolly took another turn. "I remember how I used to love making ice cream. Then the feeling went away."

"When Elizabeth died?"

He nodded, small, short jerks of his head, one thumb rubbing the nail on the other.

Ingeborg laid a hand on her son's shoulder. "Grief can be destructive in many ways, especially when you're fighting against God instead of leaning on Him and letting Him bring healing."

"Did it ever get any easier?"

"No. And yes. Death is part of life, but we have a hard time accepting that. Often it seems so unfair. Especially when the one who passes on is young, or even younger than we expected."

"Like my far?"

"Ja, and babies and children, relatives and friends. So many have gone on before."

"But the pain eventually goes away."

"Not totally. Sometimes it sneaks back and grabs you. The best way to handle that is to go ahead and cry it out, pray through it, and the sooner you can put a good memory in its place, the easier it is to breathe."

"Pa, you want to come crank for a while?" Inga asked.

He stood up and stretched, then took over the cranking.

Ingeborg patted the porch deck beside her, and Rolly plopped down to sit. Sitting still was not a skill he had yet mastered. In a moment he was up and off again. "Going to the barn, Gramma," he called over his shoulder.

He is growing up so fast. Good thing we have Grace's baby. She thought a moment. *And Rachel's too. Life continues.*

She blinked and cleared her throat. "We'll be eating out here in about half an hour, if you can get the table set up."

"Sure." Thorliff stood and waved at Kaaren and Lars, who were walking up the lane, Lars carrying the basket for a change. "Is this about all?"

"For tonight."

"We need to build another bench table."

"That we do. We'll bring this one here on the porch down as well." She waved to Kaaren. "You must be feeling better, since you're walking over."

"I am, sort of." She passed through the

gate Lars held open for her, a cough making her pause. "Before you know it, we'll be cooking for the haying crew again."

"At least we're not feeding that construction crew any longer." The enormous crew had worked long hours to build the three-story addition to the deaf school, managing to get it weatherproofed before winter hit. They were working on finishing the interior so they could welcome new students the next fall.

The cranking of the ice cream maker sang counterpoint to the conversation.

"Ice cream, even? And we don't have to walk in to the shop." Lars set their basket on the table, then helped Thorliff get both tables and benches in place.

"And to think I made two dried apple pies today," Kaaren said. "And now there's ice cream. God sure knew what we were doing long before we did."

With everyone working together, the ice cream canister was soon packed in ice and the food spread out on the table. They were all gathering around the table when Ingeborg looked around. "Where's Rolly?"

Thorliff stared at his mother, clearly trying to remember when he had seen his son last. He cupped his hands around his mouth. "Rolly!"

"We'll go look at the barn." Inga and

Emmy tore down the lane, past the well house to the barn. Ingeborg followed them as quickly as she could. "Rolly?" the girls both hollered, then paused to listen.

"Here!" he called.

"Where are you?"

"In the calf pen."

The girls climbed on the fence to look for him. "Oh my goodness, what happened?" Inga shook her head and stared at her little brother, who was picking himself up.

"They knocked me down."

"In the mud?"

"And the manure," Emmy said under her breath.

"What were you doing?" Inga demanded.

"I just wanted to pet them. Then they knocked me down again."

Ingeborg covered her mouth to stop a laugh.

"I sure hope Pa or Thelma brought extra clothes."

Emmy pulled open the gate. "Come on, supper is on the table."

"I don't like those calves." The mud on his face cracked with his frown.

"You're not supposed to come down here by yourself," Ingeborg scolded gently.

"I couldn't find the kittens." He stomped through the gate and reached for Inga's hand.

She pulled back. "Ew!"

"Let's wash you at the pump. Rub your hands together under the water." Ingeborg pulled the pump handle down and pumped three or four times before the water flowed out of the spigot.

"It's cold."

Thorliff clamped his fists on his hips when he joined them. "Roald Phillip Bjorklund, you know you're not to go to the barn alone." His tone backed up his frown.

Rolly sniffed. "I just wanted to see the kittens."

"So how did you get in with the calves?"

Rolly scrubbed his hands some more, his lower lip sticking out.

"Looks like we should dump a bucket of water on you," Thorliff grumbled.

"It's cold."

"Serves you right."

They walked back to where the tables were set up.

Ingeborg rolled her lips together to keep from laughing. "There's extra pants and shirts in my room."

"I'll take him in and clean him up." Inga shook her head. "What a mess."

"Thanks," Thorliff said to his daughter, then sent another stern look toward his son before joining the others around the table.

Ingeborg asked Lars to say the blessing.

"Lord God, thank you for this day, these people, and the food we are about to share. Thank you for your great mercies, and in Jesus' name we pray." He paused, and everyone said *amen* together.

"Pass the food around." Ingeborg started with the platter of chicken in front of her, and the others followed suit. There was Freda's chicken and Thelma's as well, so all had enough. Along with the chicken, they enjoyed the last of the potatoes, parsnips, rutabagas— what a feast.

Inga and Rolly found places to sit, their plates already filled.

"At least he smells better," Emmy whispered to Inga.

"So, Rolly, did you learn anything?" his pa asked.

"I don't like calves."

"He needs to be helping down at the barn so he won't get in trouble," Inga suggested.

"Or make sure he's always with someone older," Thorliff replied.

Rolly kept on eating.

Once they were all served, the conversation picked up again.

"I brought the letter I wrote to send out to all those I could think of. Here, I thought you could read it and see if you see anything that needs changing." Thorliff handed Ingeborg a piece of paper. "And here's the list I'm sending it to. If you have anything you'd like to add . . ." He looked across the table at Manny, who had just slid into his place. "Busy day today?"

"The woodpile at the cheese house was down, so I split some more. Took longer'n I thought. Sorry I'm late."

Ingeborg smiled. "No apology needed."

Thorliff passed the plate of chicken around the table again and asked, "Manny, why do you work so hard and so willingly?"

The young man shrugged. Paused. Thought a minute. He licked his lips. "Food. And love. When we were growing up, my brothers and me, we went hungry a lot. Ma died when I was real little, and Pa wasn't worth much. We brothers decided to go out west, where we'd get rich and not be hungry. I tell ya, we almost starved. We'd come across a hog in the woods, or a calf, and kill it and eat it. Didn't think about who it might belong to. You all know we eventually took to stealing. Robbing. Went hungry anyway."

"I remember," Thorliff said quietly.

"Then Grandma here took me in. Everyone else wanted to put me in jail, and by rights I shoulda gone to jail, but she took me in. Dr. Astrid worked a long time to help mend my broken leg, or I'd be a cripple now. And all that time, I ate. There was food to spare every day. Good food and lots of it. I never had that before. You, Grandma, all of you—you saved me. I owe you everything, but . . . well, I just want to help, whether I owe you or not. You know, just because."

They had all stopped eating to watch him.

He looked around self-consciously. "That's why."

Ingeborg felt tears burning the backs of her eyes. She glanced at Thorliff.

He too was blinking. "That's beautiful. Manny, please write all that down. I want to put it in The Book."

"Dessert's ready," Freda announced.

When they all had their pie with ice cream, Freda came around with the coffeepot and refilled cups. Emmy served lemonade to those who wanted something cool.

Ingeborg took a bite of pie and ice cream and closed her eyes, the better to savor the flavor.

"Good, huh, Gramma?" Rolly licked another spoonful of ice cream. "We should have ice cream every day, it's so good. Huh, Pa?"

"If we had it every day, then it wouldn't be so special. It would be ordinary."

Rolly pondered his pa's comment. "But sometimes we'd put strawberries on it, or maybe chocolate, and then have it plain white. Then it wouldn't never get ordinary."

"How do I argue with that?" Thorliff muttered under his breath to his mor, who just smiled.

When Freda and Thelma started stacking dishes, Emmy and Inga rose to help them, trekking back and forth to the kitchen.

Kaaren handed Thorliff a sheaf of papers. "Here's what I've thought of so far for the Book. Tell us if you want something different. I was feeling better today, but I think I overdid it. We're going home now."

Lars picked up their empty basket, and they walked off down the lane. Kaaren had another spate of coughing as they went.

Ingeborg frowned. "I think it is time she see the doctor. Whatever's ailing her is hanging on too long." She turned to Thorliff. "What is it you wanted to talk about?"

"The Book. I mentioned this before, but I want you to write your own history. An auto-biography, if you will. Everything you can remember. That would be the center, the theme of the book. Like Manny's story."

"I don't know what I'd write about."

"I've been thinking on this, and I'd like to start with some of your remedies. Especially the ones Metiz taught you, along with bits of her story. Like when you met and became

92

friends. They can be included in the book also, or maybe even in another book. You write the stories, and we'll have Emmy type them. I'm asking the same of Tante Sophie about the boardinghouse. Penny would be another good one, with the story of the mercantile. The more I work on this, the more excited I get."

"I am not certain I can do that."

"Just pretend you are writing a letter. Or telling Inga and Emmy about David. It's writing instead of talking, but pretend they're sitting there listening."

"Oh, now that is a good idea."

"Good. I'll send letters to all the relatives, including Gunlaug. Can you write about your years in Norway?"

"Maybe. A rather abbreviated version."

"I have a feeling this could become a rather large book." Thorliff lifted Rolly off the bench. "You tired?"

Rolly nodded and rubbed his eyes, then leaned against Thorliff's chest.

"When is David coming back?" Thorliff asked.

Ingeborg shrugged. "He has a lot to do there."

"Reverend Solberg and I are interviewing a young woman tomorrow for the teaching job in the grade school. We still need another teacher for the high school." He looked around. "Where's Thelma?"

"She and Freda are in the kitchen."

A few minutes later Ingeborg watched Thorliff, Thelma, Inga, and Rolly trot out the lane, dust clouding behind the cart. *Thank you, Lord, for such a pleasant evening.* The only thing missing was David.

She turned back into the house, where she heard Emmy and Manny playing Old Maid at the kitchen table. Picking up her Bible and pad of paper, she sat down in her rocking chair.

If David were here, they would still be talking out on the front porch. How could they find so much to talk about? Was he missing her as much as she was missing him?

Chapter 7

"Oh no. Now I'll be late."

Thorliff ignored the telephone ringing two shorts and a long and dashed from the newspaper office. The train whistled again, and now he heard the screaming brakes. He ran toward the depot but slowed to a trot when he saw John Solberg waiting on the platform. The conductor swung down to the worn wooden platform and set the iron step in place.

"Mornin', Reverend. You waitin' for this young woman?" His white teeth flashed as he smiled.

"I sure am." John looked over his shoulder as Thorliff puffed to a stop beside him. "Cutting it a bit close, eh?"

"Sorry. I got involved in an article for the paper and lost track of time. The train whistle finally penetrated my concentration." He looked up to see a young woman, dressed in an ankle-length skirt and fitted jacket, accepting the conductor's assistance on the step. Her matching hat with a curving feather was pinned atop a coil of thick mink hair highlighted with touches of red that caught the sun.

Her smile at the conductor's welcome turned her rather severe face into sunshine.

Thorliff and John stepped forward at the same time.

"Miss Louisa Gutenberg?" John asked.

"Yes." Her smile transformed her face again, this time revealing a dimple in her right cheek.

"We're pleased to have you today. I am

Reverend John Solberg, and this is Thorliff Bjorklund, head of our school board."

She shook hands with both of them, her smile back in hiding. Thorliff noted that her hand was strong and rough. This was a lady who worked hard and was accustomed to physical labor. Often the teachers, the lady teachers especially, seemed more delicate.

"Thank you for coming." Thorliff kept his smile. "We thought we'd show you around Blessing and then have dinner at the boarding-house."

"That would be lovely. I've heard good things about your town. My sister and her family live in Grafton."

John stepped to her left, so Thorliff moved to her right. Her stride was smooth and purposeful. John suggested, "We'll go up Main Street and then around to the school."

When they left the train station, John waved an arm, showing off the grain elevator, the flour mill, and the machinery company. The hospital, with the new wing still under construction, took up the other side of the street before the Red River.

Thorliff was struck once again by the huge part his mor had played in this town, and was still playing. She and Haakan and their children, not to mention the extended family, had built this place. The book of reminiscences was going to be not just a family memoir but a historical record of the whole town, nearly every facet of it. He could see that it would sap all his time and strength and talents, but it would be worth it. *Blessing: The Town Ingeborg Built*. He almost laughed out loud. She would never accept that title.

As they walked west on Main Street, John pointed out the obvious: the boardinghouse, the Soda Shoppe, the mercantile and other smaller shops. Thorliff was glad Miss Gutenberg was coming at this time. She was seeing Blessing at its loveliest; the houses lining the broad streets looked welcoming with their fenced yards and trees that shaded the porches, flower beds and gardens.

They passed the Lutheran church and paused at the two schools. John explained, "This is the elementary school. We now have four teachers in the elementary. The high school takes ninth through twelfth grades. We need another teacher there too."

She gazed at it. "Such windows."

Thorliff found himself smiling. "Yes, when we built this, we made sure to have plenty of windows so we didn't need to use as much electricity. The furnace burns coal, so we have central heat, and we have indoor plumbing."

"Really?" Was she beautiful? Not exactly.

Pretty? Not really, but she was striking. Her hair almost glowed, it was so silky. What would it be like to run one's fingers through that lush silkiness?

Thorliff's thoughts slapped him across the face. What was he thinking? For shame!

He knew John had been planning to take her on a tour of the school's interior, but he said, "After our dinner, I would be happy to show you the facility. We're rather proud of it."

John studied him oddly but said nothing. They continued on.

They reached the edge of town and turned back, identifying the houses they passed. The whistle at the machinery company blew, announcing that noon had arrived.

"We have reservations for dinner at the boardinghouse." Thorliff led the way.

She paused and turned to look back in the direction they had come. "This is such a pleasant place, but I'm sure you hear that often. Where will your teacher be housed? That was not mentioned in the letter."

Thorliff pointed to Ingeborg's house and barn in the distance. "Assuming it's a woman teacher, she will stay with my mother on her farm there on the edge of town. It's an easy ten-minute walk to the school. She will have a room of her own and be treated like part of the family. Mor has two sort-of adopted children living with her too, Emmy and Manny. Manny is grown now, but he still helps on the farm."

"His mother collects people like some collect china or figurines." John was smiling.

"Reverend Solberg, you said that the big building you pointed out is a school for the deaf?" Miss Gutenberg asked as they resumed walking.

"Yes, and as soon as the incoming students learn to use sign language, they are enrolled in our public schools. So we often have interpreters in our classrooms. Have you ever been exposed to sign language?"

"No, but it sounds fascinating."

"Our school is known from coast to coast and even in some other countries." John held open the door to the boardinghouse and motioned for the other two to enter.

A young woman with her hair in a crown braid greeted them. "Your table is ready in the small dining room, Reverend Solberg."

"Thank you. Can you show Miss Gutenberg where the ladies' room is while we wash up?"

"Of course, right this way."

Thorliff watched them go and followed John to the men's room.

"What do you think so far?" John asked.

"Hire her right now. I think she's an excellent fit."

Again John looked at him a little oddly. They returned to the small dining room.

Miss Gutenberg entered, and Thorliff held her chair as she seated herself. The graceful way she moved reminded him of a swan on a lake.

She scanned the menu briefly. "The pork chops sound delicious." Good! Quick and decisive, with no mumbling, hesitation, or uncertainty. Excellent and needed qualities in a teacher. She turned to Thorliff. "Mr. Bjorklund, you signed the invitational letter as the president of the school board."

"Yes. Also, John and I each teach a couple of classes at the high school. And we often engage people in the community to teach specialty classes. I also own our biweekly newspaper."

"How interesting."

The lunch went very well. Miss Gutenberg was a smart young woman; they did not have to explain something to her twice. She used excellent English and was remarkably articulate. Thorliff expected that in a teacher but it wasn't always easy to find. And she was refreshingly attractive, especially after talking with her. One might even say she glowed.

The meal ended and John stood up, so

Thorliff and Miss Gutenberg stood as well. John dipped his head toward Miss Gutenberg. "I regret that I have another engagement this afternoon, so I must take my leave. Since there is plenty of time before the eastbound train arrives, Thorliff, perhaps you would like to take Miss Gutenberg out to the farm to meet your mother after the school tour."

"Certainly." Thorliff was about to offer her his arm, but that would be too forward of him. And this was curious. What engagement did John have? Their original intention was that John would show Miss Gutenberg the school and Thorliff would go work on the paper.

"Thank you, Reverend," Miss Gutenberg said softly. "I would appreciate that." Turning, she spoke directly to Thorliff. "If you don't mind, that is."

"Not at all. Mor is looking forward to meeting you. She feels sure you are the one to be our new teacher."

Her eyes sparked question marks. "What does she know about me?"

"She read your résumé."

"Oh, I see."

But the look on her face clearly said she didn't see at all. Thorliff understood that more than most would. "My mother has been praying for us to hire the perfect teacher, and she feels that you are that person."

John explained, "His mother prays for everything. She is my stalwart prayer partner. And her counsel is always wise. We usually run decisions past her just to hear her thoughts on a matter." He checked his watch. "It was my delight to meet you, Miss Gutenberg."

"And I you, sir." She offered her hand, and they shook.

John tipped his hat and took his leave, so Thorliff walked with Miss Gutenberg toward the schoolhouse. The tour of the school didn't last long enough for Thorliff, and they even looked over the furnace room and the storm shelter. Her questions were never silly; Thorliff appreciated that.

After a quick visit to Mor, they would have to return to the train station. How to fill the conversation gap as they walked?

"Thank you, Miss Gutenberg, for coming. You said you are staying with your sister. That is the address you sent me?"

"Yes."

"Good, then I can mail any paperwork to that address."

"Yes."

Silence.

Thorliff offered, "School will begin September seventh, so if you enter our employment, you should move here by the first of September. That will give you time to set up your room and get settled."

She nodded.

He continued, "My father and mother homesteaded this section of land, which is bordered on the east by the Red River and on the north by the Little Salt, now known as the Park River. We immigrated from Norway in 1880. I was five, so I have a few memories of that trip, but now, at times, I'm not so sure if I remember the events themselves or only what others have talked about. My father's brother Carl and his family came too. That fall and winter, we all lived in a sod house."

"That sounds like my family story, only my folks came from Germany and settled west of Fargo."

As they were passing Thorliff's house, Rolly ran to the fence. "Are you going to Gramma's? Can I go along?"

"Sorry, not this time. Rolly, I would like you to meet Miss Gutenberg."

He immediately converted himself into a little man. "I am pleased to meet you," he said gravely. "Will you be visiting my gramma?"

"Thank you, I am pleased to meet you too. And yes, I am."

"My gramma is the best in the whole wide

103

world. She makes the best cookies and ice cream."

"That is his measure of a person," Thorliff muttered.

She chuckled. "How nice to hear that. Will you be in school next fall?"

"Yes, ma'am. I'll be in first grade. Inga already taught me how to read some."

"I am so glad you are starting early."

"Thank you, ma'am." Rolly could be very polite when he wanted to. Shame he didn't want to very often.

Thorliff smiled. "I'll see you later. Say good-bye to Miss Gutenberg."

"Good-bye." Pepper, his dog, came running up to his side with a stick in his mouth.

Thorliff watched his son shift gears and grab the stick to throw it. He motioned to Miss Gutenberg to continue their walk, and they resumed their conversation.

"Were there other people around here then?" she asked.

"No, they were the first, but other people soon either homesteaded or bought the land around. When the train was constructed at Grand Forks and they put a water stop here, the town began. A lot has happened in those thirty-three years. Two years after we settled here, my father died in a blizzard, and an outbreak of flu took my Onkel Carl and his two little girls. Those were hard years. An Indian woman named Metiz helped them a lot those first years. And here we are."

They entered the lane to his mor's farm just as Dr. Commons came clipping by at a fast trot in his buggy. And Mor sat beside him!

Mor called, "Emergency at Sarnoffs'!" And the buggy rattled off.

Thorliff sighed. "My mother. She is sometimes called out to help in medical emergencies. You'll meet her another day, I'm sure."

"An intriguing woman."

And so are you. "She is indeed."

They returned to the railroad station ten minutes before the train was due. They would not have had time to visit with Mor after all.

John jogged up the platform steps. "Ah. Made it. Miss Gutenberg, thank you for your interest."

"Thank you for considering me. This is a charming town with charming people. Mr. Bjorklund, your son is absolutely delightful."

Thorliff's mouth spoke before his brain connected. "Miss Gutenberg, it is my pleasure to offer you the job of teacher for fifth and sixth grades."

He instantly regretted his words. He had not consulted John, had not presented her credentials to the board, had not even introduced her to Mor. He was making a unilateral decision that was not his to make. *Oh, please*, he prayed, *say no*. Yet he was mighty concerned that she would.

She exhaled a sigh that spoke of relief. "Yes. Yes, I will accept that position. Thank you. This is perfect for me. I can teach here and still be able to visit my sister in Grafton on Saturday and Sunday."

John cleared his throat. "We would hope you'll take part in community events, including church on Sunday."

She frowned. "That was not mentioned. Is it required?"

"No," Thorliff assured her. "Desired but not required."

She looked relieved.

John explained, "Our schoolteachers have always lived here in Blessing, stayed here in Blessing, and become a part of the community. So this situation has never come up before."

"I see." Again it was clear that she did not see.

The train arrived with its huffing and puffing. Miss Gutenberg shook their hands in her usual firm way. She boarded, and the train continued east.

Thorliff watched her go with his thoughts all jumbled.

John did not look happy. "She's a nice

enough young lady, but I seriously wonder if she'll fit in here. I wish you had considered any other responses and had run it past the board before offering her the position."

Well, to be honest, Thorliff wished the same thing. But it was done now. He had offered her the position, and she'd accepted. Were they legally bound by that? What could they do by way of compromise? If only he had not been foolish and in such a hurry to make the offer. On the other hand, Miss Gutenberg was an absolutely splendid young woman, a fine addition to the school.

If only never did help much.

Chapter 8

David was knotting his tie when someone knocked on his bedroom door. "Come in."

The butler appeared. "Good morning, sir. Mr. Thomas will be joining you at breakfast."

"Did he say what he wants?"

"No, sir." The butler left, closing the door behind him.

David's son Thomas never came there just to visit, but then, neither did any of his other children. They showed up only when they wanted something from him.

Geraldine's portrait hung beside the door. In it she was smiling, her favorite fan folded in her lap. He paused before it as he did almost every morning, studying her serene face, wishing . . . wishing.

His boots clicked on the stairs as he descended, echoing in the huge open stairwell. He had once considered commissioning stair runners. A woman in Blessing made hooked rugs to order. You gave her the size and what you had in mind, and she would hook a beautiful rag rug. The children, though, said they wanted a Persian carpet runner that extended from the top to the bottom of the stairs in one long piece. He did not want that, so the project had gone on hold, probably forever. It was his house and he should be able to do as he wished. They, however, claimed that one of these days it would be their house, so their preferences should be honored.

He entered the dining room and paused. Empty. Hollow. The whole house rang hollow and empty. What his children wanted or did not want could go hang. They did not live here; he did. At least some of the time.

His thoughts turned to Blessing and Ingeborg, warming him instantly. Abruptly he turned and crossed to his office down the hall. He went in and wrote himself a note: *Get the stair measurements. Order hooked runners from the woman in Blessing.* She could certainly use the money this winter, and he would take pleasure in handmade stair runners, even if he was here only a few weeks a year. Perhaps if the stairs were padded, the house would not sound quite so empty. He returned to the dining room.

His son Thomas entered as the butler was pouring David's coffee. Posture rigid, sitting down in the chair to David's right, he nodded. "Good morning, Father."

"Good morning, Thomas. How are the wife and children?"

Why did Thomas hesitate, weighing a simple question? "Fine, Father. Just fine."

"And have you heard anything from your sister?"

"No. Not lately. I assume Lillian is fine, or we surely would have heard." Thomas unfolded his napkin in his lap.

"Surely." So David had not heard from his daughter Lillian, and neither had Thomas. And with his four younger children living in other cities, it felt like none of them were a part of one another's lives. David thought about the big, happy group that was the Bjorklund extended family. They helped each other, gathered for meals or just for fun, talked together constantly, swapped visits, and together provided alms to the poor. They were a true family. Besides Jonathan, David's children were nothing more than a bloodline.

What made the difference? Why was that family united and happy when David's was so distant?

Ingeborg! That was the difference.

Geraldine had been praised for raising their children to fit comfortably into society. Ingeborg raised her brood to fit comfortably into humanity. She taught them to honor each other and to think of others first. And you did not dare get into a petty squabble with Ingeborg nearby. Yes, there had been disagreements, big ones, but they had worked them out.

As he thought about it, he realized being a Bjorklund blood relative was not really the key. She brought in true family members from outside the Bjorklund bloodline, such as Emmy and Manny. They were a spiritually linked family in every sense of the word.

And David yearned to be a part of it.

"Father!" Thomas's sharp, irritated voice broke into his thoughts. "You're mooning again. Please pay attention. I asked a question."

"Yes, I guess I was mooning. What is your question?"

Thomas's voice sounded impatient. "I want to introduce you to a man I recently met, Lionel Hibbing. He's a relative of the people who founded the iron-mining town of Hibbing in northern Minnesota. A very important person, with a lot of money. I want you to invite him to dinner on Sunday."

"Are all of you coming to dinner?"

"We were planning to. There are several things we want to discuss."

"Good. There are several things I want to discuss as well. If this Hibbing fellow is a friend of yours, he may come."

"Thank you. Are you bringing anything special to the board meeting this afternoon, or will it be routine, as usual?"

"I am bringing a new idea of mine, which the board will study and vote on. Why? Were you thinking of playing truant again?"

"Well, frankly, yes. If it's nothing but routine, I feel I'm not needed."

"You'd better come today." *And attend to business, as you are being paid as a board member to do, instead of out playing tennis or polo or whatever.* He didn't say that last part out loud. He pondered for a moment. While he knew his son enjoyed playing polo and tennis, there had been changes in Thomas's responsibilities the last couple of years. Thomas had stepped into his role as future director of the family enterprises, yet he didn't act like it.

Again, Ingeborg's mob came to mind. Every one of them, even Inga and Emmy, worked hard and contributed to the community. What did Thomas contribute? Horse manure. David almost choked on his breakfast omelet, laughing when he was supposed to be swallowing. Nothing but horse manure; Thomas owned three polo ponies. His polo team rarely won, but the ponies remained highly productive in the manure department.

"How is your polo team doing?" David asked, hoping to get his son talking about something he cared about.

Thomas stared at him. "Father, I sold the polo team a year ago, remember? I told you."

David flinched, hoping it did not show. "Ah, that's right. Pardon me." *Better check with the chief director*, he ordered himself. What other things had he missed since he spent so much time in Blessing?

"Are you feeling all right?" Thomas narrowed his eyes, studying him.

"I am feeling wiser and wiser by the minute."

That afternoon David convened the Gould Enterprises executive board meeting. His secretary read a summary of the prior meeting minutes, and all voted to accept them. David doubted that any of them remembered the last meeting. It didn't really matter.

He nodded toward his secretary. The young man set up the big easel and laid the stack of large cardboard posters beside it. "As Arnold here will show you, this is the Holt landship."

The secretary set a large drawing of a Holt landship on the easel.

"Note the huge iron wheels. This machine is fine on smooth roadways and flat pastureland, but it cannot operate when the land surface is rough. Next picture. This is a tractor that was designed and built in England. Rather than wheels, it creeps along on what the English call a caterpillar tread. Wooden slats are bolted to chains in this picture, and the chains ride in grooves on the iron wheels. It does not need a smooth surface. It travels well over broken ground. Surprisingly, it can even creep over barbed wire fences, across ditches, even over stone walls. Next picture."

Arnold put up a series of three drawings showing how the caterpillar tread operated. David was pleased; he had prepared the drawings himself.

"There is a company in France that makes these caterpillar treads for farm machinery.

There is another company, the Jeffers Machinery in Blessing, North Dakota, that is working to develop the design of a war tank utilizing these treads into a prototype that the French company will partner with them in producing. I suggest we invest in this project."

Thomas shook his head. "Two things. First of all, I do not believe that Europe will go to war, and secondly, if they do, there is a huge ocean between them and us. Let them sort out their own affairs."

This was the part David hated discussing. "It will take probably four years to perfect and produce the caterpillar-tread landship. In spite of what you think, the rumors of war are gaining strength, and wisdom says we need to be prepared, ocean or not. As a war machine auxiliary to ground forces, this machine will be invaluable. It is nearly invincible. Bullets will bounce off it, and the landship will be able to go anywhere, delivering soldiers or supplies. Even if the rumors are laid to rest and Europe avoids war, they will certainly be building up their military presence."

"Father," Thomas barked. "We are a relatively small company in the worldwide scheme of things, and not only is this landship not necessary, we would most likely lose all of our investments in the process. I see no reason to discuss this any further and waste our time and money."

David stared at his son, and the urge to leave the room before he said something he'd regret bloomed larger and larger. *Lord, give me patience.* Amazingly, all the others around the table were staring at the papers in front of them. He sucked in a deep breath and let it out slowly. Was this what a sea captain felt like when the hands all mutinied? What had been going on behind his back these months he'd been in Blessing?

"Would anyone else like to comment?" he asked.

That was the wrong thing to say.

"If you were here more often . . . we can't afford a war . . . a war in Europe does not have to be our war . . . you know, good investors always make a great deal of money providing supplies during a war . . . remember when we lost money on . . . this is not our war . . . armaments . . ."

The room vibrated with their bickering and name-calling. He should have cleaned house with this board a long time ago. Too often discussions ended this way, it seemed. David tried to imagine the Bjorklund family bickering like this. Unimaginable!

And suddenly his patience snapped. "Enough!" he roared, slamming his gavel

115

down so hard that the handle broke and the head went flying.

The silence was instant and total.

He glared at them. "Why can't you ever discuss something in a civil tone of voice, without this snapping at one another's heels?"

Thomas said wearily, "Father, you're always like this when you come back from Blessing. Cranky, barking at us as if it's our fault. I think you ought to stay away from that place. Let Jonathan do whatever he's going to do, and you stay in New York where you belong. Mother was so right! Blessing is a bad place and has a bad influence on you." He stood. "This is a waste of time."

He turned, nodded at his cadre of support, and led them all out of the room.

Sunday evening dinner. Ingeborg's family would be gathering around the table for a light meal, for the major Sunday meal there was at noon. David's children and their spouses—at least those who lived in New York—sat at his table while the children, as usual, were eating in the kitchen. They were all dressed properly. Their manners were perfect, their conversation polite and formal. None had recently fed any chickens or milked any cows.

In fact, all of them did absolutely nothing of real value.

Thomas's guest tonight, Mr. Lionel Hibbing, sat at Thomas's right. He was a distinguished-looking middle-aged fellow with a ready smile, and although his manners were impeccable, he had a casual, easy way about him.

The cook brought out the first course, a huge tureen of salmon bisque with shallots and garnished with parsley sprigs, and set it in the center of the table. A maid brought out a smaller tureen of vegetable soup because Thomas's wife did not eat fish, and Lillian ate only vegetables. For most of David's children, it was their third major meal today. But did they know where the meat and vegetables and milk came from? Had they ever seen food produced? His children had missed out on so much. He saw that now.

"Thomas, say grace, please."

All dipped their heads, and Thomas muttered something rapidly.

Polite conversation began as the maid set bowls before each of them. David watched to see if any of them said thank you. Not that he could see. The butler poured a splash of wine in David's glass. He swirled it, sniffed it, tasted it, and nodded. The butler filled his glass and went on to fill the others. What a silly custom, to make certain the wine was not soured. The wine was never soured.

"Mr. Hibbing, Thomas says you are an entrepreneur. That is a broad term. Can you narrow it down?" David asked.

Mr. Hibbing chuckled. "I do what I love, Mr. Gould, and what I love is to take risks."

"Not many can say that."

"You are well aware that investment is a risky business. What I especially enjoy, of course, is when the risks I take pay off, often handsomely. At the moment I am looking at investment in war machines. The world is becoming an increasingly hostile place. People fear military buildup. I see it as an opportunity."

"Indeed." David nodded. Hibbing should have been at the board meeting. "What do you know about landships?"

"Landships?" His brow wrinkled, then the wrinkles disappeared. "Oh! Tanks. In Europe they refer to them as landships. Here we just call them tanks. I doubt they would be a good investment, because their movements are limited to good roads, and war is rarely waged on good roads. We won't be retiring our war horses just yet." He sipped. "Oh my. This is an excellent bisque."

Thomas started prattling about the polo game he had played that afternoon. Even though he had sold the team, he still sometimes played for pleasure. Apparently something had happened at the end of a chukker that left him all upset. Everyone around him was smiling and nodding and looking absolutely bored as they sipped their soup and he described the infraction at length.

At the far end of the table, Lillian was going on about a dress with ruffles that Aunt Mae was wearing at this time of year, when everyone knew you didn't wear white until Decoration Day. Perhaps Aunt Mae was getting a bit dotty, wink-wink.

The main course, a standing rib roast, was brought in next, and the cook skillfully carved it. The maids set out the side dishes, then gathered the soup bowls. David was getting mighty wearied by these shallow, hollow people.

Little Bessie, Thomas's oldest child, came out from the kitchen and tugged at David's sleeve. "Grandpa?"

"Yes, Bessie."

She pointed to the partly dismantled rib roast. "Artie says those little paper things on the tips of the rib bones are panties. He says leg of lamb has panties too."

"That is correct."

Giggling wildly, she clapped her hands over her mouth and ran back to the kitchen.

David smiled. Oh, if only the grandchildren could keep their lively curiosity into adulthood, but he knew it would be carefully snuffed out.

That was the word he had been looking for: lively. Mr. Hibbing was the only lively person in this room. But the whole Bjorklund clan was lively, uninhibited. Their children were curious, the adults ever open to new things. Thomas was describing a lively, action-filled game—polo—and he made even that sound boring.

David waited until dessert was served, a chocolate mousse garnished with piped sugar rosebuds and vanilla wafers. "I have some news for you this evening." He looked around at all the faces at his table. "So far I have owned the houses you are living in. As of tomorrow, I will be deeding the houses over to you. Each of you will own your own home."

He expected thank-yous and other expressions of gratitude. Instead he got complaints.

"Wait a minute, Father. Who will pay the taxes on these houses, and who will pay for maintenance and repairs?" Thomas switched from polo to affronted in a heartbeat.

"Why, the person who lives there, of course."

Thomas whined, "But you've always done that. It's just so much easier if you go ahead and continue, don't you think?"

David took a deep breath. "Tell you what. If you don't want the house you are living in, I will gladly put it on the market."

Thomas didn't look any more pleased at this idea. "My house is not worth as much as Lillian's, Father. Will I receive additional compensation?" He flapped a hand. Possibly he realized he had overstepped his bounds. "You know," he explained, "just to keep it fair so that everyone receives the same amount. You know."

Yes, David knew. He sighed heavily. Yet again, when he compared the big hearts of the Bjorklunds with this pettiness around him, he felt sad.

Blessing was a bad place, the children said. The comment still blistered David. When he thought about it, what the children were really saying was that he was incompetent or misled or just getting too old to make good decisions. But they were wrong. They had passed judgment on Blessing without ever seeing the place or meeting the people, and now they condemned him for loving it. That fact alone greatly rankled him.

Blessing was where he really wanted to be, not here. David could not wait to climb aboard that train and ride it west to Blessing and to sanity. In his pocket right now was a diamond ring to present to that matriarch of all matriarchs, Ingeborg Bjorklund. Surely she would say yes.

Chapter 9

Ingeborg stared at the calendar. June first. Why was she missing Gould so much? It was almost like the feelings she'd first had for Haakan. Not exactly, but close. And that was ridiculous. Roald and Haakan had been from her world, her culture. David absolutely was not. She did not even like his culture. The upper-crust society of New York annoyed and dismayed her. They had so much affluence and so little sense. They were useful for nothing; they could not put food on the table or love in the heart. And for all his protestations of affection for the agrarian culture of Blessing, David was not part of it. He was a foreigner.

"Don't be silly," she said aloud to herself. "You are thinking too much about this." At the same time, she found herself thinking, *He'll be home soon. I can hardly wait.*

She stared out the window, watching the

cows trailing out of the barn to get a drink at the trough and then amble on out to graze. David did not know what breed of cows these were, or how Jersey milk differed from Holstein milk. He did not know that a flood could kill a cow if the cold water reached her belly and chilled the udder, whereas a horse could survive neck-deep flooding. He had never gone hungry when the food ran out and harvest was still months away. Two worlds, and never the twain shall meet.

Freda clanged the larger of the cast-iron frying pans onto the stove. She plopped bacon grease into it.

Ingeborg returned to the stove to lift the frying bacon onto the warming shelf. "Do you have enough cornmeal sliced to fry?"

"Not really. Cleaned out the loaf pan. I thought there was another, but we already used that. I'll make more this afternoon."

"Are you going to set more cheese soon?"

"Thought I'd do soft cheese today. I got a taste for some." Freda turned the sliced cornmeal cakes.

"Good. Penny asked if we were going to have any soft cheese to sell."

Penny Bjorklund owned the Blessing Mercantile, and ever since electricity came to Blessing, she had a cooler that carried Ingeborg and Freda's cheeses. Mr. Gardner at the grocery store next door stocked eggs, butter, cheese, and fresh meat, much of which was provided by the various Bjorklund farms.

"Mm. Now I'm sure I'll make more." Freda shook the pan again.

Ingeborg glanced out the window. "Here they come."

Manny, Lars, Andrew, and two boys from the deaf school washed at the outside basin before coming into the house to sit down for breakfast. Lars bowed his head, followed by the others. "Thank you, Lord God, for this food, for your protection through the day, for the wisdom you give us to do the work we have to do. In Jesus' name, amen."

Emmy set a basket of eggs on the counter. "I think it's time for Charlie to go to the stew pot. That young red rooster who looks so much like him is old enough to take over."

"What did he do now?" Ingeborg asked.

"He killed one of the chicks and wounded the hen who was trying to protect her babies."

"You're right, it's time. He tried to attack me the other day." Freda grimaced. "Those spurs of his could do plenty of damage. I'll take care of him."

"Let me." Manny swallowed a mouthful and drank his coffee laced with cream. He might be a man now, but he still didn't like his coffee straight. Probably never would.

124

"Thank you for volunteering." Freda almost smiled. "How about building me some more shipping crates after that?"

Manny looked to Lars, who nodded. "Since we're done with the seeding, going over the machinery is next on the list. Andrew?"

"Carl is watching that sow. He's sure she'll farrow today. Ellie asked me to take down the storm windows. It should've been done a month ago, but planting always comes first."

Through the years, specialties had been divided between the three farms, with the machinery and work horses at Lars and Kaaren's, the dairy at Ingeborg's, and the pigs and sheep at Andrew and Ellie's. All the families had gardens, fruit trees, chickens, and fields.

"Thanks to Manny and the team working up the gardens, those are mostly planted too." Ingeborg nodded. "Seems like we're ahead for the first of June. Strange."

They all chuckled. Spring arriving early and the fields drying out enough to work had made that possible. The Red River had threatened to flood but went no higher than the tops of the banks.

When the men were all off to their various jobs, the girls cleaned up the kitchen and each took over a churn on the back porch, while Freda headed for the cheese house and

Ingeborg kneaded the bread she had started first thing that morning. Kneading bread always made her heart sing. She could hear the birds chattering in the cottonwood off the porch, the girls talking as the churns *thunk*ed. The songs of the meadowlarks had heralded the sunrise.

Manny swung open the screen door. "That rooster's not going to peck anyone again. He's plucked, gutted, and cooling at the well house. I'm going to the shop to cut wood for the cheese crates, okay?"

"Good for you. Thank you, Manny."

When the telephone demanded her attention, she wiped her hands on her apron and lifted the earpiece off the hook. "Good morning."

Thorliff greeted her. "Mor, do you mind if I bring Rolly out for the day? He's lonesome for the girls."

"Of course you may. Any responses to your letters for the book?"

"A couple. I'm keeping them in a file. Got to get the paper out before I can work on that. You ever thought of doing a column for the paper?"

"What ever could I have to write about?"

"Actually, some of the pieces you would write for the book. I can put them in the paper and in the book as well."

126

Ingeborg smiled at the phone. "You are really wrapped up in this book project, aren't you?"

"I believe it will be an important historical record. Also an interesting read."

Historical, yes. But important? Ingeborg writing something important. The idea frightened her, in a way.

It wasn't fifteen minutes later that Inga brought in the bowl of newly churned butter and looked out the window. "Look, Pa and Rolly are coming to the door." She turned to Ingeborg. "Did you know they were coming?"

"I did."

"Gramma? We're here!" The screen door slammed behind the body barreling toward her. Inga snatched him around the waist and turned rapidly in place. His feet flew straight out as he shrieked with joy.

"Here, you go back to Pa." She let him loose as her father came through the door. "I need to go help Grandma."

Rolly looked around. "Did you make gingerbread men?"

"Sorry, not today," Ingeborg said. "Come out and rock with Grandma."

"On the swing?"

"No, the chair on the back stoop. The front porch is too hot right now."

They got settled in their rocking chair with Thorliff next to them. As soon as he drained his coffee, he stood to leave. "You be good for Grandma now, Rolly."

He drew himself up to his full height and said sternly, "I am always good."

Chuckling, Thorliff stopped on the first step. "I left some papers I wrote on the table by your rocking chair. Would you look them over, please?"

"For the book?"

"Yes." And he left. *This book is consuming him*, she thought.

"Gramma, look," Rolly whispered. "Shh."

She looked where he was pointing. A robin hopped across the walkway, alternately watching them with one eye and watching a lady robin with the other. She was busy pulling yarn from a loose ball Ingeborg had hung near a post. With pieces of red and blue yarn dangling from her beak, she flew to a pot hanging near another post. Mr. Robin fluttered up to the yarn, pulled out one strand, and flew over to join her.

Rolly looked up at Ingeborg, his eyes as round as his mouth. "Did you see that?"

"I did. They're making a nest."

"They're going to lay eggs? And hatch babies. Right here on your porch."

"Ja, right here." With her head against the

128

back of the rocker, she smiled to herself. What could be better than sitting in a comfortable chair on a porch in late spring with a happy grandchild?

"We can watch."

Lord, what a treat you are giving us. And Rolly got to see it first.

That evening when all was quiet again, the two girls having taken Rolly home and staying to help Thorliff with the printing, Ingeborg sat in the swing out on the front porch, one foot keeping it in motion.

Manny came stomping in from the barn. "I'm going to bed, Grandma, unless there's anything else you want me to do."

"No, you grab some extra rest when you can. Good night, Manny, and as always, thank you." The woodbox was full and the split wood was stacked again on the side porch. Freda had a renewed stock of shipping crates, with plenty of wood cut for more. "You accomplished a great deal."

"Thank you, I try." He entered the house, and she could hear his footsteps on the stairs.

She looked up at the rings of the telephone. It must be David. She made her way quickly to the kitchen wall, sinking into the chair she kept there.

"Hello. Oh, David, I was hoping it was you."

"Do you miss me?"

"Especially right now."

They conversed about their days, but he knew what she meant, and she only sort of understood what all he had done.

"I have a favor to ask." His voice sounded warm and full of love, even over the miles of lines it traveled.

"Of course."

"You agree before you even know what it is?"

"If I can help you, I can agree."

"Well, this one is a bit difficult. I've invited a friend of Thomas's who is interested in the Jeffers Machinery Company. I need you to find me a housekeeper who will also cook for the week or so he is there. Not that we will have that many meals at home. Surely there must be someone."

"I know many good cooks and good housekeepers, but David, none of them would be like those in New York."

"That shouldn't make any difference."

There is a huge difference between the cook-whatever-ingredients-are-in-season cooks in Blessing and the I-make-exotic-dishes-with-weird-imported-ingredients chefs of New York. Ingeborg shook her head. Surely this could work out. After all, it was only for a week. Surely.

Then why was her stomach already knotting?

Chapter 10

If only the baby could be called by her real name.

Louisa Gutenberg leaned on the crib rails and watched the nearly two-year-old girl sleeping so soundly. Her right fist lay snug to her perfect little mouth that had nursed at Susan's breasts, not the ones that ached for her. Her wispy hair curled a tiny bit when wet and had a mind of its own, like the babe it crowned. One time Louisa had tied a tiny bow on top, but that lasted about ten seconds before that precious fist yanked it off. Louisa remembered laughing. Was it easier to laugh at the baby's antics when she was pretending to be the auntie? Jealousy stabbed through her heart, but she jerked the arrows out, wishing she could stuff them in the stove to burn. But feelings ate her insides against her will. She was an old maid schoolteacher, not a mother. She rehearsed the lie in her head. Would it be easier when she was in Blessing during the week, helping other people's children?

"Your mama got a job today, but in order to earn money to care for you, she has to be your auntie, not your mama. But at least we have a place to live with people who love us. You do all the time, but during the school year I will be in Blessing. I might not be able to come home every Friday afternoon or Saturday morning the way I want to. I could do that far more easily if I had a horse to ride or, heaven forbid, an automobile to drive."

She refused to dwell on those thoughts. She would come home to her sister's house every chance she could, to see her daughter grow up calling Susan *Mama*. But that was far better than the alternatives.

Never would she regret fighting to keep her daughter from being given away simply because her mother had no husband. She'd promised herself she would take her baby and flee rather than give her up like those people at the home demanded.

Thank God for Susan.

"Louisa, could you come help me for a moment?" The call came faintly through the closed door.

Louisa kissed the tip of her finger and

planted it on her baby's cheek. "I have to go," she whispered. She gently closed the door behind her before making her way to the kitchen, where her younger sister Susan was climbing up on a stepstool. Her swollen belly managed to knock her off kilter at times.

"I told you I would do that!" Aggravation colored and clipped Louisa's words.

"I know, but . . ."

Louisa took Susan's arm and gently assisted her back to the solid floor. She heaved a sigh of relief.

"Now, tell me what you want down, and I'll get it," Louisa said. She climbed to the second step and opened the cabinet above her. The ten-foot ceiling gave plenty of room for high cabinets. "You know Donald would have my head if you fell and lost another baby."

Susan had lost one baby to an accident and another to the inscrutable ways of Mother Nature, leaving broken hearts and shattered dreams. Louisa had given birth to Mary before Susan lost her milk, and thus the circle closed. Susan's firstborn, Zeke, now four going on five, thought Mary arrived as a present to him.

"I'm sorry, I just feel so good and so happy that I need to do some of the things I've been thinking of." She sighed. "Oh, Louisa, life is so good. I want to celebrate."

"And so . . ." Louisa looked from her sister to the cabinet to the platter now safely on the counter. "Help me understand this, please."

"I decided to make a surprise for supper."

"And what kind of surprise needs the large platter?"

"Well, if I tell you, it won't be a surprise."

Louisa inhaled. "Something smells mighty wonderful."

"I know, and now will you kindly go work in the garden or somewhere, anywhere, not in the kitchen?"

Louisa smiled at her sister, slightly shaking her head. "All right, I will gather the eggs and skim the pans in the well house. You think that will be long enough?"

Susan shrugged. "Possibly. Perhaps you could do some hoeing in the garden too?"

"At your service."

Louisa stepped out on the back porch and looked across the fields to where Donald and the team were seeding the last of the corn. The wheat and oats were already showing a hazy green in perfectly straight rows. Louisa fetched a basket out of the well house and let herself into the hen house. Most of the chickens were outside, scratching for seeds, worms, and bugs. The two broody hens inside ruffled their feathers, warning her to stay away.

"I won't bother you now, but you should be hatching chicks in a week or so. And then I will move you and your peepers to a safer pen." She picked both white and brown eggs from the other nests, since they had a variety of breeds, and returned to the well house. The eggs were all clean, since she kept straw in the nests and cleaned them out regularly.

She poured the older cream into the churn, washed the jugs, and skimmed the cream off the pans to refill the jugs. Rinsing down the gravelly floor, she scrubbed the pans to be used again. With two of the three cows freshened, they had an abundance of milk even with making sure the calves had plenty to grow on. The extra she fed to the pigs, watching the sow, since she was getting heavy and closer to farrowing.

Her brother-in-law, Donald, worked diligently from before dawn to after dusk, trying to make up for last year's poor harvests—all due to a lack of rain. Even though they had hand-watered the garden, an early frost had killed off part of it. Her paycheck would be a boon. In the meantime, she and Susan sold butter and eggs to the store in Grafton. She and Susan did the wash, and Louisa cleaned house for the two bachelor brothers on the next section over. On her days there, she cooked supper and left it ready for them at the end of the day. Often Donald teased her about taking one of them up on the offer of marriage, but she knew they were just jesting. After her fiancé died in an accident the day before their wedding, she had promised herself never again.

Carrying a basket with eggs and cream, she strode back to the house.

"Tante Louisa, Ma made—"

"Don't tell her" came from the kitchen.

Zeke clapped both hands over his mouth, his blue eyes dancing. "Oops."

Louisa wagged her finger at him, which made him giggle even more. She set the basket on the counter and watched Zeke play wooden spoons and pans with Mary, who had woken up from her nap. The racket made both the women flinch, but the giggles made them smile too. Mary picked up a spoon and a lid, and the two children marched down the hall, a new game Zeke had taught her.

"How about outside on the porch?" Susan called to them as she made sure the gate was shut. Donald had built a fence around the porch so the kids could go out to play. To Louisa she said, "I invited Grandma and Ed over for supper to help us celebrate."

Donald's mother and brother lived on a neighboring farm. "What are we celebrating?"

136

"The end of planting, for one thing, Ed's birthday is tomorrow, and your teaching position. You know Ed. He tries to be a curmudgeon, but those two make him smile in spite of himself."

Louisa immediately thought of their mother, who had loved babies so much and gave her life trying to birth the last one. Their father had always been stern, but he became bitter after her death and demanded Louisa leave her teaching and come home to take care of the younger children. Much to everyone's surprise, a year later he remarried an equally dour woman and told Louisa she could go back to teaching. They were quite a pair. His new wife didn't waste much energy smiling either. While Louisa pitied their younger brothers and sisters, she knew they were being well cared for.

"They'll be here as soon as chores are done," Susan said.

"When did you plan all this?"

"This morning. I wanted to surprise everybody."

"You most certainly did." Louisa eyed the platter. "Stollen?"

"And it isn't even Christmas." Donald was Swedish and they were German, so Susan made both julekake and stollen for Christmas, special breads from both countries.

"Donald's mother is bringing ham and her special rolls, and since our peas are not quite ready, we're having string beans with bacon."

Louisa looked down and saw Susan's swollen feet. "Have you sat down at all today?"

Susan shrugged.

"You sit down, get your feet up on the stool, and I will bring you a glass of cold water."

They kept a water pitcher in the icebox, an inherited pleasure since this was the original farmhouse when the two sections were divided between the three brothers. Donald, being the eldest, had inherited the homestead with his land.

With her sister situated, Louisa set the bacon and beans to cooking, and with Zeke's assistance, she set the table using the good tablecloth. Sandy the dog barked, sending Zeke running to the porch.

"Grandma and Onkel Ed are here. Come on, Mary."

"Donald is still down at the barn," Susan said after greeting them. "He made sure he finished the seeding before he came in."

"I know that's a relief." Mrs. Ivarsen sat down and helped Mary up into her lap. "Such a big girl."

Zeke leaned against her skirt and grinned up at her. "Mary and me played band and marching."

138

"Looks that way." Her glance at the pans and spoons on the floor said far more than words.

Louisa shot her sister a look that firmly said *do not get up.* "Come on, Zeke, let's get your band put away before supper. Pa will be here pretty quick."

Zeke picked up the wooden spoons and dropped them in the sink. The lids he put back in the cupboard. "All done."

"Good boy," Susan said.

Mary turned around and slid off her grandma's lap, chattering to Zeke. As usual, she didn't sit on a lap long. She had too much to do, following her brother around.

"Let's go out on the porch and watch for Pa," Zeke said.

"It's cooler out there," Susan said.

"Zeke, you missed a spoon." Mrs. Ivarsen pointed at one under the table.

"Oops." Zeke crawled under the table to retrieve it and took it to the sink, only to earn a *tsk* from the white-haired woman.

Louisa wanted to say something, but Susan shook her head. There was never any pleasing Mrs. Ivarsen. No matter how hard Susan tried. Louisa opened the oven and pulled out the ham to set on the stove. Susan had used the last of the canned potatoes to make scalloped potatoes for supper, because

Donald liked them and this was a celebration. In spite of Mrs. Ivarsen.

The older lady pointed to the basket. "I brought rolls and the last of the strawberry jam."

"Thank you," Susan said. "We're having your pickles for supper too. Maybe this year, you will give me your recipe so I can make them too."

Unlike most of the farming women, Mrs. Ivarsen liked to keep her specialties to herself. It was a good thing her sons had taken after their father, hardworking but with ready smiles. At least that was what Susan had said one day when she was explaining her mother-in-law to Louisa. Ever since Mr. Ivarsen had died, Mrs. Ivarsen had withdrawn more and more. On the bright side, Mrs. Ivarsen hadn't chosen to stay in this house with Susan and Donald. She felt she was needed more at Ed's.

"Pa," shrieked Zeke when the men came up to the house. Mary rattled the gate and followed suit.

"Did you hear that?" Susan grinned at her sister. "Wouldn't you know it, *Pa* would be her first word?"

"She should be talking more than that by now," Mrs. Ivarsen grouched.

"Yes, Mother." There was no need to argue.

The men came in the kitchen, each with a giggling child under his arm. "Look what we found on the porch." Ed jiggled Zeke around to set him laughing.

"Did you hear her?" Susan asked her husband.

"I did. And she said it again."

"Pa." Mary reached up and patted his face.

Zeke slid to the floor and danced around. "Say it again, Mary. Who is that?" He pointed to his father.

Mary stared down at him, then beamed at Donald. "Pa. Pa. Pa."

"First word, eh? And to think we are here for a celebration, Mother. I heard tell Susan baked something extra," Ed said.

"For your birthday, Onkel Ed. Ma said. And because the fields are all planted and Tante Louisa is going to be a teacher again." Zeke's bottom lip stuck out. "But she won't live here no more."

"But I will come home often and be here all next summer." Louisa tapped the end of his nose with one finger. "And when I am here, I will teach you to read."

"Yes!" He looked at his grandmother. "I can say almost the whole alphabet now."

She shrugged, giving Louisa a *so-what* look.

Louisa took the butcher knife out of the drawer, drew it over the whetstone a couple of times, and set to slicing the ham. While she did that, Susan pulled the pan of potatoes out of the oven and set it on a trivet on the table.

"Aren't you going to heat the rolls?" Mrs. Ivarsen asked accusingly.

"Yes, of course. They're in the warming oven."

The men washed at the sink and took their places at the table. Louisa whisked the platter over to the table and set down the bowl of string beans. "What are we missing?"

"The rolls."

"Of course. Right after I get Miss Mary in her chair." She lifted the little girl and set her in the high chair. Donald had made a stool to fit on a chair for Zeke when the new baby was ready for the high chair. After tying Mary's bib in place, Louisa broke off some bits of a roll and laid them in front of her.

Happening to glance up, Louisa caught Mrs. Ivarsen's look. That woman had not an ounce of forgiveness in her. Much like her own father. If only she could move far away, taking Susan and her family with her. If Donald and Susan were willing to live with this secret, why couldn't his mother?

Chapter 11

One of these days he had to make some changes.

Thorliff scrubbed his fingers through his hair. Three hours of sleep left him ready to fall backward onto his bed with full assurance that he would be sound asleep again before his head hit the pillow. The early morning breeze lifted the curtains but not his eyelids. He inhaled and rotated his head, hoping to find some energy in there somewhere.

He inhaled again.

Coffee. Thelma already had the coffee ready. He sniffed again and recognized the sweet fragrance of cinnamon rolls. She had rolls either baking or out cooling. Did that woman never sleep?

He staggered to his feet and into the bathroom to stick his head under the cold water faucet. It was a bit warm to start but cooled quickly. Reaching for a towel, he turned off the blast and scrubbed both his hair and his face.

Back in his bedroom, one of the pictures on the wall triggered memories and grief that came out of the blue, stabbing his heart.

Elizabeth had never fully recovered from a hard birth and, her resistance shattered, had died easily during a diphtheria epidemic, no matter how Astrid fought for her life.

Lord God, why now? He thought he'd recovered from the horrendous grief, but here it was again. He glanced at her side of the bed. No indent in the pillow, no sweet fragrance, no soft voice wishing him a good morning.

He used the towel to scrub his face again, this time of brimming tears. He could hear his mor's voice. *"Let the tears wash the grief away. It leaves faster that way. And at that same moment, thank God for her life and all she gave to you and to the rest of us."*

Thorliff sniffed and pulled on his pants. "Thank you, Lord." Through gritted teeth and a clamped jaw, he repeated, "Thank you, Lord, for Elizabeth, for Inga." Saying his daughter's name always made him smile. "And for Rolly. For Mor, for our lives here. For all this, including this day, I thank you." He pulled a short-sleeved shirt off a hanger. "And for Thelma, who is the glue that has held this family together. And for Louisa Gutenberg."

What? How did she come to mind? But she was there, and firmly planted. Intelligent and smart, and so very attractive to him. He slid his feet into his shoes and headed down

144

the stairs. Surprise stopped him. The grief was gone.

"Your coffee is ready." Thelma lifted the steaming coffeepot and poured a large cup for him as soon as he entered the kitchen.

Pepper yipped from the back porch. Letting him out for a morning run was always the first thing Thelma did, even before starting the fire in the polished iron stove. The black-and-brown-and-white pooch had shown up on their step one winter's night. He had ended up staying with them, and instead of herding cattle or sheep, he took care of the little boy who threw sticks and sometimes slept curled up with his head on the dog's soft belly. The two had become inseparable.

"Smells mighty good in here." He stood at the open window, sipping coffee too hot to drink as he watched a robin pulling a worm from the grass.

"Is your meeting here at the paper or over at Jeffers' office?"

"At the paper. Otherwise I would be late."

"How about scrambled eggs to go with a roll? I'll bring the other rolls over when everyone gets there. The coffeepot will be ready too."

"Thelma, what would we ever do without you?"

"Find yourself another wife might be a good start."

"Thelma!" He watched her shrug.

"'Bout time. Rolly needs a mother, as does Inga, and you need a wife. I've been praying for one for you."

"Okay, let's discuss this. Who in this town might fit the bill?" Miss Gutenberg settling herself at the table at the boardinghouse zipped through his mind. No, she didn't zip. She paused and stayed.

"Is Reverend Solberg coming to the meeting?" Thelma asked.

"Of course."

"Maybe you should talk to him about it." She started his breakfast of bacon and eggs.

"Thank you. If I had to cook for myself . . ."

"You would never eat breakfast, dinner would be at the boardinghouse, and supper at Ingeborg's or Astrid's."

"Or whoever invited us over. But by now I would have learned to cook, or Inga would have." He inhaled the rising fragrance from the rolls and sighed. "Anyway, thank you, and I know those at the meeting will be happy too." He ate a couple of bites and wagged his fork at her. "You spoil us all. The meeting always runs more agreeably when we are eating your rolls or doughnuts or whatever you choose to make."

She cocked her head. "Oh. I was hoping he would sleep a little later."

146

"Pa?" Rolly called.

"At the table." How one little boy could make so much racket coming down the stairs, he'd never figure out.

She pulled on the screen door, and Pepper squeezed through before she could open it completely. He ran to the stairs to greet his boy. "More coffee?" she asked.

"No, I better get over there." Thorliff paused at the giggles and toenail clicking that came from the stairs. "Bye, Rolly. Be good for Thelma today."

Rolly ran to him for a hug. "Can we go to Gramma's today?"

"Aren't you going to play with the twins at Tante Sophie's house today?"

"I guess. Can Pepper come too?"

"Sophie isn't very fond of dogs. He'll stay home and take care of Thelma."

Rolly frowned. "Thelma isn't my mor. The twins have a mother. You have a mother."

"Right." Where was this going?

"Will I ever have a mother?"

The question floored him so violently that he couldn't think what to say. "Maybe someday." He rolled his lips together. "See you later, sport. I have a meeting." He grabbed the full coffeepot and headed out the door.

Sitting at the table in the editorial office, John Solberg flipped the paper aside to greet him. "Good edition, as usual. Do you remember that Miss Gutenberg has worked for a newspaper? She mentioned that on her résumé."

"No, somehow I'd forgotten that. Hmm. I'm thinking of hiring Emmy for real, to help after school. She has become quite a typist."

"What about Inga?"

"She's my typesetter. A whiz at it. Coffee?"

"Have you ever seen me turn down a cup of coffee?" John held out one of the cups that hung on pegs on the wall.

Daniel Jeffers, head of Jeffers Machinery, arrived next with rolled diagrams and a stack of papers. "Is Gould coming home today?"

"As far as we know, he is on the arriving train. I got it straight from Mor's mouth. She can hardly speak of him without smiling." Thorliff curbed his own smile. His mother had really missed Gould this time. He could tell, even though she hadn't said much.

Hjelmer Bjorklund, president of Blessing's bank, arrived carrying a briefcase, as always. "You better not have eaten all the rolls. I could smell them clear up the street."

"You're safe. Thelma hasn't brought them out yet. But the coffee is here." Thorliff glanced at the clock. "Anyone heard from Garth?"

"I'm here," Garth Wiste, Sophie's husband, called from outside. "I think I heard the train. Here, Thelma, let me carry that."

He entered carrying a hotter coffeepot, followed by Thelma with a platter of rolls. Smiling and nodding, she refilled coffee cups and took the cooler coffee back into the house, since there was no stove burning in the newspaper office.

"Any questions we can work on before David Gould arrives?" Thorliff asked.

"I have a report on the construction at the deaf school." Toby Valders strode through the door. "Just in time." He retrieved his coffee cup from the rack on the wall, filled it, and took his place at the table. "Jonathan is meeting the train, and he and his father will come together." He held up a clipboard with a pad of paper on it. "Punch list. We're so close to being finished on that school building."

Everyone took their seats, and Reverend Solberg delivered a brief opening prayer.

"Thank you always for your wisdom and continued prayers." Thorliff looked at Toby. "Let's begin with you."

Toby ran down his list of what little remained to be done at the school and laid it on the table. "Any questions?"

Thorliff picked up one of his own papers. "I have here a request from Mr. Gardner about adding on to the grocery store."

"If we keep going the way we are, we're going to have to add on to our machinery building too, or build another." Daniel Jeffers shook his head. "So much depends on the landship David is spearheading."

Fresh from the railway station, Jonathan Gould and his father entered.

Thorliff poured coffee for them and pushed the roll platter closer to their chairs. "Welcome home."

Gould smiled. "You said the right words. Home indeed." He set his bulging briefcase on the table. "That train seems to go slower every trip." He took a swig of coffee and set a roll on his plate. "I see Thelma has been up early."

Thorliff handed him a copy of the *Blessing Gazette*. "Delivered early this morning."

"No wonder you look like you did a couple of rounds in a boxing ring." Gould shook his head. "Another thing my son Thomas is finding interesting." He and Jonathan exchanged looks of disgust.

"Bring him out here, and we'll put him on the construction crew this summer," Toby suggested.

"Too late, I'm afraid." Jonathan sat down in the last empty chair.

Toby handed him a copy of the punch list for the deaf school. "We'll talk about this later." Jonathan had become the one who kept notes on the meetings and made sure everyone received a copy.

Thorliff nodded to Gould. "Any time you're ready."

"I've compiled a report that I will get typed and deliver to each of you. We call it a landship, while others refer to the machine as a tank. I suggest we adopt that name. I received mixed reviews. Many of the people I talked with still have their heads in the sand regarding the possibility of war. They are insisting that President Wilson will keep us out of it, but I spoke with others who agree with me. We need to get ready to supply armaments and anything else we can, not just in our country, but any country. That our tank can go over any terrain will save many human lives and deliver supplies to the front in a way never heard of before. Now, *we* all understand that, so I say let's go ahead and build the prototype and do as much testing as needed. If war breaks out, we want to be as close to ready as possible."

"As I said, we need another building." Daniel Jeffers looked at Toby. "And it sounds like sooner rather than later."

"And trained machinists," Gould added. He laid construction drawings out on the table. "Like we've been discussing, this tread will change farming too. Tractors with tread will get out on the fields far sooner in the spring than our present tractors can."

"So while we are building the prototype, we will be adapting tractors too. Sounds immediately profitable." Daniel was smiling.

"I hate to throw water on your plans, but where will the money come from?" Hjelmer looked around the table. "We don't have that kind of investment money here in Blessing, although the bank will put in all that we safely can."

"I don't believe money will be an issue. I have several friends who are highly interested, and I know when we really begin looking, the money will be there. Anyone with the foresight to look ahead will be lining up to invest. We are right on the cusp of another major advance in mechanical engineering and design. I'd just as soon not go public on the stock market yet, but that is another avenue for funds."

Thorliff could almost see the energy in the room. "David, you mentioned a man who wants to come to Blessing in the near future."

"Yes, he is a friend of my son Thomas."

"Will your son come with him?" Thorliff asked. He saw a shadow cross his friend's face.

"No, he has refused to come to Blessing."

The tightening of Gould's jaw said more than his words.

"Mor said you are looking for a temporary housekeeper and cook."

Gould nodded. "I considered bringing out some of my staff, but . . ."

"Don't worry, we will find someone. He could, of course, stay at the boardinghouse."

"I thought of that too, but more as a last resort."

Thorliff looked up at the clock. "If there is nothing else for the moment, let's close this meeting so we can all get back to work. Toby, I think someone else should work on the punch list, because you need to get your pencils and rulers out. Daniel, you have some space to set him up with drafting tables with good lighting, plenty of windows, and a telephone."

Toby nodded. "I'll delegate the crew and turn the projects we are finishing over to Fritz Stauffer, move him up to supervisor, and let him choose his foremen. At least as a supervisor he won't be on the roof. I hate to say this, but we're going to need more help."

"I'll put ads in other newspapers. Give me a list of what you need." Thorliff looked around, paused for additions, and turned to John. "If you will close us with a blessing?"

"Of course." John inhaled and let silence

fall over the room. "Heavenly Father, we trust that you will provide answers for our questions and bring us the people you know we need. We thank you and praise you. Amen."

The voices together closed the prayer.

Thorliff blew out a breath. He had a feeling this was all just the tip of the iceberg.

Chapter 12

Today? Ask her today? Or wait?

David Gould pushed open the walnut door surrounded by narrow panes of etched glass on both sides and a half-circle window above. Expecting his house in Blessing to have that empty-house smell, he inhaled—and smelled coffee. And fresh bread. He set his bags on the marble floor and shoved the door closed with his foot.

"Is anyone here?"

"In the kitchen."

"Ingeborg?" He flung his hat onto the coat rack and headed for the kitchen. Green willow branches graced the table in the dining room. He pushed open the swinging kitchen door to see her sliding a pan of something into the oven.

She closed the oven door and turned to smile at him. "I didn't expect you quite yet."

He stopped in the doorway. This—this was what he wanted to come home to every evening, say good night and good morning to. The diamond ring felt heavy in his pocket.

"What is it?" she asked softly.

"You. I never dreamed you would be here. I wanted to take a shower and get to the farm as soon as possible."

"I wanted to surprise you."

"You succeeded." He crossed the room and held out both hands. "I cannot tell you how much I missed you."

She put her hands in his, then stepped into his arms. "Welcome home."

"You have no idea." He bent to kiss the lips that smiled up at him. The first kiss butterflied against her lips. The second took command. He placed his hands on her cheeks to draw her even closer. "Oh, Ingeborg. I don't want to go through this distance thing again." Holding her close, he rested his chin on top of her head, breathing deeply to slow the heart leaping in his chest. "You'd think I was thirty years old, not an older man."

"That would be far too young. We match close enough in age to be able to act with wisdom from all the life we've lived." She wrapped her arms around him and leaned into his chest. "Instead I feel like running through a field of daisies with you holding my hand and the sun and breeze blessing us beyond measure. David, am I too old for that now?"

"No, heart of my heart. We might walk fast instead of run, the better to experience all the scents and the colors and the absolute delight of holding hands."

"Would you like a cup of coffee? Dinner will be ready after we—oh no, I smell something burning." She folded her apron and used it to pull the oven door open. She retrieved the pan of little dark squares. Very dark squares. "How could I let that happen?"

David broke into laughter. "Oh my, Ingeborg. What are they?"

"Crackers to go with our dinner." She set down the pan and picked up a pancake turner. "These can go to the hens. The rest might be a bit brown, but they are edible." She looked up at him, one eyebrow cocked. "You want to eat right now?"

"I'll go wash up. Ten minutes?"

"Or more, if need be."

"You want to come help me?"

She flapped her apron at him. "I don't think that would be proper."

Proper be hanged, he thought as he squeezed her hand before letting go, picked up his suitcases, and carried them upstairs. At times like these, having household help would be a good thing. Or would it? Did he really want to share this house with servants? He had learned to shave, choose his own clothes, even fix coffee and fry eggs with bacon. Although he had slipped back into the life of New York City with great ease.

He found himself humming as he washed and shaved. He paused to figure out the tune. "Abide with Me." Hmm, what brought that to mind? They sang it at church here in Blessing, but why was he thinking of it now? He stared at his face in the mirror, smooth on one side, white-creamed on the other. The face nodded. Of course. What did he want most right now? *Lord, for Ingeborg to abide with me and us with you. I want this house filled with love and joy, like her house is. You feel it when you walk in the door.* He nodded again. He had a lot he wanted to talk over with John. He trusted John's wisdom, as he trusted Ingeborg's. He inhaled a deep breath, held it, and slowly let it out. Here he could relax, in this house, in Blessing.

He propped his hands on the sides of the sink. No rushing. Rushing was all one did in New York City. Here his life needn't be that way. While there was so much to do, here he could breathe clean fragrant air. Feel safe. That caught him by surprise too. Did he not feel safe in the city house? Perhaps it was a more spiritual safety than physical safety. Here in Blessing, honoring God came more easily.

He drained the sink and rinsed it, put his travel attire away, and pulled clean clothes off the hangers. All those things were done for him in New York, because that was the proper way to live. If one was wealthy, at least. Here, Ingeborg was waiting for him downstairs.

"Who is cleaning my house and doing my laundry?" he asked when he found her setting the table out in the back seating area with its slate floor.

"Emmy and Inga."

"Do they know how to do everything?"

"They are nearly women, Emmy especially, so they have helped with household matters and gardening, all the things women do. That's part of growing up." She watched his face. "You are disappointed?"

He sighed. "Not disappointed in what they do, but disappointed in the ways back east. Of course, that is the way of the wealthy who can afford to hire someone to do those things. Our daughters are instead supposedly learning how to run a household with servants." He shook his head. "Let's eat."

"I hope you don't mind that we are having a cold meal for dinner." She set a plate down for each of them. "We have potato salad, sliced ham, pickles, three bean salad, crackers, and something special for dessert."

He watched as she explained the meal. Peace emanated from her, and when she looked up to smile at him, he had to swallow. "Th-this is so peaceful. It's like I have stepped through a door to a whole different world." He could hear hammers pounding, saws, someone shouting, but all from a distance. Closer, he heard birds singing. A dog barked, cows bellowed. The church bell announced one o'clock, another bit of music for the day.

He took her hands and bowed his head. "Thank you, Lord God, for bringing me home safely, for all the business we wound up and began. Thank you for this food, for these loving hands that prepared it, for the land, the songs of the land, and all it produces. Thank you for my life and what you have planned for us to do, in the name of your precious Son, amen." He squeezed her hands gently before letting them go. When he looked up, tears pooled in her lovely blue eyes.

"What is it?"

"I am so very thankful." She swallowed. "And I am so very glad you are home."

He picked up his sweating glass and held it, waiting for her to do the same. "To God be the glory."

"Ja, to God be the glory." She spread her napkin in her lap. "There's plenty more in the kitchen." She held out the basket of crackers. "Deborah perfected this recipe years ago. Now we call her the cracker queen."

David ate half of one and reached for more. "These are excellent."

"A little brown."

"Tasty."

She set the basket in the middle of the table. "The challenge is to eat just one."

"Sorry, I didn't know the challenge." He reached for more.

"So, how did the meeting go this morning?"

"I'll tell you about it later."

Ingeborg leaned back in her chair. "Manny has been watering your trees."

"I probably need a yard man too." He glanced around his yard. "I see you planted some roses."

"Why do you think I did it?"

"Well, didn't you?"

"Actually, no. Amelia had some cuttings she rooted a couple of years ago, and since

160

she has pretty much filled up her yard, she thought you might like some here. If you do, she has several more to bring over. You have to decide where to plant them." She leaned forward to smile at his consternation. "Do you like what she did?"

"Yes, very much so, but . . ."

"But what?"

"But how much should I pay her?"

Ingeborg chuckled, then let the chuckles grow into real laughter. "You should see your face. You who can order big companies around . . ."

"But, Ingeborg, my love, I am not a gardener. I hire people to take care of my house and yard. What I know about plants could fit on a penny."

"You recognize beauty when you see it."

"Yes, Amelia's roses are beautiful colors, and their fragrance is wonderful, and she plants roses all over town."

"And then takes care of them too."

"People say how lovely it is in Blessing. It must be thanks to the trees and the flowers, since the buildings are nothing to write home about." He leaned back and crossed his arms over his chest. "I don't mean to offend."

"The first things I planted were the cottonwood trees to shade the house. Then the yellow rose at the steps to the front porch.

Haakan teased me sometimes about using the dishwater and wash water to water the rosebush and those trees. Our well water had to go to the livestock and to the house, and we didn't waste a drop. My mor taught me to use everything up and then give the leftovers a new use. Hauling water to the trees by hand took time and energy when sometimes we didn't have that, but look at them now." She caught his grin. "What?"

"Oh, my Ingeborg, you are such an amazing woman with the biggest heart of anyone I know. How can I be so blessed as to know you? And love you with all my heart."

She shook her head and tsked. "Uff da, how you talk."

He took her hand in his. "I have seen these hands calm a fussy baby, stop the tears of a child, knead the best bread anywhere, eviscerate a chicken, plant the tiniest of seeds, and turn the pages in your Bible." He stroked the back of her hand. "You bring healing with your hands, and you welcome the lonely and brokenhearted." He lifted her hand and kissed first the palm and then her fingers. "Such love and beauty." He cupped her hand and closed his fingers over hers. When he looked up and saw the tears running down her cheeks, he stood and gathered her into his arms. "Why are you crying?"

"I-I'm making your shirt wet."

"It will dry." He kissed her forehead and used his thumbs to wipe away the tears. "Oh, my Ingeborg, how I love you." He watched her face, those blue eyes that spoke far more than words could say. Her slight nod made him gather her close again. "We have so much to talk about."

"Yes."

He waited for more. Yes, she loved him. Yes, they had much to talk about. Yes, the sun was shining. What? *Just ask her*, that stern inner voice prompted. *What if she doesn't love me? I know that she loves me.*

"Yes?" He stared deep into her eyes.

A slight nod. "Yes, I love you." She spoke softly, like the kiss of a spring breeze.

He waited again. Had he made himself clear? That he was in love with her and wanted to marry her?

Ask her! That voice again. *But I want to make it a special occasion*, he answered. *I don't even have the ring with me.* He'd left it in his pocket upstairs.

Despite his indecision, the words burst from him.

"Ingeborg Bjorklund, I love you and I want you with me always. Will you marry me?"

She stilled as if time itself had stopped.

He waited. It seemed as if she withdrew into herself, not moving but still backing off.

"That is a big decision," she said softly. "I-I have a lot of questions." She leaned her head against his shoulder.

"Do you love me?"

"Yes. I love you. No question there." This was spoken with more surety.

"Then we can work out whatever questions or problems are troubling you."

"What do your children think of your marrying me?"

"Does that matter?"

"Yes. Even though they live across the country, it matters."

He heaved a sigh, shaking his head. "Right now I am so disgusted with some of them that if I never see them again, it would be too soon." He could feel his jaw tighten at just the thought.

"You said *right now*."

He nodded. And sighed again. "All right, we will talk about these things and, God willing, see where we are to go."

Her smile, the one that warmed and comforted his heart, broke over him. *Please, Lord, I am so sure this is your will for us. Please make this happen. Please.*

Chapter 13

Ingeborg lay in bed, luxuriating in the breeze playing with the curtains, the birds starting to stir but not up to full voice yet. Even the rooster still sounded sleepy. *David Gould asked me to marry him.* Questions paraded through her mind. If she married him, where would they live? Here in Blessing or, heaven forbid, in New York? Her entire being wanted to scream *no!* Visiting New York might be a possibility, but living there? No, no, no, a resounding *no.* The thought made even her fingertips hurt.

Do you want to marry him? That inner voice sounded reasonable this time. To wake up beside him, to lie in bed and talk about the day. To have him close beside her. Those were the things she missed most, although she and Haakan had worked so hard that there was little time for just being together. She thought of the times she and David sat on the swing, talking, laughing together, but they needn't be married for that.

She heard Freda in the kitchen, running water for coffee. Had Manny already started the stove and gone down to milk, or was he still sleeping? The rooster crowed again, this time at full volume. She should get going.

She got up and prepared to meet the day, as Thorliff liked to say.

Grateful for the indoor plumbing, she still sometimes missed the walk to the outhouse. Her bare feet in the dew-laden grass. A few minutes later she entered the kitchen, tying her apron.

"Good morning, Freda. What are we making for breakfast?"

Freda smiled. "I thought French toast, scrambled eggs with bacon, and applesauce. Good morning. Will you bring me the eggs?"

Ingeborg brought the basket of eggs in from the pantry, along with the loaf of older bread. While Freda sliced that, she broke eggs into a bowl to whisk for scrambled eggs. A little cream added to the richness.

He asked me to marry him. She couldn't stop thinking about it. The good and the bad as well.

Lars knocked and entered the kitchen door. "Kaaren is not feeling well. One of the little ones visited with a summer cold, and she caught it. May I breakfast here?"

"Of course!" Ingeborg and Freda both said together.

Lars grinned and sat down. "Kaaren has a cough and a very sore throat. She says she's better this morning, that it's not much and it will go away. At least she didn't wake up coughing during the night."

The others trooped into the house. Ingeborg poured the coffee while Emmy and Freda set the platters on the table. "Lars, will you please say grace?"

"Heavenly Father, thank you for this food and those who prepared it. Guide us and lead us through this day that we may do all to your glory. And lay your hand on Kaaren, please. Amen."

Everyone was gathered around the breakfast table when David came through the door. "Sorry, I got a telephone call. Good morning."

They all chorused "Good morning!" back at him.

"We saved you a place," Emmy said, patting the empty chair beside her.

"Thank you, miss." David smiled at Lars. "I'm glad to see you here. I want to talk with you." He took a platter from Freda, speared two pieces of French toast, and passed it on. "This is most certainly a treat."

Lars nodded with his mouth full, chewed, swallowed, and said, "Welcome back, David. I'll be in the shop. We have a lot going on today."

Finally Freda asked, "Would anyone like

more?" and received groans for an answer—even from Manny, who was like a bottomless pit. "Refills on coffee?" No takers even on that. They pushed back their chairs and the kitchen emptied, leaving the girls to wash the dishes.

Lars stopped at the door long enough to say, "David, come on over when you wish."

"And I will check on Kaaren." Ingeborg took her plate to the sink.

Freda headed for the cheese house with Manny, and Ingeborg set about getting a basket ready to take to Kaaren. Willow tree bark for tea, honey with lemon to soothe her throat, broth for nourishment, and an onion to make a poultice for her chest. She had her stethoscope in the basket and strips of old sheets for a poultice if needed.

"I'll walk as far as the machine shed with you. This seems the only way we get some time together today." David took the basket and hooked it over his arm. "Thank you for breakfast."

They took off at more of a stroll than a walk, savoring the glorious morning.

He asked, "Have you thought any more about my proposal?"

She almost blushed. "All the time."

"And . . . ?"

She licked her lips. "We must both speak

frankly now, right? I'm ashamed for thinking uncharitably, but if we were to marry, your children would become my children, and I don't want them. I don't even like them. And yet they would have equal rights of inheritance with Astrid and Thorliff and Andrew. My children work hard and make important contributions to society." She was going to add, *Your children are useless leeches who do nothing*, but she stopped herself in time.

"My children are not particularly close. They have lives of their own."

"I remember after your house was finished, you tried to get your family to visit, but Geraldine had poisoned their minds against Blessing. You said that."

"She thought you were all hopelessly rural, even stupid." His voice grew testy. "Ingeborg, my children do not direct my life."

"Oh? Then who is this Lionel Hibbing? You've never brought anyone from New York to visit before. You said Mr. Hibbing was your son's idea, not yours."

"I know, I know."

"And one more thought: How soon would it be before you yearned for your old life in New York enough to try to make our home here a little New York: a maid, perhaps a butler, a gardener—doing all the things everyone else here does for themselves."

"No, I wouldn't. In fact, I'm already putting that sort of thing behind me."

"Except that you want to have a formal dinner party one evening." They had arrived at Kaaren's gate, so she stopped. "Who would you invite?"

"You, Thorliff, Daniel and Astrid, John and his wife, Kaaren and Lars, and Jonathan and Grace.."

"I see. But, David, none of us do formal dining. We serve family-style. If this is to impress him . . ." She shook her head. "We'll do our best, but if you want something properly formal, you might consider bringing out some of your staff from New York."

"I thought of that. If Thomas had not been so insistent, I would not have extended the invitation in the first place. The more I think about it, the less I like the idea."

"And it would be terribly impolite to disinvite him."

David chuckled. "Yes, alas, it would." He handed her the basket. "You've given me much to think about."

"I will see you at dinner, then?" she asked.

"Of course."

He was still standing in front of her, but she missed him already. He continued to the machine shop. Ingeborg pushed open the gate and closed it again. They kept the heifers and some steers here, and the animals had been known to get loose. It was the same reason there was a fence and gate at her house.

She could hear hammers ringing and men talking out in the machine shop, but she went on to climb the back steps to the porch, expecting Kaaren to be resting out here where the breeze might feel cool. Instead she heard coughing from the bedroom on the first floor.

She knocked on the back door and entered uninvited. "Kaaren, it's me." She made her way to the bedroom, where a lowered shade dimmed the room.

Kaaren lay in the bed, doubled up in a paroxysm of coughing. When she collapsed back against the pillow, Ingeborg could hear her raspy breathing across the room. Why hadn't Lars told her Kaaren was this sick? Or had Kaaren hidden it from him as much as possible? That sounded more likely.

Kaaren's eyelids flickered and then opened. She whispered, "Oh, Ingeborg, how did you know to come?"

"Same way we always do. That God-prompting we've had happen so often. Granted, the telephone has taken His place at times, but here I am." She set her basket on the foot of the bed and laid the back of her hand against Kaaren's soaking wet forehead.

She had a fever, but at least she was sweating. "Were you this bad when Lars left this morning?"

"I went back to sleep after he left. I can hear them out in the machine shed, but I think I was sleeping when he checked on me. As long as I don't cough, it's not so bad."

Ingeborg stacked the pillows behind her, then, using her stethoscope, listened to her lungs.

"I thought it would get better. It's in my throat, but I'm afraid it's moving into my chest."

Ingeborg glanced around. No glasses or cups. "I'll be right back. I need to get a teaspoon." In the kitchen, she pulled out the drawer and took out a spoon. Back in the bedroom, she unscrewed the lid on the tonic, poured out a spoonful, and, propping Kaaren up with one arm, dosed her with the other hand. "That should soothe your throat. Did you not cook anything for breakfast? The stove is cold."

Kaaren sucked in another breath, and the coughing struck her again. Ingeborg held on to her while she coughed near to vomiting. When the attack passed, she poured out another spoonful of cough syrup, and Kaaren swallowed slowly.

"I'll go start the stove." Ingeborg returned

to the kitchen. At times like this she wished for something faster than a woodstove. Once flames were licking the tinder, she tucked more kindling around it before adding some bigger pieces and setting the lids back in place. She adjusted the damper to get the fire roaring and felt the reservoir. Not warm yet. The burning wood snapped and crackled. She lifted a lid and set a pan of water to boil directly over the hole.

"Ingeborg?" Then another fit of coughing.

"Coming." She found Kaaren sitting on the edge of the bed. "You need the necessary?"

"Ja. But I feel some lightheaded."

"So you waited to let me help you. I'm glad." She assisted Kaaren to her feet and held on to her as she started to walk to the bathroom that had been added on to the house. When Kaaren was finished, Ingeborg helped her back to bed. "You did fine."

"Takk." She blew out a breath. "Right now I'm thankful I did not have to use a chamber pot. I think we take so much for granted."

Ingeborg settled Kaaren back against her pillows and folded the sheet over her lap. "That we do, and indoor plumbing is one of the best things we've done. Right up there with water to the sink with a hand pump.

We've been blessed in so many ways. I'll be right back."

She returned to the kitchen. The reservoir was warming now. She fetched a washcloth from the linen cupboard, dipped it in the warm water, set it in a bowl, and returned to the bedroom.

She wiped off Kaaren's face and arms. "Do you have a clean nightgown?"

"In the clothes press, bottom shelf."

"Let's get you out of that sweaty one and freshen you up. That alone can help you feel better." Ingeborg finished with the basin bath, dried Kaaren off with a towel, and pulled a fresh nightgown over her head. Ingeborg stepped back. "You've not eaten yet. What would you like?"

"Did Lars leave some coffee? And I think I have some canned broth, if that would help. Down in the cellar, top shelf on the right."

"I brought broth for you; I'll heat it up. Lars ate at my house, so I'll make coffee. I'm going to put cream and some honey in yours. And then I'll heat up some broth. You drink that down, and we can talk about real food."

Ingeborg gathered her supplies and carried them into the kitchen, hanging the towel and cloth over the rack on the wall behind the stove. She restoked the fire, poured broth into a pan, lifted aside a firebox lid, and pulled the pan over the hole. It didn't take long. Back with the heated broth, she ladled out a cupful as Kaaren pushed herself higher on the pillows so she could hold the cup and sip.

"I could probably have made it to the table." Kaaren inhaled the aromatic steam and leaned back against the pillows. "But this feels good." Obviously feeling another coughing attack coming on, she handed the cup to Ingeborg and doubled over until the coughing left her panting.

"Do you feel like something more substantial to eat?"

"Yes, I think so." For the first time since Ingeborg's arrival, Kaaren smiled.

Ingeborg left her with the broth and carried the coffee cup back to the kitchen.

"Lord God, please bring your healing touch to Kaaren's throat and lungs. Let her heal rapidly to full strength. Give us wisdom to do what you want us to do. We give you all our thanks and praise." Ingeborg waited, eyes closed so she could focus better. "Thank you for being right here and hearing me. You said you never leave us and you always give us mercy. Thank you."

She sliced a thick piece of bread and, stabbing a toasting fork into the bottom, lifted another lid from the stove and held the bread over the flame, toasting it on both sides. After spreading it with butter and berry jam, she carried that and Kaaren's refilled coffee cup back into the bedroom.

"Why don't you pour yourself a cup of coffee, and we'll sit here a bit and visit?" Kaaren asked.

What a good idea. Ingeborg poured herself a cup, dragged a chair over beside Kaaren's bed, and sat down. "David has invited a man from New York to Blessing, and he wants some household help while the gentleman is here. Have you any suggestions?"

"So, Mr. Gould is back." Kaaren nibbled on her toast. "This tastes so good. Hmm. What about Freda's daughter-in-law, Anna? Her years of working at the boardinghouse have given her lots of experience. She would be a good housekeeper."

Ingeborg nodded. "Yes. Unless David decides he wants someone permanent." More questions to ask.

Kaaren thought for a moment, then lit up. "How about Mercy Hastings? I know she's been working at the hospital and is thinking of going to nursing school, but perhaps this would be a good break for her. And she learns really fast."

"An excellent idea." Perhaps she should talk with Jonathan. He knew far more about life in New York than she did. And then a new idea struck. Of course! Jonathan could help train someone. He understood life among the elite in the big city and what was expected of domestic help.

They chatted for a few more minutes, until Kaaren's eyelids started to droop.

"Let's set up a steam inhaler and see how you do before you sleep," Ingeborg said, finishing her coffee. "I also brought an onion to make a poultice. I'll do that before I leave. We want to keep the problem out of your lungs if we can. Freda already made chicken soup. It's on the stove at my house. I'll bring you some for dinner. Take the cough syrup as often as you need it. And drink lots of water."

Thank you, Lord, for prompting me to come.

Chapter 14

David Gould said into the telephone receiver, "Ingeborg, I've never trained household help. That is a job for the head housekeeper or the butler, and my wife ran all of that."

"Jonathan and I have been talking, and

we are doing the training, but I would like you to let them practice with you. So we will have supper at your house tonight with you and me, Jonathan and Grace, and Thorliff. And we will all be on our best manners, which are nowhere near what you grew up with."

"Why did I ever allow Thomas to talk me into this?" He tipped his head back and then to each side to stretch the cramping muscles in his neck. Heaving a sigh, he nodded. "Thank you to all of you."

"Jonathan chose the menu. He wonders why you did this too." Her chuckle carried over the telephone lines just fine. "Besides, this has been training for both Freda's daughter-in-law—who is an excellent cook, by the way—and Mercy, who says she used to deliver mended linens to houses that lived like this. Oh, and another question—which bedroom do you want him to stay in?"

"The more masculine one beside the larger bathroom." He had built the house with three bathrooms upstairs and one downstairs. And five bedrooms, so the rest of his children could come visit if they wished. None of them wished. It was far smaller than his house in New York, but he didn't plan to raise a family here. Mostly he simply hoped they would visit him. Although at this point, that indeed looked doubtful.

"Thank you, Ingeborg. What time do you plan to serve?"

"We thought six thirty would be appropriate. I know dinners in New York are usually later, but this is a compromise."

"I should be home around four. Thank you."

"You're welcome. Oh, and this is not a dress-up affair."

They hung up, and he leaned back in his chair. Some days he worked in his office at home, but otherwise he had an office at Jeffers Machinery, where he and Daniel worked on the tank designs and adapting the tractor to the use of the new caterpillar treads. As far as he could tell, it was time to bring in a draftsman and possibly an engineer. The men who worked there were already stretched as far as possible.

In the meantime, he studied the files, books, and any materials he could locate on building machinery, train engines, and diesel engines. Usually he was strictly a money man, but this time he was fascinated by this new addition to tractors and creating the tank.

"Are you staying here all night?" Daniel asked him some time later.

"I wasn't planning on it. What time is it, anyway?"

"Nearly six."

"No! Where did the time go?" He gathered the books and papers scattered over his desk into stacks and shook his head. "Thank you."

He shut the door to his office, said goodnight, and headed for home.

"Sorry I'm running late," he said as Mercy met him at the door of his house. Right now, having a butler would have been handy.

Mercy smiled. "Anna is the cook tonight. Ingeborg said to remind you that supper is being served at six thirty. Do you need more time?"

"I do. Please call the others and say seven instead." Or they could come and have drinks and appetizers while they waited. "No, never mind. Did Anna prepare some appetizers to go with drinks?"

"Yes, sir."

"Good, then start those as folks arrive, and I'll be down as quickly as I can."

"Yes, sir." She hung his hat on the pegs in the hallway.

David hustled up the stairs, sniffing as he went. Something smelled mighty good.

He laid his clothes out on the bed, took a fast shower, and could hear people laughing and talking downstairs as he finished dressing. This house needed more of that.

He paused on the stairs, listening to the

conversations in the parlor. Perhaps he should have added a butler to the staff. He watched Mercy, her hair smoothed back into a bun at the base of her neck and wearing a uniform of sorts—a black dress with a white apron but nothing on her head—moving through the group with a tray of cheese on crackers. The bar was set up, but only with lemonade and sherry. He would have to order more liquor before what's-his-face came.

Ingeborg's smile welcomed him as he strode into the room. Jonathan stood beside her.

"Sorry I'm late," David said. "Thank you for going ahead with the evening."

"Can I get you something to drink, Father?" Jonathan asked.

"Yes, please."

Mercy appeared at his side. "A canapé, sir?"

"Yes, thank you." He took a cracker off the tray, along with a napkin. "Thank you for . . ." He nodded to the chatting people.

"Mostly it was Ingeborg, sir."

"Of course." If they were married, she would have automatically been the hostess.

He moved among the group, greeting each as a guest.

Mercy stopped at the arched entrance. "Dinner is served."

Feeling like they were playacting, he tucked Ingeborg's hand around his bent arm and led the way to the perfectly set dining room table. An arrangement of irises graced the center of the table, with lit candles at either end. His seat was at the head of the table, and he pulled out the chair to the right of his for Ingeborg. Grace sat on his left with Jonathan beside her. Thorliff sat beside his mother.

With everyone seated, he smiled. "Let's say grace." Bowing his head, he took in a deep breath. The first formal dinner in his house. "Lord God, we thank you for the privilege of dining together. Thank you for these family members and friends who are helping me out with a situation that makes no sense at all. But we know you bless us and provide for us in all ways. May we do everything to your glory. Amen." He looked around the table. "Thank you all."

Despite the formality of the setting and the way the food was served, the conversation was pleasant, with everyone showing their delight over the delicious food and the proper serving. Vanilla ice cream with strawberries and lace cookies finished the meal.

"Mercy, would you please bring Anna in here before we leave the table?" David asked.

She nodded, a worry line creasing her forehead.

Anna came in wiping her hands on her apron, with Mercy right beside her.

David smiled. "I want to thank you both for working so hard to prepare and serve this delicious meal. It looks to me like you learned the formal graces very well, and I think Jonathan will agree."

His son nodded. "Very well indeed. I think we can pull off this formal dinner for my father. And I can tell you, I am grateful I no longer have to live with such formality. I like supper around the table with children included. Believe me, mine will not grow up with the strictures I did. Here we can have lots of love and laughter. And I know this house can become the same, fancy dishes or not."

"Hear, hear." David led the clapping. "And now I have a question. Do you think we should find someone to be a butler or bring one out from New York City? Or let Mercy and Anna carry the whole load?"

"We are doing this for whom? And for how long?" Jonathan asked.

"I offered Mr. Hibbing a week here, but I might come up with a reason to cut his visit short."

"This bears some thinking on, Father. Let's talk about it later." Jonathan nodded. "Anyone else have an opinion? Ingeborg, you would surely be his hostess."

She shrugged. "If need be."

No one, not even Ingeborg, the Queen of Hospitality, seemed eager to host Mr. Hibbing. David was very sorry he had listened to Thomas and invited the fellow. Oh well. At least it would only be for a week.

Standing beside David, Ingeborg watched the train come in, something she always enjoyed doing. The mighty engine huffed on past the station exactly far enough that the passenger cars stopped right at the platform. The railroad workers loaded crates of cheese that Ingeborg was sending east and unloaded crates and barrels of heaven knew what that had been shipped here.

At last Lionel Hibbing stepped down onto the platform. It had to be him, as he was the only passenger to get off. He was a tall fellow, stocky but not fat, and he stood ramrod straight. His neatly trimmed hair showed gray at the temples, and his short beard had a slight curl. Dressed like a wealthy easterner, he wore a silk frock coat and brocade waistcoat. He looked around, spotted David and Ingeborg, and came striding smartly over.

"Mr. Hibbing." David extended a hand. "Good to see you again."

"My pleasure, Mr. Gould."

This was odd. He did not even look at Ingeborg or acknowledge that she existed. Perhaps that was polite back east these days, but it was very impolite by Blessing standards.

David smiled. "This is Ingeborg Bjorklund."

Mr. Hibbing glanced at her. "Yes. Hello." His eyes immediately looked elsewhere, gazing all around him. "The village is larger than I expected."

"We're growing rapidly." David beamed. Ingeborg was glad to see that he was far more enthusiastic about Blessing than he was about New York. Perhaps if she were to marry him, he would want them to stay here.

Manny came trundling up with Mr. Hibbing's trunk in his wheelbarrow, wearing a wide grin. "Twenty-three crates of cheese just loaded on the train. That's a lot of crates."

"And some of them you built just yesterday." Ingeborg was smiling too. "Thank you, Manny. It's such a beautiful morning. After you drop the trunk off at Mr. Gould's, perhaps you and the girls should go fishing. You've all been working hard."

"Great idea! Thank you!" Manny nodded to David. "Good morning, Mr. Gould."

"Good morning to you too, Manny."

And away the young man went, pushing

the wheelbarrow faster than Ingeborg could ever have done.

"You've been sitting on the train too long. Let's take a walk, and I'll show you our town." David took off briskly, and Ingeborg fell in beside him.

As they passed the ice cream shop, the hospital, the grain elevator, the newspaper, Ingeborg got lost in her own thoughts. Not only did the Bjorklunds and their children have a hand in most of Blessing's businesses, they still ran those businesses. Ingeborg had never thought about how much the Bjorklund family had contributed to the prosperity and happiness of all these people. What a lovely gift of God. And every bit of it was God's doing. She and Haakan had followed His leading, and look what happened! *Thank you, thank you, dear Lord!*

Eventually they came to the lane leading to Ingeborg's farm.

"I usually take my noon meal at the farm. It's still early for dinner, but let's go to the house anyway. Relax and talk." David started down the lane.

Mr. Hibbing stopped. "This is all pasturage. Why has no one developed it?"

David smiled. "It probably never will be developed. This is the original farm of the family who started Blessing, essentially, and will probably remain so. It's more like a park or memorial." He grinned at Ingeborg.

She was going to agree, but Mr. Hibbing just sniffed. "Cows. Cows are grazing on some very valuable land, Gould. This should all be developed, not left as some sort of shrine of cow flops."

"Actually, Mr. Hibbing, the cows serve a purpose. They produce the milk for our very successful cheese factory. Blessing quickly sells all the cheese we can make, and our markets back east are expanding. Perhaps you noticed all those crates of cheese they were putting on the train this morning."

"I hadn't noticed, no." Mr. Hibbing frowned. "How many men does this cheese factory employ?"

David shrugged. "Ingeborg, do you know?"

"One."

David's mouth dropped open. And then he caught on. He grinned.

Ingeborg explained, "All the employees are women except Manny, who helps out in his spare time. Most of the men of Blessing are in construction or farming. The cows do not produce as much milk in winter, so four or five women can handle all the work. Eight including milkmaids. When the cows are producing more and the heifers have calved, there are fifteen."

They continued walking down the lane.

Mr. Hibbing was still frowning. "Only fifteen at most. I trust a lot of cheese comes from this."

David asked her, "Have you any idea how much they turn out in a year?"

"Freda will know. She has the sales records."

David nodded.

Mr. Hibbing looked downright testy. "Mr. Gould," he growled, "are you in the habit of letting your housemaid answer all your questions for you?"

"Housemaid . . ." David looked bewildered. Suddenly he roared with laughter. "Housemaid!" His face suggested to Ingeborg that he was planning some sort of mischief, so she remained silent.

Mr. Hibbing's assumption that Ingeborg was a servant made sense. Many upper-class easterners did not bother talking to their staff or learning anything about them, although David did. Mr. Hibbing was probably paying no attention to the housemaid, disregarding her, because he considered her well below his station in life.

David conducted Mr. Hibbing into the kitchen just as the phone was ringing. Ingeborg moved past them and picked up the receiver. "Oh, Gerald, he's right here." She handed the phone to David.

188

"Mr. Hibbing, have a seat." David took the phone.

Ingeborg saw the *Gazette* on the table, still rolled up. "Our biweekly newspaper." She handed it to Mr. Hibbing and went to the stove.

While David talked, Ingeborg put the coffee on. Freda wasn't here, but dinner was ready; a beef stew sat simmering on the side, keeping hot. She scooped flour into a bowl for biscuits, kneaded the dough, and greased a biscuit sheet. She was putting the biscuits in the oven as David hung up the phone.

He told Mr. Hibbing, "That was the machine shop. They asked me to come help solve a little problem. I apologize, but I have to leave you for a few minutes."

"Quite all right. These things come up." Mr. Hibbing smiled.

David left, and his guest picked up the paper, quietly unrolled it, and read the front page. Ingeborg sat down across from him.

The phone rang Ingeborg's rings. She crossed to the wall, picked it up, happily said, "Oh, yes," and dropped the receiver back on the hook. "My son and grandson asked to come to dinner."

"That's nice." He opened the paper, snapping it. Presently he lowered it and peered at

189

Ingeborg. "Do you not have duties to perform elsewhere?"

"No. I'll take the biscuits out of the oven shortly."

He grunted and went back to the paper. He lowered it again. "Bring me writing materials, including envelopes. I want to send a letter."

"Certainly."

She gathered the inkpot, pen, writing paper, and two envelopes from her own desk and took them out to him at the table.

No thank-you. No comment. He uncapped the inkpot and began his letter.

Ingeborg pulled her nicely browned biscuits from the oven, put them in the bread basket, and wrapped them in a clean towel.

Manny entered from the kitchen door, dragging his hat off his head as he came in. "I smell beef stew, right?"

Ingeborg smiled. "Right. Would you bring in more butter, please?"

"Freda's beef stew is the greatest." Manny left the kitchen and headed to the pump house for the butter.

Thorliff came in carrying Rolly on his shoulders. The boy had to duck to enter the kitchen. Ingeborg suspected he was on the cusp of another growth spurt.

She introduced them. "Mr. Hibbing, this

is my son, Thorliff Bjorklund. And this is Roald. We call him Rolly."

Mr. Hibbing stood up to shake hands. He frowned. "Thorliff. I remember seeing the name . . . the newspaper. You are the editor."

"That is correct."

"Who publishes the *Blessing Gazette*, may I ask?"

"I do."

David came in. "Ah, I see you two have met. Good. After dinner I'll take you over to the machine shop to meet Daniel Jeffers. He's Thorliff's brother-in-law."

Freda entered. "Oh, good. You got the biscuits made. We need butter."

"Not anymore." Manny grinned as he sat down at the table. "It's in the sink. The girls aren't coming in for dinner. They're going to eat their fish. Emmy is showing Inga how the Indians smoke fish. Then they're going to dry the little walleyes we caught."

Rolly bounced in his seat. "Oh goody! Biscuits! I want one."

Ingeborg stared at him intently.

Rolly amended his request. "Please?"

"Good man!" Thorliff tousled his head. "Always say please and thank you."

Ingeborg had a mighty hard time avoiding looking pointedly at Mr. Hibbing. She asked, "Thorliff, will you say the blessing, please?"

191

Clearly, Mr. Hibbing was not accustomed to thanking God for his food. When everyone else dropped their heads and closed their eyes, even Rolly, he did too, belatedly.

"Dear Lord, we thank you for this new friend in our midst. We ask that his stay here be pleasant and productive. And we thank you for this good food and ask you to bless it to our use. Amen."

Everyone chorused "amen," and Ingeborg ladled stew into deep dishes.

Mr. Hibbing looked at Thorliff. "As the local newspaperman, you probably know most of the people in this town."

Thorliff nodded. "Yeah, I guess I do."

"The tract of land out there where the cows are grazing. Who owns it?"

"My mother."

David was smirking. He caught Ingeborg's eye, and she found herself smirking too.

Mr. Hibbing frowned. "But I thought this woman said she is your mother."

"She is."

"But . . . that means . . ." The frown deepened. "You mean . . . ?"

Thorliff raised his voice. "My mother has helped many hundreds of people live a rich and fulfilling life here, Mr. Hibbing. You are honored to have met her."

Ingeborg smiled at the fellow as sweetly as she knew how. "Welcome to Blessing, Mr. Hibbing."

Chapter 15

A s Kaaren waved good-bye, she was smiling. "Thank you, Ingeborg!"

"You're welcome. See you later." Ingeborg left Kaaren's home happy. Her friend wasn't well yet, but she was certainly brighter and much stronger than she had been a few days ago. And her throat sounded much better.

Ingeborg closed the gate behind her. She should stop by the cheese factory on the way home.

Oh. There was Mr. Hibbing up on the corner. He spotted her and came toward her at a fast walk. "Mrs. Bjorklund! I was going to call this afternoon at your home." He tipped his hat. "You look exceptionally beautiful today."

"Thank you. You are quite dapper today as well. I would guess you slept well last night at David's, especially after that long train ride."

"Indeed, it was a long ride. Normally I just rent a train car, since I don't own one anymore. There are three different track gauges in the country, I'm sure you know. The gauge is the measurement of the space between the rails. Some rails are six feet apart, others are four. Dreadfully unhandy. And when you own a car you can only travel on one of them. So I rent a car in the appropriate gauge. Much simpler. But on this trip no car was available for rental, so I had to ride coach. One cannot sleep well in coach."

"I see." Ingeborg was a little put off that he felt he had to explain something as basic as railroad gauge to her. And didn't he know that over two decades ago they had switched nearly all the nation's railroads to standard gauge? Even in the South, the gauge was now the same as it was everywhere else. You no longer had to change gauges anywhere between here and New York. Strange that he didn't know that, and yet he was a financier like David.

Or maybe he did know, but that would be an even blacker mark against him. He would have assumed she was too stupid to see that he was, well, stretching the truth.

He took both her hands in his. "Mrs. Bjorklund, I owe you a deep apology. I was so fascinated by this beautiful little town yesterday as David was showing us around, I quite neglected you. I am so very sorry."

"Your apology is accepted, Mr. Hibbing, of course."

"Please call me Lionel. 'Mr. Hibbing' sounds terribly formal, and Blessing seems so delightfully informal a place. May I call you Ingeborg?"

"Certainly, as you wish." She put a smile on her face, but inside she was frowning curiously. He had totally ignored her yesterday when he assumed she was a maid, even when he was sitting at her kitchen table. The town certainly did not fascinate him then. When he did speak to her, all he did was bark orders. What had so thoroughly changed his mind, she wondered.

"Here. Allow me to carry this for you." He lifted her empty basket off her arm. "Oh my, that is quite lightweight."

Ingeborg was perfectly capable of carrying the empty basket she had been using for years, but she allowed him. Where was he when it had been very heavy? "Kaaren, who lives next door, is ill. I brought her some herbs and honey to soothe her throat, some soup, and a chicken dinner."

He stopped in his tracks and scowled the way a teacher frowned at children who misbehaved. "My dear lady, you are aware, surely, that practicing medicine without a license is against the law. You could go to jail. Even worse, you are not qualified to diagnose disease. This Karen"—he mispronounced it—"could be ill with a deadly disease, and you give her a little honey. She could die because of your callousness and your high-handed misdiagnosis."

"Lars and I would have taken Kaaren over to Dr. Astrid, but Astrid is very busy with several construction accidents and a surgery. My home remedies seem to be working. That is the important thing, don't you agree? To help Kaaren get well."

"The important thing is that she be treated properly by a qualified physician, not a little old lady with a jar of honey."

Anger boiled up inside her, but Ingeborg held her peace. "I have to stop by the cheese factory. You are most welcome to join me and see our operation. Then I will return home. I hope you will join us for dinner; that is, our noon meal."

He still did not look happy, but he no longer scowled. "David has a cook, as I understand it, and is arranging a formal dinner, but I believe that's not for another couple days. Yes, of course I would love to join you." He paused. "Will the others be joining us?"

196

"Others?"

"That little boy and your son the editor, and I think the other fellow's name is Lars." His tone of voice when he said *that little boy* told her very clearly that he did not enjoy children.

No wonder, she thought. Back east in high society, the children did not eat with the grown-ups. They ate in the kitchen or elsewhere, so as not to disturb the adults. But how were they to learn how the world worked if they never listened to adult conversation? "Lars will join us, certainly, until Kaaren feels better," she replied.

She led the way through the front door of the cheese house and on to the back work area.

Freda was gently stirring a vat of curdling milk. "This was slow getting started for some reason, but it's coming along now."

"That's the third slow vat this week. I wonder. Did we get a batch of old rennet?" Ingeborg picked up a ladle from beneath the vat and dipped some whey, tasting it. "It doesn't taste odd at all."

"I didn't think so either. Whatever it is affects the clotting but not the flavor." Freda kept stirring with the cheese rake.

Ingeborg led Lionel to another vat. "This one has curdled and set properly. When the curds are ready, we'll press them into a mold."

197

"You have many small pans this size. Think how much more efficient it would be to make one very large pan at a time. It would go much faster." Lionel nodded smugly. "Yes, that's definitely it. Use bigger pans."

"But if something goes wrong, such as in the vat Freda is stirring, it spoils the whole huge vat instead of just one small one. Rennet is not all the same, which means that sometimes the batch is perfect, sometimes not."

"What do you do with the imperfect ones?"

"Feed them to the hogs. It's not wasted, exactly, but losing even a small vat puts us behind. Losing a large vat would be terrible."

"Nonetheless, it's much more efficient. You should make the change." It was as if he hadn't heard her at all.

Manny was out back building more crates. Every nail he drove was exactly right. "We'll have a dozen wheels ready to go in a week or so," he said, "so I figured I should build some crates ahead of time. Then we can just send them."

"Wonderful. Thank you very much, Manny. Do we have enough wax?"

"I think Freda's ordered some more, just to be sure we have plenty. Last winter we accumulated a lot of extra cakes of wax while

198

the cows weren't producing much, but that stash is running out."

Ingeborg watched him for a few moments, admiring his thoughtfulness. Manny had come so far. What a fine husband he would be to some lucky girl; he was wonderfully industrious and cheerful. She imagined it wouldn't be long before he'd be ready for a farm and family of his own.

She started home with Lionel, who was still going on about using larger vats for the cheese, and thought about the word *cheerful*. Thorliff had been so sad and dark since his Elizabeth died. That was not only expected but proper. They had been deeply in love. But now he was coming back into his more cheerful state of mind. He had started that journey, but there were still ups and downs. How she wished she could help him more. The book they were working on was definitely helping.

Inga and Emmy came skipping up. Ingeborg noticed that their aprons needed washing. Inga crowed, "We just cleaned up Mr. Gould's weed patch."

Ingeborg frowned. "He has a weed patch?"

Emmy giggled. "He calls it a garden. Only he hadn't weeded it since the last rain."

"I'm not sure he could weed his garden when he was in New York."

Inga waved her hand. "A detail. Oh, please tell him his corn is almost ready. The silk is shriveling."

"I shall. I think he will enjoy picking it. Thank you, both of you."

They skipped on toward the house.

Ingeborg glanced toward Lionel. He was watching the girls leave with a grumpy, almost disgusted look on his face. "I'm sorry you don't enjoy children more, Lionel. They're a major part of our life here."

"Nonsense! Where did you ever get that idea?"

"Your face and tone of voice." *Matthew seven. Ye shall know them by their fruits*, she thought.

"Well, you're reading me all wrong. I *love* children. Absolutely love them."

Right. Ingeborg held her tongue, but she knew what she was seeing. You didn't listen to the words; you trusted the fleeting first expression on the person's face. And Lionel Hibbing was definitely not an enthusiast of children.

They paused at the gate to her lane.

He set her empty basket on the ground and took her hands in his. He studied her so intently that she felt uncomfortable. "Ingeborg Bjorklund, I have something very important to ask you."

"Ahem!" David came hastening up, and he did not look pleased.

Lionel stepped back instantly, looking surprised. "Ah, David. I was just going to look you up next."

"And I was looking for you. Come to the machine shop with me, please. I'd like to show you what we have in mind for the tanks."

"Certainly." Lionel picked up Ingeborg's basket and handed it to her. "You may go now." His superior attitude irritated Ingeborg.

Apparently it irritated David as well. He had not lost the frown. "Excuse me, Lionel, but she's coming with us." He smiled at her. "That business head on her shoulders is the best around."

Ingeborg set her basket down beside the gate. Why carry it all over town? "Inga and Emmy said your corn is about ready to pick. The silk is shriveling."

They took off toward the machine shop.

"And how will I know when the great moment comes?"

"The tufts of silk coming out of the top of the ears will be black or brown."

Lionel stared. "You're going to pick corn?"

David just smiled. "Not until the silk turns brown. It's not quite ready yet."

Lionel huffed.

What was that about? She tried to figure it out as they walked along, but she could not come to any firm conclusion. David was talking about the possibility of war in Europe, and Lionel was agreeing heartily. Then they were talking about the United States becoming the arsenal for the world. Again Lionel agreed enthusiastically.

When they arrived at the machine shop, Daniel was sweeping up wood shavings by the door. He grinned at them as they approached.

Lionel took charge, stepping up to Daniel. "Direct me to your supervisor." No *please*, no smile.

For a moment, Daniel seemed confused. He looked at David, then at Ingeborg, before he figured it out. "Good morning, sir. Shall I tell him who's calling?"

"Lionel Hibbing," he said expansively, pridefully. "I own an ironworks in Minnesota."

Daniel nodded. "And I am Daniel Jeffers. I own a machine shop in Blessing." He didn't give Lionel the disgusted look he deserved, but his voice hardened. "This one."

Down inside, Ingeborg was laughing, but she tried not to let it show.

Now it was Lionel who was confused. "You are the owner but you sweep floors?"

"It needed sweeping, and I was the only one who wasn't busy at the moment. We work together here, Mr.—did you say Hibbing? And we get a lot done." Daniel's smile returned. "Good morning, David. Good morning, Ingeborg." He kissed her lightly on the forehead. "Welcome, all of you. Please come in. Ingeborg, how is Kaaren feeling?"

"Better today. I'm concerned about her, though. She seems to pick up every malady that comes along."

"And seems to give Lars half of them."

"So far he has escaped this one." Ingeborg noticed that the shop had doubled its floor space by moving one wall out and extending the roof. She asked, "You're going to add side walls later, right?"

"Yeah, one of these days we'll quit making machines long enough to finish off the new floor space. During summer we don't need the walls, and I have an order for three seeders and a repair job. The machinery orders come first."

She smiled happily. "Daniel, I remember when you got started, making a few parts in order to repair seeders."

"Cedars?" Lionel scowled. "Trees?"

Daniel grinned. "Seeders. Machines pulled by horses or mules that sow seeds. Then we started building balers that are selling well, and now we're designing a threshing machine. We just keep growing."

"Astrid and I were talking a few days ago about how proud of you we are." Ingeborg smiled. "We certainly aren't going to tell you, of course. You might get swellheaded. But we are."

Daniel ducked his head. "It is all by the grace of God, Ingeborg, and your prayers sure didn't hurt any. To God be all the glory. The only thing slowing us down now is a lack of trained machinists. I have four apprentices, though, boys from the deaf school. They're good enough that they'll be journeymen as soon as they graduate."

David was frowning. "Slowing you down? Not slowing down planning the tanks, I hope."

"Your tanks are at the top of our list, David. Fear not. We have some of your spec drawings finished. Come see." He led them to the corner where drawings and papers were spread out over a long table.

Ingeborg studied a drawing of a completed tank. So this was what David was talking about. It was basically a huge iron box sitting on a chassis furnished not with wheels but with caterpillar treads. "The windows seem very small."

"Gunports with just enough space that you can see what you're shooting at," David explained. "It is self-propelled, and we have been talking about a steam engine to provide the power. Or maybe one of those internal combustion engines they're developing in Germany. They are already using them in horseless carriages here in the cities. The problem, of course, is storage space in the tank for the fuel, whether coal or oil." He looked to Daniel. "Have you figured how much material we'll need to build a prototype?"

"About a ton and a half of iron, two and a half tons of steel, a hundred square feet of lumber—I suggest starting with four-by-sixes and milling them to the sizes we need—and five yards of upholstery fabric. Seventy yards if we pad the munitions magazine, and I strongly suggest we do that." Daniel looked at Ingeborg. "We have some concern that when the tank moves over broken ground, the stored ammunition will get bumped about."

David turned to his guest. "Can you supply four tons of steel, Lionel?"

"Oh, absolutely."

Daniel nodded. "Getting iron and steel from Minnesota would be cheaper than bringing it over from Pennsylvania. We were looking at ten tanks a year to start with. That's eighty thousand pounds of material. Mr. Hibbing, can your ironworks found and ship forty tons of iron?"

"No problem. I'll repurpose a few ore cars for the shipping, if need be."

David smiled brightly. "This is a dream come true. Gentlemen . . . and lady"—he nodded to Ingeborg—"we stand on the brink of the future."

He looked so happy that it made Ingeborg feel happy.

Daniel seemed happy too. "You realize this means hiring at least five more workers. And two of those five should be trained machinists." He frowned. "Do you think we're expanding too big for our britches?"

Ingeborg didn't have to think about that very long. "It sounds like you are expanding according to God's will, as you have been all along."

"I hope so." Daniel turned to their guest. "Mr. Hibbing, you may be the answer to several supply problems we have. Northern Minnesota also has a pretty good supply of wood, does it not?"

"We do indeed. Paul Bunyan has not yet cut down all the trees."

They all laughed. Then they talked some more and debated various points about the tank. Well, David and Daniel debated, tossing ideas back and forth, sometimes agreeing, sometimes disagreeing. Lionel simply agreed with whatever they decided.

Finally it was time to eat, and the business meeting broke up.

As David, Lionel, and Ingeborg walked to her house, Lionel said, "I would like to borrow ink and paper again, Ingeborg. There's a letter I should write today."

"Certainly. If you get it in the mail today, it will leave town tomorrow at ten."

"Good. It is rather important. And I would borrow a stamp from you until I can get to the post office to buy some."

Ingeborg had grown up with her mother's voice in her ears: *Do not speak ill of strangers. You have no idea what they are going through.* So she would not speak ill of Lionel, who was still practically a stranger to her, particularly since he was David's friend and business associate. But she could not help but think that he was a moocher with far more bluster than bite.

Lionel wrote his letter that afternoon.

Howie,

Come out to a little jerkwater town called Blessing in North Dakota right away. I mean immediately. Tell them I own the largest ironworks in Hibbing and you're the superintendent. Tell them your brother owns Iron Mountain. The scam will be the same one we pulled in Decatur, but it's a thousand times bigger. These people are really ripe for the plucking. In fact, all I have to do is marry a sweet old half-witted widow named Ingeborg, and I'll have ownership of more land than you can imagine. And the town is growing fast. We can get rich just in the land sales. I'm working on her now, and she hasn't a clue. But there's more.

One of the fellows, Thomas Gould's father, seems a little sharper than the others, and he wants to build tanks—the war machines, not water tubs. He's so hot on it that I should be able to pull the wool over his eyes pretty easily. It doesn't matter whether the US gets into a war in Europe or not. We'll push for building these tanks and becoming the world's arms producer. Howie, this is going to be our biggest haul yet, and the people in Blessing are just begging to get scammed.

Chapter 16

Ingeborg heard Thorliff's buggy as she was coming down the stairs. She pulled her wool shawl off the hall rack and went out the front door.

Thorliff stood beside the front wheel. "My, Mor, you look so hoity-toity tonight." He was grinning as he gave her a hand up to the seat.

Ingeborg giggled, because she certainly felt hoity-toity in her blue watered-silk dress. "And you look just as hoity-toity in your black suit and ascot."

David's formal dinner. What an adventure this was going to be—or what a disaster. Ingeborg and Astrid had already talked about this evening. Again Astrid did not feel well, so she would not attend. And she had seemed very happy that she didn't have to. Ingeborg pretty much agreed. It was, though, an interesting adventure. And it was, she knew, bound to become even more interesting as the night wore on.

Thorliff clucked to his horse. "Normally I only wear this black suit at funerals. We will see if this dinner will be another one."

Ingeborg knew he wasn't talking about literal death.

This time of year felt so precious to her. The sun went down earlier than at midsummer, but it went down in a howling riot of color—gold, orange, red, and even streaks of pink that faded to lavender. The air was neither too warm nor too cool. She didn't really need her shawl right now, so she hung it over her arm.

She smiled at her son. "This formal high-society dinner is delightful in a way, certainly something we wouldn't do every day. I feel like we're playing dress-up."

"I certainly can't see you dressed like you are and running out to the garden to pick fresh corn for dinner."

"Or doing anything at all, except sitting around." *And yet so many of David's friends do just that*, she thought. They sat about until tea or until the next meal. Were she to marry him, would she find herself sitting around all day? What a horrible thought.

They pulled up to David's house, and there was Manny in a jacket and bow tie. Ingeborg had never seen him so dressed up. David must have loaned him the jacket; it didn't fit very well at all, loose in some places and tight in others.

Manny grinned. "I'm the hostler tonight.

210

May I take your rig?" He jogged around the front to Ingeborg's side and offered his hand, helping her to the ground. Thorliff had stepped down, so Manny gripped both lines behind the bit and led the horse off around the corner.

"A hostler." Thorliff watched his buggy disappear.

"And a butler." Ingeborg pointed to the front door, which had just swung open. There stood Fritz Stauffer! He wore a white shirt, a fancy suit coat, and a black bow tie. She paused at the door. "Am I right? Are you the butler?"

Fritz stuck his nose in the air. He said gravely, "Ja, I am, Frau Bjorklund." But then he broke into a grin. "When I was a lad in Germany, I worked in the kitchen of a wealthy man's home and saw what the butler does. So Mr. Gould is paying me to be the butler tonight."

Thorliff laughed. "Congratulations on the promotion, kitchen boy."

Fritz roared with laughter. "Promoted, ja! I am getting up in the world by falling off the barn roof, ja?" Then he led them inside to the parlor, walking slowly but without a limp. He was healing very well. He announced loudly, "Mrs. Ingeborg Bjorklund and her son Thorliff." He took Ingeborg's shawl and Thorliff's hat and left the room.

David came over to her immediately. "You are more lovely even than usual, Ingeborg. Good evening, Thorliff."

Thorliff dipped his head. "Good evening, David. Your soirée looks very fancy. The candle lanterns set all around are a lovely touch."

David leaned closer. "I must admit, we are indeed impressing Mr. Hibbing. He is highly complimentary."

"Good, good. I'm glad it's working for you."

Speaking of Lionel, he crossed the room to them, scooping Ingeborg's hands into his and kissing her knuckles. "The loveliest flower on the prairie. Good evening, celestial lady."

What should she say? She glanced at David, who was scowling at Lionel. "Thank you." It was all she could think of.

The butler announced Mr. and Mrs. Lars Knutson as Kaaren and Lars entered. Mr. Stauffer made a very good butler. Not that Ingeborg knew all that much about butlers. Kaaren still looked pale, but at least she was not coughing.

David greeted them and just as quickly led Lionel away, the easterner's elbow firmly in David's grip. Kaaren immediately came over to Ingeborg. She looked very pretty in her dark red jacketed afternoon dress. She had swept her hair up into an elegant chignon. It must have taken her half an hour.

Ingeborg wasn't certain what to say in such a fancy formal situation. Did you talk about ordinary things or important things? Did you avoid talking about other people? But then Kaaren started telling her about her pullets that had just begun laying, and her new chickens.

"I was looking through the Sears, Roebuck and Company catalogue, and I just ordered a dozen brand-new chickens by mail. They're called Buff Orpingtons. They're big and heavy, like Rhode Island Reds, and they're supposed to be very good mothers. From the catalogue illustration it appears they're a beautiful light tan or almost gold." She was so excited about her new chicks that Ingeborg forgot all about being formal. Best of all, Kaaren was almost herself again, her raspy voice nearly gone. And that pleased Ingeborg immensely.

John and Mary Martha Solberg arrived immediately thereafter, with Daniel Jeffers right behind them. Curious—when Jonathan and Grace arrived, you could tell immediately that Jonathan was born to this. He was nattily and perfectly dressed and moved so smoothly among the guests. There was just something about him that said *highborn*, like David.

The butler announced loudly, "Dinner is served." He stood beside the dining room door, holding it open.

The roomful of guests filed into the dining room, and Ingeborg was delighted to see a lovely floral arrangement as the centerpiece. She went quickly through the town's flower gardens in her mind. The yellow roses, of course, came from Amelia's rose garden, the red ones from the trellises beside the front hospital entrance. The pink double peonies, she knew, were from Sophie's foundation plantings at the boardinghouse. The iris-like flowers were blue flags from down by the river. So were the ferns artfully inserted among the flowers. And where did David find enough fancy stemware to set at each place?

"David, your table is stunning," she said.

"Thank you."

The butler was there to seat each guest. David held Ingeborg's chair for her, but Lionel slid into the chair to her right before David could get there, so he had to sit down at her left.

Mercy appeared in the kitchen doorway. "The appetizer is locally caught crayfish tails prepared in butter and served on rye crackers with cheese from our cheese house." She set a small plate in front of each guest. A dish for each guest for each course? At this rate, the

214

poor girls were going to be washing dishes half the night.

"So this is the crayfish that live in this area." Lionel nibbled his. Obviously he was not at all fond of crayfish. "Not quite the same as Louisiana crayfish. They're the best, you know. I've had them many times in New Orleans."

The soup was French onion served with a different kind of yeasty cracker. Ingeborg had been served French onion soup in a hotel restaurant many years ago, and this soup was every bit as tasty. Anna was cooking her heart out.

Lionel asked, "David, have you ever eaten at that little bistro on the Left Bank in Paris? Oh dear, I cannot recall the name."

Thorliff offered, "La Bonne Cuisine?" Ingeborg was surprised. Thorliff had never been to Paris.

"Why, yes. The very one!" Lionel bobbed his head. "They have wonderful croissants, and the tea is infused with raspberries. Quite nice."

"No, can't say as I have." David sipped his soup. "I avoid Paris. Too touristy. Everyone on the Grand Tour has to linger there. London generally offers everything I need, and they do not sneer at my attempts at French."

Ingeborg smiled.

Mercy cleared away the soup bowls, and Mr. Stauffer helped serve the entrée, carrying out two legs of lamb arranged on a large platter with lots of parsley sprigs. Mercy brought out dishes of mint jelly—oh, so that was why Anna had come by Ingeborg's mint bed this morning—roasted early potatoes, green beans in bacon drippings, and corn that tasted fresh-cut off the cob. What a magnificent feast! The yeast rolls were perfect. Anna was an excellent baker. Ingeborg even recognized the butter. It was the especially deep yellow butter that came from Gunter's Sweet Valley Farm, where the cows got a lot of rich alfalfa fodder.

David stood, and the butler handed him the carving knife and fork. David carved one leg, which seemed to be ceremonial, since the second leg was already sliced. He laid a pinkish slice on each dinner plate. The butler passed the first plate to Lionel, the chief guest, as David sliced another slab. Ingeborg was served next to last and David last. He sat down as the side dishes began to make their way around the table.

"Is the lamb from around here?" Lionel asked. "The legs seem a bit small."

David frowned. Obviously he had no idea.

So Ingeborg explained. "These are yearlings from last fall's crop of lambs. The spring crop is not ready to butcher yet. Not many local people keep sheep. Two crops of lambs and a crop of wool are very nice, but in the coldest part of winter, they have to be kept sheltered, and that means a lot of work and hay."

"My dear," Lionel cooed, "you know so much about this life. Imagine how you could enrich the steel industry if you applied your superb mind to iron manufacturing."

Ingeborg, a matron of the steel industry? Oh, honestly.

Lionel cut himself a large bite of lamb. Aha. According to David's lessons in snobbery, as Thorliff called them, no one started eating until the host had picked up his fork. Why did Lionel not know that? Or perhaps he knew it but ignored the courtesy. If so, it suggested that he considered these people to be rubes too simple to know the custom. Either way, it was an insult.

David picked up his fork, cut a bit of lamb, and stared at the ceiling, savoring a mouthful. "Marvelously tender and flavorful."

Ingeborg thought so too. Anna had prepared it perfectly—the innermost meat was slightly pink and so very moist.

The main course ended, and as they waited for dessert and coffee, Lionel started talking about his enterprises and the iron he manufactured. Talking? No, boasting. He boasted of everything, especially his travels. David sat silent, but Ingeborg knew that David traveled just as widely.

Lionel asked Ingeborg, "Have you ever been to New York? Huge city, especially for a simple country girl, I'd imagine."

"Yes." The simple country girl smiled sweetly. "I have."

David glanced at her and smirked. She smirked back and hoped it didn't show too much.

Anna came out bearing dessert, a huge, rich chocolate cake, beautifully iced. The swirls of dark chocolate frosting glistened. Mercy distributed coffee cups and poured for everyone, while the butler set out the cream and sugar.

Thorliff looked across the table at Lionel. "Every natural resource is finite, as we know, except perhaps the riches of the sea. I understand that the gold and silver of the West Coast are tapering off. Ghost towns now, where once there were thriving cities. Do you think the iron ore will ever run out in the Mesabi Range?"

"And Hibbing become a ghost town?" Lionel's tone of voice told Ingeborg he considered that a silly, stupid question. "Not in our lifetime. A mountain of ore and not half dug out. Plenty of iron for all." He paused with a mouthful of dessert. "This cake is nearly as rich and tasty as the chocolate I enjoyed in Vienna. Though I haven't been back there in several years." Next he boasted of his summer home in Vermont and a winter place in Florida, where he went each January when he wasn't traveling elsewhere. He made it clear that he thought people who stayed in one place all year long were a little slow in the brain. "My dear," he told Ingeborg, "you would love it in the South in winter. Balmy weather when people in Dakota are shoveling snow. Sarasota. Lovely little town. Palm trees. Sunshine nearly all the time."

And who would milk the cows, feed the chickens, gather eggs, and make certain the sheep were well cared for if everyone swooped off to the South? But she said nothing.

She glanced at Thorliff and realized from the stern look on his face that the moment was here.

"Mr. Hibbing," her son began, "you seem to be quite attracted to my mother."

"Absolutely! And why not? A beautiful woman, perspicacious. And wise."

"And wealthy," Thorliff added. "Don't forget wealthy."

"Well, uh, yes." Lionel suddenly looked guarded, suspicious. "That too. But of no consequence, no consequence."

David was staring at Thorliff. Then he shifted the stare to Lionel.

Thorliff continued, "Mor, you mentioned a couple days ago that when Mr. Hibbing thought you were a housemaid, he was rude and brusque with you. But when he found out that you own a lot of prime land, he suddenly became very sweet and chummy."

"I noticed that, yes," Ingeborg agreed.

Thorliff spoke as if Lionel were not present. "When a woman marries, all her wealth becomes her husband's."

"So I understand." She looked at Lionel with a steady gaze.

Lionel sputtered and opened his mouth to speak, but Thorliff interrupted. "Oh, by the way, there is no little bistro in Paris called La Bonne Cuisine. I made that up."

"Of course there is. I remember it. Are you trying to trick me?"

"I have been making some phone calls, Mr. Hibbing. There is no iron foundry in Hibbing. None. The ore is all shipped to Duluth for refining."

"Your information is based on old sources. That was in the past. My foundry, which is not too old yet—all the latest equipment, in fact—is there now. And it's out on the edge of town, you know. Not in it, exactly."

"I'm a newspaper editor and publisher, but

I also do reporting now and then. Investigative reporting. That is why I called the paper in your town. My source, the editor of Hibbing's newspaper, was talking about the present, right now. There is no foundry, and no one in Hibbing has ever heard of you. There is no one in the Hibbing family line named Lionel."

Lionel stuttered for a moment. "All right, I must confess I am something of a black sheep in the family. They've disowned me. However . . ."

"You claim that iron ore is plentiful, but most companies are turning to taconite, which is an inferior grade of ore, because the richest sources have all been used up. Oh, and incidentally, you mentioned Sarasota a few days ago when we were going through the machine shop. So I called the editor of Sarasota's daily newspaper. You are not on the rolls as a landowner, and no one there has ever heard of you either. The editor knows just about everyone of any consequence in Sarasota and that part of Florida."

"What are you saying, Thorliff?" David was scowling.

"I am saying that this man is a charlatan and a scalawag out to get our money and leave us with nothing but false promises," he said, raising his voice. "There is no iron and steel, David. He cannot help you build your tank."

"That is outrageous!" Lionel leapt to his feet. "I shall have you arrested for slander, Thorliff Bjorklund! And if a single word of this appears in your newspaper, for libel as well!"

Thorliff studied him with an almost-smile. "If you sue, you need only produce documentation that you indeed own a steel foundry and property in Hibbing or Florida or anywhere else, and you've made your case against me. In short, I am betting the farm that you cannot come up with any proof that you are not a cheat and a scoundrel."

Lionel's eyes went wide. He huffed mightily, slammed his napkin down on the table, and stormed out.

David looked grim and sad. "Thorliff, I am deeply indebted to you. I was going to give him ten thousand dollars seed money for iron and steel. He then was going to build onto his mill to accommodate the additional need. So it does not exist, you say. I would have lost a lot of money foolishly."

"I'm very sorry, David."

"I'm very sorry too." He stood up. "I'm also sorry this lovely meal ended on such a sour note. The food was splendid, all of it. Now I will go help Mr. Hibbing pack. He will be leaving tomorrow. Count on it."

"It did not end on a sour note. We all have

been saved from making terrible mistakes. That is certainly not sour, and our dinner was marvelous." Ingeborg stood up too. "And since I no longer have to be formal, I will go out to the kitchen and help the girls wash all these dishes."

Chapter 17

SEPTEMBER 1913

O h, I hate to see you go."
Louisa sniffed and hugged her sister. "I know. I never realized how hard a parting can be."

She looked across the room at Zeke and Mary playing in the corner with the various pieces of wood Ed had made for them. Zeke would build a stack, and Mary would knock them down and chortle with glee.

"Mary, you have to wait until I tell you to hit 'em." Zeke's tone sported a touch of impatience.

Louisa swallowed and returned to her packing. How could she possibly leave? She had to remind herself for the umpteenth time that she was *auntie*, not *mama*. But how she would love to be *mama*. Maybe someday she would find a good man and have another baby, one she could keep.

"You met the woman who owns the farm you will be living on?"

Louisa turned to her box of books and added one more. "Sort of. Her name is Ingeborg, and she is a widow and a grandma and seems to be the heart of Blessing. The walk is easy to the school, since the town of Blessing started at the southern edge of her farm. All of her family lives in Blessing; in fact, her older son is the head of the school board and owns and runs the local newspaper."

"I think you are rather impressed with the town and the people."

"I am. If only it were close enough for me to teach there and live here. I'd even buy a horse to get back and forth."

"Or one of those new automobiles."

"Don't be silly. That will never happen." Louisa rolled her eyes, shaking her head at the same time. "I'll take a horse any day. Besides, no one in the country or small towns will ever buy one of those noisy things."

Although Blessing had both telephones and electricity, at least in the town. Mrs. Bjorklund's house had those services too.

Tomorrow Louisa would get on the train in the morning and be there in little more than an hour. Far better than even a horse. Surely someone would be meeting her, but who? After all, she had her trunk of clothing and personal things and several boxes of books and teaching supplies she had kept from her former position.

A wail arose from the corner.

"What now?" Susan asked.

"She knocked the blocks over and one hit her. I didn't do nothing." Zeke glared at his little sister. Obviously even his long patience could get worn thin.

Louisa kept herself from responding. Susan waddled over and sat down on a chair to pick up Mary. She kissed the finger that the little one held up and murmured comforting things.

Louisa closed her eyes and tipped her head back so tears would not run down her cheeks. She failed. Digging in her apron pocket, she used a piece of a worn-out dish towel, soft enough to wipe tears from eyes that felt swollen. Probably red too, she thought as she stuffed the damp bit back in her pocket. That was something else she needed—handkerchiefs.

While folding the last of her skirts and waists into the trunk and checking to make sure it would close, she thought of the people she had met. Particularly Mr. Bjorklund. She'd brought an older copy of his newspaper home with her. She had truly enjoyed writing for the newspaper in Fargo. Perhaps if she offered, he might agree to let her do the same in Blessing. His pride in his paper was justly earned.

"Auntie Louisa, would you please read to us?"

She jerked her thoughts back to the present. "I will at bedtime." The last time for at least a couple of weeks. Would her returning home on the weekends cause problems? Mr. Bjorklund and Reverend Solberg had both reacted when she mentioned her plan. How could she bear to stay away longer?

Mary leaned against her knees and babbled something. Louisa cupped the little one's face in her hands. "I don't know what you said."

"She said, read to us now, please."

"Oh, really. Are you sure?"

Zeke nodded and shrugged. "She was pretty clear."

"Then I guess if both of you are so insistent, we will do just that. Come, let's find the rocking chair." She kept one book by the rocking chair and one by Zeke's bed. She picked Mary up, and together they went downstairs to the parlor, where the chair sat. She settled the little girl in her lap and made room for Zeke. "All right now?"

He nodded and Mary babbled, reaching for the book.

"This is a new book, and I think the illustrations are lovely. Beatrix Potter is the author. That means she wrote the book, *The Tale of Peter Rabbit.*" Mary opened the book for her and patted the pages. "'Once upon a time there were four little Rabbits and their names were—Flopsy, Mopsy, Cotton-tail, and Peter.'"

Mary pointed at the words and babbled something.

"She likes this book, 'specially that rabbit," Zeke translated.

Louisa kept on reading. Zeke turned the pages when she paused. His little sister clapped her hands. *Oh, Lord, how will I bear leaving?*

Later that evening after supper, she read to them upstairs, sitting on Zeke's bed. Mary drifted to sleep first, but when Zeke started to nod off too, Louisa closed the book and set it on the chest by the bed. Scooting off the bed, she picked up the baby and tucked her into her crib. After kissing the downy cheek and flipping a sheet over the little girl, she watched her sleep, Mary's thumb finding its

227

way into her mouth. *Oh, Lord, protect these little ones of yours. Bless this home and family as you know best.* She turned and knelt by the bed.

"'Night, Auntie Louisa. We will miss you." Zeke never even opened his eyes.

She kissed his cheek. "Good night."

The next morning, as soon as he finished milking, Donald harnessed the horses and drove her to the train station in Grafton. "Let me know when to pick you up. I hope you like your new job. I know how much you love teaching."

"Thank you." She had managed not to cry earlier while the others waved her good-bye, and she would not cry now either. "The way time flashes by, it will come soon." She knew she was speaking to herself even more so than him.

The train screeched to a stop, the conductor shouted, "All aboard," and she took his assisting hand. She had barely gotten seated when the first small jolt said they were moving. She waved out the window one more time, but Donald had already turned back to the wagon.

It won't be long. Lord, please help me get so involved I'm not homesick, or I will be crying all the time. She dug her journal out of her carpetbag and, using a pencil, started a list of what she needed to do first as she settled into her new life in Blessing.

When the train whistled the news that it was about to stop, the conductor paused beside her. "Your trunk and boxes will be unloaded right away, and I know Thorliff will be there to meet you. You did tell him you had baggage?"

She nodded. "Yes. Thank you." She tucked her journal into her bag.

The train screeched, steam rolled past the window, and the conductor swung down to set the step in place. As soon as the train fully stopped, she rose.

"I'll take that for you." The conductor again.

"Thank you for being so kind." She took his hand and stepped into her new life in Blessing.

"We brought your new teacher," he called to the man striding forward.

Mr. Bjorklund smiled radiantly. "Thank you, we're glad to welcome her. Good morning, Miss Gutenberg. You remember my mother?"

"I most certainly do. She was in a doctor's buggy, flying past us at a brisk trot."

"Welcome to Blessing." Ingeborg shook her hand. "We have been so looking forward to your arrival. Thorliff will load your things in the wagon, and we'll be off to your new home."

"There's even a bit of breeze." Louisa lifted her chin to feel it. "Thank you for coming to greet me."

"My privilege. We are all so excited to welcome you. The girls, Inga and Emmy, wanted to come too, but instead they are helping Freda make something special for dinner. They wouldn't tell even me what it is."

When the train left, the stationmaster helped Thorliff load her belongings in the back of the wagon, then stopped next to the two women and assisted them up onto the seat.

"Not the most comfortable transportation, but it saves a trip," Ingeborg said.

"Blessing is so lovely. Who planted all the roses and trees?"

"You'll meet Amelia Jeffers. She lives in the house right across from Thorliff. Her garden is spectacular." Ingeborg pointed down the street. "She starts her own roses and then finds homes for those she has no room for. As you can see, she starts plenty."

"In fact, she is out planting some around the front doors of the school as we speak," Thorliff said.

"All those around the hospital too?" Louisa asked.

Ingeborg nodded. "Oh yes. She took clippings from my yellow rose that came from Norway, so all the yellow roses are from that. It's so fitting, since so many of us immigrated from Norway. Nowadays we have immigrants from several different countries, so Amelia teaches English, both speaking and reading, to anyone who will make the effort to come to her classes."

"Something I would love to do as well. My family is from Germany, so I grew up speaking two languages." She looked ahead to see Thorliff's son hanging on the fence.

"Hi, Gramma, can I come too?" Rolly waved and giggled.

"Not now, Rolly, but maybe later," Thorliff answered.

"He could come," Ingeborg murmured, but when Thorliff shook his head, she raised her voice to address her grandson. "Maybe later."

"Rolly, come help me bake cookies," an older woman called from the porch.

Rolly jumped down and headed for the porch steps. He waved. "Later, Pa."

"The way I understand it," Louisa said, continuing their conversation, "teaching sign language is similar to teaching any foreign language."

"Except you use your hands and learn all

the symbols," Thorliff said. "We all learned sign language at home and in school. My cousin Grace was born deaf, and her mother, my tante Kaaren, learned first and taught Grace, who can both sign and speak. Grace is one determined woman, and now she has people from across the land and even foreign countries all coming here to learn from her."

Louisa shook her head. "What an amazing story."

"Someday I'll tell you about the other businesses in Blessing, all owned by women. My mother ships Bjorklund cheese all over the country."

Louisa smiled at the woman beside her.

Ingeborg's eyes twinkled. "I had to do something with the milk from our cows, and now we use milk from other farms too. Whoever dreamed things like this could happen?" She shrugged. "We'll probably have some of our cheese for dinner. I have a feeling the girls are baking crackers. They're delicious if you don't bake them too brown. Deborah figured out the recipe. You'll meet her at church tomorrow."

"And tomorrow after church, there will be our usual family dinner at the farm. Then whoever wants to play baseball will gather for probably the last game of the year. Since we are still working on the ball field at the school, the game will be out in one of our pastures, like it has been for the last several years." Thorliff pointed to a field ahead on their left.

"The cows haven't been pastured in that field for the last few days," Ingeborg assured Louisa.

Thorliff stopped the team at the front gate of the fenced yard. "Is Manny here?" he called to the two girls leaping off the porch and running to the wagon.

The girl who was introduced as Inga, Thorliff's daughter, joined them, her blond hair flying. "He's out at the cheese house."

"Run and get him please. We'll take the lighter boxes up to the porch."

Inga charged out of the yard.

Thorliff climbed down and came around to assist Louisa and Ingeborg to the ground.

"Thank you." Louisa turned toward the rear of the wagon.

"You and Mor go on in the house. We'll take care of this." The other girl was already lifting a box. "This is Emmy. She lives here with Mor."

"Good to meet you, Emmy."

"Welcome back to Blessing."

A young man who must be Manny came running up.

"We'll leave these on the porch until after dinner," Thorliff told him, then grabbed one

233

leather handle of the steamer trunk. Manny took the other, and together they started toward the steps.

Before taking the second trunk to the porch, Manny tied the near horse's lead line to the fence post. "I'll put the team away as soon as we're done. Freda said dinner is ready. We're going to eat on the back porch."

"Sounds good to me."

Louisa glanced at Ingeborg.

Ingeborg nodded and laughed. "Ja, it's pretty much always like this." She tucked her arm around Louisa's. "You get used to it."

So she's a mind reader on top of everything else, Louisa thought. They strolled up the walk, arm in arm. "Your yard is so lovely. I see Amelia's rosebushes. I assume you planted all these trees too."

"I was insistent we had to have shade trees for the house. They were just seedlings we found along the river. Cottonwoods are the fastest growing, and since I kept watering them, they grew even faster than usual. We started out with a sod house but built this one after a couple of years. The barn went up first, of course, but we've added on to it."

"So this was all . . ."

"All tall grass a man on a horse could get lost in." Ingeborg stopped on the front porch. "I always wanted a house with big porches. These go almost all around the house. Haakan, my husband who died a while back, enjoyed porches as much as I do."

"I'm so sorry to hear that." Why did people always say that when they had never even met the deceased?

Louisa's trunk and boxes were stacked by the front screen door, and she heard Manny talking to the horses as he drove them to the barn.

"Would you like to freshen up a bit before dinner?" Ingeborg asked.

"I would, thank you."

Ingeborg opened the screen door. "Right this way. Your bedroom is upstairs, but please believe me when I say this is your home for as long as you want. You needn't ask permission to use anything here."

Louisa stopped by a treadle sewing cabinet, feeling her eyes widen. "Even your sewing machine?" She couldn't believe she'd just said that.

"You like to sew?"

"I do, but I've not used a machine."

"Easy as pie. I'll teach you any time you want. I do a lot of sewing, and our church women make quilts to give away, but we never get a lot of extra sewing done in the summer."

Louisa trailed her fingers over the cabinet

235

as they went by. She'd be able to make dresses for Mary and shirts for Zeke.

"And here is our bathroom. Indoor plumbing has been such a blessing." She showed Louisa how to flush the toilet and use the faucets. "No matter how long you are on a train, that coal smoke makes everything dirty."

"No outhouse?"

"No outhouse."

Louisa heard the others laughing and talking while she used the toilet and watched the water flush down, all the while shaking her head. She washed her hands under the running water and dried them on a towel hanging on the wall. No hurrying to the outhouse when it was raining or snowing. Someday they would put this in her sister's house. Probably her father had such luxury in his house by now.

She stared in the mirror and tucked a tendril of hair back in the chignon at the base of her head. So much to get used to. To think they had plumbing like this at the schoolhouse too. And she would not have to go to school early to start the stove to warm up the room. This job was looking better all the time.

Chapter 18

"L etter for you, Grandma."

"Thank you. Will I like it?"

"Oh, you most certainly will." Inga handed it to her. "It's from Minnesota."

Ingeborg clasped the letter to her chest. "How wonderful." She slid a knife blade under the back flap and drew out a sheet of paper, filled on both sides with close lines of writing. "Where's Emmy?"

"Out in the cheese house, helping Freda." Inga leaned on the back of Ingeborg's chair. "Can I read it when you're done?"

"Of course." Ingeborg reached up and patted Inga's cheek. "Takk for bringing the mail." She flipped the letter back to the beginning.

Dear Ingeborg,

I am still thanking God that we can communicate with each other again. So many years went by, and it makes me enjoy each letter from you more and more. Yes, we are very busy, just as you are. Farming is both the same and so different from home. Oh, sorry, I promised myself that I must call here home, no longer Norway. Although I miss my family I left behind. Rune writes to the others, saying he will pay for their tickets, but they do not want to leave Norway, just like their father. I do not give up hope, though, praying that God will change their minds.

School is about to start, and Knute complains that he wants to work on the farm and in the woods with the big trees, but Signe has insisted that he finish school. We do not have many acres left of the big trees. Rune has begun planting a grove of maple trees so we can harvest sap for syrup in the spring. Leif has a way with animals here on the farm, but he has his nose in a book whenever possible. Nilda has promised he will be able to attend any college he desires, but that is still many years away.

Little Kirstin is playing with the kittens right here under the table while I write. She is only four, but Leif has already taught her the alphabet and numbers, and he is now teaching her to read. She thinks the sun rises and sets on Leif.

I am weaving rugs as always, some of them from our own wool.

You are probably getting tired of all

my news. I so look forward to hearing more about your life in Blessing.

With love and joy,
Your cousin Gunlaug

"How I would like to see those big trees. So different from our prairies," Inga said, handing the letter back when she was done. "Emmy says there are big trees in the mountains near where she grew up."

Ingeborg nodded slowly, thinking hard. "We had trees in the mountains of Norway. But I believe those in Minnesota are far larger."

"Mr. Gould keeps saying he will pay for your ticket to go there."

Ingeborg nodded again. "I know. Maybe someday."

Inga heaved a sigh. "Well, that's better than the *no* you've been saying. I think I'll tell him there is hope. When is he coming back this time?"

"I wish I knew, but he said it might be a while. He is traveling for the machinery company now." She caught back a sigh. "I'm beginning to think he just likes to travel. He does it so much." He'd already been gone more than two weeks and still wasn't sure when he would return. Would a life with him be this constant waiting? Probably.

In a big way, Ingeborg wished he had never proposed to her. Since then, there had been a tension between them—very faint, but there. Their conversations about marriage often grew intense, as much as Ingeborg hated that. David didn't mind heated arguments. He said that was many times the way business got done. Ingeborg abhorred arguments.

Lionel Hibbing, or whoever he really was, had been right about her land. It was very valuable as lots to be developed as this town grew, not as cow pastures. Perhaps she was being too careful about preserving it in the family. Perhaps—a ghastly thought—it really ought to be developed. Development would benefit many. But to simply hand it over to David's lazy children? No. She would not permit that, as much as it would be in her power to prevent it.

I'm so sorry, David. You have told me you want to be with me forever, but I'm afraid to make your desires come true. I'm so very sorry.

Inga knelt beside her. "Are you all right, Grandma?" Her Bjorklund-blue eyes stared up at Ingeborg as if trying to see inside her grandma.

Ingeborg sniffed and cupped Inga's face in her hands, nodding all the while. "Ja, my dearest one, I am always all right because

God keeps me that way. His word is always my comfort and my peace. He says to lean upon Him, and I take Him at His word. When concerns come into your mind, you just step back and wave them on to our heavenly Father. Doing so takes a lot of practice, so He gives us chances to do just that—practice."

Inga laid her cheek against her grandma's hand. "I think practice hurts sometimes."

"You are right. And so we can pray for one another and share all the love and wisdom He gives us."

"So you pray for Mr. Gould all the time?"

Ingeborg stroked Inga's white-blond hair. "Oh yes, and I thank God for each one of us. Just think of all He gives us. Why, even this rocking chair that Haakan made for me those many years ago. Think of all the times you have sat in my lap and we've rocked, and all the others this chair has held."

"Rolly liked to rock in this chair too."

Ingeborg smiled. "I think he still does."

"And we pray for Miss Gutenberg?"

"Of course. She doesn't know it yet, but she is now part of our family too."

"She's going to be our teacher this year."

"Indeed she is."

"I think something is bothering her."

Ingeborg puffed out a breath, nodding as she thought. Inga had been given an instinct about people beyond what most had. Especially anyone her age. *Lord, protect her and teach her how to use this gift she has been given. Actually, she and Emmy both.*

Ingeborg leaned over and dropped a kiss on Inga's hair. Hearing footsteps on the porch, she straightened and sniffed. "I think the pie is ready to come out."

Freda came in, letting the screen door slam. "The pies."

"We were just going to check on them."

Freda opened the oven door. "Perfect. Manny will be dancing for joy."

"Let's invite Tante Kaaren and Lars for supper," Inga said. "Strawberry rhubarb is his favorite kind of pie."

"Good idea. Go ahead and call her."

"The new cheese is all set, so we waxed the wheels, and now they can age." Emmy had followed Freda inside and was washing her hands at the sink. "But we brought some in for supper. I have a hankering for cheese soup."

"Sounds delicious," Inga said. "We could bake crackers too."

"Cheese soup, crackers, salad from the garden, and strawberry rhubarb pie." Freda set the first pie on the rack on the table to cool, and then the second. "After we have some strawberry lemonade and bread and jam out on the porch, I'll go pick the lettuce."

"Sounds wonderful." Ingeborg inhaled. "This kitchen smells heavenly. Inga, call Kaaren."

Ah, how I wish I could call David and make sure he was coming for supper. At that moment, the pang of missing him stabbed her in the middle. Would it be any different if they were married, or only worse? If only she had agreed to go with him—not that he had invited her this time. He said it was because he was going to be gone longer than usual, but was that really the case? *Lord, please bring me peace of mind here. I give you my fears and worries, but I have to confess, sometimes that is very difficult. Not the giving them up, but the leaving them with you and waiting. I know you've been working on that for years with me. Patience.*

Rocking the chair gently with easy pushes of her foot helped her clear her mind and focus.

"Grandma, are you all right?" Emmy asked.

"Oh yes. Thank you for asking."

"We're set up out on the porch," Inga called.

Ingeborg smiled. Where had her mind gone? She stood and stretched. "Kaaren and Lars are coming for supper? Good." After she settled in her chair, she shook her head. "What were we doing in the house when it is so much more pleasant out here?" She shrugged as Emmy handed her a glass. "I know, we can't make raspberry jam without a hot stove."

"Four batches of jam, and that is pretty much the end of the raspberries. How many quarts of sauce?" Emmy turned to Freda.

Freda shrugged. "Lots. I didn't count when we took them down. But I know we have forty quarts of string beans. Another couple of canners, and we can pick for bean britches and then let the remainder dry on the vine. I thought we planted too many rows of beans, but perhaps they didn't bear as well as other years. Aren't you keeping a journal of what we've done to help us for next year?" Freda asked Ingeborg.

"So far," Ingeborg replied. "We planted more corn this year." She rolled her eyes. "Wait until we tell Manny he's going to have to work up more ground for the garden and move out the fences." She smiled. "I never could have dreamed we'd have a garden this size and need more."

"Grandma, you feed half of North Dakota." It was Inga's turn to roll her eyes.

Here comes Miss Gutenberg. "If we'd known you were coming back early today, we'd have waited for you."

Louisa paused at the bottom step. "It is

244

so much cooler here. You all look so comfortable."

Inga went inside and returned with another glass. She poured the icy drink into it and pointed to her chair. "Please sit there where the breeze can cool you."

A smile tugged at the corners of Louisa's mouth as she sank into the chair. Pulling the pin out of her straw hat, she took it off and, reinserting the pin, laid the wide-brimmed hat on the floor. Blowing out a sigh, she accepted the glass. "Thank you, Inga. I hope I'm not disturbing anything."

"Not at all," Ingeborg reassured her. "Welcome home."

This time Louisa's smile made it to her face. She held the sweating glass to her cheek before taking another sip. "This is so delicious. What do you call it? Do you have a recipe?"

Inga and Emmy stared at each other, then shook their heads as if one.

"We mix lemon juice with whatever berries we have. Right now these are raspberries. We add sugar, water, shake it all up, and pour it over ice." Emmy shrugged. "It's different all the time."

"Sometimes we add vinegar to make swizzles," Inga added.

"And extra sugar." Emmy raised the pitcher. "More?"

Louisa held out her glass. "Thank you."

Freda stood and went into the house, returning with cookies on a plate. She held it out to Louisa. "Here, you need more refreshment." Then she set the plate on the low table. "I'm going back out to the cheese house for a while. Manny finished some more crates so we can get another shipment out." She left.

Ingeborg smiled at the young woman across the table from her. "So, are you pleased with your classroom? Did you have enough bookshelves?"

Louisa studied her glass and nodded. "Tomorrow we have staff meetings, so I might be back here early again."

"Yes, some of us are bringing dinner over to the school. Kind of a tradition we started a couple of years ago." Ingeborg sipped her drink.

"Really?"

Ingeborg smiled at the surprise crammed into that one word. "The people of Blessing are very proud of their schools. We have quite a few immigrants here—well, really all of us are, but I was thinking of more recent ones. They will do anything to make sure their children have an education." In her mind she finished that statement with, *Like they were never able to have.* "School starts on Tuesday, correct?"

Louisa nodded.

"We'll be having dinner here after church. You will be here, right?"

Louisa nodded again, but Ingeborg could see shadows drifting across her face like clouds, some turning a bit gray.

"I'm glad to hear that. People here are looking forward to getting to know the new teachers. We have one at the secondary school too, so you are not the only one."

Louisa nodded and pushed herself to her feet. "I think I will go to my room and put on something lighter. Do you have anything I can help with? If not, I will work on my teaching schedule."

Inga and Emmy looked at each other. "It's done, or will be, but thank you for offering."

Louisa watched them go through the gate, her head wagging slightly, then went inside.

Ingeborg breathed deep and exhaled slowly, smiling inside as well as out. *Lord, please keep me from ever taking my family for granted. I know how blessed I am, most of the time.* She paused again and looked around her. Blessings innumerable.

Now if only David will call tonight.

He didn't.

Chapter 19

I just want to go home."

David stared at his face in the mirror, half-hidden by shaving soap. Here he was shaving when he could have told his man to come and shave him. Having a man along was a help but no longer necessary. He didn't have a man at home in Blessing. Didn't need one. He sharpened the shaving blade on the strop and went ahead, flinching once when he nicked himself. *I have too much on my mind to be shaving myself.* He washed off the remaining bits of white foam and applied pressure to the bead of red.

"You have to pay attention—to everything," he said aloud to his now-cleanly-shaven face.

If only Ingeborg were with him. They could go see some of the sights and—and what would she do while he was in these interminable meetings? Granted, they were for a good cause. He was finding suppliers for building the tanks. Never again would he be hoodwinked and made a fool. Now he had to set Thomas straight. Face to face. He was afraid Thomas was continuing his friendship, if you could call it that, with Lionel. When David laid all the evidence in front of his son, whom would Thomas believe?

He patted aftershave on his skin and put away his toiletries. All the things his man would do. Including help him dress.

A knock at the door. "Breakfast, Mr. Gould."

"Come in." He could hear the cart, and the valet setting the table while he finished dressing. The table stood in front of the window drapes that were now pulled back.

"Coffee, sir?"

"Yes." He sat in the chair the valet pulled out, sipped the coffee, and nodded a dismissal. "Thank you."

"How else can we serve you?" the man asked.

"You can arrange my transportation." David glanced down at the list he had compiled and read off the address. "In fifteen minutes—no, make that half an hour."

"Yes, sir."

David checked the time. "That will be all." He ate his meal, all the time reading through reports and making notes. Down in the cab, he set his briefcase on his knees and watched the city go by. His mind flew back to Blessing. He'd not telephoned Ingeborg for the last two nights. The excuse was meetings lasting too late, but the truth was that he didn't know what to say. That small voice inside his head lambasted him. *You were a fool and you need to apologize. You were the one to introduce the snake in the grass, and she recognized him for what he was sooner than you did.* The whole thing left a horrible taste in his mouth.

Just get through this day, he commanded himself. *Pay attention. You will set things right with her tonight, at least as much as you are able over the telephone.* Somehow that plan did not fill him with peace.

Today was his last stop, a visit to a chainworks. The foundry made nothing but chain, they said, chain that would not break. He had seen samples. Now he was showing up unannounced on their doorstep. The company president himself, shocked that a customer would appear in person, showed him through their facility. David asked him the question he asked all of his suppliers: *Do you, sir, believe European war is imminent?* The gentleman grimaced and nodded. The tour made David's final decision. Yes, the Jeffers Machinery Company would buy five hundred feet of oval-link forged steel chain in this exact size, with more orders to come. They shook hands.

The fellow cleared his throat. "If I may ask a question, sir. You could have easily completed this transaction by mail. Why did you come here to do so in person?"

David smiled, but it was a sad smile. "If not for the research of a very dear friend, I would have been hoodwinked out of ten thousand dollars by a charlatan who could not deliver what he promised. I am making certain you have the facility to make good on your promises. And now, kind sir, would you like to join me for a late supper tonight at my hotel?"

The company president nodded. "Good. Thank you."

When David finally called Ingeborg after the dinner meeting, he was grateful for the time difference. Even so, she was most likely getting ready for bed.

"This is Ingeborg." The sound of her voice rolled over him like waves on a seashore.

"I know this is late, but . . . please forgive me."

"For what?" Gentle but with a touch of—of what?

He paused, searching for the right words. "For introducing a snake in Blessing."

"An apt description." Her voice seemed to smile. "Your apology is accepted, of course. You were misled by a very capable confidence man."

He sighed thankfully. That bit of business

was over with. "I wish you were here, but more than that, I wish I were there."

"How is your trip faring?"

"Well. You can be assured, I am being far more careful regarding the people I am willing to work with." The static made him hold the earpiece away from his ear. "I can't hear you."

"Take care of yourself." Her voice now came through loud and clear.

"I am. I have so much to tell you, it will take a week." Or more.

More static. Surely there were ways to improve the reception. He heard her say goodbye, and the line went dead.

He set the earpiece back on the prongs. A desk telephone was far easier to use than a wall phone, but still the static and the cutoffs happened far too often. Should he call her back in the hopes they could talk without all the static, or give up for tonight? He leaned back in the leather chair and closed his eyes, the better to see her on the backs of his eyelids. Telephones were being improved; if only humans could be. He hadn't told her when he would be home. Tomorrow night . . . he would do that tomorrow night.

When he finally caught the train east to New York, it was all he could do not to get on a westbound train instead. He sat in his com-

252

partment, staring out the window without seeing anything. If only this discussion with Thomas would go as well as most of those he'd had the last few days. *Lord, please give me wisdom on how to handle my son. It's like we're yelling across a lake to each other, catching only bits and pieces.*

Back in New York, he let the cab go and stood before his house. He wanted Ingeborg to come here and enjoy some of the pleasures of New York, and get to know his other children and them her. That was one of those miracles he prayed for—unity in his family. And bringing her here might just be the answer to that. How could they not love her once they knew her?

The maid—not the giggly, efficient little Emmy—opened the door when he was partway up the walk. "Mr. Gould, I didn't know when you would be arriving."

"Sorry, I should have informed you." He kept a smile to himself. As if he were required to do so. "Whatever Cook fixes for supper will be just fine." He knew this would send the cook into a flurry.

The butler pushed past the maid to take his bags. "Welcome home, sir. Would you like us to prepare a bath?"

David followed them inside. Flowers on the credenza, someone to take his hat and his baggage. All the comforts of home. Hardly. "No to the bath for now. I'll be in my office for a while. Could you bring in a tray with tea and a little something?"

"Yes, sir. Right away."

David strode to his office across the hall from the library. When he closed the door, the silence hurt his ears. There was never silence like this at Ingeborg's. If not people talking, there would be cattle lowing, or birds singing, or a rooster making himself out to be a big shot. He crossed to the French doors overlooking the fountain, which was in the center of a broad green circular space with mosaic paths that branched out in four directions. Water splashed from the fountain, so he opened the doors to hear the music. A round wrought-iron table and chairs awaited him on the slate-tiled veranda that stepped down to the lawn. What would Ingeborg think of all this?

"Come," he said, answering the maid's knock at the office door. He turned. "Set it on the desk please."

She did so and poured a cup for him. "Would you like milk and sugar?"

"Not this time, thank you." He sat down in his leather chair and glanced at the tray. Small triangle sandwiches, cookies. Did he really want them? Everything made him wish for Ingeborg to be there.

"Will there be anything else, sir?" the maid asked.

"No, thanks. Oh yes, please tell Cook I would like supper at seven. Something simple, served in the morning room, not the dining room."

"Yes, sir."

He picked up his teacup and saucer and spun his chair to look out over the fountain to the grove of elm trees that screened the estate behind them. What would Emmy and Inga think of this? They could set up a croquet game or play badminton. His children used to do that in what he now thought of as another lifetime.

He picked a sandwich from the plate and took a bite. Definitely not Ingeborg's bread, although Cook made good bread or had it delivered from a bakery. He wasn't really sure which. Not that it mattered.

The telephone on his desk interrupted his musings. "Hello."

"Father, I didn't realize you were coming in today."

"Don't worry, Thomas, I will see you at the office in the morning. The board will meet then, and we will have dinner here in the evening. I'd appreciate it if you let your siblings know, if they're in town. The usual time."

"I see. I will."

David set the receiver back in the hook of the telephone. Talk about not wasting any words. Although he could hear the surprise in Thomas's voice. David Gould did not usually change plans like this.

Morning did not come soon enough. He arrived at the offices of Gould Enterprises before anyone else. Two hours until the board meeting. He gathered his papers together, making sure he had everything. When he entered the board room half an hour early, he surprised the man setting up the coffee table.

"I'm sorry, sir, I—"

"Just go ahead with what you are doing."

David went to the blackboard and wrote in large letters. *Every day is a new beginning.* Dusting off his hands, he crossed the room to stand in front of the windows. The streets of New York City teemed with conveyances hauling supplies, pedestrians hurrying to somewhere, a policeman on a horse, another on foot directing traffic, carts of ready-to-eat foods. Patrons of the food carts were grabbing breakfasts they had no time to eat at home. The noise made it through the window. He shuddered. So much he had taken for granted.

Lord, please get me out of here quickly. He watched the other board members filing in, taking their places at the table and nodding to the young man serving them. David watched their faces when they noticed the saying on the blackboard. Most expressed consternation as they greeted him and welcomed him back.

Thomas, followed by several of his staff, was the last to arrive. "Good morning, Father." He set his briefcase to David's right as usual. No mention or pardon that he was late to the meeting.

David banged his gavel. "We have a lot to do today, so let's get started on time."

He studied the board members while the minutes were being read. They expressed utter boredom. Not one person seemed to be paying attention. His secretary, Arnold Meyer, finished reading and looked to David.

"Additions or corrections?" David glanced at the men around the table. Most shook their heads without even looking up. He could feel the heat of anger rising within him. "Approved?"

Hands went up lackadaisically.

"Before we proceed further, I am calling a second meeting here in the morning so that we can finish all our business. I expect all board members to attend."

A few of them were now looking at him.

"I know some of you believe that even if

257

there is a war, the United States will not be a part of it. But even though the coming war will not be fought on our land, we will need to support the side that believes in freedom, or one day the fighting may be in our streets, with our children dying and our homes and businesses destroyed."

Two heads nodded, the others appeared to be deaf to his entreaties.

"Any discussion?"

One man leaned forward. "I have a question."

David nodded. One out of eleven. "Proceed."

"I assume you are leading toward that machine you want to build, the tank?"

"Yes, but that is only a part of what we need to do. I've been talking with the steel companies in Pittsburgh, companies that build the parts we would need. 'Find a need and fill it' is a wise saying. We need to become both creator and supplier. We—" He looked over and caught Thomas yawning. David clamped his teeth together before he made a serious mistake. If he were going to reprimand his son, he would not do so in front of this group. However, the thought of turning this company over to Thomas made him shudder. He'd sent Thomas to college to learn about economics and business principles, and then set him to work in various departments to have a clear understanding of the company he would one day be head of. And yet Thomas seemed to care only about what the company could give him, not what the company itself did.

Perhaps it was time to search for someone else to train, just in case. How long could David run the company long-distance like this? Probably indefinitely, but did he want to? The thought of moving headquarters to Blessing floated through his mind, but he couldn't picture that either.

David turned to the others. "I believe we can be an example for other companies. A prototype, if you will." He waited to see if there were any other questions. Then, heaving a sigh, he shuffled another page to the top of his agenda. "Department reports. Please have your P&L statements ready to hand around. We'll do two now before lunch and two when we return. Any questions? All right, who would like to be first?"

By the time the first two department heads were finished, the chef's assistant opened the doors and announced, "Lunch is being served in the dining room."

Thomas did not need a second invitation; he was first out the door. David and Arnold brought up the rear.

"How much longer will you stay in the city?" Arnold asked.

"I'm hoping to catch a train tomorrow evening." *I'd rather make that tonight, but since I arranged for the family dinner tonight, I better be there.* He turned to the man who walked beside him. "Arnold, have you ever thought of living out west?"

"How far west are you thinking?"

"North Dakota. Blessing, to be exact. I don't mean to be nosy, but is there any young woman with whom you are thinking of spending your life?"

Arnold shook his head. "No, I am free to go where I will."

"So when you graduated from college, what did you see yourself doing?"

"Exactly what I am doing."

"And would more travel be a good addition?"

"Yes, sir."

"You speak what other languages?"

"German, French, some Spanish, and I can get by in Italian."

"I see." They reached the small dining room and entered. "We'll pick up this discussion later."

"Thank you, sir."

That night David joined his children, who were enjoying canapés, drinks, and gossip.

David could tell immediately that Thomas was not particularly eager to be there, but Thomas wisely refrained from bringing it up to his father.

Since women were present, the conversation around the table was not all about business, nor politics, and when those topics sneaked into the discussion, Thomas's wife deftly changed the subject so that the women could be included too.

After dessert, the women excused themselves, and the men gathered in the parlor. Over drinks and cigars, they picked up the discussion about the possibility of war.

"Why are you so insistent that if the war does break out in Europe, the United States will be involved?"

"Thomas, how can you not see what is happening right before us?" David replied.

"Father, it is more than three thousand miles across the Atlantic Ocean. It takes weeks for cargo ships to cross. Who in their right mind would spend all that time and money to attack us? We are safe here."

"We also are the source of minerals and natural resources, along with millions of young men to recruit. We have a big resource in all our businesses. No other country has all these resources."

Thomas shrugged. "All the same, I say

Wilson is right and we mind our own business. There are enough opportunities to make us wealthy without diving into international waters."

"If you had given any thought to the news, you'd see that we cannot take a chance on the possibility of remaining neutral, like President Wilson advocates. If you question the things I've been saying, go back and look at history to see who profited from any war. The needs of any kind of war will force every industry to produce more and faster. That is us. Those German U-boats have already been discovered in American waters. How many submarines does our country have to keep our seacoasts safe?"

Thomas huffed and went to refill his drink. David watched him sadly, wondering if he and his eldest son would ever find common ground again.

David was getting mighty tired of board meetings. He thought briefly of that garden plot the girls called his weed patch, and they were right. There was not a weed to be seen in Ingeborg's garden. How he yearned to make his own garden look like that, to invite people for a meal and serve them vegetables from his own labor. With a sigh, he entered the boardroom and called the meeting to order. Sitting down in his padded leather chair, he thought that perhaps he would bring this chair with him to his office in Blessing.

Arnold was already seated, his piles of papers neatly stacked in front of him and his notepad open. He cleared his throat and read the minutes from yesterday's meeting. He had summarized some of the discussion very nicely.

David looked around. "Additions or corrections?" Silence. "Approved?" Bored silence. "Passed. Old business?" No one offered any.

"Very well. Since none of you seem to have done anything worthy of reporting, we will move on to new business. I have decided to retire earlier than I first intended. The company is on solid footing, and I will remain a major stockholder. Before I leave, I want to—"

His receptionist stuck his head in the door. "Mr. Gould? An urgent phone call."

"Thank you, Roger. Excuse me momentarily. I shall return as quickly as possible." He left the room.

Out in the hallway, the receptionist, Roger Dawes, sat at a small table with a mahogany-encased machine containing a round fabric-covered speaker. He smirked at David and threw a switch. "Let's see if this newfangled listening device works."

Instantly they could hear what was going on in the boardroom. The sound was scratchy, but they could make out most of the words.

David whispered, "But they cannot hear us, right?"

"Right." Roger did not bother whispering. "No speaker in there. I hid the microphone in your chair."

One of the board members spoke. "I knew he'd retire soon, but I wasn't expecting it quite yet. Not with his landship idea just getting started."

Thomas's voice was clear. "The first thing I'm going to do as chairman is dump that idiotic project. We're not going to spend a lot of money tooling up for a foolish idea like that one. Tanks. Honestly."

Another voice, too far from the hidden receiver to be clear.

A closer voice: "I agree. The social duties he talks about corporations having are all right for small companies, but we are expected to turn a profit, not make some common laborer's day happy."

Another: "You're both wrong! What he's doing is excellent, and we should pursue it. You do want to go to heaven, don't you?"

"Baxter, Martin Luther proved you don't

have to do good works to get to heaven. When I retire, I want a nice fat bank account to curl up and rest on."

Other voices chimed in, shouting and arguing.

David wagged his head, especially since Thomas's voice was one of the loudest. "Less than five minutes, and they're at each other's throats already. This whole board needs to be replaced. Mr. Dawes, you have been urging us to adopt the latest technology. How about you head up our new technology department?"

"I would love to, sir. Our company is lagging behind in that, and we need the latest innovations. This very device is a form of wireless technology that we need to explore. It's not all ships at sea."

The noisy arguing was still rattling the windows in the boardroom.

David felt sad in a way, happy in another. "Take your listening device back to your office. It has served us well. Thank you."

"Gladly, sir."

David went back into the room. It instantly got quiet. He looked around at his board. "How many of you have read the company's bylaws lately? Our code of regulations and procedures?" No one moved. "How many of you have read them at all?"

Baxter shrugged. "When I came on. It's been a while."

"I will refresh your memory. The code specifies that the chairman and only the chairman has the power to name board members and remove them. I suggest you read the code carefully, especially section three, particularly parts D and E."

Thomas frowned. "You aren't thinking of replacing any members of this board, are you?"

"I am indeed, including me. Mr. Meyer here will succeed me as chairman."

Arnold's mouth dropped open, but Thomas bolted to his feet. "Wait! You promised me! I'm the eldest!"

David kept his voice quiet and even. "I promised you nothing, Thomas. Arnold Meyer has attended every meeting, even long before he was my secretary. Your attendance record is something like three or four meetings in ten. You love the money and the prestige, but you seem unable to take on any of the responsibilities. Mr. Meyer cares about the company, and he is wise. He will direct it wisely."

"That illiterate mob in Blessing has turned you against me, haven't they?" Thomas glanced at the others. "Yesterday evening you tried to tell me that Lionel Hibbing is a thief and a liar. That's slander! He's a fine man and a well-traveled financier. For some reason you don't like Mr. Hibbing, so you're trying to turn me against my friend. This is coercion, right? If I end my friendship with a man I like, you'll reconsider and let me be chairman. That's what you're planning, isn't it?"

"I will not argue with you here before this board. You're off the board. I'm putting you on the Manhattan gas line project. Let's see how you do as a project manager."

Thomas was his son, and the look of rage on his face surprised even David. What had David just done?

Thomas roared, "This company is going to ruin with your cockamamie ideas, and I'm glad to be rid of it!" He stormed out, slamming the door behind him.

"Do you think he'll do something extreme?" Baxter asked.

David sighed. "Quite probably."

"What are you going to do?"

"Continue this meeting. Harlan, your report on the railroad acquisition."

Thomas's fury burned hot for only a little while. Doubt and uncertainty put the fire out. Where would he go? What could he do? Why had his father betrayed him like that? How had that Blessing mob managed to turn him against his own son? And against Lionel? Poor Lionel, smeared with those ridiculous accusations.

Thomas left the building and stood in the busy street. Men in a hurry brushed past him. Horses and buggies and horseless carriages wove in and around one another. Walking in New York was just plain dangerous.

The bank. He would go to the bank and find out how much he had available. Since his father had deeded his house over to him and quit paying for the maintenance, Thomas was no longer certain how much money he had.

His regular teller was working down in the end cage today. The young man smiled brightly as Thomas stepped up to the window. "Good day, Mr. Gould."

"Here is my passbook. How much has been added and subtracted?"

The teller took the passbook, checked it against the ledger, and totaled it. He handed Thomas the paper of calculations.

One of Thomas's stock holdings had just yielded him a nice amount. This was good news to counter the bad news of the fight with his father. "I am withdrawing it all. Give it to me in fifty- and hundred-dollar banknotes."

The teller looked startled, then puzzled.

"Yes, sir." He had to go to the vault because he didn't have enough cash at his station. He brought out the money, and the manager, Mr. Mooney, came out with him.

"Good day, Mr. Gould." Mr. Mooney looked perplexed. "Is there a problem?"

"No, not at all." Thomas realized what he would do next. "I am taking a trip, is all." He was immensely satisfied with this sudden decision. "Yes, I will be traveling."

Chapter 20

He's coming home today. He's coming home today.

Her excitement set the words to music, rippling from the top of her head to the tips of her toes. Ingeborg lay in bed one more moment to revel in the joyous feelings. "Lord, thank you for keeping him safe. Thank you for trains that go so fast." She knew David wasn't to Grand Forks yet, but . . .

The clanging of the stove lids said that Manny was up and started on his chores. She'd hear Freda greet him any moment.

How blessed she was to be able to lie here these few more minutes and let others do the early morning chores.

Finally she threw the covers back, including the quilt she had recently added as the nights began hovering close to freezing. Setting about dressing and brushing her hair, she pondered what to wear to the station to welcome David home. Was he as excited to see her as she was him? "Uff da!" she muttered, standing in front of the chifforobe that held her better clothes. Surely there was something in between church and her work-at-home clothes. She settled on an ankle-length skirt, a white waist with leg-of-mutton sleeves and lace cuffs, and a red vest she had knit during one of the long winters, then donned an apron to protect the outfit from stains.

Entering the kitchen, she found Freda feeding the maw of the polished black cookstove, a never-ending job, and asked, "What have you decided we will have for breakfast?"

"Sourdough pancakes with chokecherry syrup, sliced ham, and scrambled eggs. I set the starter last night." Freda paused, eyes twinkling. "My, but don't you look nice. Couldn't be that you'll be seeing a certain gentleman today, could it?"

"Whatever gave you that idea?" Ingeborg went to the icebox in the pantry to fetch butter and buttermilk, supplies they used to keep in the water trough out in the well house. The hams and other smoked meats still hung in the perpetual coolness of the well house. "You know, the spikachit hanging in the haymow must be ready to eat."

Spikachit was always such a treat and one good reason to keep sheep. After butchering, they soaked the mutton haunches in a salt solution, then hung them on pulleys at the highest peak in the haymow. This year they had hung four so each family could have one. Drying mutton like this was another way to preserve meat. When they were completely dry, they were brought down and hung in the well house.

Bringing back the supplies, Ingeborg glanced up at the clock. Nearly four hours until the train arrived. In half an hour, the milking crew, plus Emmy, who was taking care of the chickens and feeding the calves, would come trooping in. With Freda slicing the ham, Ingeborg stirred up the sourdough to be ready to pour the pancakes. The yeasty fragrance floated throughout the house and even out the door.

"Grandma, you look so nice today." Manny stopped to grin at her when he came through the door at the head of the crew.

"So you don't think she looks nice all

the other times?" Emmy teased, coming right behind him with a basket of eggs on her arm.

"Well, no—I mean, well . . ."

Emmy chuckled. "Gotcha, didn't I?"

Manny tugged on her braid. "Two can play that game."

"All right, children," Freda scolded.

They burst into laughter at the frown Freda tried to apply to her face.

Ingeborg tsked and poured more batter on the griddle. "Are you washed up yet?"

Even with breakfast being a lively affair, time seemed to move slower than a limping turtle. While Emmy was cleaning up, Ingeborg added more flour to the leftover pancake batter and began kneading in grated cheese to make cheese biscuits for dinner. This was one of David's favorites. Not that she'd been thinking about him.

"You leaving now?" Freda asked a while later, when Ingeborg removed her apron and checked her face and hair in the mirror.

"Ja. You need anything from the store?"

"No. You look lovely, and there is no need to hurry back."

Leaving the house, Ingeborg strolled along the lane that turned into a street before she reached Thorliff's house.

"Gramma," Rolly called from the porch

and came running down the steps to the fence. "Where are you going?"

"To the train to meet Mr. Gould."

"Can I come?"

"Sorry, Rolly, not today. Where's your pa?"

"At work."

She heard the train whistle from the east. "I better go. Why don't you throw the ball for Pepper?"

"Okay. I guess." He stepped down from the lower frame on the gate and stuffed his hands in his pockets. The drooping shoulders and hanging head made her feel sad, but she would not be late for this train.

She picked up her pace and arrived at the station just as the whistle blew again, and the screeching wheels made her want to clap her hands over her ears. The train screamed to a stop, with steam billowing from around the wheels. The conductor swung down and set the steel steps in place.

"Good morning, Mrs. Bjorklund. I think I have that man you're waiting for."

"Good thing." She watched the shadow of the open door and managed to keep herself from cheering when, after two others stepped down, she saw David appear.

"Have a good day, Mr. Gould," the conductor said, touching the brim of his hat.

"Thank you. And you let me know how your son is doing."

"I will, sir."

David's face lit up when he saw Ingeborg. He dropped his valise and reached for her with both hands. "I thought I would never get here."

Her hands warm in his, her smile could have lit up the station. "I so agree." She stepped into his arms and tipped her head back to see his face. "It feels like you've been gone a year rather than a month." Exhaustion had grayed his face. "Welcome home."

He rested his chin on the top of her head. "Yes, home indeed. I cannot begin to tell you how good this feels." He stepped back and grasped her shoulders, shaking his head. "The telephone has been a godsend, but nothing can take the place of seeing your smiling face." He pulled her close again, this time kissing her forehead.

She leaned her head against his chest. His heart was thudding just like hers.

"Let's go home," she said.

David heaved a sigh. "I need to stop by the office first."

A groan inside nearly made it out. Why did he have to do that? He'd said they would spend this day together.

"Do you have more luggage?" she asked stiffly.

274

A curtain seemed to have dropped in place between them.

"I do." He nodded to some boxes on the platform. "I'm seriously thinking of hiring a secretary. I'll ask Thorliff to run some ads for me in other papers around here, or perhaps I'll bring one out from New York." He picked up his briefcase and motioned to his valise, speaking to the stationmaster. "Put this with the other boxes, please, and deliver one to my office at the machinery plant and the others to my house. They're labeled. Thank you." He turned back to Ingeborg. "I shouldn't be long."

"I'll be at Amelia's."

He nodded and, with a slight wave, strode off.

Ingeborg watched him go. What was going on? She understood his excitement over his tank project and the progress on that, but surely that could wait until after dinner, at least. Something big was eating at him.

She turned and walked back the way she had come, grateful she had worn a shawl. The nip of fall had progressed to the bite of October. The leaves were fully dressed in fall colors, and the blossoms on the rosebushes had succumbed to the three frosts in a row, the final one a killer.

Turning into the gate at Amelia's, Ingeborg found her trimming her rosebushes. "You have time for a cup of something hot?"

"Why, Ingeborg, what a surprise. I thought you were spending the day with Mr. Gould." Amelia tucked her shears down in her basket. "I guess I'll have that little Drexel boy, Vinnie, come and pile up the clippings. I can burn them later."

"He's in school, isn't he?"

"Oh yes. But he comes to help me when I ask, and I pay him something. I think his family can use the money." She locked arms with Ingeborg. "It's too cool out here on the porch, so I guess we better move inside."

"Where's Danny?"

"Taking a nap. He woke up this morning with a touch of the crankies. He was over at Sophie's for a while yesterday so he could have some children to play with. Astrid is at the hospital. She was fussing about all the paper work she has to do these days."

"David mentioned hiring a secretary to help cope with his paper work. I guess finding good clerical help is not easy."

"Probably not in a small town like Blessing." Amelia hung her sweater on a hook by the door and tied on an apron. "Now, let's see about getting this stove roaring as quickly as possible. You know that, what with the baby

276

coming, Astrid is thinking about cutting back on her hours, don't you?"

"I wondered, the way she has been feeling so poorly with this one. She mentioned nausea too. Hopefully that's passed by this stage." She smiled to herself. Another grandchild. "She's wise to do that. She looks tired."

"Well, I'll believe it when I see it."

The two women smiled at each other, shaking their heads.

Ingeborg got up and went over to stare out the window. She was sad to see the few roses still in Amelia's backyard blackened by the frost, gone for the winter. She was sad to see David look so sad.

"Something is bothering you."

About to deny it, Ingeborg instead paused. "Not sure it is anything, but David seemed a bit off. It's not something I can describe."

"A trip like he's been on would make anyone exhausted. Might that be it?"

Ingeborg nodded slowly, for she was still pondering. Something kept her thinking it was more than that. Something had happened, she was sure of it, but was it something she had done or said?

"Come sit down and try this coffee cake I baked this morning. I hope it is good, since I sent a pan of it over to the hospital for when the staff have a cup of coffee."

Ingeborg sat down, deciding it was time to change the subject. "How's the construction going on the new wing? Is Astrid pleased with it?"

"I think she is still in shock that her dream is coming true so soon." Amelia looked in the coffeepot on the stove. "Almost ready." She returned to sit at the table. "You know, I was looking in the Sears, Roebuck and Montgomery Ward catalogues, and they have electric stoves now. Instant heat, can you believe that? Of course, they are outrageously expensive, but just think. A twist of a dial, and a burner heats up."

"You wait, Penny will have them in her store as soon as she is able."

"And Sophie will buy the first one, and we'll all be invited for tea to see it."

"Hard to believe, such progress." Ingeborg shook her head. "I remember when we were cooking over campfires and progressed to fireplaces in the house, and then the joy of having a cookstove."

Amelia got up and poured them each a cup of coffee, pulled the coffee cake out of the warming oven, and placed everything on the table. She sat down, and they both picked up their forks for a first bite of the new recipe.

With a smile, Ingeborg said, "This is delicious. Where did you find the recipe?"

"I made it up. Had some applesauce to use

up, and chopped nuts always make something better, and then I mixed butter and brown sugar with a bit of flour and spread it over the top." She took another bite and nodded. "I'm sure I'll make this again."

"What if you used chopped fresh apples?"

"Sounds good too. Oh, here come Mr. Gould and Daniel."

Ingeborg's heart fluttered. Honestly. You would think she was a schoolgirl.

Daniel led the way to the kitchen, David right behind him.

David grinned. "Now I get to walk you home."

Ingeborg couldn't stop smiling. "And I get to let you."

"Sit," Amelia ordered. "Have some coffee cake, if it won't spoil your dinner." She brought two dessert plates to the table and went for the coffee and two more cups.

Ingeborg cut pieces for them.

"Just a little one for me. Save the rest for Astrid," Daniel requested. "We stopped by for some notes on my desk."

"Sit and have your coffee." Amelia plopped down. "Do you know if Astrid is coming home for dinner?"

Daniel thought a moment. "I doubt it, but I think she plans to quit for the day around two. She was there at six this morning."

Ingeborg wagged her head.

David and Daniel were both wrapped up in this project. Just now they were debating upholstery, of all things. David wanted cushioned seats for the soldiers because of the rough, bouncy ride. Daniel wanted steel seats to minimize anything flammable in that small enclosed space. Fire was a danger.

Ingeborg listened for a few minutes. There was a lull as Daniel cut himself a second piece, despite his initial protests. "This is so good!"

Ingeborg suggested, "Why not make cushions an option and let the buyer decide whether their operators should burn up or be uncomfortable?"

Daniel and David looked at each other and burst out laughing. "The perfect solution!" David jotted a note. "We can build a whole list of options, add-ons. More profit."

Daniel grinned.

The men finished their coffee. Ingeborg picked up the plates and cups, set them in the sink, and said her good-byes. The two men followed her out the door, as did Amelia. Daniel went back to the factory, Amelia returned to cutting back roses, while David and Ingeborg headed out for the farm.

"Your briefcase?" she asked.

"I had one of the youngsters over at the plant take it to my house."

Ingeborg raised her face to the sunshine. "Oh, this feels so good. I'm glad I didn't wear a hat after all."

"You decided not to be proper?"

She nodded. "I want to soak in every moment of sunlight that I can."

He looked about him. "It seems strange to have all the children in school. It's so much quieter."

"It's the same at home. I miss the girls. Did things get any better with your family in New York?"

And the ice instantly formed so thick that you could skate on it.

She stopped, turned him to her, and studied his face. "What is it?"

Obviously, he was thinking of not telling her. But then it poured out. "I have fired my board . . . the whole board. The company is mired, nearly at a standstill, and I want to turn it around, but I'm not certain how."

"You're a capable businessman and an aggressive one. You take a problem on and solve it. There's more than that bothering you, David. I can tell that's not all of it."

"Thomas is gone."

She clapped her hands over her mouth. "Dead?"

"No one knows. He and I got into a violent argument about Lionel Hibbing. He still

281

thinks it is Blessing that turned me against that scoundrel. The next day in the board meeting, he exploded and stormed out. He drained all his liquid accounts, leaving his wife and children with nothing. She doesn't have a dime, and he's disappeared. Left town, as far as I can tell."

"But . . . but . . ." How could that young man do such a thing?

"He claimed he knew Hibbing well. Lionel was friendly, jovial, and well-dressed, and I was either lying about him or simply misled by all those rubes in Blessing, ignorant people jealous of Lionel's wealth. He wouldn't believe me."

Her eyes filled with tears. "Oh, David, I feel so sorry for you. But do you see now why I am so afraid to marry you?"

His voice rose in anger. "Thomas is not like my other children! They would never do such a thing! You can't judge them by his standards!"

"A short time ago you would have said the same thing about Thomas."

His face filled with fury and something else. What was it? Fear. Overriding fear, for Thomas, for everything. "Perhaps you can find your own way home from here." He wheeled and quickly walked away.

She stood there a moment, the tears flowing freely. Then she turned and continued down her long, lonely lane.

Dawn had not lighted any part of the sky the next morning when, after a sleepless night, Ingeborg lit the kerosene lamp by her rocking chair and gathered her Bible and journal. The house was silent, and the predawn chirping of the birds was not even a possibility. She sat quietly with her hands folded on her Bible.

Lord, you know David asked me to marry him. He said he has prayed over this, and I am sure he has. But is this you guiding him, or just what he feels? I feel torn. I love my home and my farm and all that you have given me here. All these years of hard work, first with Roald and then Haakan. All the blood and sweat we have put into this land, these people too, this town.

What do you want? The voice whispered in her heart.

I love this man. She stared at the words she had written. She nodded. *Yes, I do love him. I love to be with him, and I missed him terribly while he was gone. Like the sun is dimmed by clouds. Somewhere in me, I knew this was coming. But I love this house, this place. Can I—you—we make that house into a home?*

She tipped her head back to rest against the rocking chair. This chair that Haakan had spent so many hours making for her. For her to hold and rock their babies in. *And many others since you chose not to give me any more babes of my own.*

If I marry David, if you want me to marry David, Lord, you must make it so clear to me that I will throw away all my doubts and questions and . . . She shook her head. *Oh, Lord, thank you for your unending patience with me. I trust you. I trust that I do not need all the answers, like cows in a line, coming to the barn for milking. I will trust you. After all, you have never deserted me in the past. Even in those times of horrible despondency, you did not let me go. You provided Kaaren to lead me out of the pit. You will show me and us your perfect will, at just the right time. I trust you, the Lord my God. Forgive my doubts and fears.*

Seek my face. The words echoed around and within her. She blew out a breath, and surely the doubts and fears with it.

Yes, Lord, I will seek your face. I do seek your face.

She heard the rooster crow and Manny come down the stairs. He stopped when he saw the kerosene lamp lighted beside her chair.

"Grandma, are you all right?"

She turned to him with a gentle smile. "I am now."

"Why the kerosene lamp? We have electric lights. They're so much better."

284

"Ah, yes, but this old lamp has seen me through many years. It is friendlier."

He stared at her, shook his head, and kissed her on the cheek. "I'll get the fire started." He paused. "And a hunk of cheese and bread before I go to the barn."

"Ah, Manny, I thank God for bringing you to us, to me. You are like another son to me."

"A grandson, perhaps? An always hungry grandson?" He chuckled as he cranked the grate to let the ashes sift to the tin catcher below, and whistled as he laid the wood and the starter.

Thank you, Lord. Ingeborg set the chair to singing its familiar song. Freda would come into the kitchen any time and the day's work would begin. A smile creased her face as the song of the meadowlark heralded the rising sun.

Chapter 21

It seems to me you are spending more time here than usual."

"I had those papers to bring you and . . ."

Thorliff was sure he wasn't stuttering. He grinned at the school principal.

John Solberg tipped his chair back. "I know, I know, the duties of the president of the school board. I thought you came to inspect the ball field. They just finished up the bleachers—but then, you know that. But since you're here, let's go take a look."

The two men left the building and headed toward the high-fenced field. Thorliff nodded as he walked past the backstop over to the bleachers. Five tiers of board seats lined the fence. He turned to John. "It's hard to believe we really got it finished, and before the weather turned bad. How are the kids liking it?"

"I think they are still in awe. You know that last donation?"

"You mean the one from the deaf school?"

John nodded. "I know, it has David Gould's fingerprints all over it. But as far as the community is concerned, they did it." He slapped the seats. "I'll get some of the older boys out here to paint these so the winter won't be so hard on them. Did you see that we could attach chains to the frame and move them around with a team of horses? Not that we will ever need to do that, but it was a good idea."

"Right."

The two men swapped grins and headed back to the front door just as the bell rang for dismissal.

John clapped Thorliff on the shoulder. "Enjoy yourself."

Thorliff shook his head and made his way through the crowd, answering the many greetings he received, to the door to Louisa's classroom. He waited until the last of the students exited and then stepped inside.

"Hi, Pa," Inga said as she came in from the hall. "You want to pound erasers?"

Louisa looked up from sorting papers on her desk. "Hello, Mr. Bjorklund. You don't have to do that."

"I know, but if we get the chores done, I thought we might go for sodas." He looked at Inga. "Where's Emmy?"

"She'll be here in a minute. You mean all of us?"

He nodded, looking to Louisa. "If that's all right with you."

"I haven't had a soda in a long time. I'd love to."

Within a few minutes, the chores were finished and the four of them were walking toward the soda shop. A breeze, tinted with fall, lifted the brim of Louisa's straw hat and played with the girls' skirts.

Louisa lifted her face to the sun and inhaled.

"Fall is in the air, that's for sure. How long does the soda shop stay open?"

"Until six o'clock for now, but Rebecca closes it down for the winter once it really turns cold. It becomes the town gathering place during the summer, though. She sets tables out under the trees in the spring, and that announces the soda shop is back in business."

"Inga, what's your favorite flavor?" Louisa asked.

"Strawberry when she had fresh berries, but most of the time chocolate." Inga turned to Emmy. "What's yours?"

"I tried them all this year, but chocolate is still my favorite." The two girls looked at Louisa.

"Chocolate."

"Then we're unanimous." Thorliff held the door open, then raised his voice. "Four chocolate sodas, Rebecca. Is Benny home yet?"

"No, he's working on something at school. Four it is. Nice to see you, Miss Gutenberg. I've heard good reports about your classroom."

Thorliff made introductions. "Miss Gutenberg, have you officially met Rebecca Valders? You'll often hear her husband's voice on the telephone. He's the head operator."

"Not officially, but I remember you from church." Louisa and Rebecca exchanged smiles and nods. "And Benny is your son?"

"Our adopted son and the light of our lives." Rebecca scooped ice cream into four glasses, added the fizzy and long-handled spoons, and set them on the counter.

Thorliff handed them around before digging in his pocket for the payment. "Thanks, Rebecca. Outside or in?"

They sat around a table outside to enjoy their sodas and visit, as comfortable as if they'd known each other much longer than a few weeks.

Louisa turned to Thorliff. "I have a feeling there is a story behind Benny. That boy amazes me."

"He amazes most of us. Astrid, my sister, went to Chicago for surgical training. Benny was brought in one day with mangled legs, having been run over by a wagon. They never thought he would make it, since he lost both legs, but he and Astrid got to be close, and she decided to bring him back here, since he had no family. He got the care he needed in our hospital and was adopted by the Valders family."

Inga added, "That summer, Emmy and I stayed with him as much as we could, so we're all best friends. Now, during the summer, he drives a wagon for the construction company."

"They helped him learn to use his crutches and artificial legs to walk. He also uses wheels."

"Wheels?"

"A flat board with four wheels attached. He kept up with the others pretty well."

Inga licked her spoon and dropped it back in the glass. "Does Grandma know where we are?"

"Probably not." Emmy gathered up their glasses. "Thank you, that was so good. But I've got chores to do."

"Inga and I will walk you both home," Thorliff said.

He thought back on their soda break that evening as he got ready for bed. He and John had done a good job in hiring Miss Gutenberg. Getting to know her better made him smile. Maybe next time, he'd make sure the outing was just the two of them.

The world was his. Where would he go?

Thomas relaxed in his beach chair, courtesy of Montauk's luxury hotel, sipped his cocktail, and gazed out to sea. He didn't particularly want to sail to Europe. It was always crowded with tourists. Africa? Nothing worthwhile in Africa once you'd seen the pyramids, and he'd done that when he was ten.

How about somewhere here in America? Perhaps Philadelphia. A lot of upper-class people seemed to love Philadelphia. But no, its reputation was Quaker Conservative, and that certainly was not his style. Chicago? Rotten weather often, even in summer. Florida? Too hot now. New Orleans? The same. How about San Francisco? Now there was an idea. Yes, he would make San Francisco his first stop to celebrate his new freedom.

The beach boy paused beside his chair. "Do you wish anything, sir?"

"When do the trains leave for Grand Central Station?"

"On the hour from six until ten p.m., sir, and one at two a.m."

"Good. Bring me another drink."

The lad hustled off.

Thomas had plenty of money with him, but he didn't have much in the way of clothes. In his haste, he had left home with only his valise, taking some of his favorite shoes and shirts. But that was certainly enough for the train trip across the United States. He would tog himself out properly when he reached San Francisco.

A little voice at the back of his head whispered, *You should take your wife.*

Are you joking? That shrew would suck all the fun out of his new freedom. Besides, she had to stay home and oversee the house and children. No, Thomas would take no one with him, least of all her. He would be a brand-new man, free of responsibility.

An unencumbered man of the world.

Chapter 22

"L ouisa, will you be going to Grafton this weekend?"

Louisa looked at Ingeborg's calendar on the kitchen wall. November already. Where had the time gone? Much too soon, it would turn into the year 1914. "I was thinking about it, but since I went last Friday . . ."

"It will be nice to have you with us this weekend." Ingeborg smiled at her. "We're having supper here tonight with Thorliff's family to work on The Book."

Louisa knew now what book Ingeborg was talking about, the story of Ingeborg's life, which was becoming the history of Blessing. "I've been thinking of asking Thorliff if he

292

could use more help. I've written for a news-paper before."

"Oh, how wonderful. I know he hates to admit it, but he is drowning in work, what with the newspaper, running the construction company, and adding the Book into that."

"Thank you for inviting me to the supper. I'll see you tonight." Louisa pinned on her hat, gathered up her satchel, which included her dinner pail, and headed out the door. The leaves were gone, the cottonwoods bare. A straw hat was not the smartest headwear at this point in the season, and she clamped one hand on the top of her head to foil the west wind as she made her way to the school. Of course, her dainty little felt hat was no warmer.

"Let me help you." The male voice made her smile.

"You snuck up on me." She turned to see Thorliff, feeling the smile warm her face.

"Hardly." He reached for her satchel. "I hoped to catch you before you left the farm."

"Thank you. Now I have both hands free to save my hat." She reached up, pulled out the pin, and, outsmarting the determined wind, clamped hat and pin under one arm. "Is it always this windy?"

"Pretty much. At least it is coming from the west, not the north. That's when we get really cold." He pulled his own hat down tighter. "I've been wanting to talk with you. You mentioned that you once worked for a newspaper, and I'm wondering if you can find the time to work for the *Blessing Gazette*."

"I would be happy to."

"I mean, I can't afford—" He stared at her. "Did you say what I think you said?"

"I did. I really enjoyed writing for the paper in Fargo, but when my sister needed help, I moved to Grafton." At least this part of the story she could tell.

"I'm hoping you can help me with this history book too. Do you type?"

"No, but I learn fast."

Together they mounted the steps to the school. He opened the door for her, and they stepped into the warmth of the building.

"I have a meeting with John, so . . ." He started to hand back her satchel but then motioned her down the hall. "When can you start?"

"Whenever you want me to. I'll be here this weekend. Your mother told me about dinner tonight and invited me."

"Good, we'll talk more then." The intensity of his gaze made her clear her throat. Standing outside the door to her classroom, she felt like she was drowning in a lake of blue.

With a shaking hand, she reached for her satchel. He slowly released it without breaking eye contact. "Th-thank you." Her words came out in a whisper.

"You're welcome."

"I'm ready anytime you are," Solberg called from his office door.

"Coming." Thorliff blinked and released the satchel. "Yes, er, have a good day." Turning without waiting for an answer, he trotted down the hall.

Louisa stared after him. What in the world had just happened?

She opened her classroom door and entered, then set her satchel on the table and hung her coat on the peg by the door. She hung her hat, looking slightly worse for the wear, on a peg above it. Emptying her bag, she put her dinner pail in the bottom drawer of her desk and stacked the papers on top, all the while in automatic motion. Whatever was the matter with her?

The bell rang, and she stood to greet her students. *Pay attention*, she ordered herself. *No confusion like that allowed.* She guessed that was as good a word as any.

She signed *good morning* to Josiah, as he was the first in line, and received a big smile in return above his flashing fingers. The others followed him, all hanging their coats on the pegs and setting their dinner pails on the shelf above. All in all, a normal day—she hoped.

Birgit, who spoke with a heavy accent, stopped at her desk. "I brought you a roll that my mother made. I hope you like it." She set a napkin-wrapped bundle on the corner of Louisa's desk.

"I'm sure I will. Please thank her for me."

Birgit nodded and made her way to her desk.

While Birgit answered when a question was directed at her, this was the first time she had volunteered to speak. Louisa felt like dancing.

At the noon recess, Louisa joined the boys on the ball field. "I've been watching, and I believe I could help you hit the ball more consistently. Now, with the looks I am getting, I figure I better show you what I mean. Who's pitching?" One of the older boys raised his hand. "Good. Pitch to me."

He took the ball out to the mound, shook his head, and lobbed the ball toward her in a gentle arc.

Louisa grinned at him and hit the ball way over the fielders' heads. "You want to pitch another?"

This time he wound up and pitched straight in and fast.

She shrugged, swung, and connected

296

again. "That would have been a ball, but I adjusted."

All the eyes followed the drive of the ball as it bounced off the back fence. The pitcher caught the ball thrown to him and stood on the mound, smacking the ball into his glove. "Where did you learn to hit like that?"

"At home from my older brothers. Now, how about you pitch, and I help the younger boys?"

"Okay."

"I'm going to show you all some tricks." She held up her bat and stepped into the batter's box. "First, place your feet like this, so you are swinging the bat over home plate. Grip it like this and hold it above your shoulder. The most important thing is to keep your eye on the ball. Okay, pitcher, let 'er fly."

The ball came in, she hit it, and this time it went foul.

"See, that shows that I swung a bit too low. You want to hit the ball right in the center. And what is most important?"

"Keep your eye on the ball," they chorused.

"Now, who wants to be first?"

Several boys raised their hands, and she motioned to one and led him through the drill of correct positioning. "Okay, pitcher, pitch as straight as you can, but easy on the speed."

"Yes, ma'am." He threw the ball, the batter swung, and the ball thumped into the catcher's mitt.

"You did well. Watch the ball."

The boy hit the second pitch. It didn't go far, but he made contact. All the boys cheered. The batter turned to her with a grin that nearly split his face. "I hit it!"

"Yes, you did. Very good." She looked up to see Thorliff and Reverend Solberg on the other side of the fence, clapping and cheering. The warning bell rang, and the boys picked up the gear to take inside.

"Thanks, Miss Gutenberg, for helping us," the pitcher said.

"You are most welcome. If you would like some coaching on pitching, I'd love to help you. You are doing well already."

"Thank you. Could you maybe meet with some of us after school and—and coach?"

"I would like that, but I probably need to talk it over with Reverend Solberg."

She met the two men waiting for her. *You shouldn't have done that without asking permission first*, she scolded herself. *Now you're in for it.*

"Well done, Miss Gutenberg." John Solberg nodded and smiled at her.

"I wish I'd known you could hit like that," Thorliff said. "You could have been on my team for the ball games."

She relaxed, realizing they weren't upset. "I grew up playing with my brothers. I felt sorry for the little guys, because they weren't getting good instruction." The bell rang, making her flinch. "I'm going to be late for my class."

"Yes, go on." The reverend smiled at her.

Louisa caught up with her class as they walked back into the school. Once they were in the classroom, they clustered around her, asking questions and replaying the recess.

"All right, everybody, take your seats, and let's get back to school work. Take out a paper and pencil for the spelling test I told you about yesterday."

Groans greeted her announcement, making her roll her eyes. The universal pre-quiz reaction.

"You had your spelling list to work on, so let's begin. We are studying American history, so all these words are from our history lesson." She watched the interpreter sign the words. When she finished announcing the ten words, she told the students to pass their paper to the person behind them, and then she spelled the words so they could grade their classmates' tests.

When the last half hour of class rolled around, she could see her students checking the clock. To put them out of their misery, she announced, "Time to put away your things. Your homework for this weekend is to read the next chapter in your history text and write down three points that caught your attention. Any questions? Good, then we'll end the day with chapter three of *Black Beauty*."

Louisa loved to read aloud, letting her mind see the pictures the author wrote.

The bell ringing caught her by surprise. "That'll be all for today. See you on Monday."

"Thank you for reading," nearly all the students said as they passed her desk.

"You're welcome, have a good weekend."

"You want us to do the blackboards?" Inga asked as she entered a few minutes later.

"Please."

Louisa looked up to see Thorliff standing just inside the doorway. Her face smiled before her mind reacted.

"I've never read that story," he said. "Do you mind if I walk you home?"

"Not at all. I have a couple of things to do first." She looked up as another girl entered the room. "Hi, Emmy. Thank you."

While the girls washed the blackboards, Thorliff took the erasers outside and clapped them together.

"You didn't need to do that," Louisa said when he came back in.

"I know, but it's getting colder outside, so I thought we might want to hurry."

They all finished and buttoned up to brave the weather. Louisa tried to stuff her straw hat into her satchel, but when it wouldn't fit, Inga offered to carry it.

"Don't you have any books to take along?" Louisa asked.

"Not this weekend."

The four of them stepped out of the building and were blown all the way to the farm.

"Brrr." Louisa shuddered when they mounted the stairs to the back porch. "Monday, or perhaps Sunday, the winter coat comes out."

"It might bounce back to warm sunny days for a bit before we settle into winter for good." Thorliff held the door for them all.

Inga grinned up at him. "Thanks."

"You think it'll swing to the north?" Freda asked him as she followed them into the house.

"I hope not, but the way that sky is darkening, we might have rain tonight."

"Take off your coat and stay awhile," Ingeborg said with a smile, lifting the coffeepot.

"Okay, one cup, and then I'll go get Thelma and Rolly."

"You want Manny to go for them?"

"No, he needs to be here for milking."

"Grandma, Miss Gutenberg spent noon recess teaching the boys how to hit the ball better," Inga announced. "Carl said she whacked that ball right over the fence."

Ingeborg's eyes twinkled when she handed a full cup to Louisa. "You did, did you? Where did you learn to play ball?"

"My older brothers taught me. They thought it was funny that their little sister could smack the ball." She sipped her coffee, still standing by the stove. She wasn't sure which was warmer, the man standing beside her or the stove at her back. *Louisa Gutenberg, get thoughts of him right out of your head. If you have any ideas about this man, remember, you'd have to tell him everything first. No more secrets.*

But, she tried to argue back, *but . . .*

"Please excuse me," she said, suddenly overwrought. "I need to go to my room."

Without another word, she set down her coffee cup and slipped past Thorliff to go up the stairs. She threw her distraught body across her bed. *I can't tell him. What if he blows up like my father and bans me from teaching here? I can't afford it. You promised you would never be interested in another man, remember? You won't be allowed to teach if they know. Think of Susan and Donald, how much your pay is helping them. If you get fired, then what?*

She rolled over and stared up at the ceil-

302

ing. *A fallen woman, that is what I am. I can teach as long as no one knows, but I am living a lie.* She heard the front door slam shut. Thorliff was off home. She could tell he was attracted to her, and her body failed her by reciprocating the attraction. Traitorous body. *Lord, help me be strong and not hurt others by my weakness.*

Silly. Aren't you blowing this all out of proportion? This voice sounded more reasonable. Surely . . . surely. She ordered herself to her feet. *Change and go down the stairs.* She could work for the paper. The extra money would come in very handy.

When she went downstairs a while later, Mr. Gould had arrived with Thorliff and Thelma. Rolly was already kneeling on a chair at the table, eating a cookie.

"So, Miss Gutenberg, I hear you are going to help Thorliff with the newspaper. I think that is a fine idea." Mr. Gould filled his mug from the pot on the stove.

She nodded. "Thank you, but I have a favor to ask of you."

"Really? Well, of course. What is it?"

"Could you please call me Louisa?"

He nodded and smiled at her. "That is certainly an easy favor to grant. Thank you, Louisa. But you realize that means you must call me David."

"Thank you, sir, I'll work on that." She could feel her face responding to his smile by flushing. Calling an older man by his first name? Her father would have tanned her hide to be so presumptuous. But here in the Bjorklund home, it was the most natural thing in the world. They seemed to simply overlook formality. Might her fallen nature, her sin, also be overlooked?

Conversation was lively around the supper table, including plenty of laughter. But there seemed to be an unnatural coolness between Ingeborg and David . . . or was that just Louisa's imagination? She was not good at reading unspoken feelings in others. At least the frost, or whatever it was, did not dampen the good cheer.

Louisa wished her family could enjoy a meal like this. Her father felt that children should be seen and not heard, so meals were a silent affair unless he found something to complain about. Louisa had frequently been the recipient of his tongue-lashings. Those days were behind her, she hoped, but if her stepmother were to die or leave, and he asked her to take care of him and the children still at home, would she go?

There at that cheerful table, she decided no. The past had passed.

Inga stood up and carried her plate to the

sink. "Thank you, Grandma. That was very good." She looked at her pa. "Are we working tonight?"

"If you want. The ads and back pages are ready to set." He looked at Louisa. "Do you want to start tonight too? You ever do any layout?"

She shook her head. "I just wrote articles. But I'd like to learn."

"Good. Emmy types the articles I've written, I do the layout, and Inga both sets and cleans the type. The day or two before the paper releases are always rush time."

"When will it come out?"

"The *Gazette* always comes out on a Monday. Well, mostly. We'll be printing Saturday afternoon and evening. I try not to work on Sunday."

"If everyone is finished, pass your plates around," Freda announced. "Who'll have a piece of apple pie?"

"There is nothing like the apple pie at this house." Mr. Gould passed plates to clear the table.

Inga and Emmy picked up the dishes, scraped them, and put them in the soapy hot water in the dishpan in the sink.

Mr. Gould propped his elbows on the table. "So, Louisa, what's this I hear about you helping the boys with baseball?"

"It just seemed a shame that the younger ones aren't learning to bat the best way."

"I think us girls should get to play ball too." Inga passed the dessert plates around while Thelma poured the coffee.

Ingeborg shook her head. "Thelma, you are supposed to be a guest. Let us serve you for a change."

"I just can't sit still and watch others work."

"It takes practice." Ingeborg smiled at her from her chair. "I should know."

"We almost had to tie her in the chair, right, Grandma?" Emmy patted Ingeborg's shoulder and set a plate of pie in front of her.

The girls slid into their chairs after making sure Freda did so too.

"Thank you, Lord, for apples." Ingeborg inhaled the scent of apples and cinnamon rising from the pie. "This is what fall smells like to me." She watched Mr. Gould close his eyes. "Good, isn't it?"

"Better than good. Who do we thank?"

"Grandma and Freda. The pies were baking when we came home from school." Emmy nudged Manny. "Don't take such big bites, it'll last longer."

Manny poked her back. "This way I get a second helping."

"What if the pie is all gone?"

"Then I'll eat yours."

Louisa looked up to see Thorliff smiling, not at their foolishness, but at her. Her heart seemed to skip a beat. Perhaps going to work with him was not the best idea.

Chapter 23

I feel like I am totally useless there."

Louisa stared up at the slanted ceiling in her bedroom that night. She had no idea what it took to put out a newspaper. Well, she did now, but would she be any assistance on this edition? But what a delight it had been to watch the three of them in action. How a thirteen-year-old girl could set type with her fingers flying like that, and Emmy entered into her own world, typing away. But come to think of it, those two girls could knit as if the needles were attached to their hands. Louisa heaved a sigh. At least she knew she was a good teacher. And what fun it had been to see the surprise on the boys' faces when she hit the ball.

Sunday at church she would ask Reverend

Solberg if she could teach the girls too. *When* would be the problem. So much depended upon the weather.

As late as it is, morning is going to come even more quickly than usual. Lord, thank you for bringing me here. She rolled over to her side.

The next thing she heard was Manny starting the fire in the cookstove. She could hear Emmy getting dressed, so she forced herself to throw off the covers and get moving. Another good thing about living here: she needn't make the trek to the outhouse.

Immediately after breakfast, she and Emmy donned their wool coats and knitted hats and left for the newspaper office. "How old were you and Inga when you started helping at the newspaper office?"

Emmy thought for a moment. "I must have been ten or eleven."

"And Inga is three years younger than you."

"Thorliff started her with it to learn her letters and numbers. It's probably why we both read so well. I learned right along with her."

"How old were you when you came to be with Ingeborg?"

"I must have been six or so. My uncle brought me here because he knew Grandma could take better care of me than he could, just for the winter, so I wouldn't freeze to death or get sick like so many of the others. When he died, I stayed here with Grandma, but she takes me back to the reservation sometimes. She and the women of the tribe teach one another all kinds of things."

"Did you go up this last summer?"

"Yes, but our visit was real short. We took a wagonload of clothing, some quilts, and seeds for planting. Tante Astrid sent some medical supplies too."

"And you want to become a teacher so you can help them?"

"I do. There is supposed to be a school near the tribe, but the children have to leave the reservation to go to school while they live there. I would like to build a schoolhouse where they live."

"You have big dreams."

"I know." She pushed open the door to the newspaper office and motioned for Louisa to go ahead of her.

"The coffee is in the pot. Thelma said she'd be out with rolls in a while." Thorliff stood from his desk chair. "Good morning. Thanks for coming."

His smile made Louisa's heart leap. *Stop that*, she told herself. *This has to be just a friendship, so don't encourage him.*

Don't be rude, the bossy voice in her head retorted.

Louisa poured herself a cup of coffee and watched as he moved pieces of typed columns around on the layout to make them all fit without leaving spaces. He had explained that last night. "How can I help you?"

"I'll lay it all in place, kind of like a jigsaw puzzle, and then you glue them onto the paper for Inga to set type from."

She nodded as he daubed glue on the back of one column, laid it back in place, smoothed it out, and moved on. Standing next to him, she inhaled the fresh fragrance of shaving soap and a hint of ink. Everything about him made her smile.

"Okay?" he said.

"Yes, I think I can do that."

"We start working on the next edition on Monday. Any suggestions for articles are gladly accepted." He turned to warm her with his smile. "Oh, and we have the keyboard chart for the typewriter. Emmy will show you the fingering."

"Good. I have so much to learn. Typing, signing, and Ingeborg said she would teach me how to use her sewing machine." She daubed glue on her first column and carefully set it into place, smoothing it with her fingertips as Thorliff had done. It was crooked.

"Pick it up quickly and reset it before the glue dries." He handed her a rag from his back pocket. "Use this to smooth the copy in place so you can keep the glue off your fingers."

"Thank you."

"Inga, where might we have another apron?"

"Thelma probably washed them. You want me to go find one?"

"I'll do it." Emmy pushed back from her typewriter. "You take those inky fingers of yours in the house, and . . ." The two girls giggled.

Louisa could tell there was a story behind that too. She glanced up to find Thorliff smiling at her. She swallowed hard. Emmy returned a minute later with several heavy aprons, ink-stained but clean. She handed one to Louisa and took the others to a closet where cleaning and other supplies filled the shelves.

"Here, let me tie that for you so you don't get glue on the strings." Thorliff dropped it over her head and tied the strings at her back. Having him behind her, fussing with the strings and breathing on her neck, made her swallow again. She seemed to be doing a lot of that.

"Th-thank you."

Thelma pushed open the outer door and announced rolls and hot coffee.

Thorliff poured the dregs of his cold cup into a jar beside the plate of rolls. "Thank you, Thelma. What's Rolly doing?"

"He went over to play with Danny. Amelia called and asked if he could come. Astrid is at the hospital, and Rolly keeps Danny entertained."

Thorliff nodded. "And out from under our feet."

"Ja, that too." She set a pitcher of cream out for the girls. "Beef vegetable soup for dinner."

Louisa set her coffee down on the ledge where Thorliff had set his and returned to her gluing. She'd just finished one page when he took that and laid another one in front of her.

"Good job. Do you want a stool?" he asked.

"I think so, yes." She stretched her shoulders and rolled her head from side to side. "I'm not used to staying in one position this long."

"It'll go faster the more you do it." He set a stool beside her.

"How many pages are there?"

"Twelve. Everything is done in sets of four. That will be three sheets of paper to run through the printer. Each sheet has four pages on it, and we print, assemble, fold, and fold the finished in half, then bundle them. Early Monday morning, they're distributed to places like the hospital, the mercantile, Gardner's Groceries, and the boardinghouse. They also get delivered to the homes of customers in town."

Louisa settled on the stool and continued gluing. *I have to stay away from him.*

Don't be silly, he's your employer. This is just a job.

She reached for the cup of coffee and knocked it over—onto the sheet she was nearly finished with. "Oh no. Where's a rag or something?" The coffee spread.

Thorliff handed her an old towel, and she mopped up the coffee. *Stupid, stupid, stupid,* she yelled in her head. *How can you be so clumsy?*

"Don't worry about it," Thorliff said. "We'll let it dry and continue on. Not the first time that's happened."

"We all have to do that at least once," Emmy added.

"Some of us more than once," Inga called from the printing room.

"See?" Thorliff raised his hands. "It happens."

"But shouldn't I start over?"

"No, just let it dry. Inga can read it, stains or no stains."

A bell clanged.

"Dinner's ready. Don't worry, this'll be

dry by the time we get back out here." Thor-liff ushered them ahead of him and shut the door. "That soup smells mighty good."

"Thelma makes good soup," Emmy said as they mounted the steps to the back porch.

"Thelma's like Grandma," Inga agreed. "She makes good everything."

"Inga, please call Amelia and have her send Rolly home for dinner," Thelma asked as they came in the door.

Inga did as requested and then headed outside to wait for him. When Amelia said good-bye to him at the top of the steps, Rolly waved at Inga.

"I'm coming." He jumped off the bottom step, ran to the gate, and charged through.

"Shut the gate, Rolly," Inga called.

"Oh." He turned around, pulled the gate shut with a slam, and ran across the street. "You done with the paper yet?"

"No, sorry." The two siblings climbed the steps, hand in hand.

Louisa watched them come in the door. Rolly obviously adored his big sister. *Make that sisters*, she thought, as he ran to Emmy and hugged her.

"Can you come play with me this after-noon?" he asked. "I'm building a whole town out of blocks. I don't know how to build the steeple."

314

"Not today, but tomorrow we can play."

"The paper will be done?"

"That it will. Let's eat. Wash your hands."
They washed their hands together at the sink.

"Did Thelma bake cookies?" Rolly asked.

"I have no idea."

"I know, you were working on the newspaper."

Obviously the whole family was involved with the paper. Louisa smiled at Rolly. "Did you have fun playing with Danny?"

He nodded and grinned. "He's little, but he's cute. It's fun to teach him new stuff."

Thorliff said grace, Thelma filled the soup bowls, and Inga carried them to the table. Emmy passed the cracker basket to Rolly, who sent it on to Thorliff. The children in all the Bjorklund houses were treated pretty much like adults, and they took their responsibilities as adults, or almost so. Another important difference between Louisa's present and her past.

Later, out in the newspaper office, Louisa asked Inga, "Is Rolly always funny like he was today?"

"He can be. He's so smart. Emmy and I have fun teaching him. But then other times he can be, well, difficult. Challenging."

"Most people are like that." Wasn't that the truth?

By the time the paper was all bundled and ready to send that night, the clock had struck ten. The four of them washed their hands in the sink, hung up their aprons, and Thorliff went out into the dark to harness the horse to the buggy.

"We could have walked home," Louisa said to Inga. "It's not that far."

"Usually Emmy stays here with us, and actually, we finished earlier than usual."

"I never knew what a big job putting out a paper is."

"There are newer printers that Pa dreams of having, but he doesn't want to invest the money right now. He said he'd have to expand the business were he to do that. I guess we'd need a bigger building, for one thing."

"He's ready." Emmy pulled open the door.

Thorliff helped Louisa up onto the seat, and the girls climbed up themselves.

"You didn't leave much room for me," Thorliff said as he mounted to the seat.

Louisa felt crushed into his side, his warmth keeping the cold of the air from all but her face. The trotting horse and jingling harness added another level of comfort.

A candle beckoned them from the window of Ingeborg's house. When Thorliff stopped the horse at the gate, Emmy jumped down. "Thank you."

Thorliff's warm hand sent a tingle up Louisa's arm as he helped her down. She looked up at him and had to swallow. What if . . . ? She nodded. "Thank you." And stepped back. If her voice was shaking like she felt inside . . .

"See you in the morning." Even his voice did something to her middle. *This has got to stop*, she ordered herself as she strode up the walk to the back porch. *Do not look back at him*. She heard the buggy turning around and heading back to his house.

"Are you all right?" Emmy asked softly.

"Yes, yes of course." *Liar*.

Emmy blew out the candle in the window, and they climbed the stairs to their rooms. "'Night."

"'Night." Louisa shut her bedroom door softly behind her. How would she ever keep from drawing closer to him? If only . . . if only she did not have such a secret to keep.

Rain sluiced down the windows when she woke up. A gray day when she already felt gray and tired. She rolled herself out of bed and washed in the cold water of the basin in her room. The furnace was blowing warm air up through the big square vent in the hallway, so when she opened her door, she went to stand over it. She could hear Ingeborg and Freda talking in the kitchen. Emmy

317

and Manny would both be out doing chores already.

"Good morning," Ingeborg greeted her when she stepped down into the kitchen. "How did getting out the newspaper go?"

"We got it finished, and then Thorliff brought us home in the buggy. I had no idea what it takes to put out a newspaper." Louisa rubbed her hands over the stove. "Those two girls are amazing. They do the work of grown women and know so much. I have a feeling much of that is thanks to their grandma."

"Right you are," Freda agreed.

"Now, how can I help with breakfast?" Louisa asked.

"You could slice those three loaves of bread. We're having French toast today." Freda pointed to the loaves on the table.

"Gladly. You sure feed a lot of people."

"It could be more. Andrew usually goes home, as do Lars and Samuel. The two schoolboys always eat here. By the time they get back to the school, the breakfast is cleared away. Today they'll all be here—no, wait, Andrew is going home." Freda shrugged. "We just make plenty of food. I remember what it was like to go hungry, and I don't want anyone to go through that."

Louisa nodded. Never had Freda talked this much. The fresh bread fragrance rose from the loaves as she sliced them.

Ingeborg answered the rings of the telephone. "Good morning. Yes, I can see it is raining. Why, thank you, that would be very nice. Good, we'll see you then." She hung the earpiece back on the prongs. "That was Thorliff. He is going to bring the buggy with the canopy up to take us to church. I'm sure Lars was planning the same thing, but this will be nice."

Is there some way I can say no? Could I plead a headache? But then she blushed. *You know you want to see him.*

Some time later, even though the sun was peeking out, Thorliff drove up with the buggy. "I dropped the others off at the church so we'd have room for everyone." He and Manny helped the women in, and then Manny announced he would walk.

"Don't be silly," Ingeborg said. "We can squish together back here. Emmy, you sit in front with Louisa."

I couldn't sit in the back without being rude. Louisa smiled at Emmy as she stepped up to the seat and gathered her skirts closer to her as she moved closer to Thorliff. Was everything conspiring to put them together?

The same thing happened at church. Thorliff managed to sit next to her with Rolly beside him.

The boy looked over from behind his pa. "'Morning, Miss Gutenberg."

319

"Good morning to you too, Rolly."

Reverend Solberg greeted the congregation and announced, "Our opening hymn is 'Holy Holy Holy.' Most of us probably know this one by heart."

Thorliff pulled a blue hymnal out of the pew rack and looked at the large plaque on the wall that gave the hymn numbers for all of today's songs. Thorliff held the hymnal for Louisa, so she held up her side. How could singing out of one hymn book be so—so perfect? His baritone and her alto blended well. *Louisa Gutenberg, pay attention to the music.*

The same voice repeated that command over and over as she focused more on the warmth at her side than on the words being preached. Somehow it sounded an awful lot like her father. That was enough to make her snap her mind back to the man at the white pulpit. The scrollwork at the back and along the sides of the intricate altar made her feel right at home. It looked so much like the church she had grown up attending in Fargo. She wanted to ask who had made the altar but promised herself she would later.

Rolly was doodling on a scrap of paper, slumped against his father's side. Inga sat on the other side of Rolly with Emmy next to her. Mr. Gould, Ingeborg, and Freda sat in front of them, but they were surrounded by

320

Bjorklunds. What was it like to be part of such a large family? After two months in town, Louisa hadn't even met all of them yet.

As they stood to leave after the benediction, Rolly leaned across his pa. "You're coming to Gramma's for dinner too, aren't you, Miss Gutenberg?"

"Rolly," his pa reminded him, "she lives there."

The urge to tuck her arm through Thorliff's made Louisa lock her fingers together. She looked down as a small hand sneaked into her own. Rolly's smile warmed her heart.

Next Friday, she promised herself, *I will get on that train to Grafton. I won't do this again.*

Or, on the other hand, maybe not.

Chapter 24

So this was Chicago. Black smoke belched from a hundred factories. Lorries and freight wagons rattled about everywhere. It was a town as crowded and bustling as New York.

Leaving the train station, Thomas climbed into a hansom cab. "I want a good hotel."

"I recommend the Palmer House, sir, or the Burnham."

He had heard of neither, but then, he knew no one who lived in Chicago or even came here often. He himself would only be here a day or two, but since he was passing through, he figured he might as well see the place. "Palmer House."

The driver clucked at his black horse, and they rolled away. A few minutes later, the cab came to a stop at the impressive Palmer House. Chandeliers, white marble, gilded trim—it all felt like home.

Thomas registered, then strolled back outside. It was too early to go to bed, so he would go for a walk.

He followed a promenade along the lakeshore for a while, as did a number of well-dressed couples. He felt at home among these fashionable people, but he wasn't really seeing the city this way. He turned west and entered the busy streets.

Did they have a Macy's or Gimbels in this city? Apparently not, but he found he was walking past a large store that could be the equivalent, Marshall Field's. He ought to go inside and look around, but it was getting dark, and he should probably return to the hotel soon.

Within a block or two, he realized he was totally, helplessly lost. Michigan Avenue. Was that his street? His hotel was on a street that started with an *M*, but this didn't sound right. He would have to ask a local or take a cab. He approached a fellow leaning against a big brick building.

"Excuse me, sir. Can you direct me to the Palmer House?"

"Palmer House. Aye, that I can. Ye wouldn't spare a fellow a quid, would ye?"

Irish. Of all the people in this city, Thomas had to ask an Irishman, the scum of the earth. "Never mind. I'll find it." He turned away.

"Sure and ye will not. Not goin' that way, ye won't," the fellow called after him. "Half a quid, mayhap."

Thomas kept walking. The streets got shabbier and shabbier, and no hansom or trolley was to be found. He walked on. It was quite dark now. The streets were becoming quiet. Too quiet.

A fellow appeared out of nowhere, it seemed, and fell to walking beside Thomas. "You look a little lost, sir." Good. No Irish accent.

"I'm staying at the Palmer House, but I seem to have missed the street."

"Ah. That's way over on Monroe Street."

"Monroe! That's it. Can you direct me to Monroe?"

323

"I surely can. This way. The route is a little complicated, so I'll walk with you. I've nothing more important to do just now."

"Thank you. I'm grateful." Thomas admitted to himself that he had been feeling uneasy about walking alone in these strange streets at dark on the seedy side of town. He welcomed the company. "What is that nasty smell?"

"Stockyards. You know, sir, Chicago has the world's largest and best stockyards. You sound like you're from New York. All the beef you eat in New York came from these very stockyards."

The fellow turned suddenly and entered an alleyway, so Thomas followed. Apparently they were taking a shortcut. Good. Thomas was starting to get weary.

Thomas suddenly noticed a very large, burly man lurking in the shadows. The fellow stepped forward and stopped Thomas and his companion. He growled, "Quite a nifty suit y're wearing there. Cost a good ten or twelve dollars, I'll wager."

"Bet your pappy is rich," said Thomas's traveling companion. "Gimme your money."

Terror nearly froze him. "I-I-I'll call the police!"

"Not in this neighborhood."

The burly fellow hooked an arm around Thomas's neck and began to choke him as the other man yanked his jacket open. Buttons flew everywhere.

"Inside pocket here," the fellow crowed. "Look at the banknotes!"

The burly one whistled.

Thomas was going to beg them not to take it all, but the burly fellow threw him against the brick wall, stunning him. Cackling like magpies, the robbers ran off, their footsteps fading quickly.

His money was gone, just like that.

He lay still for a moment, trying to recover his wits. He couldn't think. Finally he sat up. What to do? He could find a phone and call his father, but no. He would die before he called his father. As lost and penniless as he was, dying was a possibility.

He should find a police officer. But what would the police do? Take his statement, probably, but his money and the robbers were long gone.

He should go to a hotel, any hotel, but he had no money for a room. He knew no one who lived here. Not in Chicago, not in Illinois, not in Indiana.

He stood up shakily. Nothing seemed broken. He staggered back out to the street. Deserted. Surely somewhere, something . . .

He began to walk, aimlessly headed nowhere. The stockyard stink grew stronger.

Thomas hung up the manure shovel and picked up his buttonless jacket. His job was done for the day, thank heaven, and it was payday. He hated mucking out the stockyard cattle pens, but he hated mucking these pigpens even more. He'd been reduced to doing this for over two weeks, because the stockyards here were the only place willing to hire him. Again he invited a curse upon the whole city of Chicago. He shrugged into his jacket and took his place in the payday line.

One by one, the laborers in this stockyard stepped up to the bursar, told him their name, and received their pay. They were all uneducated lowlifes. He would be rid of them soon, and gladly.

"Thomas Gould."

"Here ya go." The bursar checked off his name and handed him some bills. "Seven dollars."

Seven dollars. A week's pay for back-breaking, stinking work. Thomas looked at the blisters on his hands. Seven lousy dollars.

But his luck was about to change. He did still have one friend: Lionel Hibbing. He never had believed the lies his father told about Lionel. He knew the fellow well; Lionel was friendly, jovial, and well-dressed. Father was either lying or simply misled by those rubes in Blessing, ignorant people jealous of Lionel's wealth.

Thomas would go to Lionel in Hibbing, Minnesota. He had paid for Lionel's needs willingly once when his friend had forgotten his wallet in Jersey City. He had promised to pay Thomas back as soon as he retrieved his wallet. Lionel owed him.

Chapter 25

Thorliff laid his knife and fork across his plate. Saturday breakfasts at Ingeborg's were always a special treat. "Mor, that was mighty good. Thank you for inviting me."

"Yes," Louisa agreed. "It was delicious."

Inga looked at him. "Emmy and I were supposed to pick squash, but if we set type, we won't have time to do both."

Across the table Astrid said, "I know. You girls go set type. That's the more important job. I'll pick squash." She looked at Thorliff.

"And your pa will help me. We might as well shock the sweet corn while we're at it."

"Hey, wait a minute," Thorliff protested.

But Mor bobbed her head. "Good. Manny, let's you and I do the dishes today. Give Freda a rest."

Freda stood up. "I have to run down to the cheese house, but then I'll rest."

"And I want to help with dishes." Louisa stood up. "With all of us working, it will go quickly, and then we can all rest."

Thorliff was going to send Astrid a dirty look, but why? It was actually a pretty nice job, picking squash. It was even intellectual in a sense. You matched wits with vegetables that were trying to hide from you. The thought struck him as so funny, he voiced it out loud as he and Astrid grabbed their jackets and headed out to the garden, bringing all the baskets on the back porch. She laughed too.

They pawed among the vine leaves, pulling cornstalks as they worked. The leaves were dead now, and their bristly sandpaper texture was rough on his hands. He should have brought gloves. Thorliff found a nice little acorn squash hiding under the broad leaves of a pumpkin vine. "It's been a long time since I picked pumpkins and squash."

In the next row over, Astrid giggled. "Looks like some of the seeds got mixed up.

Here's a crookneck where it shouldn't be." She stood erect, arched her back, and looked at him smugly. Her belly seemed to be growing by the day.

Thorliff hated when she looked smug. It meant she knew something he didn't. "So what's on your mind? You never volunteer for garden work."

"Just wondering when you and Louisa are getting married, is all."

His brain screeched to a halt like a rusty locomotive. He forgot about squash. "Whatever gave you that idea? Besides, it wouldn't be ethical, the school board member marrying a teacher."

"Ethical or not, you're in love. No, I'll go further. You're obsessed with her. I've watched you when you're around her. So has Mor, and she agrees with me. Don't lie to yourself, you think about her all the time. And why not? She's smart and pretty. And you're not getting any younger, you know."

"You're nuts." He bent over and pawed viciously at the dying leaves. Here was a zucchini that had won the game of hide and seek. It had to be well over two feet long, yellowed on the bud end, and probably weeks past being edible. Its only purpose in life, to go on Mor's table and feed her family, had been killed by old age.

Old age. *Never too early to think about your own old age, Thorliff.*

They ran out of baskets. He hurried to the barn and brought back the last of the bushel baskets. The peck baskets were too small to hold much, but he brought them anyway.

Astrid had it nailed down like a cheese crate. It was getting so that Louisa was just about all he thought about. But marriage? For one thing, she would have to quit teaching, and they needed her. But then, perhaps if he pled her case before the board . . . He never understood why Blessing wouldn't allow married women to teach.

Thorliff caught himself up short. What were Louisa's feelings? He had no idea. Astrid probably already knew, but he'd be hanged if he'd ask her.

By dinnertime, they had gathered most of the squash. Thorliff's brain was still spinning. The others chattered and laughed while he pondered. Astrid and he went back out to the garden.

Astrid swiftly, from years of practice, braided corn leaves into a rope. They gathered half a dozen cornstalks and bound them into a triangular teepee shape using the rope. Then they started stacking other stalks against them all around. While Astrid finished one shock, Thorliff started another. The ten fat corn shocks they ended up with would help feed the cows during the winter. The cobs had all been dried and thrown into the corn cribs for feeding cattle, hogs, and chickens.

And look at the overflowing baskets lined up along the garden edge.

"Bumper crop this year," Astrid observed. "Almost enough to feed Manny."

Thorliff laughed. "Almost. He sure can pack it away."

"He works hard. Of course, Mor will give squash to Thelma, so you'll get to eat your share."

"Of course."

When they finally returned to the kitchen, the sun was low above the trees, the dinner dishes were all put away, and Louisa was just finishing sweeping the floor. Thorliff could hear his Rolly and Danny laughing in the other room.

Louisa smiled brightly. "You two sure got a lot done this afternoon. Ingeborg and I looked out at you now and then."

Astrid laughed. "Lots of practice. I'll gather up Danny and head home. Good night."

"Good night," Louisa said as she hung up the broom and dustpan and took off her apron.

Thorliff found himself saying, "It's getting

cool out, but the evening is so pretty. Would you like to go for a walk?"

"I would love it," Louisa answered, and she fetched her heavy cape. He held it for her and dropped it over her shoulders.

They ambled out the lane and up the street in silence, apparently at random.

She asked, "Have you any idea where we're going?"

"Nope. Maybe down to the river to watch the sun set. It does that most every evening, you know."

"So I've heard." Her giggle partnered with his smile as they set out.

Strolling beside her like this made his whole body tingle a little. He admitted to himself that Astrid and Mor were right—he was obsessed. Overwhelmed. Was this love? These were not the same feelings that had possessed him when he and Elizabeth were courting. They were, curiously, similar and yet different. But then, why should he expect them to be the same? He had been younger then. Did being older and wiser make a difference? Probably. Besides, this woman was not Elizabeth, she was Louisa. And like Elizabeth had, she had captured him completely. *Dear Lord God, what shall I do?*

Louisa was smiling. "I am so impressed with your mother. Here she is in her fifties, and she zips around like a twenty-year-old, constantly busy. And she has done so much good in her life. When someone needs something, or is ill, instantly she's there. She amazes me."

"Would you believe she has slowed down these last few years? She used to be the first one up every morning and the last one to blow out the lamp." He thought about this. "Looking back, I think I saw the change begin when Haakan, my stepfather, died. The two of them were one person, and his death hit her terribly hard. I think a little piece of her died with him."

"That is very sad." She too seemed thoughtful for a bit. "I so wish I could have a marriage like that, where the two are truly one."

So do I.

They reached the riverbank and just stood there awhile. The sun was half visible through the distant trees and half gone. The day was turning from pink to gold, the glorious colors splashing across a few thin clouds, dancing and sliding along the water's surface. The river was running low, but it always ran low this time of year.

"This is so beautiful," she said quietly. "Thank you for bringing me here."

She stood very close to him, so he wrapped

an arm across her shoulders and drew her in closer. She did not stiffen or try to move away.

He might destroy the quiet, lovely moment, but he had to speak. "Louisa, I care for you. I care about you more than I can say." That was true. And he was supposed to be a wordsmith.

She stiffened instantly and stepped aside. Her lovely face was twisted with emotion. "No! Please, not that!" She turned away, struggling to fight back the sob that shook her shoulders.

What was going on? All he'd said was . . . "Louisa, what's wrong? Why are you crying? Please tell me."

"I don't deserve you. I'm not worthy of you. Please go away!"

Worthy? What? He gripped her shoulders and turned her to face him. "Louisa, do you care about me?"

"Yes! Yes, I do. I care for you so very much. That's why . . . we can't . . . I won't . . . no!"

"What is going on? Tell me."

She shuddered a deep breath. "You're a magnificent man. You serve the community in many ways, and you have wonderful children, and your mother adores you. I am not worthy of all that." She was looking at his shoes.

He lifted her chin. "Louisa, look at me. What is this all about?"

She looked at him as tears streamed down her cheeks. "I was so afraid this would happen. Please . . . I love the children. The children in my class."

"What does that have to do with it?"

"If I tell you, I'll lose my job. Please, let it go. Just let it go."

He found himself yelling, "You will not lose your job." He made his voice drop back to normal. "I promise you will not lose your job. Tell me."

She looked briefly into his eyes, then focused on his throat. "It was a Friday night. We were going to be married the next day, in less than twenty-four hours. Johnny begged me to, uh, let him . . . you know. He said it was only a few hours and we'd be united for life, and . . . and I loved him so much. So we . . . did something we shouldn't have. And then the next morning, I was getting ready for the wedding, and my sister came to me and said Johnny had been . . ." She stopped, sobbed, sucked in air.

Thorliff waited.

After a few deep breaths, she continued, "Killed. He was dead. It was a freak accident. He and his cousin were milking a cantankerous cow. It took two of them, one to

335

hold her and one to milk. The cow kicked him right here." She laid her hand on Thorliff's breast at the bottom of his ribcage. "It killed him. A month later I found out I was pregnant."

Thorliff's heart went *thud*. No, his whole being, his whole body and soul went *thud*. "Keep talking."

"My sister was pregnant too. Then she lost her baby like she'd lost two others. She and her husband already had Ezekiel, but they wanted more children. So when I gave birth, we all said it was hers. Zeke and Mary call me Aunt Louisa. I'm Zeke's aunt and"—her voice broke—"and Mary's mother." She was weeping now, hiccuping sobs.

What could he do? His brain was mush. Well, he knew what he could do first. He pulled her in against himself and wrapped his arms tightly around her. She struggled only a moment, then melted against him, still sobbing. It gave him time to get his muddled thoughts together.

The sun was well gone now, the limpid blue sky at the horizon turning darker. They should start back.

"And now you'll hate me. And I deserve it." She turned her tortured face up to Thorliff, sucked in a sob, and grimaced. When she stepped back a little, he loosened his hug.

"We were so careful to keep the secret, and here I've told the man who writes a newspaper." She wagged her head. "And is head of the school board where I used to teach."

Already he had made a couple of decisions. "Your secret is safe, and you will still teach at the school."

She shuddered a sigh. "What are you going to do now? You can't unlearn the truth."

"Nothing has changed, and nothing will change for now."

"But, Mr. Bjorklund . . ."

"My name is Thorliff." He smiled at her. "And I love you."

The train made its usual steamy, screechy, jerky stop at the Grafton station. Louisa stood up. She still was not certain this was a good idea, but they were in it now. Thorliff stood as well, dragged their valises off the overhead rack, and ushered her down the aisle to the door.

She stepped out onto the platform with Thorliff right behind her. It wasn't raining, exactly, but the mist was heavy. She waved to the man standing beside a buggy near the station. "That's my brother-in-law. I'm happy to see he put the cover on the buggy."

She led the way to the buggy. "Donald

Ivarsen, this is Thorliff Bjorklund. Thorliff, my brother-in-law Donald Ivarsen."

Both gentlemen were grinning as they shook hands.

Donald whipped a fat cigar out of his coat pocket. A cigar? Donald didn't smoke! He handed it to Thorliff. "Brand-new son, born today."

Louisa clapped her hands over her cheeks. "The baby is here! When?"

"Probably when you were getting on the train." Donald was all grins.

"But he wasn't due for a couple weeks yet."

"Shows you how much the doctors know. Hop in."

He lifted the cover, slid the valises into the boot, and buckled it down again. Then they clambered up over the wheel and crowded into the buggy, barely fitting on the seat. Thorliff pocketed his new cigar. As far as Louisa knew, he didn't smoke either.

Donald clucked to the horse. "I've got some chores to get done yet tonight, even though it's getting dark. The baby messed up our schedule. So I'll go down to the barn, feed and milk and all, and be up to the house as soon as I can."

Thorliff clung to the side rail as the buggy bounced over a pothole. "I grew up farming. I'll help you get it done faster."

338

Louisa giggled. "Not too long ago, you picked squash."

"That I did. And shocked corn."

At the house, the men headed off to the barn and Louisa hurried inside.

"Susan?"

"In here" came a voice that wasn't Susan's.

Louisa strode to the spare room on the main floor.

Susan lay on the old four-poster, swathed in blankets, and at her shoulder lay a tiny bundle. "Oh, Louisa! You're here! Louisa, this is our midwife, Ellen."

They exchanged how-do-you-do's. Ellen said, "I'm so glad you're here. I didn't want her left alone, but I have to leave." With that, Ellen hastened out.

Louisa sat on the edge of the bed and gently lifted the tiny baby. "He's so tiny and perfect. I remember when Mary was this size."

"But only for a minute or two. She grew so fast."

"What is his name?"

"Heinrick Mayling Ivarsen."

Louisa looked at her sister. "I hope little Heinrick doesn't get the nickname Hank, like his grandfather did."

"We'll try not to. Your letter said your friend Thorliff was coming with you."

"He's here. He and Donald are finishing up in the barn." She put the baby down.

"Prop me up a little, please." Susan arched forward, and Louisa arranged pillows behind her. She dropped back against them. "That's better. Now we can talk. Who is this Thorliff? A beau?"

What should Louisa say? How much should she—? Wait. This was Susan, her sister and closest confidante. Louisa poured it all out, finishing with, "When we got back to the house, he repeated that my secret was safe. And he said he would like to meet Mary. Since you were close to term, I figured this would be a good weekend to come down."

Susan smiled. "And it turned out perfect."

"Perfect. You're obviously very tired. What shall I fix for our supper?"

"Donald says he'll bring the last ham when he comes up from the barn, and there are potatoes in the kitchen bin."

"Good." Louisa squeezed her hand. "You rest." She got up to leave the room.

"Louisa?" Susan's voice was dreamy. She lay staring at the ceiling. "I realize I'm getting way ahead of things, but let's say Thorliff proposed and you accepted. Would you take Mary with you to complete your family?"

Louisa's heart sank. The only honest answer she could give was "I don't know."

The next morning, after chores and breakfast, with Zeke entertaining Mary, Louisa refilled the coffee cups, set a plate of cookies in the center of the table, and took her chair. She looked to Thorliff, and at his nod, she began. "There's been so much going on that Thorliff said he wanted to come and meet you since we—since I . . ." She sucked in a deep breath and blinked, hoping to forestall the tears burning behind her eyes.

Thorliff stepped in. "Louisa told me her whole story and how much she loves you and wants us all to be a family."

Louisa nodded. "And to come right after your baby was born made it even more special."

"Speak of the angel," Susan muttered when the baby, swaddled in a warm blanket in the cradle at her feet, began to whimper. With her foot, she gently set the cradle to rocking.

Louisa swallowed. "I told him about Mary and how I am Auntie Louisa and you, my dear sister, are her mama." She looked at Donald. "And you are her papa. And two of the most loving and generous people I know."

Susan looked from her husband to Louisa. "I-I have to ask again. If you two are . . .

341

I mean . . . will you want to change that? To take Mary into your own family? I know this is rude, but I have been so afraid you would want to reclaim her."

Louisa slowly shook her head and reached for her sister's hand. "And I now have an answer for you. Deep in my heart, I would love to have her with me, but I cannot do that to her nor you. This is her home, and you are her parents." Tears spilled over and meandered down her cheeks. "And I love you all and am so grateful for what you have done for me. And Mary."

Susan nodded, wiped her eyes, and clung to Louisa's hand. "Thank you. Oh, thank you."

Both men cleared their throats. Donald nodded to Louisa. "Thank you. When you decided to come on such short notice, I feared the worst too."

"I just wanted to meet you and thank you for helping Louisa," Thorliff said. "As far as my family is concerned, she already has a place in our hearts. My mor wanted me to tell you that there is always room for you to come visit, but since we've always had milk cows, she understands how difficult it is to get away."

Zeke came to Susan's side. "Ma, tell Mary she can't throw the blocks." His voice said he was at the end of his rope.

"I will. How about you two come have cookies and milk with us?" Susan looked up to check with the others, who all nodded.

"I'll get her." Louisa stood.

Susan nodded. "Thanks."

With Zeke holding her hand, Louisa walked to the parlor. She picked up Mary and squeezed her to make her giggle. *Oh, child, your mother will have her hands full.* Back in the kitchen, she handed Mary to her pa and retook her seat. When she looked up, Donald held a glass of milk for his daughter to drink. His daughter who somehow already had cookie crumbs around her mouth and down her front. Louisa's heart ached, but she smiled.

The baby in the cradle went from whimpering to demanding. Susan stood and picked him up. "We'll be back in a while." She headed for the bedroom.

"Why don't you take a much-needed nap when he's done?" Louisa suggested.

"Thank you. I think I will."

On the train the next day, Louisa and Thorliff leaned against the back of the seat. "Thank you for choosing to do this."

Thorliff nodded. "Their relief was so evident. You are a wise and generous woman, Louisa." He took her hand. "And I love you more than I can say."

She felt like she was sinking into the blue sea that was his eyes. "Thank you." She paused and nodded with a sniff. "Thank you."

Chapter 26

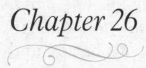

Dear Louisa,

All is well here, and Henry is such a good baby. His grandma thinks the sun rises and sets with this little one. Mrs. Ivarsen likes boy babies so much more than girl babies. It's sad, in a way. But she has been such a help. Mary calls her Momo and runs to greet her when she comes in the door.

We are invited to Grandma's house for Thanksgiving, so while I will prepare some things, I needn't do the entire dinner. You are welcome to go with us, but if you would rather stay in Blessing, we truly understand. I am so thrilled for the new life you are building there. And really, you are not terribly far away. It's

*just that we can never leave the live-
stock, but Donald says he will perhaps
ask his uncle to take over for a few days
if need be.*

*Oh, little Henry is reminding me that
he is hungry. So I will bid you good-bye
for now. Please write soon. Some good
news: We might be getting a telephone
and even electricity. We'll be coming out
of the Dark Ages.*

*I love you always,
Your sister Susan*

*Well, that answers my questions about
Thanksgiving without even having to ask them.*
Since Louisa had originally been planning to
spend the long weekend with her sister and
family, now she could answer Thorliff when
he asked. Again. He had been pretty insistent that she remain in Blessing. Did he have
something up his sleeve?

At least the newspaper came out the week
before the holiday, although he'd been mutter-
ing about a Thanksgiving special edition. His
staff—she, Inga, and Emmy—had pleaded
against it.

Louisa tucked the letter away in her
pocket and joined the others in the kitchen,
the general gathering place. She watched all

the busyness. This house was always busy. Just now they had swatches of fabric all over the dining table, sorting and cutting pieces.

"I thought Thorliff was coming out," she said. "He said he was."

"He's meeting first with John." Ingeborg turned from cutting out pieces of fabric on the table. "Do you need anything?"

"No. I just learned that my sister has un-invited me for Thanksgiving."

Inga clapped her hands. "Wonderful, then you'll be here all four days? No school, no newspaper to put out. We can play games, eat great food, and work on Christmas presents."

"Now, that sounds like plenty." Louisa picked up a cup and turned to fill it at the stove. "Anyone else?"

"No, thanks, but there are cookies in both cookie jars." Freda nodded toward the pantry.

"I'll get them." Inga bounced into the pantry and returned with a plate piled high with both ginger and sugar-sprinkled sour cream cookies. She served Louisa first and passed the plate.

"I can't eat a cookie without coffee."

Emmy handed Freda a steaming cup, and Inga poured one for Ingeborg.

"Please do not spill coffee on the fabric," Ingeborg warned.

The sound of boots scraping on the porch

announced Thorliff. "Brrr. That north wind is cold." He unwound his scarf and hung his hat, scarf, and coat on the tree by the door.

"How did you know we were eating cookies?" Inga asked.

"Observation. Because you always have cookies, and most of the time you're eating one." He crossed to rub his hands over the stove's heat. Taking a cup from the shelf on the back of the stove, he poured himself a cup of coffee and clasped both hands around it. "We got it sent out."

"What sent out?" Ingeborg placed the next cut-out piece of fabric on the growing pile.

"The letter to the state superintendent of schools." He caught Louisa's eye and smiled at her. "Hey, Inga, you think you could get your freezing father a cookie to go with his coffee?" Inga rolled her eyes and held out the plate for him. "Mor, how are you coming on those last stories you have to write?"

"Finished the writing, Louisa edited them, and they are in Emmy's pile to type."

"Thank you. I sure wish the others were as faithful as you. Did you write about those early years with Agnes and Joseph Baard? Their children were too young to remember the earliest days."

"Penny wasn't. She turned in several stories, including about when they drove in with the covered wagon. Agnes and I became best friends almost overnight. They were going to move on but decided to stay after a couple of days with us." Ingeborg paused. "God gave me a wonderful gift in Agnes. Losing both her and Metiz left big holes in my life, let alone my heart."

"After reading bits and pieces like this, I'm sure looking forward to reading the whole thing," Louisa commented.

"Pa, good news," Inga piped up. "Miss Louisa won't be going to her sister's for Thanksgiving."

"Really." His smile nearly blinded her.

Louisa shrugged. "I got uninvited, sort of. They are going to Donald's mother's house instead of the whole family coming to Susan's house. It takes the big burden off her shoulders."

"Good. You can see how we do Thanksgiving." The smile that made his eyes dance also made a shiver polka down her spine. She swallowed and nearly choked on a bite of cookie.

"We better get this table cleared and set for supper." Freda put her coffee cup in the dishpan. "Thorliff, you staying for supper?"

"Nope, sorry, I have a meeting tonight. Inga, it's a school night."

"I know." She went to retrieve her coat

and kissed Ingeborg on the cheek. "See you tomorrow."

As the two of them went out, David Gould entered. "Evening, everyone. Is the welcome mat still out?"

"For you, always." Emmy took his coat and hung it up. "Coffee's hot, if you would like some."

Freda smirked. "But if you would not like some, the coffee is hot anyway."

Emmy looked perplexed.

Louisa laughed. "Emmy, I see we ought to sit down and learn about dependent and independent clauses."

David headed for the hot coffee. "Thank you, I *would* like some. I saw the lights all on out at the barn, so I'm not too late. We don't have evenings anymore." He stepped out of the way as Emmy brought a stack of plates to the table. "I guess I'll take my paper in the other room."

Ingeborg lifted her stack of cut fabric. "Louisa, if you'd like to come, I can give you a lesson on the sewing machine."

Louisa looked to Freda, who shooed her on.

"What are you making?" Louisa asked as she followed Ingeborg to the sewing cabinet.

"Dresses for a couple of the girls up in the tribe. I double stack the fabric when I cut it, so this is really two dresses. Speeds things up." Since her sewing machine was all set up, Ingeborg pulled out the chair and sat. "Bring another chair over. This is so simple. I still have the treadle kind. I heard that they have new ones with a little electric motor so you don't use the treadle. Amazing." She snagged a piece of paper from her letter box. "I'll use this, as it's easier for you to see." She put the paper in place, lowered the foot, and pushed the treadle to start. With her feet rocking, the stitches showed up nice and even and easy to see. "Now you try it."

Louisa followed the instructions carefully, and sure enough, the stitches followed the way she moved the paper. "Kind of like dancing with your feet." She looked up to see David watching them rather than reading the paper.

"Would an electric machine be a big improvement?" he asked.

Ingeborg shrugged. "I have no idea. I've not looked at any of them, and this one works fine." She placed two pieces of fabric together, slid them under the foot, set it, and stitched from one end to another. Laying them open flat, she beckoned to Louisa. "See how tight the seam is? Much faster than hand sewing."

The thumping and clunking from the porch

clearly announced the milking crew cleaning their boots. They washed in the kitchen sink, then trooped to the table. Louisa and Ingeborg put their sewing aside to help serve.

Supper passed with the usual grace, the passing of food, Manny's teasing, and the food disappearing as if by magic. The camaraderie still amazed Louisa.

David, sitting on her other side, leaned closer. "Takes some getting used to, I know."

"It makes me feel sorry for my youngest brothers and sisters still at home. Even though my father remarried, I'm sure that mealtimes are no more pleasant now than when I was a child. One of my sisters wrote that the stepmother is pregnant, so there will be more babies." She shook her head. "Sad."

"Do you keep in touch with some of those siblings older than you?"

"Somewhat. Susan hears from them the most. We exchange Christmas cards or letters. I plan to write to my oldest brother, who was adamant that his little sister learn to play ball, and tell him how grateful I am."

David grinned. "You're a big hit with the school children and their families."

"Well, we won't be playing again until spring, I'm sure."

"You mean you don't want to go searching for the ball in the snow?"

She chuckled. "We could set up a way to practice batting inside if we didn't have to use the dining room for eating."

"You are determined."

She shrugged. "I love teaching, and I have a bright and willing bunch of students. It's a far cry from some of the others I've had."

"Inga speaks very highly of you."

"She is one sharp girl. Have you seen her set type?"

He nodded. "I hear you want to learn to type."

"I do. I would be more of a help to Thorliff with his newspaper, and I can see so many other ways to use it. For one thing, it is faster than handwriting if you are practiced at it, and, of course, it saves paper."

David looked at her oddly. "I grew up in a world of wealth. There was always paper. It was just there. You just showed me how valuable common things are if you need them and don't have them. And not everyone has them. Thank you for that important insight, Louisa. You are a blessing to me."

She didn't know what to say. So often she had fallen short in her father's eyes. Today, to a fine gentleman from her father's generation, she was a blessing.

Her heart sang. She was a blessing!

352

As Thanksgiving drew nearer, the weather grew worse, and Louisa thought about Thorliff even more. If only she had not told him her secret. However, they were more than good friends. She helped him when she could, and he kept on at his breakneck pace, trying to balance the paper and the construction. The men were working furiously to get the big addition to the machinery plant roughed in so they could work inside when the weather grew worse. She had never dreamed she would want to learn so much about building houses and barns. What fascinated her the most was the story of Blessing. She was able to read everything as she edited and rewrote what so many people sent in. She'd taken to sending thank-you notes to all who contributed, and to some she asked for more information, sending a list of questions.

Thorliff read one of those follow-up letters one night. "What a grand idea. Thank you. I never have time to do these extra things." He laid a hand on her shoulder, and she felt it zing clear down to her toes.

One day when she was sorting the mail, she saw a letter from the state superintendent of schools. Her heart thudded down to her ankles. What had Reverend Solberg and Thorliff written for, or about?

She finished editing a menu for the board-inghouse and laid it in Emmy's pile to type. While she'd started learning to type, she still made too many mistakes to work on some-thing like this. Emmy's fingers flew over the keys, like Inga's did when setting type. When Thorliff came in, they would begin the layout for the next paper. Inga was already typeset-ting the back pages. Many were the same since the last edition, so they were ready for her.

Gathering up the typed columns, Louisa began tacking them to the board, looking for both style and interest. Several columns were always on the same page and other things worked around them. The editorial page would be filled in with business ads. It wasn't routine yet for her, but the rhythm was now familiar.

"Sorry I'm late." Thorliff slammed the door behind him. "Thank you all for starting without me."

"There's hot coffee." Emmy pointed to the pot on the top of the heating stove.

"Bless Thelma. I never know how she senses when I am coming, but the coffee is usually waiting." He poured himself a cup and checked on each of their stations. "You started without me?" he asked Louisa, eyeing her burgeoning layout.

"I thought I'd try. Nothing is glued down."

Thorliff studied each page and nodded. "You could fill this space with the ad for the dental office."

"The ads for the mercantile and the grocery each take half a page, right?"

"Mm-hmm. What about these small spaces?"

"I didn't know what to do."

"Usually I slip in a question or a quote I've heard." The look he gave her made her swallow.

"You ever put jokes in?" she asked. "Or Bible verses?"

"In a newspaper?"

"What if we interview women of different nationalities, get their stories, and then include a couple of recipes from their homeland?"

Thorliff stared at her, nodding all the while.

She shrugged. "Other newspapers do things like that. The one in Fargo did. If you build pages, you can build readership. Unless you don't want people out of town reading your paper."

"Let me think on this. Go ahead and lay out those pages. We'll put 'Happy Thanksgiving' in those blank spaces this time. Inga can fill those in."

"How about next year, we ask groups of people—like a classroom, or employees from the machinery company—to make a list of all the things they are thankful for. Men, women, kids, some mixtures, like a family."

"It's a shame you didn't start here earlier," he said, smiling.

"Thank you. Oh, the mail is on your desk."

The clanging of the supper bell brought everything to a halt, and they headed to the house. Thorliff closed the door behind them all and caught Louisa around the waist. "Thank you," he whispered in her ear. "What a treasure to come back to the office and find you working there."

"You're welcome." She felt heat creeping up her neck. She leaned into him for just a moment, then drew away and hustled up the stairs. *Louisa Gutenberg, what are you thinking?*

"Miss Gutenberg!" Rolly leapt up from playing with the dog and ran to her. "Are you staying for supper?"

"I am." She reached down and shook his hand. "But I have to wash up."

"Me too."

Rolly soaped his hands and passed the bar to her. As she soaped up, she happened to glance toward Thorliff. He was grinning broadly. She and Rolly shared the towel for drying.

They took their places at the table, with Louisa beside Rolly, Inga and Emmy across from them, and Thorliff at the head of the table. Thorliff said grace, and conversation flowed as the dishes were passed around.

When they were done with supper, they hurried back out to the office and were finished by nine.

"A miracle," Thorliff said. "We can print tomorrow and not work half the night. Thank you all. I'll get the buggy."

"Why? We can walk it about as fast," Louisa offered.

"Then I'll walk you both home."

"Emmy's staying here tonight," Inga said. "Did you forget I asked you?"

"I did. Well, Miss Louisa, it's just us, then." He tucked her hand in the crook of his elbow and patted it as they stepped outside.

She lifted her face to watch the moon. "Now that the wind has died, it's lovely out here. Walking feels good."

He pulled an envelope from his pocket. "Here's your first salary from the paper."

"Thank you." The thought of buying presents for Zeke and Mary made her do a little skip.

"It's not much."

"It's more than I had."

When they reached the gate to the farm-house, he paused and wrapped her in a hug. "I've been wanting to do this all evening."

Louisa leaned against him. She'd not had a hug like this for so long. She rested her cheek against the scratchy wool of his coat. Hopefully there would be plenty more.

"Louisa, this isn't the way I wanted this to happen, but I love you and I want to marry you. Could you possibly feel the same?"

She tried to swallow her tears, but instead they leaked down her face.

"Did I offend you? Is something the matter?"

"With all you know about me, how can you ask that? I mean, ask me to marry you."

"Do you love me?"

"Yes, I do." There, she'd said it. "But . . ."

"But you don't want to lose your job."

She nodded. "I don't want to let down my students. Thorliff, I love what I do."

"But if you would not be sacrificing your job?"

"Then yes, I would be honored to marry you." She threw her arms around his neck and melted into his kiss. *Married. I could be married.*

"Let's just keep this a secret for now, all right?" he said when they pulled apart.

"All right. Your mother will figure it out, you know."

"I think she already has." He kissed the tip of her nose, opened the gate, and walked her up to the steps. "'Night."

She heard him whistling as she opened the door to the kitchen. What a night. What an amazing, wonderful night.

Chapter 27

So you agree, then?"

John Solberg nodded. "I've always thought that was a stupid rule anyway. As if a woman loses her ability to teach when she gets married." He shook his head. "I remember when Kaaren was teaching and brought her baby to the classroom. He just slept in a basket near the stove. But back then we were so grateful to be able to have a school at all, let alone a small school teaching signing to deaf children and adults. Several of those early students work for the deaf school now."

"Miss Gutenberg is an excellent teacher, and her students love her."

"As does the president of the school board."

Thorliff sheepishly shifted his weight. "That obvious?"

John leaned forward. "My biggest concern is what has happened to her. What secret is she carrying?"

"I know what it is. She told me one evening."

"Do you want to talk about it?"

"We will both come to you, if you are willing."

"Thorliff Bjorklund, you know I love you like my own brother or son. If there is any way I can help you, I will."

"I have asked her to marry me, with the thought that we would wait until school was out. But since that letter gives us the go-ahead, I will announce our wedding at Thanksgiving, and we will be married sometime before Christmas. In my mind, the sooner the better." He smiled sadly. "I'm not getting any younger, you know."

"What about what she wants?"

Thorliff grinned. "Guess I better ask, eh?" He paused. "What if she wants a big wedding?"

Solberg shrugged. "From the sounds of it, she's not in touch with most of her family except her sister in Grafton." John glanced up at the clock. "School's about out. Tell her to come talk with me."

"Thank you."

"You have no idea how happy this makes me." They shook hands.

Thorliff strolled down to wait outside Louisa's classroom door. The bell rang, and he could hear kids putting their things away in all the classrooms. Children poured into the hallway, many of them greeting him as they walked past.

He stepped into Louisa's classroom to find her talking to one of her students. Inga soon came in to wipe off the blackboards, and one of the boys was taking the erasers out to clean.

"Reverend Solberg would like to talk with you," he said gravely after their greeting.

She paused to stare at him, then shrugged and left the room.

"Hi, Pa," Inga said. "Just think—two more days until Thanksgiving, and we get Friday off too."

"I know. Where's Emmy?"

Inga shrugged. "She said she'd be late."

Thorliff fetched the broom and started sweeping, wishing he were a mouse in the corner, listening to the conversation happening in John's office.

He paused when Louisa returned to the

room. Her smile brought a lump into his throat.

"You knew, didn't you?" she said.

Thorliff nodded. "But it was his job to tell you."

Inga looked from one beaming face to the other. "Something's going on."

"We'll talk about it later," Thorliff said. "Let's get this room cleaned up and head on home."

Emmy caught up with them as they were going out the door. "Are we riding or walking?"

"I brought the cart." They loaded in, and he set the horse to a trot to Ingeborg's. The cart bumped and jerked over the frozen ruts, throwing the riders into one another. Giggles erupted from the two girls, but Thorliff didn't slow until they reached the gate.

Thorliff let the girls go ahead and turned to Louisa. "Since you can keep teaching, I think we should have the wedding between Thanksgiving and Christmas. I know that's not much time, but is there any reason to wait?"

Louisa thought a moment. "I doubt my sister could come anyway. I would like for her to stand up with me, but . . . ." She smiled up at him. "Just not the same weekend the paper comes out."

Thorliff broke out in laughter. "Oh, my so-very-practical Louisa. That I promise. I'd even skip an edition or postpone one, if that would help."

"My, my, our wedding must be rather important to you."

"I have no words to describe it." The laughter had left his face and coiled around his heart.

"You don't need words. The love is beaming from your face." She reached up and kissed him. "Let's go tell the others."

Louisa waited by the door while Thorliff shut it behind them.

"We have an announcement to make." Thorliff paused, waiting for the room to quiet. "I asked Louisa to marry me, and she said yes. We have a special dispensation from the state superintendent that Louisa can marry and keep teaching."

Emmy and Inga stared at them and then at each other. Emmy squealed. "Inga, you'll have a mother again!" The two girls hugged. Inga's grin nearly split her face.

"I guess that means you approve?" Thorliff asked her.

"Does Rolly know yet?"

"No, you are the first we've told."

Inga looked at Louisa. "What will I call you at school?"

Louisa shrugged and looked up at Thorliff, who also shrugged. "I guess you will call me Mrs. Bjorklund, like the others."

"Mrs. Bjorklund. That has a good sound to it." Thorliff smiled at his daughter.

"But outside of class, Rolly and I can call you Ma?" The look on Inga's face socked Thorliff right in the midsection. "As soon as you're married, that is."

Louisa cupped Inga's face in her hands. "Yes, Inga, you can call me Ma, and I will be thrilled clear to my bones." She pulled Inga into a hug. "I have wanted to hug you ever since I met you," she whispered in his daughter's ear.

"And Rolly too?"

"Oh yes, and Rolly too."

Inga was still beaming. "This will make Thelma so happy. I heard her tell Pa that he needed to find a wife."

Thorliff rolled his eyes and caught his mor's smiling look. Snagging Louisa around the waist, he moved her over to Ingeborg. "I hope you are happy."

"Oh yes, the good Lord bless and keep you both. Louisa, welcome to our family. The wedding will only make it official. Thank you, Lord, another prayer answered."

Inga took the calendar off the wall and laid it on the table. "So, can we set a date?"

Thorliff tried to cough politely but took one look at his mor and broke out in a roar of laughter. "Leave it to Inga." They all leaned over the calendar, and Thorliff noted when the paper was due out. "Louisa asked that we not have the wedding on a weekend when the paper comes out. That leaves Sunday, December 14. Comments, anyone?" He sent Louisa a questioning look.

"Fine with me." Louisa blinked a couple of times but smiled around the tears.

"Mor?"

"After church? Dinner here?"

"How will we celebrate? We probably can't play baseball then," Inga pointed out. "No kittens in the barn for the little ones, no pony rides. Guess we'll just have to . . ." She stopped and turned to Thorliff. "What will we do after dinner?"

Thorliff shrugged. "If there is snow, we could have a snowball fight."

"On your wedding day?" Freda shook her head. "We'll have dinner and probably open presents, and then most of the people will go back to their houses because it gets dark so early, and I think Inga and Rolly and Thelma should spend the night here, and then it is Monday morning as usual. But Louisa will not be here for breakfast."

"And since tomorrow is school and a

regular workday, what if we get together on Friday after Thanksgiving and plan the wedding? We'll have a little over two weeks," Ingeborg suggested.

Louisa nodded. "Are there any holly bushes around here? Where do you get your Christmas trees?"

"From over on the Minnesota side, but up out of the Red River Valley," Thorliff answered. "Why?"

"For decorating the church."

He nodded in understanding. "We usually go and bring back a wagon or sledge, depending on the snow level, full of trees and greenery. Sometimes snowberries and bittersweet. The last few years, we've taken several wagons. There's a farmer over there now who has planted Christmas trees. We used to have to tramp through the woods to find and cut a tree."

"The church has big red or white bows for the ends of the pews," Ingeborg added.

The rest of them chimed in with other decorating ideas. Thorliff was always amazed at how quickly and efficiently women planned social events, including a wedding. It would have taken him weeks.

"Yes, but right now we have a crew to feed," Freda reminded them. "They'll be here shortly. Girls, get the table set."

And the bride-to-be pitched in with the others to get out the flatware for the table.

Thanksgiving started with putting two stuffed geese—Andrew had shot them out in the cornfields—in the oven, and then everyone trekked off to church. By the end of the special holiday service, it seemed everyone had heard of the coming wedding and made sure to congratulate both Thorliff and Louisa.

"I should have just announced it from the pulpit and made it easier on everyone," John said as he greeted them at the door after the service. "The news of the day. We are all overjoyed."

"Thank you. We would like an appointment with you before then," Thorliff said.

"Of course. How about this Saturday afternoon?"

They both nodded. "One o'clock?" Thorliff asked.

With Astrid's, Andrew's, and Thorliff's families all present, the house felt stuffed as full as the geese that were now resting on the back of the stove. Each family brought part of the meal, Thorliff carved the meat, Freda made the gravy, and everyone found a seat at one of the three tables. Emmy and Inga took care of the table with the smaller cousins. They went around all the tables, with each person saying something they were thankful for.

"Your turn, Rolly. What are you thankful for?" Inga asked him.

"Food and pie." He grinned at his big sister. "Now you."

"I'm thankful you and I are going to have a mother again."

Thorliff took Louisa's hand under the table. A tear trembled on her eyelashes before slipping down her cheek. "Soon," he whispered in her ear. "Soon."

Saturday afternoon, they met with John Solberg at his home office, since the church was not heated until Sunday morning.

"I'll put the coffee pot on," Mary Martha called.

They sat down, and John pulled his chair in to form a triangle. He held out his hands. "Let's pray first. Lord, bless this meeting, and thank you for being right here with us. We ask your guidance and thank you for your mercy and grace. Heal our hurts and deepen our love. In Jesus' name, amen." He cleared his throat. "I have a prepared discussion for most who come for pre-wedding counsel, but first I think we should start with you, Louisa. How can I help you?"

"I-I need to tell you my history."

"All right."

"I had a baby out of wedlock."

"I see."

Stumbling and sniffing, she told him all that had happened and where Mary was now. "I told Thorliff all this so that he would know why he could not marry me and why I would lose my teaching position."

"Do you love Thorliff?" John asked.

She nodded and used a tightly wound handkerchief to wipe away her tears.

"And he loves you?" John looked to Thorliff.

"No matter what," he answered.

"And now that the superintendent has sent us his permission, you are planning to marry."

They both nodded.

"So . . . ?" John raised his eyebrows.

"So, I am not worthy." Louisa struggled over the words. "What I did was against God's ways. And . . ."

"And do you know that God has forgiven you?"

"How can He forgive something so bad? My father said I would always be a sinner."

"Ah, my dear, when Jesus died on that cross, it was for everyone for all time. Did you confess your sin?"

She nodded and blinked. "I cried and pleaded, but I still feel unworthy."

"Let me give you one of my favorite verses. 'If we confess our sins, He,' meaning God our Father, 'is faithful and just to forgive us our sins, and to cleanse us from all unrighteousness.' So often Jesus said to people, 'Your sins are forgiven.' And Louisa, yours are too. Now, you confess, tell Him your sin."

"Jesus, Father in heaven, I gave in to temptation with my fiancé, and he died and I had a baby, and now I have given her to my sister who loves her like I do, so that I could teach school. I've been living a lie."

John placed one hand on her head and the other on her folded hands. "Louisa Gutenberg, I now declare to you the Father's forgiveness for all your sins. He has washed you clean and white as snow. You are forgiven. You are free."

"I am forgiven," she whispered. "No matter what my earthly father says, my heavenly Father said so."

"Do you believe it?" John asked.

"I do."

"What are you going to do the next time that voice inside you says you aren't worthy of love?"

Louisa let out a long-held breath. "I am going to tell that voice that I am forgiven because Jesus said so. So get away, I don't believe you anymore."

"The closer we walk with Jesus, through His word and the Holy Spirit, the more we can believe His word and make it ours."

"Now, about the baby," Thorliff said.

Louisa sniffled. "I would love to have her, and Thorliff agreed, but my sister Susan and brother-in-law, Donald, took her in when she was born, and Susan nursed her, and Mary is their daughter. I agreed and, Reverend Solberg, as much as it hurts my heart, I love her too much to drag her away from her home and her family. I-I will always be her auntie Louisa."

"And now I am her uncle Thorliff, or will be after the wedding. And as far as I'm concerned, all this can now be put behind us as we begin a new life together."

"It takes great courage to love enough to let go. Were there legal papers drawn up?" John asked.

Louisa shook her head. "Do we need to do that?"

"Let me look into it and get back to you. Not as far as I'm concerned. Just think, Rolly and Inga will have three new cousins."

Louisa nodded. "Thank you, Reverend Solberg."

"And now I have something for you." He pulled an embroidered and framed picture from his desk and held it out. It said, *Do unto others as you would have them do unto you.* "If you live by this rule, your marriage will grow stronger all the time." He turned to Thorliff. "And remember what Paul said: to love your wife as Jesus loves and died for our sins. Love your wife as Christ loved the church. Keep that in mind for sometime when you get really angry at her, for you will, because you are human." He smiled at each one of them. "And remember, His Word is always the answer. Any questions?"

"Not at this point, but thank you." The three of them stood, and Thorliff reached out to hug John. "Thank you." He stumbled over the words and sniffed. "You've seen me through a lot. You and Mor."

"The Lord bless and keep you both. And so it is to be December the fourteenth, right after church."

"Cake and coffee downstairs afterward."

"Good. Good. You can stay for coffee, can't you? My wife will be so thrilled to welcome you into the family, Louisa."

"Thank you." She blinked again. "I'm free."

Sunday, December fourteenth, dawned clear and cold, the rising sun glittering on the snow-studded fields, glinting like diamonds. It had warmed to above freezing by the time the bells in the church steeple called the people of Blessing in to worship.

In the announcements before the service began, Reverend Solberg invited the congregation to the wedding following the service and to enjoy the wedding cake and coffee served afterward.

Louisa, wearing the lovely blue silk dress that Ingeborg had worn when she married Haakan, sat between Ingeborg and David Gould and couldn't quit shaking. *This is my wedding day. I am free.*

Thorliff, wearing a dark suit with a blue silk tie, sat between his brother, Andrew, and his sister, Astrid. *They are so close, these brothers and sister*, Louisa thought.

After the benediction, no one moved. The time had come.

Reverend Solberg walked to the center of the altar, turned to face the congregation, and opened the book he carried. "Dearly beloved, we are now gathered here to witness the marriage of Thorliff Bjorklund"—he nodded to Thorliff, who stood with Andrew and moved up the aisle to stand to the reverend's right—"and Louisa Gutenberg." He nodded to her, and Astrid moved first, then Louisa stepped into the aisle and looked at Thorliff. She joined Astrid and handed her new sister-in-law the spray of pine and winter-berries with a white bow and streamers.

Louisa wished her sister were here. She even wished, in a way, that her father were here. Most of all, she wished her father could have talked to John about her freedom.

"Who gives this woman to this man?"

The entire congregation said, "We do."

"Then let us begin with prayer. Heavenly Father, you made the gift of a woman from the rib of a man and taught them about love. And the sacred gift of marriage, we here celebrate. Bless this couple and all the couples and the families here, that we may all learn to love each other more deeply, always learning from you what perfect love is. We rejoice in your name, amen."

Sacred gift. Louisa had not thought of it that way before.

"Lars, would you please read the love chapter? First Corinthians thirteen."

As Lars read, his baritone voice resonating, Jonathan Gould softly played the organ, the music and the words floating around the room.

As they said their vows, Thorliff and Louisa looked into each other's eyes, and there was no doubt in her mind that they both meant every word.

John nodded to Inga. Obviously she had

been coached beforehand, because she and Rolly, hand in hand, came forward to join the couple, standing shyly between them. Louisa's heart was bubbling over; it was the only way she could describe it. She pulled Inga tightly to her side.

"I now pronounce you husband and wife, and family of Inga and Roald. Thorliff, if you can manage it, you may kiss your bride."

"I'll manage."

Louisa laughed with everyone else. Thorliff stepped in a bit closer and, leaning over Rolly and Inga, wrapped an arm around Louisa's shoulders and kissed his bride. What a wonderful kiss it was, not a token peck. Rolly hugged Louisa around the waist, so she leaned down, and he kissed her cheek. "I have a ma!"

John raised his arms. "Please rise. And now may the Lord bless us and keep us, may His face shine upon us and give us His peace. In the name of the Father and of the Son and of the Holy Spirit, amen."

The organ broke into the postlude, and the congregation swarmed in close around the new family, everyone laughing and hugging and congratulating.

Louisa heard someone say, "This is the best wedding I've ever been to."

They all moved downstairs, enjoyed the

coffee or fruit punch and the cake, and the newlyweds were congratulated one more time before the people headed home on this glistening December day.

"Shall we go, Mrs. Bjorklund?" Thorliff asked, dropping her coat over her shoulders. "You look gorgeous in that dress," he whispered in her ear.

"We shall." She slipped her arms into the sleeves. "And you are one handsome man." She tucked her arm through his. And stopped. "Do you know, Thorliff, ever since I learned I was pregnant, I have been in chains. But now I'm forgiven. The chains have fallen away. I am truly free." Her teary eyes bubbled over like her heart. "And now I am Mrs. Bjorklund."

Chapter 28

Peace. Dinner was over, and for a few moments, Ingeborg's house was quiet. She was in her rocker, and David, in the big armchair, sat in front of her fireplace, the logs crackling, and sipped his coffee. It was always a pleasure, simply watching him. Why could she not say yes to him and make everybody happy? Because she would lose her lifestyle here, would live in his house rather than this one with all its comforting memories, and most of all, his children would be waiting to cash in on the Bjorklund holdings.

She asked, "Have you heard anything about Thomas?"

"No. I hired detectives from the Pinkerton agency to find some trace of him. If they can't find him, he can't be found. I have no idea whether he's alive or dead."

Her heart wrenched. To lose one of her children that way . . . She'd best change the subject, or she'd get teary-eyed. "Christmas is only a few days off. Are you going to New York?"

David shook his head. "All those holiday parties and dinners that I have both given and gone to . . . I can't even abide the thought of them."

"But your grandchildren?"

"I've sent plenty of money for their parents to purchase the desired gifts that will say, 'With love from Grandfather Gould.' I will receive the dutiful thank-you letters, usually before the New Year—that is the polite way, you know. I will not miss the noisy open house we always had on Christmas Day, with mistletoe over the entryway. Or the five-day trip to Vermont for skiing, where the parents and the older children go out on the slopes, and nannies tend the little ones. Always that division, those who do and those who aren't old enough." He heaved a sigh. "Ingeborg, they won't miss me, and I won't miss them."

"I'm sorry."

"For what? You have nothing to apologize for."

Ingeborg shrugged. "I'm not apologizing for anything. I'm just sorry. If your Christmas is like that, it's not really celebrating the birth of Jesus."

"No, it isn't. True, there are all the rituals and formalities proper people must do. Church on Christmas Eve with a midnight service, but get it over with quickly, because everyone wants to go home. That was the one service of the year that was memorable, although there was quite a bit of ritual activity during Easter week too." He paused. "The tree in the parlor was huge. Nothing like the one in Rockefeller Square, but impressive." He looked directly at her. "This year I want to spend the holiday with you, your family, and Jonathan and his family. By the way, he agrees with me about Christmas in New York City."

"Grace and Jonathan usually go to Kaaren's

for Christmas. We have a Christmas Eve service at our church, with the children's program and then a candlelight service. Jonathan plays the organ. Linnea, Penny's daughter, learned to play from Elizabeth before she died, so now she is on the piano, and Joshua Landsverk and Johnny Solberg play their guitars. Lars will probably play the fiddle too. Christmas Day after dinner, we all go out and visit the other houses."

"If everyone goes out, who's left to visit?"

"Some choose to stay home, like Kaaren and me, and some of the older folk do. It works out. So many years I have spent at the hospital, helping and praying there. Now we have enough doctors and nurses, so we only need to be on call."

"You and John are always on call." His smile made her warm inside.

"David, being called to pray for someone sick or injured is one of my greatest joys. Our God is always so faithful. We've had more than one baby born on Christmas Eve or Day." She leaned forward. "I cannot begin to number all our Christmas miracles."

"That is why I want to stay here. Something beautiful will happen, and I will be with people I love."

"And who love you."

He nodded. "That too."

"Sometimes in years past, we had a real baby in the manger for the program, but this year I can't think of any woman who has a newborn. Astrid is due later in January."

Ingeborg stood up, fetched the coffeepot, and refilled both their mugs. It felt right on a cold December day. It was snowing outside, but not blizzard conditions. Blizzards always frightened her, ever since Thorliff's father died in one. That was . . . oh my. Over thirty years ago now.

She sat down again and watched David. He was obviously struggling in some way. "What is it, David?"

"Thomas." David slowly shook his head. "How that man—no, that wayward boy—could do something like this to his family is beyond me. His wife, Bernice, promised me the last time I spoke with her that she would let me know if and when she heard from him. When I talked with his sister Lillian, she was so angry at her brother, she could hardly talk coherently about it. Lillian has always looked up to Thomas and tried to copy what he did. And I had such grand plans for him." He shook his head. "Not now."

"Have you been praying for him?"

The question fell into the quiet of the room with a thud.

"Once in a while. I had to get over the disgust first. Maybe that's part of why I do not want to go back to New York. Although I will have to be at the board meeting in January." He looked at her. "You've been praying for him?"

She nodded slowly. "Several of us have been."

"You don't know him."

"Ah, but I know his father and his brother, and I love them. So it makes sense to pray for the rest of the family as well."

"But they don't even like you."

"Jesus said to pray for those who spitefully use you." She could see he was growing disturbed, restless, perhaps angry.

"When John preached on that, I wanted to argue with him, but how do you argue with a direct command from Jesus? So it was easiest just to ignore it. I never dreamed then that I would be in this position now. And now I can't do it." He pushed to his feet to stride about the room. He spun back to glare at her. "Sometimes God asks too much."

Ingeborg slowly rocked her chair, the rhythm creaking softly. The quiet stretched. "But then look at how much He gave."

David stared at her. He grabbed his coat from the rack by the door and strode out, pulling the door shut and letting the screen door slam behind him. He stomped down the steps, and she waited for the slam of the gate.

Lord God, keep him safe as he walks and works this off. Please speak so he can hear you and come closer to understanding how much you love him. And his family too. Thank you for keeping Thomas in your sight, even though no one else knows where and how he is. Keep watch over his family, and please show me how to help.

When the telephone sounded with her pattern of rings, she rose and padded to the kitchen. "Hello?"

It was David. "I'm so sorry, Ingeborg, but don't worry about me. I went home. I'm not fit company right now."

She could hear the tears in his voice. *Oh, my dear man, wrestling with God is never easy.* "Remember, joy comes with the morning, even after the blackest of nights. I love you, David Gould, and God loves you far beyond how much any of the rest of us do."

"Bless you, good night."

She hung the earpiece back on the prongs, shut off the lights, and made her way to her bedroom. Moonlight made bright squares on the floor, giving her enough light to get ready for bed and crawl between the sheets. Pretty soon it would be cold enough for heating rocks to warm the bed. She said her prayers and, as always, closed with the Lord's prayer.

The cat left her box behind the kitchen stove and jumped up on Ingeborg's bed.

She padded up to sniff Ingeborg's hair, now braided for the night, walked back down, and curled up at her feet. Even the purr felt warming.

David gave his present to everyone early: electric lights for the Christmas trees, including the one at the church. With the threat of fire from candles no longer an issue, Christmas trees could be seen through windows as people passed by, bringing even more delight. Probably the tree at the hospital brought more joy than any of the others.

When the snow started falling the morning of the twenty-fourth, memories of blizzards made everyone a bit anxious, but softly falling snow only created more beauty, and when it cleared to a star-studded sky, with the biggest one in the east, people arrived at church in awe. The music swelled, the carols lifted in praise, and even the little children felt the glory.

Ingeborg let the tears run down her face. With David by her side and her children and their children all around her, she rejoiced and, like Mary, pondered the meaning of it all in her heart.

Carl played Joseph in the pageant, and Inga was Mary, and as always, one of the angel's wings fell off and she went running to her ma. The sheep tried to get away from a shepherd, and Carl saved the day. He was used to handling sheep and completed the pageant with the wayward ewe firmly locked between his knees.

After the program and the carol singing, every child received a present, putting stars in some of the children's eyes.

Back at the farmhouse, the piles of presents around the tree grew. Ingeborg rocked beside the fireplace as David sprawled in the armchair.

Rolly stood in front of the tree with Inga. "Some people open presents on Christmas Eve, did you know that?"

Inga nodded. "So I've heard." She glanced at Ingeborg, smiling.

"We could too." He waited, then drooped. "But we have to wait until morning, huh?"

"That's right. Not until morning."

He perked up. "If we go to sleep soon, maybe morning will come sooner."

"Maybe. At least it will seem that way." Inga pulled him in close against her.

"I'm glad I get to stay here at Gramma's tonight." He leaned his head against his sister's arm.

"Why?" she asked.

"It's closer to the presents."

From the kitchen, Thorliff called, "We're

going home now, Rolly. You sure you want to stay here?"

Rolly nodded.

Thorliff came into the parlor, Louisa following, and gave Rolly a hug. "See you in the morning."

"G'night, Pa." Rolly hugged Louisa's waist. "G'night, Ma."

"Good night." Louisa hugged him back. She hugged Inga too. "Thank you."

"For what?"

"For helping this become the most special Christmas of my life."

"Ours too," Inga whispered back.

Ingeborg's heart swelled with happiness watching Thorliff and Louisa and their children.

"Come on, David, we'll give you a ride," Thorliff said.

"Thank you, although it would be a beautiful walk." David got up and reached for his heavy coat.

"Right, beautiful and cold. The temperature is dropping by the minute."

"Tomorrow will be a beautiful sleigh day." Ingeborg closed the door behind them. "Good night, everyone. Chores come first, and then Christmas breakfast."

Rolly slept on a pallet in the girls' room, buried in quilts, and in the early morning, they managed to slip out of the room and leave him sleeping. They swallowed their giggles until they reached the bottom of the stairs.

"Merry Christmas, Grandma and Freda," they chorused.

"It already smells good down here," Inga said.

"Merry Christmas!" Ingeborg returned. She thought a moment. "Let me help with chores this morning. It will go faster." She grabbed her sheepskin coat off the peg.

They bundled up, and out the door they went. Only a faint lighting in the east announced that the day would soon dawn and bring the white world alive with sparkles on trees and drifts, fence caps and rails. Manny was chopping the ice off the cattle tanks so the cows could drink after milking and return to the barn for their hay. Hand watering all the cows and horses took a lot more time once the cold set in.

"Merry Christmas," they called as they headed for the chicken house.

"You want to take a turn chopping tonight?" Manny called as he headed for the milking parlor.

Inga giggled. "No, thanks."

They stopped at the corncrib to pull out a

dozen cobs. With all the used straw bedding banking the walls of the chicken house, it was warm when they stepped inside. Clicking on the overhead light, they rubbed the cobs against each other, rasping off the kernels. The corn scattered thickly across the floor. They filled the feeders with mash and checked the nest boxes, just in case someone laid late or really early.

"We'll need plenty of milk and buttermilk," Ingeborg said, so they stopped at the well house, skimmed the pans for cream, and returned to the house.

"Good thing you brought the buttermilk." Freda waved a wooden spoon. "The pancake batter is waiting for it."

"Pigs in blankets?" Inga asked hopefully.

"As Manny says, pigs in blankets means Christmas." Freda brought a rope of small sausages in from the pantry and cut them apart into the pan.

"Is it Christmas yet?" Rolly asked, entering the kitchen. He rubbed his eyes.

"It sure is." Ingeborg hung up her coat and crossed to wash at the sink.

"You done with chores?" he asked.

"We are."

"Did they give the cats milk?" He snuggled against Ingeborg, not yet fully awake, obviously.

"I'm sure they did."

"Is Pa coming for breakfast?"

"I think they intend to eat at home."

Freda looked at Rolly, then at Inga. "So many questions. We'll handle breakfast if you like." She winked at Ingeborg.

Ingeborg took the hint and herded Rolly into the front room by the fireplace. She was happy to see that Freda had built the fire up again. It crackled cheerfully. "You're too big now for this, but let's do it anyway."

She settled back in her rocker and pulled Rolly into her lap.

He curled up, snuggling, and watched the fire. "We'll open presents soon, right?"

"Like always. First your father will read the Christmas story."

"You've already heard it lots of times, huh, Gramma?"

"And I love to hear it again."

The men came thumping and tumbling in, brushing the snow off their boots. Rolly joyfully yelled "Breakfast!" and ran to the table. Manny said a rather rapid prayer of thanks for all the good food, and the platters of sausages-rolled-up-in-pancakes passed from hand to hand, the big bowl of apple-sauce following right behind. Emmy poured coffee all around and started another pot.

As the platters came by, Rolly asked, "How come we only get these on Christmas?"

388

"Good question!" Manny grinned. "I think we oughta get these at least once a month."

"We'd run out of sausage." Freda took an extra one.

"This place never runs out of anything." Manny took an extra as well.

An hour later, with everyone helping, the kitchen was put back to rights, the second ham was in the oven, and the table was set for guests. Platters held slices of *julekake* and apple bread, *fattigman*, *krumkake*, *sandbakkelse*, peppernuts, frosted sour cream cookies, and a whole platter of *lefse* rolled with butter, cinnamon, and sugar.

Bells announced the arrival of the first sleigh.

Rolly ran to the window and announced, "Pa and Ma. Thelma and Mr. Gould." He ran to the door and leaped into his pa's arms when they came in. "We waited for you."

"I'm sure you did." Thorliff gave him an extra squeeze. "Merry Christmas, everyone. *Gladlige Jul.*"

More bells out front announced Andrew and his family, and finally Astrid and hers. When all was brought in, the children sat on the floor and the adults in chairs, filling the parlor and part of the kitchen. The adults smiled happily and nodded as the Christmas

389

story was retold, and the children squirmed as if they had ants in their pants, to quote Freda.

Rolly announced, "Finally!" as Inga and Emmy started reading off the names on the packages and Carl delivered them. Emmy had made Danny a teddy bear out of rabbit skins that he never put down. Ingeborg had knitted David a natural fleece-colored cable knit sweater that he pulled on and never took off. Manny had carved a little lady wren that Ingeborg kept in her lap, stroking now and then. Andrew had made Carl a baseball mitt out of a tanned cowhide and used the rest to make Thorliff a leather apron for printing.

When all the packages under and on the tree had been opened, people started to gather their things and get up, but David and Thorliff held up their hands.

"One more thing." They both rose, grabbed their jackets off the coat tree, and hurried out the back door.

Ingeborg looked to some of the others, but everyone shrugged. An *ouch* came from the back porch. David called, "Ingeborg, cover your eyes and no peeking."

Carl got behind her rocker and held his hands over her eyes. "She can't see now," he called.

"Don't smother her, Carl," Andrew cautioned his son.

Someone held the kitchen door open. Ingeborg could feel the rush of cold air, and she heard the shuffling feet of two men. What was going on?

"Okay, Mor, you can open your eyes."

Carl giggled as he stepped back. Ingeborg opened her eyes and saw Thorliff and David flanking a large, bulky object covered in a quilt.

"Ready? One . . ." Everyone joined in the counting. "Two. Three!"

They whipped off the quilt covering.

Ingeborg stared from David to Thorliff and back.

Thorliff raised both hands. "Not me. I just helped get it in here. That man, he made this for you in Lars's woodshop." He pointed at David.

A roomy rocking chair.

"You made that?" She clasped her hands under her chin.

David grinned. "I figured you needed a rocker at my house too. That Lars is an admirable teacher. Kaaren made the cushions. I forget what she called them."

Tears streamed down Ingeborg's face, and her smile wobbled. "It's beautiful." David gestured to her, and she rose and sat in her new chair. "It's comfortable too." Stroking the smooth arms with her hands, she tipped her head to rest against the back. "Thank you." Even her eyes smiled. "A couple of years ago, you didn't know how to wield a hammer."

"But the fine men of Blessing taught me building skills, and Mr. Stauffer taught me how to finish wood in my house, so when I asked Lars to help me do this, he didn't have to start from scratch. The next addition to my house will be a woodshop. After the porch and greenhouse, that is."

The others broke into applause.

"So pretty much everyone knew about this but me," Ingeborg said.

"Pretty much, I guess. How we all kept it a secret seems to be a real Christmas miracle."

"So some of the times when I thought you were at the office, you were . . ."

"I was in Lars's woodshop."

"With me," Manny added. "Besides carving the wren, I made the toy train engines for Danny and Rolly. I got one started for Astrid's baby, if it's a boy."

"Sure kicks like one," Astrid answered, and flinched after a hefty movement lifted the hand she was resting on her stomach.

"Thank you, Inga, for the lovely apron. I didn't realize you knew how to use the machine also." Louisa hugged her new daughter.

"Grandma taught us both long ago. Emmy sews more than I do." Inga grinned at Louisa. "You didn't give us much time to get presents made, you know."

All those around them joined in the laughter.

"Dinner is about ready," Freda called from the kitchen. "Thorliff, you want to say grace?"

"I'd like to do that, if you don't mind," David said. "But I'm going to need some help. Rolly, you want to help me?" At the boy's astonished look, David beckoned. They stood together. "Now, are we ready? *I Jesu navn går vi til bords . . .*" The two voices blended, and all the others joined in. "*. . . så får vi mat i Jesu navn.* Amen."

Everyone clapped, and Rolly and David shook hands.

"Just help yourself at the food table, fill your plate, and sit wherever you want," Freda instructed. "The low table here is for the children."

They had just finished eating when the first of the sleigh bells announced visitors, and the stream didn't stop until the sun was throwing reds, oranges, pinks, and purples across the snow. The last of the visitors went home, and those still at the farmhouse divided up food to take home. The lefse was

393

all gone, and the rest of the cookies were put back in the tins. They sliced more julekake, buttered the slices, and gathered for a final cup of coffee.

Andrew and Ellie took their family home, and then he came back to help milk. Thorliff finally gave in to the teasing and joined the other milkers, all of them laughing their way to the barn.

"I want to go watch," Rolly insisted, so he and the girls headed for the barn too.

When Thorliff brought him back to the house, the girls having gone to their chores, Rolly ran to Ingeborg. "Can I learn how to milk? That was so great. Pa milked two cows, and he even squirted some milk into the cats' mouths."

"And my hands hurt so bad." Thorliff rolled his eyes. "I'd put out a paper every week rather than go back to milking."

Ingeborg laughed. "Andrew is never going to let you live this down."

Thorliff nodded. "Figures."

She fetched her liniment from the pantry and handed it to Louisa. "Rub this in before he goes to bed." She turned to Thorliff. "And remember what happens if you rub your eyes after applying the liniment."

"Burns like all get out."

After the chores, Emmy and Inga came

to Ingeborg. "Grandma, not tomorrow but the next day, can we make popcorn balls?"

"Why not? We have plenty of popcorn."

"Remember the times we did the taffy pulls?" Inga said.

"So we do popcorn balls first and then the taffy pull. We could invite Carl and Linnea, Johnny Solberg and his older sister."

They looked to Ingeborg, who shrugged. "Fine with me. Freda, what do you think?"

"As long as they clean up afterward."

David stayed until all the others had gone home. He and Ingeborg each sat in a rocking chair in the parlor.

"I have never seen such a heart-stirring, loving, charming Christmas. Your descriptions didn't even begin to do credit to yesterday and today."

"Every year is different. But now you see why I would never go somewhere else. Although, as the families grow, this house seems to get smaller."

"My house is plenty big. Something to think about." He tipped his head against the back of the older rocking chair while Ingeborg sat in the one he had made. "Just think—what if my children ever came out here for Christmas? Tomorrow I'm having dinner with Jonathan and Grace and some of their staff. Between their house and mine, we have room for the others." He heaved a sigh. "Maybe I'm just dreaming."

Lord, give him a heart for his children. Help them learn to care about people more than society. They have so much. Thank you that Geraldine saw the value in what our school does and helped support it, even continuing on since her death.

"Ingeborg, remember what you said about not getting between me and my children?"

She nodded. She still believed that most heartily.

"Well, since they won't come here, will you please go with me to New York? Let them see who you really are for themselves. Go with me in January, when I have to be there for the board meeting."

Lord, I don't want to go back there. Not at all. But she heard herself say, "Yes, I will."

Uff da. Sometimes her mouth just got away from her thoughts and feelings. *Please, Lord, if this is your will, let me be at peace with it.*

Chapter 29

The New Year rang in with a cloud hanging over Ingeborg's head.

"Lord, I agreed I would go to New York with David, but that doesn't mean I have to be thrilled to go. Yes, I was just reading about a sacrifice of praise, and this most assuredly is a sacrifice. But I'm not praising well. In fact, I'm not praising at all. I am far closer to grumbling and being resentful." She stared at the frost-painted window that broke the rising sunlight into ever-new patterns. It was lovely, but it took mighty cold weather to make it happen.

You said you would turn bad into good for those who love you. Lord, I love you, but . . . She knew what John would say about the "but. " *Lord, please help me here. Help me put aside the way they have wounded their father, wipe off that old slate, and write something new on it.*

Her bags were packed, and they would be on the eastbound train this morning. David had ordered an executive car to make the trip more comfortable for her. What was wrong with one of the sleeper compartments?

She remembered the trip from New York to Grand Forks, with hard wooden benches lining the car, and how she and her family carried their bundles and satchels. At least they had brought quilts, so they were warm enough. The car was warmer near the stove at the end of the car, but the cigar smoke was horrid there from all the loud men who played cards and smoked and were generally obnoxious. Even young Thorliff had stayed close by. And they were hungry. Their money had nearly run out, so after the basket of food that had been packed by the wonderful woman at the boardinghouse, all Roald would buy was one hard roll apiece each day.

Her memories of that train ride were bad, but when she had gone to Chicago to the hospital for the surgery, the ride had been far more pleasant, except for the pain. The few rides she'd taken to Grand Forks were also pleasant, watching the scenery stream past. Still, she was no fan of railroads.

Freda called to her, "An hour before they'll be here."

Ingeborg tucked her Bible into her bag, along with a tablet to write upon and pencils. Envelopes and stamps were already packed, as were a selection of herbs, teas, and simples, her just-in-case supplies. She knew they had drug stores in New York, but the thought of going out on the streets of the city again did not sit well.

She'd made a list of the grandchildren. Thomas's wife was Bernice, and they had three children: Elizabeth, seven; Benjamin, five; and Herbert, three. Bessie, Benny, and Herbie. Even the thought of Thomas made her tighten her jaw. He had not contacted anyone since he left, as far as they knew.

David's daughter Lillian was married to Stephan, and they had three children. She'd already managed to forget their names. Stephan had been on the board that was fired. As far as Ingeborg knew, Lillian had never written to her father or telephoned him since he had started living part-time in Blessing. The same with the twins, Daniel and David, who were managing Gould Enterprises' assets in Boston and Charleston. Mary Anne, the youngest daughter, was in her last year at a women's college in Pennsylvania and only came home for holidays. Thomas had been the one David heard from the most. Jonathan never heard from his siblings either. He'd told her one day that as far as his siblings were concerned, he had fallen off the edge of the world when he married Grace. His comment was "good riddance." What a sorry family.

When she heard the sleigh bells, she latched her bag and stood to stretch. She'd said good-bye to Emmy and Manny this morning and the others after church on Sunday.

"Now, don't you go worrying about us," Freda ordered as she tucked some cookies and who knew what else into Ingeborg's bag. Her small trunk contained more of her simples and her clothes. David had told her she needn't bring anything, they could shop for whatever she needed, but she ignored him. She had packed her blue silk dress in case she had to attend a more formal supper.

Thorliff and David entered the house. Her son picked up her trunk, and David held her wool coat for her to slip into. He squeezed her shoulders and whispered into her ear, "Thank you."

Thorliff tucked a packet into her bag. "Louisa wanted you to have a good book to read on the train."

"Tell her thank you for me." Ingeborg hugged Freda. "I promise to pray and not to worry. Besides, I can at least use the telephone."

David put his hand on her shoulder. "Come, now. We don't want to be late."

"Go with God," Freda said and blew her a kiss.

Ingeborg wrapped her long scarf around her neck and over her hat. With gloves on and a shawl wrapped around her shoulders, she let

Thorliff and David tuck her into the sleigh. If she didn't believe so strongly in keeping her word, she'd have backed out of this trip. With the heavy robe pulled up to her nose, she reached for David's hand as soon as he climbed in, and Thorliff started the team. They set off at a trot, the sleigh bells ringing merrily.

"Rolly wants to wave to you, so watch the kitchen window," Thorliff told her as they rode by his house.

Ingeborg freed her hand from the warmth, ready to wave. Rolly and Thelma both waved from the window, so she waved back and blew them a kiss.

The eastbound train pulled into the station, the car at the end far cleaner and more elegant than the others. Ingeborg hugged Thorliff and let the conductor greet them and assist her up the stairs, setting her bag on the floor of the car. The door to their car was open, and Ingeborg stepped inside. Velvet draperies and comfortable chairs with tables, a velvet upholstered sofa, fine wool carpet on the floor, a private bathroom, and two bedrooms. The windows sparkled in the sunlight.

"Oh my." Ingeborg turned around to take it all in. "How lovely."

"Let's get seated so we don't end up on the floor when the train starts." David helped her take off her coat and scarf, handing them to a man in a white jacket and black bow tie, who hung up both their coats. She sat down and unpinned her hat, but before she could see where to set it, he took that too.

"Welcome. My name is Carver, and I will be serving you this trip." He turned to David. "William will be joining this train in Chicago. He said for me to tell you."

"Thank you, Carver. You did a fine job on my last trip."

The train jolted and eased out of the station. "May I bring you coffee?" Carver asked. "I know the pastries just came out of the oven."

"Yes, thank you. And we will have dinner at one o'clock, so please bring menus."

"Yes, sir." Carver looked to Ingeborg. "May I bring you anything else?"

She made sure she smiled. "No, thank you. Coffee sounds perfect." She rubbed her hands together, almost wishing she hadn't taken off her gloves.

"Carver, can you please turn up the heat in here?" David requested.

"Yes, sir."

Ingeborg watched him go, swaying with the train. "You didn't need to order this fancy car, you know."

"True, I didn't need to, but I wanted you

to enjoy a bit of luxury. Let someone wait on you, for a change."

Snow covered the land, sparkling white in the country and dirty gray in the cities. Ingeborg sat at the window, enthralled with the passing scenery. In the cities there were automobiles and trucks, along with horse-drawn conveyances and electric street cars. Minneapolis–St. Paul, Chicago, Pittsburgh—all had sprawled across the country far more than she dreamed possible.

With her knitting needles clicking, she carried on conversations with David and thanked Carver and, later, William. David had spoken about William and how they had become friends—including how David helped William's children go to college.

The railroad station in New York City made the one that she remembered from her last trip seem puny. But both thronged with people.

David made sure her arm was tucked securely under his after the conductor helped her out onto the platform. "You needn't be concerned about our luggage. It is all taken care of. I didn't think you'd want a tour of the city right now, so I called for a limousine to transport us home. Through the windows, you'll be able to see quite a bit."

She snuggled down under the lap robe the

driver laid over their legs, which helped hold in the heat from the vent at their feet. "So many people." And all in such a hurry. *Lord, I would so much rather be in Blessing.* But as they drove farther out, the scenery changed to elegant homes with snow-covered lawns and trees. Black-frosted snowbanks edged the streets, nothing like snow in the world she came from.

The driver turned onto a curved drive to an intimidating three-story granite home.

The door opened, and a butler in striped trousers stepped out. "Welcome home, Mr. Gould." While he spoke, he made his way down the shoveled walk to assist Ingeborg from the car. "Welcome, madam. I hope you will enjoy your stay in New York." He led the way inside. "Let me take your coats and hats." He tucked her gloves into a coat pocket and hung it not on a peg but on a wooden hanger. "Would you care for tea or coffee to help you warm up? Lunch will be ready in half an hour. You may freshen up here, if you choose." He pointed to a closed door off the hallway.

Ingeborg turned to David.

"What would you like?" he asked her with a smile. "I know, how about coffee in the morning room? The fireplace there is always welcoming."

She smiled back at him. "You read my

mind. If I could first stop in the necessary, that will be perfect."

"Of course."

A water closet on the first floor? To Ingeborg, that was a greater luxury than were the lovely carpeting and mahogany woodwork. In the bathroom, a beautiful arrangement of various evergreens with spikes of red berries graced the table, with a gilt-edged mirror above it to reflect the beauty.

A few minutes later, she crossed the morning room to the windows that reached nearly from floor to ceiling. Lace curtains framed the snow-covered backyard, with its trimmed shrubs and both deciduous trees and evergreen. "How lovely." Two potted evergreens at the outer edge of the slate veranda reminded her of miniature Christmas trees with snow ornaments.

"Your coffee, madam."

She turned to see a young woman in a black dress, white apron, and perky cap setting a tray between the two armchairs facing the fireplace. "Thank you. I'm sorry, I don't remember your name."

"I'm Rebecca," the maid said with a smile and a slight curtsy, "and I will be serving you downstairs."

"And I am Ingeborg." She glanced at David, who was trying hard not to smile.

"Yes, Miss Ingeborg. May I pour your coffee?"

Ingeborg nodded as she sat down on the brocade seat. Oh, what a comfortable chair.

"Will you have cream and sugar?"

"No. Black, please." She eyed the tiny cookies. Manny would need a handful to equal one of those baked in her kitchen. She took two when the plate was passed to her. "Thank you. The design on these is delightful."

"I'll tell the cook you liked them."

After Rebecca left, Ingeborg looked at David. "Am I allowed in the kitchen? I would like to see how things are done here."

He laughed. "Of course you are. You are the world's leading expert on kitchens."

She held the gold-rimmed saucer in one hand and the matching china cup in the other. "This coffee is delicious."

"Good. I told them in advance that you prefer it strong." He settled into the chair beside hers. "We will dine here tonight. Tomorrow morning I will take you to meet my daughter Lillian and Thomas's wife, Bernice."

"Will I get to meet your grandchildren too?"

"I told them you would like to."

"Do I have to be called *Madam* or *Miss Ingeborg*?"

He shrugged. "That is the way they are trained."

She stared at him. *So what?* She took another sip of coffee and finished her cookies.

"To call the help, pull the cord in the corner." He pointed it out. "Now, let me show you around."

"Yes, please." *This house is so huge, I might get lost. It's more like a hotel without any numbers on the doors. Not that I've stayed in very many hotels.* She swallowed and ordered herself to straighten up. "Are you sure we have time for a tour before dinner?"

David smiled at her. "People in New York call the noon meal lunch and the evening meal dinner." He shrugged. "Just a minor thing, but . . ."

"I see. Any other terms I should know so I do not embarrass you?"

He lifted her hand and kissed the back of it. "Nothing you do embarrasses me, but I thought you might feel more comfortable if you knew the differences."

She inhaled and exhaled, nodding all the while. *Lord, please watch over me and keep me from . . .* She wasn't sure what lay ahead in the next several days, but perhaps keeping her mouth closed might be best. She had already realized that people here had a different accent than at home.

He led her upstairs. "This is your room. My room is that one over there." He pointed across the hall and down a door. "Tug that bell pull by your bed for assistance."

She looked around, her head shaking just a little.

"What is wrong?"

"Nothing is wrong, but this is so big—and beautiful."

He showed her the door to her own personal bathroom, the closet where her few clothes hung on padded hangers. Even her Bible was out, waiting for her on the nightstand.

"This used to be Lillian's room."

A tap on the open door caught their attention. "Lunch is being served," a different young woman announced. Her uniform was the same, but her red hair was forced into a bun, with springy curls escaping in front of her ears. "My name is Kathleen, and I am your personal maid." She had a lilting Irish accent, much like a former priest in Blessing, Thomas Devlin.

"I see. Please call me Ingeborg."

"Yes, Miss Ingeborg. Can I get you anything before you go down to eat?"

Ingeborg shook her head.

"Whenever you like, I will draw you a bath, and perhaps you might like to rest a bit."

"Ah, yes, thank you." All of a sudden, the thought of a bath and lying down for a nap in that lovely bed made her wish for it right now. But instead she joined David in the hall, and he escorted her down the curved stairs. Wouldn't Inga have loved sliding down these banisters? Probably not now, but when she was younger. No, probably now as well—she had not lost her little-girl joy in life.

While they were enjoying the soup and grilled sandwich, David smiled at her. "Do you mind if I invite my daughter and my daughter-in-law for dinner tonight? An informal meal so I can learn what has been going on, especially regarding Thomas."

"Would it be better if I were not here?"

"No, I want them to see how easy it is to talk with you. If the men are here, they dominate."

And the women are trained to let them. Ingeborg nodded. "But we will still call on them tomorrow?"

"Yes."

"Then, if you don't mind, I would like to take the bath Kathleen offered and lie down for a while. Then I would like to call home and tell them we made it all right."

He took her hand in his. "Ingeborg, you can do whatever you would like. Dinner will be served early, at six."

"Thank you. Now, if you will excuse me." He came around to pull her chair out, dropping a kiss on the top of her head. She stood and shook her skirts. "One other thing. I would like to go to the kitchen and meet your cook. What is her name?"

"Mrs. St. John. She's been with us for ten or twelve years."

Ingeborg pushed open the door the servers had come through and stepped into a narrow room with cabinets from the floor to the ceiling and a waist-high counter. She could hear people talking ahead, so she walked through another swinging door into a kitchen with big windows, a huge stove, and the cook, the butler, and the maid staring at her.

"Is everything all right, miss?" the butler asked.

"Everything is fine. I just wanted to see the kitchen where such delicious cookies were made. You're Mrs. St. John?"

"Yes'm," the cook replied. They stood about nervously, all of them.

Ingeborg's kitchen at home was bigger than most in Blessing, and it fed a lot of people. But this kitchen was cavernous, with cupboards and a row of large polished pots hanging from pothooks over a huge oaken table in the middle of the room. She pictured her family sitting at that table, laughing and

410

eating cookies, and a wave of homesickness washed over her. Homesick already!

"I am pleased to meet you," she said. "Now, if you could show me the way to the morning room and call Kathleen for me, please."

"Come with me, please, Miss Ingeborg." Rebecca led her out into the hall.

David was waiting for her in the morning room. "I'd like to show you my office and the library later, but for now, enjoy your rest. Rebecca, please take Ingeborg upstairs when she's ready."

"Yes, sir."

A bit later, Ingeborg found herself in the biggest bathtub she had ever seen, with a sloped back to lean against, hot water with bubbles, and a delightful fragrance.

"Would you like me to wash your hair?" Kathleen asked as she tucked a little pillow behind Ingeborg's neck.

"How would it ever get dry?" At home they dried their hair at the open oven door in the winter.

"You could sit in front of the fire, and I will brush it dry. Then if you like, I could style it for you."

"I think I would rather have a rest today, but another day, that would be lovely."

The bath completed, she used a little stool

to climb up in the bed while Kathleen closed the drapes and promised not to let her sleep more than an hour. The door clicked behind her, and Ingeborg heaved a sigh. Uff da. Napping in the middle of the day. But oh, the bed felt so good.

A tapping sound brought her awake. She definitely was not in her bed at home. The tapping continued.

"Miss Ingeborg?" a voice called.

"Yes, come in." With the curtains drawn, she had no idea what time it was. Had she slept clear through the day and night too?

Kathleen entered with a smile. "Dinner will be in about an hour, so I will help you get ready." She opened the doors to the chifforobe and studied the two skirts and three waists hanging there, then pulled out the navy serge skirt and the laciest waist. "Your silk dress is being pressed."

"Are the daughters coming for dinner?"

"Only Miss Bernice and Mr. Stephan. Miss Lillian is sick in bed."

"Did she say what was wrong?"

"No, ma'am. Will you want the woolen underskirt also? I think you might find it too warm. This house is well-heated. And the camisole?"

"The clothes I was wearing?"

"Are down in the laundry."

412

No wonder David asked about buying more clothes. "Is dressing up for dinner an ordinary thing here?" She had read about that somewhere and thought it a waste of time.

"Yes, ma'am. If I may assist you."

"But I . . ." Closing her eyes, Ingeborg huffed out a breath. *Be polite and just do as you are told.* Her bossy voice made her want to roll her eyes. "Do you do this for everyone?"

Kathleen grinned at her. "Yes, ma'am, all of our guests and family members."

"How long have you worked here?" Ingeborg held up her arms so Kathleen could do her job.

"Four years."

"And your lovely accent?"

"I come from County Kerry in Ireland, ma'am." Kathleen buttoned her skirt in the back and motioned Ingeborg over to the seat in front of the mirror. Picking up a brush, she removed the pins from Ingeborg's hair and began brushing it.

"Oh my, that feels so good."

"At home, my sisters and I brushed each other's hair. Our curly red hair is far more difficult to tame than your lovely golden hair. Do you mind if I do something a bit different for you?"

"Is that part of your job?"

"It is." She held up Ingeborg's hair, then

413

rolled and twisted it, stuck pins in to hold it, and then pulled some little wisps out around her face. Handing Ingeborg the hand mirror, Kathleen stepped back.

Ingeborg's eyes widened. "My land, but you did that so easily." She touched the French twist with one finger. "Thank you."

"I'm glad you like it. Now, do you have any jewelry with you, to dress this up?"

"No, I don't wear much jewelry."

"Just sit there a moment. I'll be right back."

Ingeborg stared at her reflection in the mirror. When Kathleen returned, she nestled a blue stone pin at the center of Ingeborg's throat and hung matching earrings from her ears. With a soft brush, she added some pink to Ingeborg's cheeks.

"There now, what do you think?"

"I don't know who she is," Ingeborg said, staring at her reflection.

"I think Mr. Gould will be very pleased."

A tap on the door caught her attention. "Are you ready, Ingeborg?" David asked.

Kathleen nodded.

Ingeborg stood and crossed the room to open the door. "I am."

"You most certainly are." He offered her his arm, and she slid her lotioned hand into the crook. "I was beginning to wonder if you were still sleeping." The look in his eyes said far more than his words. He led her down that intriguing curved staircase.

The butler announced, "Mrs. Bernice Gould and Mr. Stephan Everidge."

David greeted them both, then brought them over and introduced them to Ingeborg. "Lillian was too sick to come?" he asked Stephan.

"Yes, she has been bedridden for the last several weeks."

David frowned. "She's been seen by the doctor?"

"Oh, yes, but he has pretty much given up. He thought she would be past this stage by now."

"This stage?"

"She is with child, is all, but this time is far worse than the others."

"I see. Well then, we will go see her in the morning."

"Yes, sir."

Ingeborg thought the younger man might salute, he was so rigid. Then she remembered. He had been a member of the board that David had fired. No wonder he was so stiff and icy.

Only ingrained manners kept the conversation going at all, mostly from David asking questions.

When Ingeborg said, "I'm looking forward to meeting your children tomorrow," Bernice just nodded.

Ingeborg made sure to smile. *Oh, my Bernice*. What would it take to build a friendship there? Were she to marry David, all this would be hers—the warm, soft luxury and the frigid family relationships.

She could do without all of it.

Chapter 30

*L*ord, *please let these things I bring be a help.* Ingeborg checked to make sure she had all she might need in her bag and then made her way downstairs to find David in the dining room.

"You're up early." He greeted her with a smile and laid his newspaper on the table.

"Good morning, Miss Ingeborg." The butler wore a white towel over his arm and no smile. "Would you prefer coffee or tea?"

"Oh, coffee, please." She smiled up at him as he seated her.

After pouring her coffee, he nodded to the

buffet on the wall, now covered with heated pans. He listed the foods therein and finished by adding, "Or, if you prefer something else, Mrs. St. John will prepare that for you."

"No, this is fine." *More than fine. There's enough food here to feed the milking crew two times over, including Manny at his hungriest.* "I help myself, then?"

"Yes, ma'am. Unless you would prefer I fix your plate."

She could choose her own breakfast, thank you very much. She picked up a lovely rose-decorated plate and lifted the lids. Shirred eggs, sausages, ham, scalloped potatoes. Oh my. Freda would just laugh at the fancy foods and dish up more sourdough pancakes.

The butler seated her again. "Thank you." She glanced over at David, who was draining his cup. "You're already finished?"

"I will sit here with you."

"What time is it?"

He checked his pocket watch. "Barely seven. Most women do not come to the table this early."

"Oh. At home, we'd be feeding the milking crew by now."

"I'm aware of that. And that you actually slept in this morning."

"A wonderfully comfortable bed. So, when will we leave here?"

"Probably about ten. Calling earlier than that is just not done."

It sounded preposterous to her. "Even when it is your daughter? What about the children?"

"Their nanny is taking care of them."

"All the time?"

"Well, yes. They will see their mother during the day—usually."

"And when do they see their father?"

"Sometimes in the evening, or perhaps on Saturday or Sunday. Sunday is usually considered family day."

"Between ten and four, I presume?" She glanced up to see David wiping his mouth with a napkin, but his eyes danced. "So they never joined you for breakfast?"

"When they became older."

"How old? Ten, fifteen?"

"No, by fifteen they were in boarding school. Usually between ten and twelve."

"I see." But she didn't. "Are all families like this?"

He shrugged. "I suppose not. Probably only the wealthy."

Ingeborg tried to be polite, but her head shook before she could stop it. *How would I ever adjust to this way of living? It is so cold.* Or did she even want to? "How old are Lillian's children?"

"I think the youngest, Joanna, is not yet two. Jonah is four, and Jason, I think, five. School, or a tutor, will start for them at six."

"Will you stay with me at Lillian's?"

The lines deepened in his forehead. "Is that necessary? I had planned to go to the office and have you call me when you are ready to go to Bernice's."

"No, that's fine." She would soldier on without him, as she had done nearly all her life. "David, with all these servants and nannies and tutors, what do the women do?"

He shrugged. "Well, they run the household, they meet with other women, pay social calls, volunteer. Uh, needlework, music— whatever they choose to do."

And look beautiful for dinner and dress for calling or being called upon and plan balls and soirees. Ingeborg kept her thoughts to herself. After all, Geraldine had been interested in the deaf school and donated both funding and efforts to encourage her friends to do so also. Jonathan and Grace had named the new addition to the school after her for that very reason.

Ingeborg finished her meal, started to stack her dishes, and caught David's slight shake of his head. She stopped and glanced at the butler.

"Would you care for more coffee?" He towered over her.

"Yes, please."

He brought the carafe and filled her cup. Steam rose off it. Good and hot, just like she preferred it.

She most certainly had a lot to learn. One thing she knew for sure: she did not want to live like this. But could she visit like this? After all, if she married David, coming here to visit would be necessary. Hmm, not that Geraldine had ever felt the need to please her husband by coming to Blessing. She finished her coffee. So much to think about.

"How far is Lillian's house from here?"

"Less than a mile, but no, you can't walk. Walking might be acceptable in the summer, but not in icy winter. The snow is plowed off the streets and mounds up where you would be walking."

"And how far is Bernice's?"

"About the same distance the other way."

"Do people ever ski around here?"

"Out in the country I'm sure they do, but not around here." He checked his pocket watch. "Nearly eight. A driver will be here at nine-forty-five."

"You mentioned a library when we arrived. Do you mind if I visit it?"

"Of course not." He motioned to the butler. "Lay a fire in the library for Ingeborg, please."

"Yes, sir." The butler left.

David stood and extended his hand, smiling. Ah, David. Maybe she could live like this if it was with David.

When they stepped into the library, the butler had just finished starting the fire and was putting a screen in front of it. He nodded and backed out, closing the door with a click. Ingeborg stood in the middle of the room and gazed in awe at the books on shelves tall enough that a rolling ladder graced the long wall that also housed the fireplace. Two overstuffed leather chairs sat on an ornate crimson rug.

David pointed. "The painting above the fireplace is by Albert Bierstadt, known for his paintings of the West. Here is one of the Hudson Valley School."

Ingeborg stared at the mountains. "They're so different from the mountains in Norway. At least the ones I knew."

"Yes, they are."

"You have seen the mountains of Norway?"

"Yes, when I toured Europe after college. I always have liked mountains."

"That is one thing missing in North Dakota."

David laughed and put his arm around her shoulders. "We shall have to visit the

421

Rocky Mountains sometime." He dropped a kiss on her hair, which was bundled in a snood. "If you have any questions, I'll be in my office right across the hall."

Go see the mountains. He acts as if that were no problem at all. He'd even suggested taking a trip back to Norway to see her relatives. Or to Minnesota to see Gunlaug. As if she could just leave all the work at the farm behind.

Ingeborg moved to read the titles on the shelves of novels. Most of them were leather-bound. She pulled out *The Adventures of Tom Sawyer* by Mark Twain. She'd read that one last winter. Jack London—she'd heard of him. *The Call of the Wild.* She opened the book, inhaling the fragrance of leather and printed pages, and settled in one of the chairs in front of the fire. *"Buck did not read the newspapers, or he would have known that trouble was brewing, not alone for himself, but . . ."*

The sound of the opening door brought her back from the wild woods to where she sat.

"Are you ready to go?" David asked.

"Oh, of course." She looked around for something to mark her place.

He crossed to the desk and brought her back a strip of leather. "Use this."

"Thank you. Every winter I read aloud at night before bed. For Manny, Emmy, and

Freda, and whoever is staying with us. One of winter's pleasures. I've not read a book by Jack London before. I will ask Thorliff to order this one for me."

"Why don't we go to the bookstore and buy one for you? And maybe a few for the school library. Didn't Louisa say she needed more books?"

Ingeborg stared at him. What would it be like to go to a real bookstore? She laid the book on the table between the two chairs and gave it a pat, to say she'd be back.

"It is sunny out but still cold, but you needn't wear your boots. Do you need anything from your room?"

"No, I have it all in the bag near the door."

The driver helped her both in and out of the automobile, and David tucked her arm in his to walk up the three low steps to the front door of Lillian's home. While this house was granite also, and big, it wasn't half as large as the family house.

A butler ushered them inside as if he'd been waiting for the bell to chime. "Welcome, Mr. Gould. It is good to see you again. Let me take your things, although Miss Lillian is not having visitors today."

"Thank you, Arthur. We are not visitors, and you needn't show me the way."

They left their outer things with the rather

nonplussed butler and mounted the stairs to the upper floor. Ingeborg could hear children playing off to one side of the stairs, but they turned the opposite way, passing several closed doors until David tapped at one.

A sour older maid blocked the door. "Miss Lillian is not seeing anyone today."

"I am not a visitor. I am her father. This is my friend, Ingeborg Bjorklund, and she is well-known as a healer where she lives. I believe she will be able to help my daughter, so do whatever she asks of you."

"Well, I . . ." The maid harrumphed as she was forced to step back or get run over.

The room was so dark that Ingeborg could hardly see the form in the bed. The entire room reeked of sickness and despair. She walked over to the drapes and pushed them back to let in the light.

The woman in the bed didn't move.

"How long since she has had anything to eat or drink?" Ingeborg asked the maid. "By the way, my name is Ingeborg, or Mrs. Bjorklund. What is yours?"

"Matilda." Did the dour lady always look so displeased? "She had a bit of broth last night, but nothing stays down for her."

"I see." Ingeborg laid the back of her hand against Lillian's cheek. "Not even plain warm water?" Taking out her stethoscope, she listened to Lillian's lungs and heart. Weak but clear so far. Lying in bed like this could turn into something far worse rather quickly.

"Sometimes. The doctor is certain this will pass with time."

"And in the meantime, she suffers." *Astrid would never let a woman languish this long.* "Please bring me a kettle of boiling water and then start a fire in the fireplace to keep it hot."

The maid glanced at David. "Yes, ma'am. Right away, ma'am." She hustled out the door.

"Now, if you would crack the windows, please, David. Just a little to get rid of the stale air. Is there a bathroom here?"

"Try the doors." David bent to his task, finally getting the windows open.

Two closets later, Ingeborg found the bathroom, located a pan in the linen closet, poured water into it, and laid a small towel and washcloth on the chair by the bed.

Matilda brought a tray with a steaming kettle and two teacups into the room.

David pointed. "Set it there, please."

Ingeborg mixed scalding water with the water in her pan and tested it with her fingers. She bent over the patient. "Lillian. Lillian, please wake up." She touched the young woman's shoulder. So pale and frail. *Please, Lord, care for this one, your daughter.* She wished John were there to help her pray.

A frown creased Lillian's forehead, and her eyes blinked open. "Who are you?"

David joined Ingeborg and laid his hand on his daughter's shoulder. "Hello, Lillian. I brought Ingeborg to help you get well again."

"The doctor said . . ."

"I know what he said, but I believe God has something better for you than lying here like this, being miserable for weeks on end." Ingeborg smiled down at her patient. "I'm going to wash your hands and face. That will feel really good. And here is a cup of warm water. I want you to keep this in your mouth and then spit it out, all right?"

Lillian almost nodded. "Father, you came back. I . . . I was beginning to think I . . ." She paused, her eyes fluttering closed. "I thought you were never coming back."

Ingeborg slid an arm behind Lillian's neck and shoulders, lifting enough for the ill woman to sip from the cup. "There, good. Rinse it around. Good, now spit it out. I'm going to put another pillow or two behind you." She did so as she spoke, each word gentle. Dipping the washcloth in the warm water, she wiped her patient's face and throat, then arms and hands.

"Th-thank y-you."

"You are welcome." Opening the packet of her own mixture, Ingeborg poured boiling water over the herbs and tea leaves. While it steeped, she pushed the heavy drapes back even farther and glanced out the window. David did the same for the other windows. "It's so lovely out. I'm sorry you've been cooped up in here so long."

She checked the teapot and saw there were no more floating particles, so she poured a cup of the weedy brew and stirred in a spoonful of clover honey.

"This tea, for lack of a better word, has helped many young women with this same problem." *This and prayer*, she thought. She sat down on the chair and, holding the cup in one hand, spooned some out. "We'll go really slow, but swallow this for me, please."

Lillian opened her eyes and stared into Ingeborg's, then opened her mouth. She worked the liquid around inside. "It's sweet. And delicious."

"I know. The honey is from our own hives, and our bees love the clover fields that we cut for hay for our cows."

Lillian swallowed and opened her mouth again.

"Two swallows is all we'll do for now, but if this stays down, I'll give you more." Ingeborg turned to Matilda, who was standing at the foot of the bed, fingers clamped over the carved wood. "Could you please go down and see if the cook has chicken broth? Canned or fresh, either is fine."

"Yes, ma'am." The maid hustled out the door.

David placed a hand on Ingeborg's shoulder. "If there is nothing more I can do to help you, I will go on to the office. Call me immediately if you need anything."

Ingeborg nodded. "I will. I plan on letting her rest a bit, then trying some more tea." She looked at Lillian's face. Was that a smile on her lips?

David picked up his daughter's hand. "I'll be back later."

She barely nodded. "Papa, will you see Bernice today too?"

"We'll see." He squeezed her shoulder and left.

Ingeborg watched him go, then turned back to her patient. "Since you kept the first spoonfuls down, let's try some more." She took her time, spooning in one sip, then another. And waited. "Do you have any idea how far along you are?"

"No. The doctor says four months. I don't think it's three."

"And when did the vomiting start?"

Lillian opened her mouth for more tea, and Ingeborg obliged her with three more spoonfuls.

"The vomiting started two or three weeks after I missed my time of the month and just kept getting worse."

Ingeborg nodded, aware that Lillian's words were getting spaced more apart. "You take a nap now, and we'll try another dose when you wake. In the meantime, I'm going to the nursery to meet your children."

"I miss them so."

"If you continue to do well today, we'll see about them visiting tomorrow." She patted Lillian's hand. "Let me take some of those pillows away now so you can rest better."

Her patient was asleep before she finished.

A tap at the doorway, and a young woman pushed it open with her hip, carrying in a tray. "I brought you some lunch. Matilda said you like coffee better than tea, but I have both."

"Thank you. I was just going to visit with the children, but I'll eat first, unless . . . ?"

"They have already eaten, and Joanna is about to go down for a nap. The boys sit and read or color, and Jason likes to build things."

"With wood?" Ingeborg chose a chair in front of a window, and the girl set the tray on the lamp table.

"Anything. Paper, cardboard, wood. He built a little house out of sticks last summer. It's up on one of the bookshelves." She looked around the room. "It's nice to see some light in here. No wonder Miss Lillian has gotten so weak. All that darkness."

"She's holding down the tea I brought her. That is really good news."

When the young woman left, Ingeborg fell to her meal. Breakfast seemed years ago. *Thank you, Lord, for this food and this family. Thank you that she was able to keep down the tea. Guide me, please, and I will give you all the glory. Amen.*

After eating, Ingeborg checked on her patient, who was sleeping comfortably, so she asked Matilda to show her to the nursery and then return to stay on watch duty. "And please come get me when she wakes. If she is up to it, we will give her a bath and change that bedding."

Matilda showed her the nursery and tapped on the door. A middle-aged woman wearing a dark-colored street dress answered the knock. "This is Georgina Haines, the children's nanny," Matilda said. "Mrs. Bjorklund is a friend of Mr. Gould's who is visiting from North Dakota and wants to meet all of his family."

"Arthur told me. I'm pleased to meet you, Mrs. Bjorklund. Welcome to New York." Her voice flowed like music as she extended her hand. "I'm sorry, but Joanna is sound asleep. I'll take you to peek in at her. The boys are having their quiet time, but they will be delighted to see you."

"Thank you." Ingeborg stepped into a room with shelves of books and toys for all ages, large windows that let in the sun, several doors to other bedrooms, and a closed door where she was sure the little one slept. A spinet piano stood on one wall, and a giant world map covered another.

They paused for a few moments in the doorway of Joanna's room. A doll house, dolls, and girly toys lined all the walls. And books. This house held more books than did all of Blessing's schools combined. The little girl lay curled on her side, thumb and forefinger in her mouth. They backed out and closed the door.

"It is about time for tea. Would you like to join us?" Mrs. Haines asked.

"I would be delighted."

"Good, then I shall introduce you to the boys. Jason is the eldest at five, and Jonah is close to four." The boys were seated in two child-sized armchairs, Jason with a tablet and pencils, and Jonah glaring at a jigsaw puzzle on a low table.

"Boys, this is Mrs. Bjorklund, and she has come from North Dakota to visit your grandfather."

Jason stood up. "I am pleased to meet

you," he said formally. He poked his brother, who looked up and said hello, then stared back down at his puzzle.

"Thank you. What is that you're drawing?" Ingeborg asked.

Jason held out his tablet. "I think I need a ruler to draw straight lines."

The paper was covered in three-dimensional cubes. "You drew these boxes? How old are you?"

"Almost six."

"You draw very well for your age. Where might a ruler be?"

"Mrs. Haines said she would find me one." He seemed so much older than five.

Jonah looked up at her. "You talk funny."

"Jonah, that's rude." His nanny scowled at him.

"Well, she does."

"I have an accent because I grew up in Norway before coming to America. Do you want to see where that is on the map?" Both boys joined her at the wall map. Ingeborg pointed high on the wall to Norway. "This is Norway, and I took a ship to England and from there to America, here in New York. We rode a train west across this country to North Dakota to build a farm."

"That's a long way." Jason pointed with his finger. "In summer, sometimes we go up in the Catskills. It's a long way, and it's only from here to here. Your house is a *really* long way!" He looked up at her. "Do you still have the farm?"

"Do you have animals on your farm?" Jonah asked.

"Yes and yes." She grinned down at both of them. "We have cows, pigs, horses, sheep, and chickens."

"It must be a big farm."

"It is. Oh, and we have a dog and cats."

Jonah looked sad. "I want a puppy, but Mother says no. Maybe when we get bigger."

"When they say *maybe* that really means *no*, but we keep asking," Jason finished for his brother. "Do you have grandchildren in North Dakota?"

"I do. Inga is the oldest. She is thirteen. Carl, who loves to go fishing, is twelve, and—"

"Goes fishing in a lake?"

"No, a river. The Red River." She noticed Mrs. Haines pulling chairs up to a table. "Can I help you?"

A tap at the door, and a maid brought in a large tray to set in the middle of the table.

"You boys go wash your hands," Mrs. Haines directed.

"Don't leave," Jonah said with a grin as he did as he was told.

"You can sit in a larger chair if you would

like," Mrs. Haines told Ingeborg. "I had her bring both tea and coffee for us."

Ingeborg chose one of the children's chairs and sat down carefully. The boys returned and joined her. "What a nice tea." Small sandwiches cut in various shapes, cookies, and orange slices waited for them.

Jonah reached for a sandwich, but his older brother tapped his hand. "Company first."

Ingeborg smiled her thank-you, bubbling with chuckles. She chose some of each and held her cup for Mrs. Haines to fill.

"Do you have tea at your farm?" Jonah asked, after helping himself.

"Not as fancy as this, but usually when the children come home from school, we have cookies and milk or coffee." She ate one of the sandwiches. "Delicious."

Jonah mimicked her. "De-licious."

She'd just set her coffee cup down when a tap on the door brought Mrs. Haines to her feet.

Matilda waited outside. "Miss Lillian is awake again."

"Thank you, I'll be right there." Ingeborg turned to the boys. "Thank you for the visit and sharing tea with me." She smiled at the nanny. "I'll see Joanna tomorrow when I come."

434

"Us too?" Jonah asked.

"Yes, you too." She stood.

"Can we go see Mother?" Jason asked.

"As soon as she feels well enough to have you there."

Back in the sickroom, Ingeborg checked to make sure the tea was warm enough, then poured some in the cup with the spoon.

"I've been visiting with your boys. In fact, I had tea with them."

Lillian's nod was more than she had done before.

Ingeborg replaced the pillows and picked up her cup and spoon. "You ready?" She held the full spoon to Lillian's lips and smiled when she opened her mouth. Again three spoonfuls, and she paused. "Do you feel at all nauseous?"

A small movement but definitely a *no*. "Just weak."

Three spoonfuls. Wait. Three spoonfuls. Wait.

"I was going to give you a bed bath, but I think we'll wait until tomorrow. Can you take more?"

Lillian raised one finger, so Ingeborg smiled and did the three spoonfuls again. Already her patient's eyes were drifting closed.

"Cook said she has chicken broth any

time we are ready for it." Matilda moved the kettle closer to the heat.

Ingeborg nodded. "I think we'll try a couple of spoonfuls of that later. She and that baby are in desperate need of nourishment."

Dark had fallen when David tapped on the door, but the white of the snow reflected into the room, keeping Ingeborg from closing the drapes. Her heart leapt when she heard his voice.

"How is she doing?" he asked.

"She has kept the tea down, so next we try chicken broth." Ingeborg laid her cheek against his hand on her shoulder. "Matilda, please call for that."

"Will you be staying the night or coming home with me?" David asked.

Ingeborg looked to Matilda.

"I will be sleeping in here, and I hear every noise. If we need you, I will telephone you."

"Has she been restless at night?" Ingeborg asked.

Matilda shook her head. "Not since she quit vomiting about two days ago. But I was afraid to force her to drink. She refused everything."

Lying there waiting to die. *Lord God, thank you for your grace and mercy.* She looked up at the man smiling down at her. "Will you visit with the children?"

He nodded. "Has Stephan been home?"

"I have no idea. I only left the room to visit the children. Joanna was asleep, but I had tea with the boys and their nanny. Did you apologize to Bernice for us not coming there?"

"I did and asked her to join us for dinner."

The broth arrived, and Ingeborg woke her patient. "Now, Lillian, since you kept the tea down, we'll try broth."

A slight nod was her answer. The process was the same. Three spoonfuls and wait.

David went to visit the children. Ingeborg wished she were a mouse in his pocket to see how they acted with him.

Later, in the automobile returning to David's house, she felt like every bit of energy she had drained right out the soles of her feet. When she closed her eyes, she could see her kitchen and everyone gathered around the table, Manny teasing Emmy, and Freda giving him her stern look. *Oh, Lord, I want to go home, where there is peace and love and laughter.*

"Are you all right?" David asked as he helped her from the noisy box on wheels.

She nodded. "I will be."

The butler took their coats. "How is Miss Lillian?"

Ingeborg looked up to him. This man cared. The idea caught her by surprise. He always acted so formal. Did he know the situation? "She is keeping liquids down." Was that relief she caught in that instant? Gray hair and a lined face told her he was up in years. She resolved to ask David about him later, if they ever got a chance to talk without anyone else around.

"Set a place for Bernice. She'll be joining us for dinner. And tell Cook we'll be ready as soon as our guest arrives." David looked to Ingeborg. "Unless you need more time."

"No, anytime is fine with me." The thought of the hot bath and bed in her room appealed to her more than the cold and formal dining room. Tomorrow she would take her Bible along. Reading to Lillian while she slept would be a good thing.

Dinner was strained. Ingeborg would ask a question, one of them would answer, and the silence would return, smothering them in sadness. Bernice looked pinched and drawn. Her face was probably quite pretty, but grief and worry had etched it. Mrs. St. John served a delicious chicken Florentine. Where did she get fresh spinach at this time of year?

After dinner, the three of them sat with their tea and coffee in the morning room in front of a snapping fire.

Bernice sipped at her tea. "I still have no money, and my father is being quite difficult.

He took over paying the help. I'm grateful for that, but he put them on half wages, and already three of them have quit and found positions elsewhere. I don't really blame them. Our home is so unstable at the moment." She heaved a sigh. "My father is insisting that I divorce Thomas. I don't want to break my marriage vows, but Daddy says when Thomas abandoned us, he was the one who broke the covenant. I thought he would be back anytime, but . . ." She shrugged and stared down at the handkerchief she had twisted around her fingers. "At first I was worried and then too sad to get out of bed, and then I grew angry. And now I don't know where else to turn. I guess there is something inside of me that still hopes he'll show up one day."

David nodded. "I hired detectives to find him, but they failed. Have you been exploring options to discover if he is still alive?"

She wagged her head. "I checked at his club several times, and the maître d' says if he shows up there, he'll tell me. And I talked to the police and the morgue. There has been no body found that fits his description."

David sat back, talking more to himself than to the women. "I would guess he's nowhere in New York. He would buy railway or steamship tickets with cash, and cash cannot be traced. No wonder the Pinkerton boys had no luck."

Bernice's voice was soft, querulous. "Mr. Gould? If we can't find him, will you disinherit the children and me?"

David looked stunned by the question. He leaned forward. "Bernice, my dear, no matter what he has done, he is still my son. And you are my daughter-in-law. There will be no disinheriting."

Ingeborg could hear the pain in his voice no matter how he tried to disguise it. *Lord God, help.*

January in Hibbing, Minnesota, was a lot colder than it got in New York City. Thomas figured that out the moment he stepped off the train.

Here came the stationmaster. Excellent. He would know where Thomas could find Lionel. But the stationmaster simply swatted Thomas's arm with the back of his hand. "No loitering here."

"Wait!" Thomas called, but the fellow was gone into the mail car.

Thomas began walking toward the downtown area. Hibbing was a nice little place, clean and quiet. It looked wholesome, freshly painted, and well-scrubbed. On the main

440

street was a barber shop, marked by the big candy-striped cylinder all barber shops displayed. And every barber the world over knew every person in town and everything that was going on. Thomas went inside.

Two patrons and the barber all gave him dirty looks, then otherwise ignored him. And why not? He was unshaved, untrimmed, and unkempt. His clothing was filthy and ragged, and most of the buttons on his jacket were missing. His cash had been stolen, every bit of it. He was destitute. Penniless. But that would all change shortly. Once Lionel paid Thomas back, everything would be okay.

Thomas cleared his throat and addressed the barber. "Excuse me, sir, I'm looking for Lionel Hibbing. I'm a friend of his."

The barber scowled at him. "No Lionel Hibbing here. Go seek elsewhere."

"Do you know where he lives? His address?"

"There isn't any Lionel Hibbing. Now, go find someplace else to loiter." The barber continued snipping.

"Who around here would know him? Is there a county clerk's office? I know—out at the ironworks. They'll know him. I'll ask at the ironworks."

"Good plan." Snip, snip, snip. "The train to Duluth leaves this evening."

"No, the local ironworks. Here in Hibbing."

The barber did not lose his scowl. "No ironworks in Hibbing. We ship everything we dig to Duluth."

"Of course there is. Just outside of town. A new facility, modern equipment."

The barber's customer spoke for the first time. "Look here, young man. You've got the wrong Hibbing, understand? My mother is a Hibbing, so we go to every family function there is. I know all the Hibbings in Minnesota, the young ones and the old ones and the historical ones. There ain't no Lionel and never was."

"But the ironworks—"

The fellow insisted, "And we've never had anything like a smelter or foundry in Itasca County, or St. Louis County either."

"But—"

"You calling me a liar?"

Thomas shrank back. He staggered over to a vacant chair and flopped down. He needed Lionel. He had come to Hibbing certain that he would be taken care of here by his friend. And now . . .

He suddenly felt as if he were being crushed by a ton of ore. It slapped him hard: His father had been right all along, absolutely right. Thomas had argued so hotly in support of his friend, but now he had to admit the reality. He had dismissed his father as a dotty, out-of-step old geezer, led astray by those rubes in Blessing, but his father was wise beyond comprehension.

Lionel Hibbing was a liar and a scalawag.

And Thomas's father was well justified to disinherit him. Through his own stupidity, Thomas had just lost everything.

Chapter 31

Thomas, oh, Thomas.

Thomas, his firstborn, who had started out pushing to be the head of everything, had turned into a playboy and now disappeared. Was he dead or alive? That was the biggest question. David stared at the fire in front of him. Snapping sparks, nearly white coals. The natural order of things. If you wanted heat along with beauty, you started a fire. If you wanted something mesmerizing to take your mind away from a problem you couldn't resolve, you started a fire. Or drowned it in drink. His gaze switched to the bottles on the cart. Temporary relief was no real help at all. Another lesson he'd learned the hard way. Two loud crackles brought him back to the fire. That and a chunk of burning wood falling and creating a shower of sparks.

Thomas, where are you?

The anger from his son's actions at the board meeting, the temper that had driven him to fire the lot of them, had abated. Appointing Arnold as the chairman had turned out to be a good thing. Between them they had created a new board that had learned to work together and begun to make progress again.

His thoughts turned to Ingeborg. They'd been friends all these years, but now were far more than friends. He wanted nothing more than to spend the rest of his life with her in Blessing but with the freedom to return to New York when he wanted or needed to. He wanted to show her the world, but she was content with her life in Blessing. But she said she loved him. He *knew* she loved him. He desired to marry her. She said she would not divide him from his children—and grandchildren.

His brilliant idea to bring her here to meet his children so they could fall in love with her too had started out well. But Thomas . . .

Everything came back to that.

The sad thing is I let those months go by without trying to contact him. I should have done something about it. But then, perhaps not. I guess I was waiting for him to come to his senses.

Lord, between Ingeborg and John, I have learned to turn to you. Or is it that I am learning to turn to you. You know where my son is. I don't. All I ask is that you protect him. He is in your hands. I trust Thomas to you. I have seen you turn evil into good. Thank you for bringing John and Ingeborg to be my closest friends. Gifts beyond measure. I believe that marrying Ingeborg is in your plan for us. I am trusting you will work that out.

Another log fell. He studied the fire. *Amen.* Heaving a deep sigh, he stood and leaned against the mantel. *Thank you. Lord, I praise your name. May my praise and petitions rise to you as on the smoke of this fire.*

Upstairs in bed, he drew his Bible out of the nightstand drawer and turned to Psalm 139. If God knew him inside and out like the psalm said, he most certainly knew where Thomas was. David slept fitfully.

Ingeborg came to the table early the next morning, ready to leave.

"Did you have a hard night?" she asked. The butler quickly came and helped seat her.

"The night was fine. After a rather difficult time in front of the fire." His head moved

445

from side to side, in spite of his usual self-control.

"Wrestling?"

He stared at her. "Where did you come up with that idea?"

"It seemed to fit. About Thomas?" She lifted her steaming cup of coffee, blew gently on it, and inhaled the fragrance. "I'll help myself, thank you." She smiled up at the butler, who had just poured her coffee. When he left, she placed her hand over David's on the table. "Besides, I've been there a few times. I've read Jacob's story many times through the years."

"Where he wrestled with the angel? Or was it the Spirit of God?"

"Talk with John about that." She pushed back her chair and went to choose her breakfast. "When will you be ready to leave?"

"Anytime you want. I have plenty to do at the office. If I hire a Pinkerton detective again to see what he can learn of Thomas, is that not trusting in God?"

"Good question. Ask Him."

"Now you sound like John."

"I accept that as a great compliment. I want to be at Lillian's side as soon as I can."

"Then you eat, and we can leave."

He dropped her off at Lillian's and proceeded on to his office. Early as he was,

Arnold was there before him. He had taken over Thomas's office and had an assistant of his own in the reception area.

"May I have an appointment with you at about ten?" Arnold asked.

"Of course." David proceeded on to his office and greeted Robert, the young man who had been the typist before. "Please bring me a cup of coffee with whatever is on the table, and we'll begin in half an hour."

"Yes, sir. I hope you are enjoying your time here."

"Thank you, I am." *And will even more so when we get some of these things started, let alone finished.*

He and Arnold had just finished their meeting when Robert rapped on the door. "Your son-in-law would like to speak with you."

"Show him in."

Lillian's husband, Stephan, entered. The young man was growing prematurely bald, a rather mousy little fellow. David didn't quite know what Lillian saw in him, but they had been married for the last eight years and had a fine family.

"Yes, Stephan?"

"May we talk, sir? Is now a good time?"

"As good a time as any." David waved toward the chair beside his desk.

The young man perched on it. "When

you fired me from the board, I was very angry. I wanted to protest, and to start with, I decided to make a list of everything I had done for the company in this last year. But I couldn't think of anything significant. Then I decided I'd make a list of everything I'd done on the board for the last three years. I couldn't think of anything there either. Oh, we passed a few resolutions, but they were merely cosmetic, you might say, to make the company look good. Nothing to make us do or be better. And I realized why you consider me a do-nothing. All of us. It is because we did nothing."

"You argued a lot."

Stephan smiled weakly. "We are all rather opinionated, aren't we?"

David snorted. "An understatement. Have you discussed this with Lillian?"

"Not yet. Her pregnancy is very trying for her, and she is still upset because her husband is no longer a senior board member. Apparently my position was quite important to her."

"I can believe that. It's the way her mother raised her. What will you do now?"

"Are you familiar with Rogen and Sons?"

"Yes."

"I have applied for a position there. A senior position in their financial department.

448

The fact that I was on the board here at Gould Enterprises is a big plus in my favor."

David nodded. "Rogen is a good company." He thought for a few moments, studying Stephan's face. In fact, this was probably the first time he'd ever really looked at his son-in-law. The young man appeared timid and mousy, but there was obviously more to him than that. "It took courage to come to me and admit that the board was weak. In fact, it takes courage to apply for a senior position at Rogen. They are very careful in their hiring."

"Thank you, sir. I've heard that."

David laid his hand on a stack of papers. "I was just browsing through some of the annual reports for the last few years. The plant in Rahway has been struggling. Shaky finances, high employee turnover. Do you think if you took over as director, you could turn it around?"

He brightened. "I would love to try, sir."

"My daughter will probably not appreciate living in New Jersey, but you could take the train over. Let me set you up there."

Stephan licked his lips. "Sir, I did not come here to seek a position."

"I know."

Stephan was an in-law, not a son by blood, but at the moment, he was a bright spot in David's dark world.

Ingeborg opened the drapes and looked down at her patient. "How did she do through the night?"

"I gave her both broth and warm water as you said three times during the night. I had to wake her each time," Matilda reported.

"So you got some sleep too?" Ingeborg watched as Lillian's eyes fluttered open.

"I did, ma'am, thank you." Matilda nodded, a smile fighting to change her face.

Lillian gazed at Ingeborg. "You're back. I thought I dreamed an angel had been here."

Ingeborg felt the young woman's forehead and listened to her lungs. *So far, so good. Thank you, Lord.* "Not an angel, just Ingeborg. I was looking forward to meeting you, but not like this. It looks like you are doing better."

Lillian nodded. "I am, thank you."

"We're going to try more at a time today, so let's get you sat up." She and Matilda took care of the pillows, and Ingeborg sat to spoon out more broth. "How's that feeling?"

"Not cramping."

"Good. My plan is to give you a sponge bath, then move you to the chair while we change your bedding. Tell me the instant you start feeling nauseated or crampy."

Lillian nodded. "Can I see my children

this afternoon, or do I look so bad it will frighten them?" She had to catch her breath at the end.

"Yes, and no. They will be so thrilled to see you. Jason asked about you yesterday." Ingeborg smiled. "You have two fine boys, about as different as day and night."

Lillian nodded and smiled. "Thank you. I am so thirsty."

"Good." Ingeborg picked up the glass of water. "If Matilda holds you up, do you think you can sip from the cup?"

Ingeborg only allowed Lillian three sips before stepping back. She watched as her patient smiled and drifted back to sleep. Taking her Bible out of her bag, Ingeborg settled herself into the comfortable chair by the bed and began to read, starting with the Psalms.

When Lillian woke again, Ingeborg dosed her with nearly half a cup of broth and then let her rest. After spreading towels beneath her, she and Matilda soon had their patient bathed, dried, and in a fresh night dress. "Now, how do you feel?"

"So much better, thank you. And before you ask, yes, please change this bed."

Together, Ingeborg and Matilda helped their patient over to the chair and tucked her in a blanket that had been warming in front of the fire.

"Oh, thank you. What a grand idea."

With the bed redone and the bundle of used sheets out the door, they helped her back to bed, where she was asleep before they had her covered with the quilt.

"Ring for coffee," Ingeborg said. "We need it."

When the tray came, there was one cup for the coffee. Ingeborg smiled gently at the maid. "Please bring up another cup and whatever there is to go with it."

"But, miss—I mean, I can't . . ."

"Matilda, we have earned a rest with a cup of coffee, and I don't like to drink alone. So please do me this honor, and I promise not to tell a soul."

Matilda rolled her eyes. "Miss, you are one determined lady."

"That I am. And I much prefer being called Ingeborg, since that is my name."

"Is that an order?"

"Yes, ma'am, it is."

Later, when they were finishing their coffee, Ingeborg asked, "Would it cause a problem if I had lunch with the children?"

"I'm not the one to ask, Mrs. Haines is. I can go get her for you."

"No, thanks, I can do that." Ingeborg stood. "I'll be right back." She returned in a couple of minutes to tell Matilda that she'd be back in an hour or so with the children. Then she returned to the nursery.

Jonah charged up to her as soon as she entered. "You came back."

"I said I would."

"Adults always say they'll do something, but then they don't." Jason remained at the table with his sketchpad.

Ingeborg exchanged looks with the nanny. "I'm sorry to hear that, Jason. What is it you are working on?"

"Turning the boxes into houses."

She walked over to see his paper. "I see you found a ruler."

He nodded. "I looked at some of Leonardo da Vinci's drawings."

"Who is he?"

Jason looked at her with raised eyebrows. "He was Italian and an artist of all kinds and an inventor too." He pointed at a book on the table. "We have one of his drawings framed on the wall in the library."

"A real one," Jonah added.

"Do you mind if I have lunch with you?"

Both boys stared at her. "I don't want to go to the dining room!" Jonah's voice rose to a near shriek.

Ingeborg stared at him. "We're eating here."

His mouth snapped shut, and a smile instantly appeared. "Good."

Jason shook his head. "He always gets in trouble in the dining room."

"Oh." She looked to Mrs. Haines, who had just reentered the room. She held a blinking, curly-haired little girl who looked so like her mother that they could be twins.

"She just woke up from her nap," Mrs. Haines explained. "Just in time for lunch, little Jo."

Joanna pushed back and demanded to be put down, then hid behind her nanny's skirts.

"Come on, boys, let's clear off the table." Both of them scrambled to obey and put chairs around the table. "Jason, please get a wet cloth and wipe off the table."

"Will you sit by me?" He donned his angelic look and smiled up at Ingeborg. "Joanna sits in the high chair. She's messy."

Jason dried the table too and returned the cloths.

"What time will lunch be here?" Mrs. Haines asked.

"Twelve noon, when both hands of the clock are straight up," Jason said directly to his little brother, obviously trying to teach him properly.

They all stood at their chairs until the clock said noon, but nothing happened.

454

"We might as well sit down." Mrs. Haines settled Jo in her high chair and clicked the tray in place.

A tap at the door brought on a hoot from Jonah, earned him a frown from his older brother, and caused Ingeborg to fight back a smile.

"Jason, answer the door, please."

He opened it, stepped back, and said thank you. The maid set the food on the table. "How nice to have a guest today. If you need anything else, just call." When she was out the door, Jason closed it and came to sit down, earning a nod from Mrs. Haines.

"Thank you, Jason."

"You're welcome."

The serving dishes were passed around, with Joanna banging her spoon on the tray, yelling, "Food, food."

Mrs. Haines rolled her eyes but put cut-up potatoes, carrots, and bread on the tray, which earned her a grin of approval.

Ingeborg nodded. "You know, my youngest grandson, Danny, is about your age, Jason."

"Can I come see him?"

"Who knows? Perhaps one day."

"Tomorrow?"

"No, we live far away. You saw on the map yesterday the distance from New York to North Dakota. It takes a train two or three days to get there."

"Does he live on your farm?"

"No, he lives in town, but that is very close by. He comes to the farm to visit as often as he can."

The conversation continued, making Ingeborg more homesick by the minute as she described her life and family in Blessing.

When they'd finished the meal and cleaned up the table, the boys were excused, and Joanna was set on the floor to toddle after the boys.

"Their mother really wants to see them," Ingeborg told the nanny, "so I'll go see how she's doing. I'm hoping this is a good time."

Mrs. Haines nodded. "The tutor will be here after I take the boys to run around. I take them outside every day that the weather is decent."

"Do they enjoy the snow?"

"Oh my, yes, they have such a good time. Jo is good until she gets tired of falling down. Jason pulls her on the sled sometimes."

Ingeborg returned in a minute. "Now is good."

"Boys, come here, please. Good. Now, we have a surprise, but you have to behave quietly. We are going to see your mother, but remember that she has been very ill, so we can't stay long."

456

Jason nodded and jerked his little brother's arm to make him stand still. Mrs. Haines picked up Joanna, made sure her face was clean, and motioned for Ingeborg to open the door. The two boys marched quietly to their mother's door, until Jason saw his mother and tore over to the bed, where she was sitting propped against pillows. Matilda grabbed him and made a shushing motion. When he nodded, she let him go.

"Oh, I am so glad to see you." Lillian hugged each boy and then Joanna when she was let loose on the bed. Joanna crawled up to her mother, murmuring, "Ma, Ma, Ma" the whole time. Lillian kissed her baby's cheek and looked up to smile her thanks at all the women. "Now, Jason, what are you drawing?" He held out his tablet, and she smiled. "My goodness, cubes and houses. Why, you might be an architect someday."

He grinned at her. "I hope you get better soon."

"Oh, me too. And Jonah, did you win at checkers yet?"

He shook his head. "Jason won't let me win."

She stroked his curly hair. "That would not be right, to let you win."

Joanna sat right beside her, in the circle of her other arm.

"Are you all being good for Mrs. Haines?"

Both boys nodded, then looked at their sister and shook their heads.

Ingeborg watched the energy leak out of her patient. "I'm sorry, but we need to let your mother rest. Say good-bye." The boys did, Jonah clinging for a moment longer, looking about to cry. Joanna let out a scream and stretched both arms out toward her mother when Mrs. Haines reached for her.

As soon as they were out the door, Lillian collapsed against the pillows. "Thank you."

Ingeborg gently removed the excess pillows. "You lie back and rest now. You did very well."

"Sometimes I wonder if I will ever be well again."

"You will be, but it takes time to get strong again. You watch, each day will be better, as long as you can keep food down. For dinner tonight, how about some applesauce? If that works, half a piece of toast and more broth."

"Ingeborg, thank you." Lillian's eyes closed, and her breathing deepened.

That evening after dinner, the butler came into the library where both Ingeborg and David were reading. "Telephone call for Mrs. Bjorklund."

"We'll take it in my office." David led the way and handed Ingeborg the receiver from the desk telephone.

Her heart pounding, Ingeborg swallowed. *Please, Lord.* "Hello."

"Mor, it's Astrid."

"Is everything all right?"

"Oh yes, everything is perfect. When you get home, you can meet your new grand-daughter, Elizabeth Amelia Jeffers. She is all of four hours old and already nursing well. Actually, she's a little pig, doesn't want to let go."

Ingeborg lost the battle of fighting tears. "And how are you? You sound wonderful."

"I am. In labor only four hours, and once she decided it was time to come, she did. Seven pounds, four ounces."

Ingeborg sniffed and wiped her eyes with the handkerchief David handed her.

"You're not supposed to cry, Mor. I know those are happy tears, but now you have me crying too."

"Thank you for calling me. Everything else all right?"

"Everyone's fine. We had a bit of a blizzard, but it didn't last long. I hope all is well there. Do you know when you're returning?"

"We'll probably be home before a letter would get there. Thank you so much for calling to let me know."

"We love you. Good-bye."

Ingeborg set the receiver in the prongs. She turned and let the tears pour on David's shoulder.

"Tears of happiness?" he asked.

She nodded. *And sorrow that I wasn't there, but they are all right. Lord, please make sure they stay all right.*

"Wait! I know. Astrid gave birth, right?" he guessed.

Ingeborg nodded against his shoulder and stepped back. "You heard the story of Rolly's mother, Elizabeth, who was also a doctor. The baby is a girl, seven pounds four ounces, Elizabeth Amelia Jeffers."

David smiled, gave her a big hug, and wiped her cheeks with his handkerchief. "And life goes on."

Chapter 32

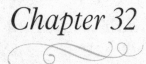

David watched as Arnold called the meeting to order. When the young man prayed that God would bless this meeting and these people, and guide the direction of this company, he had to take a deep breath. Those were the same things he had been praying for, and he hadn't mentioned that to Arnold. He could almost hear John say, *"Surely God is in this place."*

"Next on the agenda is a message from David Gould." Arnold shook David's hand and sat down.

Standing at the head of the table, David looked around the room at all those gathered. A wave of enthusiasm seemed to be washing over him. "Thank you." He wiped his forehead as if wiping away perspiration. Little did they know how close he had just been to tears. "As I look around this room, I am filled with joy. I sense a new purpose and energy. I see men, good men wanting to do their jobs right, fill their positions to the best of their ability. I see this as a new beginning for this company I began so many years ago, with little money but great enthusiasm. The timing was right then, and it is right now.

"I've heard it said that I'm related to King Midas—you know, the one that everything he touched turned to gold. I think it is a fairy story, because I have learned in the last months how much of our success must be laid right at God's door. He blessed us, and then, when we turned another direction, He caught us just in time. I thought I was

461

resigning, but Arnold and some of you encouraged me to stay on as part of this board, with the tank as my department." He pointed to the technical drawing on the wall behind him. "You and I both know there are rumors of coming war. I hope and pray that doesn't happen, for it will tear our world apart. But we will be prepared and on the forefront of a new type of weapon, unlike anything else in existence. A vehicle that can go over any terrain and carry its own armament. This vehicle will protect those driving and manning the guns. The prototype for this tank is being built as we speak, and we are working with those who will build a larger fleet than we can."

He paused. "So thank you all in all you do. As Tiny Tim said in Dickens' *A Christmas Carol*, 'God bless us, every one.'"

Arnold stood as the others clapped politely, smiling and nodding. "Thank you, David. Now, we all have the minutes of the last meeting in front of us. I hope you read them, as we will deviate from Robert's rules of order by just accepting them as they are and as part of our history. Our old business is also included. So we will now move on to department reports." He nodded to the man on his right. "Joseph, will you begin?"

David did not go back to the meeting after

dinner even though he had enjoyed the gathering for the first time in . . . he wasn't sure how many years. One of the motions that had been introduced, having quarterly instead of biannual meetings, had passed, which surprised him.

He knew Ingeborg was at Bernice's house, so he had the driver drop him off there. He thought of going home instead, but he had so much to tell her. Tomorrow he would meet with his attorney, and the next day they would board the train west.

When he dropped the knocker on the door, he was surprised when Bernice answered. "Is everything all right?" he asked as he stepped inside, removing his hat as he entered.

"Yes, I can truly say things are all right." She hung up his coat and hat.

"Where's your butler?"

"He's taking a few days off while I, with Ingeborg's help, am trying to see what I want to do."

"I see." But he didn't see at all. He followed her up the stairs to the nursery, where Ingeborg was reading to the children.

"Hi, Grandpa." Bessie came over to him. "Would you like to sit down with us?"

"Perhaps he might like a bigger chair," Bernice whispered.

The little girl paused a moment. "Grandpa,

if you would like a bigger chair, there is one out in the hall you could bring in."

David looked over to see Ingeborg fighting to keep from laughing out loud. "Why, I think I just might do that. Would you like to show me the chair you mean?"

Bessie nodded, her blond curls bobbing. She took him by the hand and led him out into the hallway. "That one."

"It looks mighty heavy."

"I could help you."

So he turned the chair and dragged it by the back, and she pushed from the front. When they got it into the room, he sat down and turned to her. "Since you helped me so ably, would you like to sit with me?"

She looked at him and then at the chair. With her pointer finger on her chin, she said, "I would have to sit on your lap, you know. That chair isn't big enough for both of us."

"I would be honored if you sat on my lap." David tried to ignore the laughter coming from both his daughter-in-law and Ingeborg, but his grin gave him away. "Read on, madam. May I ask what you are reading?"

"I am reading about tea parties," Ingeborg replied. She had the three-year-old on her lap, and the five-year-old sat on the floor.

David sat listening to Ingeborg read, watching the children and surreptitiously studying Bernice. Was this the same woman who had been frantic the other day? He'd not even given her his news yet. He wanted to wait until the papers were signed with the attorney. She would have the money she needed to run her household, and thanks to a forfeiture clause in the original title, she would control the house.

When Ingeborg closed the book, Bessie leaned against him and sighed. "I like fairies." She looked up at him. "Don't you?"

David thought a moment. "I have never met one, so how can I know if I like them?" He could feel Ingeborg's approval in her warm glance.

When they said good-bye to the children and their mother, Bessie hugged Ingeborg and said, "I wish you did not live so far away." Ingeborg hugged her back. Bessie looked up at her grandfather. "Why did you move so far away? Will you come stay in your house here? We can visit you there, or you can come here."

David stooped to her level. "Yes, we will come visit again, and I think that when we do, we should go to the zoo. And maybe somewhere else that you can choose."

She grinned at him, one of her front teeth missing. "Really?"

"Really."

"But we don't do those things."

"Then I guess we will have to learn."

He helped Ingeborg into the automobile. She turned and waved to the family standing in the doorway. "What a day. Is anyone coming for dinner tonight?"

"No."

She bobbed her head. "Good, then let's eat in the morning room and read and talk in the library."

"Do you not care for the parlor? There's a big fireplace in there."

"It's not a friendly room like the others."

"I see." But the puzzled look on his face must have given him away.

She laid her head on his shoulder. "I'm sure it is a fine place to have company. May I call home tonight?"

"You don't have to ask my permission to use the telephone."

"I just thought it was polite."

He stared at her, shaking his head. This woman continually surprised him. "How would you like to go to the bookstore tomorrow? If we buy a lot, we can bring them to Blessing as luggage or simply ship them in boxes."

"I thought of two titles besides *The Call of the Wild*."

"I know, but you don't have a lot of books at your house."

"Because I give them all away."

"I know Louisa wants more for her shelves. Perhaps it is time for the school to have a library. Let the people of Blessing use it too." He handed the driver several bills. "See you in the morning."

"Yes, sir. Same time."

When the butler opened the door and welcomed them, he asked, "Miss Bernice did not let her butler go, did she?"

David said, "I heard he was taking a few days off." News certainly traveled fast among the hired help.

Ingeborg chimed in, "He asked if he could have a few days off for a family crisis of some kind. He was shocked when she said yes." She smiled at David. "Bernice and I had several long, lovely conversations. She's a brilliant young woman when she hasn't been blindsided. She seems to be more sure of herself now."

"And Lillian seems much better. You are a tonic for all the Goulds, lovely lady."

"I'm sad that she is having such a difficult pregnancy with this one. Did she tell you? She has decided to summon a different doctor, one a friend recommended. He is much younger and seems to specialize in childbirth."

David smiled more to himself than at

her. "I wonder where she got that idea." He paused. "I'm serious about the bookstore. I have several meetings in the morning, but I'll make sure you have a driver to deliver you."

"I could take the trolley."

"It doesn't come clear out here. And no, you can't walk to it." He caught the twinkle in her eye.

Two days later, with far more luggage and boxes than they came with, Ingeborg and David mounted the steps to the last car on the passenger train, possibly the same one they'd had on the way east.

"Are you pleased with all you accomplished?" she asked David as they settled into the comfortable chairs by the windows.

"I think so."

"But you look troubled." She laid her hand on his arm. The conductor cried "all aboard," the steam billowed by the window, and the car jerked as the wheels ground their way forward. Ingeborg leaned her head against the well-padded backrest.

"I was hoping to hear some news regarding Thomas from the Pinkerton men. I have a feeling they will not find much, but I know nothing about finding someone."

"If he is still alive."

"If he is dead, Bernice needs to know that so she can begin a new life."

"And you?"

"And I can . . ."

She saw the shine in his eyes and leaned over to take his hand. "This is something John has told me more than once. He said, 'You do the best that you can, you pray about it, and you leave the rest in God's hands.'"

David inhaled and released a breath before nodding. "He has said the same to me."

"Grief is a heavy burden to bear."

He nodded slowly. At a knock on the door, he blew out another breath. "Come in." He smiled. "Ah, yes, glad you are on this train."

"Have you done all you needed on this trip?" William wore his black jacket and pants with a white shirt and black bow tie with both pride and ease.

"I hope so. And how about you? Your boy doing well?"

"Yes, sir. He loves that college, and they love him. Thanks to you, sir."

"Good. Good. Glad I could have a part in it. You let me know when he graduates and if he wants to continue his education."

"I will. May I bring you a pot of coffee and something to go with it?"

David caught Ingeborg's nod. "She hasn't had enough coffee yet today, so thank you."

Ingeborg rolled her eyes. "Blame it all on me? Just for that, please make it a small pot."

William chuckled. "I'll be back soon." The door clicked behind him.

"How many young people have you helped in this way?" she asked.

He shrugged. "I have no idea. But I know several are now working for us and doing very well. They learn the new technology and pass it on to the rest of us. A good investment, I'd say."

"I'd say you are right."

"You do the same thing, only you go about it a different way."

Ingeborg gave him a puzzled look.

"Think of how many immigrants have come to Blessing to find good work, learn the language, have good schools for their children, and are welcomed into the community. Some then have gone on to other places and done well."

"I guess I'd not thought about it that way. See, you helped there too. You found us workers and sent them on."

Another tap on the door. "Come in," David called.

William set his tray on their table and poured the coffee. "Black, right?"

Ingeborg nodded and eyed the small platter of various pastries. "How can your cook turn out such perfect and delicious croissants while swaying on a train?"

470

"Experience, ma'am. I don't think he re-members he's on a train. Now, can I get you anything else?"

"Lunch is served until three?" David asked.

"Yes, sir."

"Please bring us a menu at about two o'clock."

William handed them two menus. "I'll check back with you." He grinned at their laughter. "You're good for him, ma'am. When he's alone, he works all the time."

They heard him whistling as he went out the door.

"That is one happy man," David said as he decided which pastry to eat. "More than once through the years, he has reminded me to be grateful."

Ingeborg looked out the window. David saw they were beyond the dirty city and get-ting out into the country, where clean snow sparkled on the hills and trees. "We live in such a beautiful country," she said softly.

"We do." David reached into his briefcase and pulled out a thick sheaf of paper. "And now we have some business to complete."

"Business?"

"I sat down with my attorney and drew up some papers for us. He has served me faithfully for years, transferring property and seeing to the best interests of the company." He handed her a small packet of paper. "This is my latest will, on file at the lawyer's office."

"Your will?" Ingeborg read the first paragraph. "Oh no! Do you have a serious health problem?"

"I was afraid that was the first thing you would think of. No, there are no health problems. I also had a will drawn up for you."

"For me? I already have a will." The look she gave him clearly expressed that she thought he was being presumptuous.

David gave her one more paper, a single sheet. "I ask that you read both wills carefully. They do not depend upon whether we marry. This is a brief summary of the two wills without all the flowery phrases and jargon that attorneys seem to insist upon." He sat back. "Basically, they say that everything you own will go to the people you designate— your side of the family. And everything I own will go to my side of the family, even if we marry. Our two families will have no right to the others' inheritance."

"And your grandchildren will be taken care of?"

A feeling of gratitude swept over him. If he had not come to know the Bjorklunds and to see how much better it was when they made the little ones an active part of the family, his own grandchildren would not have the advantages he was about to give them, advantages far beyond wealth. "Yes, they will. Ingeborg, I owe you more than I can say."

Ingeborg watched the lovely farm country of Ohio pass by outside as she finished her breakfast. Perhaps it was Indiana now. They looked so much alike from the window of a speeding train. "I've been thinking." She set her coffee cup on the table.

"About?" David laid his napkin beside his plate.

"I read both wills carefully. Incidentally, that is a very good summary page. It is true to fact, I suppose you could say. An honest summary. The will you had made for me is marvelous. It is exactly what I wish. You know me very well."

"I should hope so."

She smiled. "There are a few items I want to add, bequests for Sophie and a few others, but all in all, it's perfect."

"We can add those things as codicils even after the will is ratified."

Her heart trembled. "Then I believe the answer is yes."

"Well, I'm glad to hear that, but what is the question?" He looked into her eyes. "Such glorious blue eyes," he murmured, almost under his breath.

"I love you, David Jonathan Gould, and yes, I will marry you."

He sucked in a breath. "You're sure?"

"I wouldn't be saying this if I weren't."

"You did say you would marry me? If it seems I am having trouble grasping this, it is only because I am." He took her hand.

"Are you teasing me?"

"I love you, Ingeborg, and now you have added the perfect note for today and always." He leaned over and gently touched his lips to hers. With a smile, he cupped her cheeks in his warm hands. "We can talk to John as soon as we get home."

"I think June would be the best time."

"That's a long time to wait."

"It'll be here before you know it." She leaned closer and kissed him back. "I love you." His smile warmed her face. "And by the way, your daughter and daughter-in-law are planning to come visit this summer."

His eyebrows arched. "Do they know about the wedding?"

"No, they want to see what is so wonderful about Blessing that you and Jonathan want to live there and not in New York."

"I guess we'll have to suggest they come in June so they can attend our wedding."

474

She sat in the circle of his arms and leaned her head on his shoulder. "They both said you were different this trip."

He laid his cheek on her hair, and she willed the westbound train to travel faster. So much to do before June.

Chapter 33

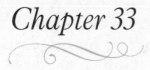

JUNE 12, 1914

Why do I get the feeling there are things going on that I don't know about?" Ingeborg asked.

Inga shrugged, and Emmy did the same. But when they looked at each other, they broke out in giggles.

Ingeborg shook her head. "Uff da."

The girls went from giggles to bent-over laughter.

My wedding day. Whoever dreamed that I would be marrying again? Heavenly Father, sometimes you have an amazing sense of humor. I'm an old woman, and you have stripped years away so that I feel young and so happily in love again. You have given and taken from me two fine men, and now I am starting another all-new life. She gazed at the lovely rich cream gown hanging on the door.

Freda came to the bedroom door. "Ingeborg, there is someone here to see you."

"Really? Who?"

Freda backed up, both hands held up in front of her. "You must come and see."

Ingeborg heard her two girls trying to stifle laughter as they walked to the kitchen. She heaved a sigh. "All right." The hilarity seemed to be contagious. Had she heard a wagon drive up? Emmy and Inga met her at the door.

"Come on, Grandma. To the parlor." They took her hands and pulled her along.

Ingeborg stopped in the arch to the parlor when she saw the room's occupant. Her chin nearly bumped her chest. "Gunlaug? Is it really you?"

"I was afraid you would not recognize me."

The two women met in a hug in the middle of the room, both of them weeping and sniffling.

"When? How?" Ingeborg asked.

"Your Mr. Gould sent me the tickets and said he would come and get me himself if I didn't agree to come, that I had to be here for your wedding. That I am one of his presents to you."

"Oh my, that man." Ingeborg hugged Gunlaug again. "Did you come by yourself?"

"No, Ivar came with me. He's always dreamed of coming to Blessing, and now he and Thorliff are getting acquainted. We came on the train, and Thorliff and Mr. Gould met us." Gunlaug shook her head. "Oh, Ingeborg, this place is so lovely. Your little town is everything you said it was."

"Are you hungry or thirsty? What can we get you?"

"I think you are supposed to be getting ready for a two o'clock wedding."

"All I have to do is put on my dress. Everyone else is doing all the fussing. The church is ready. I am told the supper is taken care of."

"We had breakfast on the train, but as always, a cup of coffee would be good."

"I have it ready. You two go sit on the porch, and we'll bring things out," Freda ordered.

"You met Inga and Emmy?" Ingeborg asked her cousin.

"Of course. They met us at the gate. Thorliff drove us on a tour of the town—a quick one, because he was afraid someone would come tell you and spoil the surprise."

The two women settled into the rocking chairs on the back porch.

Ingeborg reached over and took Gunlaug's hand. "This is such a dream come true. But I had a suspicion that a stop in Blackduck would be part of our honeymoon trip. David wanted to go to Europe, but with all the unrest and tension over there, I flatly said I didn't want to go. We can go to Norway another time." She paused, and her eyes lit up. "Maybe when we do decide to go, you can come too. And no, don't go thinking you could never afford that. David keeps reminding me he will provide whatever I want." She leaned closer. "But look around. What more could I possibly need?"

Freda set a tray on the table and handed each of them a cup of coffee. "And there's cookies."

"Why, look at that," Gunlaug marveled. "Sandbakkelse and sour cream cookies."

Inga brought in another plate. "And fattigman."

Emmy another. "And rosettes."

"And it isn't even Christmas." Gunlaug sounded shocked.

"They asked what were my favorite cookies, so I told them," Ingeborg explained. "And we had a grand time making them all."

"We made lefse too, but that is being saved for the supper after the ceremony." Inga sat down at her grandmother's feet, Emmy on the other side.

"I feel I should be doing something," Ingeborg said, "like we're forgetting something, but I don't know what."

Freda checked the clock. "We will go to the church in one hour and fifteen minutes. Thorliff gave me the schedule for the day. You and Kaaren will dress at the church. You may not see Mr. Gould until you walk down the aisle. Now remember, these are the instructions your son and daughter came up with. None of this is my doing."

Gunlaug laughed. "And just think, I get to be here to celebrate with you."

Ingeborg blew out a puff of air. "Takk. It's not like I've never done this before, but I never dreamed this would happen again."

Inga and Emmy leaned against her knees. "Things will indeed be different," Emmy said. "But it's not like you are moving to New York, only across the field."

"I just wish some of David's family had come. I look around, and I have all of you around me." She sighed and nodded. "At least Jonathan is here."

Emmy and Inga clapped their hands over their mouths, trying to stuff back laughter.

"All right, you two, what else do you know that I don't?"

The girls looked at each other and up at Freda, who shrugged. "Why not?"

Inga leaned forward, her face shining up at Ingeborg. "Well, since you won't be able to tell Mr. Gould . . ."

Emmy nodded. "Go on."

"His daughter, her husband, and his daughter-in-law both arrived at Jonathan's yesterday with a tiny baby. The men kept Mr. Gould busy at the machine shop so he wouldn't see them."

Ingeborg laughed so hard, the tears streamed down her cheeks. "Oh, oh my. They both told him they couldn't make it in June, so they'd come in August instead." A black cloud descended. "That Thomas . . ." She shook her head. "So sad." She shook her head some more. "It took a lot of courage for Bernice to come when her husband is so against us in Blessing."

Gunlaug patted Ingeborg's hand. "He has no idea what he is missing. Love and family are more important than wealth and prestige." She used the Norwegian words in places she stumbled over the English.

Ingeborg nodded. "I think that is why David chooses to live here. Life is more simple in some ways, although he has managed to find more investing to do here, but he saw family here, along with love and acceptance.

He also learned the satisfaction of working with his hands and muscles when he joined Thorliff and the crews in building the new addition at the deaf school. He found out he liked working with wood and tools, and discovered another side of life he had not seen."

"How did you meet him?" Gunlaug asked.

"In New York after we left the ship, got through the inspection, and were trying to get a train to North Dakota. It's a long story, but I got lost on the streets of the city and nearly tripped off a curb, and he kept me from falling. We've been friends all through the years. He has found us workers and all manner of other things when we asked for his assistance. Uff da, we have so much catching up to do."

"But my pa has been collecting stories from all through the years," Inga said, "with all the families who have come and gone. He put them in a book. I am sure you will get a copy." Emmy gave Inga a look, making Inga flinch. "Sorry," Inga whispered.

Ingeborg rolled her lips together and nodded slowly. She leaned over and hugged Inga. "I won't tell anyone. It will be a surprise."

"It looks like this day is full of surprises." Gunlaug's smile mirrored Ingeborg's.

Ingeborg clasped her hands under her chin. "What a day this is turning out to be."

"And the wedding isn't even here yet," Freda muttered as she turned back to the kitchen. She looked up at the clock. "One hour until you go to the church."

With a thump of his tail, Patches tore off the porch and down the lane, barking his happy bark.

"Must be Thorliff," Emmy commented.

Gunlaug looked at Emmy. "How do you know?"

"Patches has a family bark, a visitor bark for people he knows, and a stranger bark."

"Come to think of it, our dog has at least two, a friendly one and a fierce one. But he would never bite someone, even though he sounds like he would."

"What's it like, seeing those giant trees?" Inga asked. "The trees we have around here are the biggest I've ever seen."

"You will have to come visit us when Ingeborg comes and meet your cousins. I think if Mr. Gould has his way, we'll all learn to ride the train between our farms."

Thorliff and Ivar tied up his horse and came through the gate and up the steps.

"Well, I finally get to see my cousin Ingeborg." Ivar took Ingeborg's hand. "This is quite a surprise, isn't it?"

"You should have seen the look on her face when she came into the parlor where

I waited." Gunlaug's joy made her words sing.

Ivar nodded. "That's how we felt when we received the tickets from Mr. Gould, along with the admonition to keep the secret."

Ingeborg held out both her arms to wrap him in a hug. "You are welcome to stay as long as you like."

"Thank you, but I know I am needed at home. Between the farming and the tree-felling, there is never a slack moment."

"Have you had dinner?"

"Thelma made sure we had something to eat." Thorliff poured himself and Ivar a glass of the strawberry lemonade Emmy had made. "So, Mor, Lars will take you and Tante Kaaren, along with Emmy and Inga, to the church to dress, and I will bring the others."

"That's what they told me." Ingeborg smiled at her son. "As far as I can see, this is a day of amazing surprises, let alone a wedding. Every time I ask about something, they say not to worry, it is all taken care of. I don't know how that can be. Have you seen David today?"

"Yes, and he seems content with the way things are moving. We about had to hogtie him to keep him from coming over here, but he will live through this. We assigned John to be his keeper today. Louisa is the backup."

"One thing's for sure, there are some good secret-keepers in this family." Ingeborg stood. "You all go on visiting. I'll be back in a bit."

"Can I get you anything?" Freda asked.

"Not that I can think of. I'm going to wrap our dresses in sheets to take to the church."

"The girls will take care of that. Kaaren is about to leave."

"I've never felt so taken care of in my life."

Freda nodded in satisfaction. "Good. Now, I figure Gunlaug could have your room, and Ivar can sleep in Louisa's old room, so I had Manny move all their bags here. After you leave, the rest of us will get ready here and go over to the church. I heard they've reserved the front rows for family, but as near as I can figure, that'll take up half the church, at least."

"I won't feel like all this is real until I hear John pronounce us husband and wife. Otherwise, perhaps it is a dream."

"Clara has Mr. Gould's house all ready. She is so pleased to have that job."

"You trained her well."

"No, we did. Sometimes when I think back to that girl who came here, so terrified she couldn't even talk . . . ." Freda puffed out a breath. "And now we are stepping into another change."

484

And I won't be living in this house anymore. Except when David was traveling. Ingeborg felt a pang in her heart.

She heard a horse whinny out by the back gate. "Lars is here. Have him and Kaaren come meet Gunlaug and Ivar. I'll be ready in just a few minutes."

Later, down in the church basement, where the women were dressing, laughter overflowed right up the stairs. Someone had brought over an oval full-length mirror, and both Sophie and Astrid were there to help. The girls held up their arms, and Sophie and Astrid dropped their sky blue dresses over their heads.

Emmy stroked her hands down her hips. "I've never had a dress that felt like this before."

Inga twirled so the skirt billowed out. "Me either." They turned to look at Ingeborg as the two dressers dropped the ivory gown over her head. "Oh, Grandma, you are so beautiful," they breathed together.

Ingeborg watched in the mirror as Sophie buttoned up the back. The simple princess-style gown draped down to her shoes and swayed with every movement. Ingeborg slowly shook her head. Her braided hair, now a mix of silver and gold, was wrapped around her head like a crown. A fall of lace was pinned in the back and cascaded down to the hem of the dress, floating freely as she moved. Three-quarter-length sleeves draped over the gathered-back gloves.

"I've never worn a dress that felt like this either, so we can all feel shimmery."

Astrid and Sophie tucked some daisies into the coronet of braids and stepped back to see their handiwork.

"Oh, Mor, you grow more beautiful every year." Astrid sniffed back tears. "That dress. Wait until he sees you. I can't keep back the tears."

Sophie tucked another daisy in Ingeborg's hair. "Like you are a queen with a daisy crown."

Ingeborg looked in the mirror to see Kaaren dabbing at tears also. "All right, all of you. Stop the tears, or they will think we have been sad. There is no regret here."

Sophie got herself under control. "No, only an appreciation of love and beauty. I will bring in the photographer now so he can do his job. Are you all ready?"

Ingeborg rolled her eyes and shook her head.

"Mr. Gould brought this man here and said he was to take pictures. Right, Tante Ingeborg?" Sophie said.

"Yes." Ingeborg sniffed and straightened her spine. "We are ready."

486

The next few minutes couldn't go by fast enough for her. They all did what the man ordered, and then he bowed, smiled, told them they had done well, and left the room. They could hear the organ playing in the sanctuary.

"The pews are all full, and chairs fill every possible spot, and they are setting up chairs outside." Rolly came halfway down the stairs to tell them, then ran back up.

"Five minutes," Astrid called down.

"Okay, let's go upstairs to the waiting room." Sophie supervised them going up the stairs. She retied a bow on Astrid's braid.

They had just adjusted to the new room when a tap on the door announced Reverend Solberg. He stepped in. "Everything is fine, and the men are about to move to their places, so let us pray. Heavenly Father, we thank you for all the blessings you are pouring out on this couple as they bless so many people. Make this a union of such love and faith we can all rejoice. In the name of the Father, and the Son, and the Holy Spirit." They joined him at the *amen*.

Ingeborg frowned. "John, shouldn't you be up at the altar to preside?"

A devilish twinkle filled his face with joy. "Oh, I'm not going to marry you two."

"Who is?"

"Father Thomas Devlin."

Ingeborg felt her knees wobble. "Father Devl—is . . . he's here?"

"Yes. Thomas, Anji, and the children. The whole family came back to Blessing for this and they're going to stay. Father Devlin is going to start that church here that he wanted to start years ago. And I will help him all I can."

"Oh my." Surprises! The only disappointment in this day was Thomas Gould. If only . . .

"You girls ready?" Sophie asked.

Inga and Emmy both nodded.

"All right, get lined up. Inga, when the organ changes, you let your Tante Sophie count for you." John smiled at Sophie.

Astrid hugged her mor one more time, handed her the bouquet of pink and white peonies and white daisies, and slipped out the door to go sit with her family.

Sophie and Inga stopped just behind the door. "You okay?" Sophie asked the young girl.

Inga nodded. And swallowed.

The organ changed into Mendelssohn's "Wedding March." Sophie whispered, "Go."

Inga, holding one pink peony, started down the aisle. Emmy followed her when Sophie told her to go.

The music changed again, and Kaaren

started down the aisle. She and the girls lined up opposite from the men at the altar and turned to watch Ingeborg and Thorliff framed in the doorway.

The music broke forth, Ingeborg smiled at her son, and together they walked down the aisle.

"I love you, Mor," he whispered.

"And I you." She raised her eyes to see David smiling at her, the love beaming from his face. His smile grew wider as she drew nearer. Through her tears, she could see tears on his cheeks also.

Thomas Devlin, glowing with happiness, stood by the altar with John Solberg right behind him. He raised his voice, that wonderful lilting Irish voice. "Who gives this woman to this man?"

"I do." Thorliff spoke loud and clear. He placed her hand in David's. "Take good care of her," he whispered.

"Oh, yes."

Ingeborg sniffed at their exchange. David tucked her arm against his side, and they turned to face the altar.

Father Devlin smiled at the couple in front of him. "Dearly beloved, we are gathered here in the sight of God and this company to join this man and this woman in holy wedlock."

Ingeborg couldn't quit smiling. She glanced up to see David smiling at her, his heart in his eyes. She nodded and made herself return to the ceremony. They all bowed their heads as Father Devlin prayed.

Both of them spoke their vows in clear, ringing voices.

"Do you, David Jonathan Gould, take this woman to be your wedded wife?"

"I do."

"Do you, Ingeborg Bjorklund, take this man to be your wedded husband?"

"I do."

"With this ring, I thee wed." And David slipped the gold band onto her finger.

The ceremony continued with the two pastors taking turns, but it was Reverend Solberg who announced, "David Gould, you may kiss your bride."

David cupped her jawline with both hands and kissed her tenderly. "I will love you forever." The kiss was long and sweet and overflowing with promise.

Father Devlin boomed, "I now pronounce you husband and wife. Friends and family, 'tis me boundless joy to introduce Mr. and Mrs. David Gould."

Those gathered broke out in applause.

Reverend Solberg encouraged everyone to go downstairs to enjoy cake and coffee, and

Thorliff stood up to add to that announcement.

"Many of you know we've been working on a memoir that has become a history of Blessing. There are copies for everybody who would like one at the reception. Most of you are in it, and I thank you all for your assistance in bringing this project together."

Kaaren gave Ingeborg back her bouquet. Inga hugged her grandmother and then looked up at David. "Can I hug you too?"

"You most certainly can, and you know, I am now officially your grandfather."

"So I should call you Grandfather instead of Mr. Gould?"

"If you would do that, I would be honored." He turned. "And you too, Emmy."

Her dark eyes dancing, Emmy nodded. "Welcome to our family, Grandfather."

With their attendants going ahead of them, David and Ingeborg started down the aisle. Until he stopped, and his mouth dropped open. "Bernice and Lillian, I thought . . . but you came. And the baby! You brought my brand-new grandson! Thank you! And Stephan!"

Stephan was grinning as he enthusiastically pumped David's hand. "Mr. Gould, sir, I have discovered that Blessing is much nicer than Rahway. And friendlier."

Lillian hugged him one-armed, his newest grandchild in the other arm. "Yes, Father, we are so delighted that you and Ingeborg are now married."

Bernice nodded. "And we want the very best for you."

Ingeborg hugged each of them. "Thank you," she whispered in their ears. "Thank you so much, and welcome to Blessing."

"Did you know this?" David asked her under his breath.

"Not until about an hour ago. There have been so many secrets created and kept around here, my love."

"It's been fun, eh?"

"Oh, yes."

They continued toward the front door, but it was blocked by a thin young man Ingeborg had never seen.

David's lip quivered, and he gasped. "Oh, thank you, God. Oh . . ." He bolted forward to the doorway and wrapped his arms tightly around a man who had to be Thomas Gould.

Behind them, Bernice yelped a wordless cry.

Suddenly Thomas dropped to his knees. "Please forgive me, Father. I'm sorry. I am so very sorry."

David gripped handfuls of the young man's jacket and dragged him to his feet. And hugged him again. Tears streaming down his face, he turned to Ingeborg. "Ingeborg, my oldest son, Thomas. He was dead to me and is alive again."

Bernice rushed forward and into her husband's arms. Lillian and Stephan ushered the reunited couple out of the church, and Ingeborg knew they would be waiting for David as soon as their duties were complete.

She and David stepped out onto the landing at the top of the steps to greet the people as they came out. Those sitting on chairs and benches and standing outside broke into applause too, shouting greetings and good wishes.

As they chatted with each person and shook hands or hugged, Ingeborg had to dab at her leaking eyes every once in a while. She looked now and then toward David. He was the happiest that she had ever seen him. And that made her heart rejoice as well. Her life had been so enriched by the appearance of her long-lost cousin Gunlaug, and David's life was complete now that his son Thomas was back in the fold. So many blessings at once!

Rolly hugged her. "Don't be sad, Gramma."

"Oh, Rolly, remember we talked about how tears can be happy too. So much happiness that it just leaks right out and makes tears." She kissed his cheek. And then, hand in hand with David, she led the whole big happy congregation off to the reception.

Ingeborg sat on the front porch of David's home, sipping coffee and watching the clear June sky change color as the sun went down. "I'm so tired, but I am still all wound up, like Rolly on Christmas morning."

David sat so close beside her that their chairs touched. He chuckled. "Me too." He stared out across the yard. "It's a good thing we're doing this in June. June has the longest days of the year, and we needed a long, long day to squeeze all the surprises in."

She laughed, then sobered. "I knew Bernice and Lillian were coming, but I was as surprised by Thomas as you were."

"He told me something of his months away. He was robbed, and when he finally made it to Hibbing and discovered Lionel's chicanery, he had no money left. He found a job in a tannery to make enough to live on and save for the trip to Blessing. He called Lillian a few days before she came, so she knew he was coming. That was her secret to contribute."

"Bernice seems to have grown a lot in self-confidence. His absence helped her grow,

494

but I certainly wouldn't recommend it as a good method."

David nodded. "The surprise I'm proudest of was getting Gunlaug to come. Astrid told me about your history—that when you were young, you two were inseparable, but her father broke the family up over something he got mad about." They were silent for a moment, enjoying the coffee and sunset and each other. "Who is Thomas Devlin? He's a wonderfully warm and cheery soul."

Ingeborg took his hand in hers. "He lived here for about two years. He was here when Elizabeth died. In fact, he carved a beautiful caduceus for her coffin. He's a fine woodworker, and I think you two will get along very well."

"So many surprises. Have you noticed that all of them are specific answers to earnest prayer?"

Ingeborg didn't have to think about that very long. "That's true. Some of the greatest blessings take a long time coming, as God works out His plans. Like today, there are many blessings to cherish."

"Do you suppose we value them more because we have waited longer?" David asked.

"I don't know, but I think we have the rest of our lifetimes to find out." She kissed him. "And I have a feeling we have this new life to learn, with two such different lives combined."

"Blessings to cherish." David nodded. "I like that. You are the greatest blessing God has given me, and I plan to cherish you for the rest of our lives." He got up and opened the door to his house. "Welcome home, Mrs. Gould." He picked her up and carried her over the threshold. "Our new life begins."

A Letter from the Author

Dear Readers,

This Red River of the North series—often known as the Blessing books or the Ingeborg books—has been quite a ride, surprising many people, including this author. Many of you have let me know that you will miss Ingeborg. I'll let you in on a secret: *A Blessing to Cherish* has been far and away the hardest book I've ever written. Looking back, I can see ways that might have made it easier, but what is done is done. Thank you for your patience with me as my editors and publisher have had to reset the release date. And thank them for their extreme patience. But now we are seeing light at the end of the tunnel, and it is not a train coming. So when you read this, rejoice with us all that it is finished.

I keep reminding myself that Ingeborg is not a real person, that I made her up. But she will always live in my heart and in my head. And I could go back and read the books too.

Ingeborg is a combination of my mother,

Thelma, and her older sister Inga, two of my lifetime heroines, and I've always said I want to be like Ingeborg when I grow up. She is an amazing woman, a wise woman, to be sure. Thank you for the many letters I've received through the years about the way Ingeborg has impacted people's lives. I believe that is the Holy Spirit at work, and I am so thankful to be part of this team.

Thank you also to the many people who have shared their family stories with me. While I have never knowingly used a real person as a character, I have included many events that people shared with me and real history of the times. But the final line is that I strung the beads together to be the necklace for these stories. To God be the glory.

As I wrote this novel, I took some creative license with the timeline of the development of tanks, moving it up a few years so that David Gould and Daniel Jeffers would be able to work on their project. I tried to include characters from past books, but since the story could not be a thousand pages long, my granddaughter Danae and I put together a list called "Where Are They Now?" describing where some of the characters from the series are in 1914. I often wonder what will happen to Inga and those of her generation and following. These people have stories to tell, so I gift it to your imaginations. Go and play with that.

My gratitude, too, to all those special people at Bethany House Publishers who have helped me tell these stories. Their hard work is what took my manuscript pages and made them into each of the books that comprised the entire Red River of the North series. I can never thank them enough for the privilege of working with them and for sharing their advice, their skills, wisdom, and love. I am so incredibly blessed.

Another team I am blessed to be part of is the Books & Such Literary Agency, with my agents Wendy Lawton and Janet Grant. Thanks to Deidre Knight, another agent who helped with earlier books. None of us ever dreamed this series would continue for this long.

Now I'm moving on to a new series, and one of my real challenges is to create new characters who are not Ingeborg. The title is Leah's Garden and the stories are about her four daughters, Larkspur, Forsythia, Delphinium, and Lilac, after the Civil War. I think you are going to come to love these characters.

Thank you again for staying with me through all these years and pages, and for telling your friends and relatives about Ingeborg and this, her series. I know Ingeborg is deeply humbled by your regard.

Blessings,
Lauraine

Where Are They Now?

By Danae Hiltner and Lauraine Snelling

After marrying in Duluth, Reverend Jorge Gunderson and his wife, Mary (Landsverk) Gunderson, settled in Bemidji, Minnesota, with Mary's two sons, Norbert and Hank. Jorge and Mary had two more children: another son, whom they named Edgar, and a daughter named Vera. Hank grew to be an ordained preacher like his father and married a woman named Eva, who died in a wagon accident four years later. Norbert married a Bemidji woman, and they took over running a farm that belonged to his wife's family. Edgar worked in town as a carpenter, eventually settling down with a woman he met through his father's mission work. Vera married a rancher from Beach, North Dakota.

Following their marriage in 1893, Baptiste and Manda LeCrue moved to Montana with Manda's father, Zebulun MacCallister, to raise, train, and sell horses he rounded up in the wild. Baptiste and Manda had four children: Katie Marie, John Pierre, Gray Beaver, and Running Fawn.

Katie Marie had a talent for training even the most difficult horses and went on to become a well-known trainer in Montana and much of the west. John Pierre and his younger sister, Running Fawn, were skilled trainers and riders and went on to join a traveling Wild West show. Each married fellow show people years later.

Gray Beaver remained in Montana, where he worked on the ranch while running his own leather-making business on the side. He met and married a woman from a neighboring ranch, and they settled on their own place and remained there until their deaths.

Zeb MacCallister ran a successful horse ranch for years after moving to Montana and was known for his reputable character, business, and training of the horses he sold. He never married again. In later years, Zeb turned the horse work over to Baptiste and Manda, due to age and illness. He spent his time pondering life and caring for the chickens and other smaller farm animals. He was a doting grandfather to Baptiste and Manda's children. At his passing, he was found with a smile on his lips and his beloved deceased wife's shawl pressed to his chest.

Kane and Augusta Moyer ran a successful ranch in South Dakota for years after their marriage in 1889. They raised three children: Katy, Thomas, and Stephen. Katy had a love for music like her father and would go on to become a folk musician. Thomas loved life on the ranch like his father and worked it for as long as he could, later marrying another South Dakota woman. Stephen joined the military his father sold horses to, and after his time there, met and married a widowed soldier's wife. They moved to live near Kane and Augusta.

Margaret Louise Claggett, Kaaren's first deaf student, graduated from the Blessing School for the Deaf and returned home to live with her family. She met and married a man who'd lost most of his hearing due to prolonged exposure to loud noise, and was able to teach him sign language. Margaret Louise had a skillful hand for painting and spent many years designing the posters for the theater where her husband worked, as well as interpreting plays for any deaf guests who attended. She and her husband later bought the theater and continued to run it for years. Margaret

Louise ran events for children who were deaf or had other physical or mental impairments. In their final years, Margaret Louise and her husband sold the theater and retired from show life. Margaret Louise passed away first, followed by her husband only a few hours later.

Phillip and Annabelle Rogers remained in Northfield, Minnesota, for the rest of their lives. Phillip continued to run his newspaper business, and Annabelle kept up with her charity work and social events. After the death of their daughter, both became strong supporters and advocates of studies in women's health in order to prevent other parents and families from enduring the grief that befell them when they learned Elizabeth had passed. The couple exchanged letters with their grandchildren and even managed to visit them more than once over the years. They were diligent in donating to the Blessing Hospital in honor of their daughter to help with any expenses and to keep Elizabeth's (and Astrid's) dream alive. In later years, Phillip sold his newspaper but continued to write small articles for it. He and Annabelle lived out the remainder of their lives peacefully.

George and Solveig Carlson managed to keep their farm going in spite of bonanza farms diminishing. Though the farm grew smaller, the property remained in the family for years. They had four children: Arne, Anna, Clara, and a second son, Henry. Arne would go on to inherit the farm. Anna and Clara married into farming families, and Henry drove a stage-coach all over North Dakota.

The Geddick family remained in Blessing for years. Abram and his wife, Cora, were active in the church and in their community. Joseph and Elmer, their two older sons, worked in construction. Heinz worked building houses, and in Drayton, North Dakota, he met a woman and married her. Ida Geddick, the only daughter, worked with her mother, traveling with the threshing crews and cooking for them. When not away with the crew, she cooked at the Blessing Hospital as well. She befriended a maintenance worker at the hospital and eventually married him. They remained in Blessing for years.

Ina Odegard worked as a switchboard operator in Blessing for years before moving back to Chicago, following her father's death, to be near family. She met a clockmaker named Mathew Hill in the city. They became close friends, then later married. He taught her how to assemble clocks, and she ended up working in the shop regularly after discovering she had a knack for understanding them. Later, her work having gained her an admirable reputation, the mayor chose one of her clocks to be erected in the city. She and her husband ran a successful business for years before retiring and passing it on to their children.

After completing his work at the Morganstein Hospital for Women in Chicago, Dr. Red Hawk returned to his people and helped them in numerous ways for years to come. He mentored other young adults wanting to join the medical field, and many trained at the Morganstein Hospital as he had before them. Dr. Red Hawk also reduced barriers between people by tending to the ill outside his reservation. He married a half-Indian woman from another reservation, and she often assisted him in his work. They adopted three half-Indian children, orphaned when their parents died of illness.

Maisie Christopherson, the former dressmaker in Blessing, married Joshua Landsverk and became the manager of the boarding-house dining room. Months later, Maisie's mother sent for her when her ill younger brother didn't have much time left. Joshua accompanied Maisie home and ended up taking over the failing family business that would have died completely otherwise. Joshua and Maisie remained with her mother, running the family business and giving Maisie's mother a home. They had four children. Their fourth child, a girl, was born with a condition that required her to wear leg braces for much of her life.

Rachel Anderson, Ellie Bjorklund's cousin, continued to live with Ellie's parents in Grafton. She had a love for trees and plants, and throughout her school years, she pored over books about plants, as well as illustrating them. She attended college for arboriculture and later became a professor at the same college. There she met a fellow professor, a scientist named Dr. Hartmann. At first, they didn't get along, but then he accidentally saw an illustration of hers, and their relationship changed. Soon she was illustrating images for him to use during lectures, as well as joining his lectures. They often researched together as well. Together, they assembled a stunning indoor garden to further educate students and bring enjoyment to people beyond the college. The two later married and had one daughter together. Their only son failed to survive infancy.

Lauraine Snelling (www.laurainesnelling .com) is the award-winning author of more than seventy books, fiction and nonfiction, for adults and young adults. Her books have sold more than five million copies. Besides writing books and articles, she teaches at writers' conferences across the country. She and her husband make their home in Tehachapi, California.

Sign Up for Lauraine's Newsletter!

Keep up to date with Lauraine's news on book releases and events by signing up for her email list at laurainesnelling.com.

You May Also Like...

Only while trick riding can Ella Fleming forget the truth about who she really is—the daughter of a murderer. Phillip DeShazer buries the guilt he feels for his father's death in work and drink, and his guilt continues to grow the more Ella Fleming comes to his rescue. Will they be able to overcome their pasts and trust God to guide their futures?

What Comes My Way by Tracie Peterson
BROOKSTONE BRIDES #3, traciepeterson.com